Advance Praise for *Synapse*

"A groundbreaking, mind-bending adventure. *Synapse* is next-level suspense that keeps the pages turning combined with next-level writing on par with the great literary masters. Isaac Asimov meets Thomas Aquinas in the front car of a runaway roller coaster. *Synapse* is not merely a thriller you should read—as 5G approaches and advances in AI snowball, it is the thriller you can't afford to miss."

—James R. Hannibal, award-winning author of *The Gryphon Heist*

"Perfectly timed and thought-provoking, *Synapse* is a smart, intense thriller that keeps the suspense building until the final page. Steven James once again delivers a perfect amalgam of character and plot, totally immersing the reader in an irresistible narrative."

—Simon Gervais, international bestselling author of *Hunt Them Down*

"If you've never worried about a future with artificial humans, now is a good time to start. They'll look like us, talk like us, and think like us. Only they'll be faster, stronger, and smarter. But will they also wrestle with questions about God like us? *Synapse* is a snappy, savvy thriller about a future that's coming. Start sweating now."

—Randy Ingermanson, author of *Son of Mary*

"Wow! I will say it again: Wow! With *Synapse*—a near-future thriller firmly grounded in today's realities—Steve James has accomplished that rare feat of blending phenomenal storytelling, a captivating plot, intriguing characters, and thought-provoking themes. And it doesn't stop there. At the risk of gushing (you're going to see a lot of that over this story), the action is exhilarating, the suspense nail-biting, the twists stunning and perfectly timed. Through it all, it'll have you pondering faith, the essence of God and grace, and what and why you believe. Entertaining, provocative, and intelligent, *Synapse* is as close to a perfect thriller you'll read this year, or any year."

—Robert Liparulo, bestselling author
a *Horseman* and The Dreamhouse Kings

"With *Synapse*, Steven James hurls us into a near-future where technology collides head-on with what it means to have soul. A complex and riveting thriller that invites you to ponder the deepest questions of existence while at the same time leaving you on the edge of your seat."

—JAMES L. RUBART, FIVE-TIME CHRISTY AWARD WINNER

"The technology of tomorrow poses so many dangers and questions, and Steve James explores this in the exciting *Synapse*. While it's set in a realistic near future, this well-crafted tale deals with fundamental issues we all have like grief and faith. They just become more complex when mixed with science and high-tech. I really enjoyed this imaginative novel."

—TRAVIS THRASHER, BESTSELLING AUTHOR OF *AMERICAN OMENS*

"Steven James—a name synonymous with deep books and even deeper characters. I found myself irritated with life for intruding on well-placed truth bombs, as well as the more incendiary kind. *Synapse* is a book that makes you think, rethink—and think again! A realistic and an intelligent look into our future, *Synapse* takes the reader deep into the minds of the characters, both human and artificial, to smartly explore AI and eschatology. Thought-provoking and compulsive—this is a book you can't afford to miss!!"

—RONIE KENDIG, BESTSELLING AUTHOR OF *THE TOX FILES*

"A futuristic thriller that explores the raw power of technology woven with the world of tomorrow and the debate of God's sovereignty."

—DiANN MILLS, BESTSELLING AUTHOR OF *FATAL STRIKE*

SYNAPSE

Also by Steven James

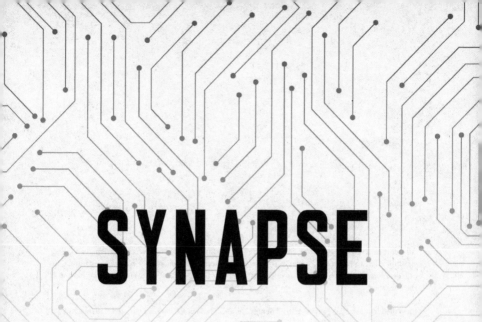

SYNAPSE

STEVEN JAMES

THOMAS NELSON

Since 1798

Published in Nashville, Tennessee, by Thomas Nelson. Thomas Nelson is a registered trademark of HarperCollins Christian Publishing, Inc.

Interior design by Emily Ghattas

Thomas Nelson titles may be purchased in bulk for educational, business, fund-raising, or sales promotional use. For information, please email SpecialMarkets@ThomasNelson.com.

ISBN 978-0-7852-2526-3 (e-book)
ISBN 978-0-7852-2529-4 (audio download)

Library of Congress Cataloging-in-Publication Data

Names: James, Steven, 1969- author.
Title: Synapse / Steven James.
Description: Nashville, Tennessee : Thomas Nelson, [2019]
Identifiers: LCCN 2019016535 | ISBN 9780785225256 (softcover)
Subjects: | GSAFD: Suspense fiction. | Christian fiction.
Classification: LCC PS3610.A4545 S96 2019 | DDC 813/.6--dc23 LC record available at https://lccn.loc.gov/2019016535

Printed in the United States of America

19 20 21 22 23 LSC 10 9 8 7 6 5 4 3 2 1

To Amanda

"Humanity, in its desire for comfort, had over-reached itself. It had exploited the riches of nature too far. Quietly and complacently, it was sinking into decadence, and progress had come to mean the progress of the Machine."
—From *The Machine Stops* by E. M. Forster, 1909

30 years from now

1

Tuesday, November 4
Cincinnati, Ohio
4:14 p.m.

You do not hear your baby cry.

"What's wrong?" you ask, but you're still weak and the words seem to come from someone else, someone not on this bed, someone who has not just born life into the wide, bright world beyond the womb.

Yes, Naiobi should be crying, but she is not.

A chill runs through you—every mother's worst fear: silence after the birth of her child.

You hear the beep of monitors and the hurried, hushed words of doctors, and then a nurse's measured reassurance that "the doctors are with her," but from the infant warmer, only silence.

"Tell me she's okay," you beg the nurse. "She is okay, isn't she?"

"Shh," she says. And, "It's going to be alright" and to "Just rest."

"Tell me!"

"Shh."

No.

Your baby.

You force yourself to sit up higher to see for yourself. The pain roaring through you is disorienting. You bury it.

And catch a glimpse of your daughter, the neonatologist intubating her, another doctor doing compressions on her delicate chest, lightly and with two fingers, and yet firm enough to break ribs.

Your baby is tinged gray instead of vibrant and alive. A pale and lifeless color.

Oh, God, no. Please, no.

The nurse was wrong. This isn't going to be okay.

You pray, yes, a gasping and frantic prayer: *God, don't do this. Bring her back. Take me instead. Punish me, not her. Oh, please, please spare her life.*

No child should die in a place like this. If she must die, let it be at home surrounded by stuffed animals and soft blankets, by warm candles and a loving family, but not alone in a hospital infant warmer, hemmed in by these strict square walls, alone and unhugged in harsh, unforgiving light.

No baby should—

Please, God.

The nurse isn't saying anything now. Instead, she's just holding your hand and squeezing it tightly, too tightly.

Yes.

She knows.

And she cares in her own way. You realize it now—yes, she does—but it's not going to matter.

The doctor continues the chest compressions.

Thoughts flash through your mind—the times you held that music box against your stomach to calm Naiobi when she kicked too much. The nursery you prepared and painted for her. The songs you sang for her. The prayers you offered for her.

Nine months.

The doctor stops the compressions.

"Keep going," you gasp. "Try again!"

"It's too late," he mutters.

"It can't be!"

After a short hesitation he starts them again, perhaps just to calm you.

Okay, this time they'll work. Naiobi's going to come back.

You feel a shiver, soul-deep and terrifying.

This isn't really happening. She can't be gone. There's been some mistake. Maybe that's someone else's baby over there. Maybe this is just a bad dream that you need to wake up from, that you need to wake up from *now*.

Wake up, Kestrel!

Finally, the doctor is done. He turns and looks at you with heavy eyes. "I'm sorry."

You scream. You can't help it.

"Let me hold her. I need to hold her."

"Yes, okay." After removing the tube they had used to intubate her, he signals to the nurse and she brings your daughter to you, wrapped in a blanket that serves no purpose anymore, save to keep your baby's limp body from view.

You tenderly accept her, even though it strikes you that it's too late for tenderness to matter.

She has fairy-like eyelids that will never flutter open to see the world.

"Naiobi." You're barely able to speak her name.

With a soft whisk, the door closes and the staff leave the two of you alone.

Somehow you manage to hold back your tears.

You realize that you'll never blow out a birthday candle for your daughter when she turns one, or say goodbye to her on her first day of school, or build sandcastles with her at the seashore.

The big things and little ones. The good and the bad.

A lifetime never lived.

She'll never struggle with her homework, get bullied, cry into her pillow. She'll never lean her head against a boy's shoulder on the dance floor, never have him awkwardly kiss her good night on the cheek afterward.

This baby, your baby, will never know what it feels like to be held to her mother's breast, to be comforted and cooed to and hugged.

You glance out the window.

Not even the whisper of a breeze unsettles the few remaining leaves that still cling to the trees surrounding the hospital. Even the clouds are still—dark slats layered low in the heavens, encasing their cold November rain in the vast and lonely sky.

It's almost as if the day is mourning for Naiobi.

Or turning its back on her.

As tired as you are, you don't want to sleep. It feels like a betrayal, however slight, against the love you have for your daughter. How could you sleep at a time like this? How could you even consider it?

The nurse knocks softly on the door and asks if you would like her to take her. You have no idea how much time has passed, but it has not been enough.

"A little longer," you say.

She offers to help you, to take a photo of her for you to remember her by, but you don't want a picture. Not of Naiobi now. Not now.

Not of her corpse.

Such a terrible way to refer to her. Terrible but true, as the truth so often is. Terrible in its unforgiving, searing way.

The nurse disappears.

Afternoon settles into dusk.

"I love you, I love you, I love you." You find yourself saying the words aloud, even though you know your daughter cannot hear them, will never hear them.

She has a tiny, feathery, disobedient tuft of hair. You calm it down with a gentle, moistened finger. This is a moment you must remember. You tell yourself that, and you close your eyes to take in all the sounds and smells that you can.

You kiss Naiobi's cheek and it feels much too cool, more like clay than the cheek of a child.

With all of your heart, you will her to breathe, you beg her tiny heart to beat, but all the love in the world is not enough to bring her back.

She's in heaven now.

She's happy and at peace.

She's in the Lord's presence.

These are the things you tell yourself. These are the words you use to try to convince yourself that what you believe is true—the glory and goodness of the Lord. The laughter of a child in his everlasting care. But the words and comfort seem as cold as Naiobi's corpse in your arms.

Right now, heaven is only wishful thinking to you, an unreality.

Finally, the nurse returns.

The darkened window tells you that nighttime has fallen over the city. There's no clock in here, and for all you know it might be the middle of the night.

After a final, wrenching goodbye, you hand Naiobi to her.

You know the nurse is going to take her down to the morgue. You know this because you are no stranger to what happens in this building, to the pain and anguish that the walls hold for so many patients and family members. You know this hospital's ways. It's part of your job.

"Would you like to speak with a chaplain?" the nurse asks you softly. "I can send one in."

You're not sure if it will help, but it might. "Alright."

Then she leaves, and you weep and you wish you were anywhere else other than the room where your precious child died.

The doctor tried to explain what went wrong, but none of it really registered with me except the part about it being a difficult birth and Naiobi not getting enough oxygen—but he didn't use her name and referred to her simply as "your baby."

I wanted to correct him: *She has a name!* but I held back. He was just doing his job the best he knew. I understood that.

I'd wanted to have a child before I turned thirty-five, but time was running out and I'd finally decided not to let the lack of a man in my life stop me from having the baby I'd always dreamed of.

The law allowed me to choose the sex of my child, her height and eye color, her personality, her resistance to any number of genetic disorders—all choices related to DNA manipulation that wasn't possible even just a decade ago—but I chose not to design my baby.

And now, it wasn't anger that I felt toward God, but abandonment.

It was as if someone had ripped away all the good that I had believed about him—that he was loving and caring and kind and that he sacrificed to give us hope for eternity. Now when I needed him most, I didn't sense his peace. Only his absence.

Nothing made sense.

Not my faith.

Not my God.

Not my job.

No, a pastor shouldn't have those kinds of questions, this kind of heartache. A minister should have more hope at a time like this. Much more.

A knock at the door.

The chaplain.

"The nurse told me what happened, that you might want to talk?" he said as he entered the room.

But since that nurse had left I'd changed my mind and didn't want my doubts known by anyone, even a chaplain who, out of confidentiality, would keep them to himself.

"It turns out it might be better if I don't."

Bearded and well-groomed, he approached my bed. "I'm Grayson." He carried a stiff Bible. It looked like it might never have been opened. "Is there anything I can do for you?"

"No. Are you new around here?"

"Just a couple weeks. Moved down from Milwaukee."

Silence.

"I'm a minister myself," I told him. "Methodist."

"Okay." A pause that was hard to read. "Is there anyone you'd like me to call?"

"No."

And it was true. There really wasn't anyone to contact. My brother, Trevor, lived out in Seattle, but we weren't talking. He would have been the only one to call. Besides, if he was interested, the Feeds would give him all the information he would ever need at the prompt of his voice or the touch of his fingertip. He knew I was going into labor. I just didn't know if I was ready to give him the news about Naiobi yet. Eventually, but not yet.

My congregation members would hear the news soon enough. A pastor often finds that it's difficult to make friends with people in their flock. There's an odd power dynamic at play that keeps people at a distance.

"I can sit with you," Grayson offered.

"Yes. Okay. But please don't tell me that God has a plan for me. Don't tell me that everything will work out for good in the end. Don't tell me that God loved Naiobi enough to end her suffering. Don't tell me anything."

He acquiesced and said nothing as he sat on the chair beside my bed.

I'd thought that having him here might help in some way, but it didn't. The silence between us eventually grew too awkward and I asked if I could be alone.

"May I pray for you?"

"That won't be necessary." Only after saying the words did I realize what an odd response that was. But it felt honest in the moment, and I let it stand without explanation.

"Okay," he said. "Shall I talk to the hospital about memorial service arrangements?"

Since the nurse had left I'd thought about this. "Thursday at two at Saint Lucia's Chapel, over by the river."

"I know the place." He verified the availability, then he left me a link on the Feeds with a form to fill out.

After he was gone, I asked the staff if I could be taken to another room, and they transferred me. At least that way I wouldn't be looking at the infant warmer where they'd tried and failed to save my daughter.

Wednesday, November 5

In the morning I confirmed the reservation for the chapel, and as I was preparing to leave, one of the representatives from Terabyne Designs showed up, a visit I'd been expecting.

It was standard in a case like this, although I'd already made my decision regarding getting an Artificial.

The man introduced himself as Benjiro Taka. During the times I'd come to the hospital to comfort congregation members who had just lost loved ones, I'd crossed paths with a few of the Terabyne reps, but I'd never met this one.

Terabyne's regional production center was close by, just off I-75—in fact, my car would take me past it on the way home—and Terabyne employed hundreds of employees, many of them sales reps, so it wasn't very surprising that our paths hadn't crossed yet.

"First of all," he said, "let me tell you how sorry I am for your loss. My deepest and sincerest condolences."

The words sounded genuine, and maybe they were. Or maybe he'd recited them so many times that he'd learned to make false sympathy sound authentic.

"Thank you for saying so."

"Terabyne Designs would like to do all we can to help you navigate through this difficult time in your life."

Yes, and I knew what was coming next.

He went on, "Many people find it helpful to have—"

"A replacement."

"Well, a surrogate. A specially-designed, unique, and personalized Artificial. We have models this size. We can replicate everything about your daughter for you down to her fingerprints. And we offer our units at a greatly reduced price for people in your situation."

"In my situation."

"For anyone who has experienced the recent loss of a loved one."

I knew it was his job, that some people found solace in an Artificial at a time like this—a newborn-sized robot that could cry and be comforted, that would mimic the sleep cycles of a Natural. Far more than simply a technologically advanced doll, the Artificials this size looked so real, acted so real, that it was almost chilling. I'd seen them. I knew. They help some people.

I didn't mention it to Mr. Taka, but my brother, Trevor, was the vice president of global security at Terabyne's headquarters out west. With his high-level position I could get an Artificial any time at cost, but I'd never had any desire to acquire one, not since what happened to our parents when I was in grad school.

I didn't want a robot in my life, especially one that was intended to fill the void left behind from my daughter's death.

"No thank you, Mr. Taka. I'm not interested."

"Of course." He swiped a chip-implanted finger through the air to pass along his contact information to my slate the way someone in the past might have offered me his business card. "If you change your mind."

I knew that wasn't going to happen, but I didn't want to be rude so I accepted the data transfer.

Then he left and I passed through the silent and sterile hallways toward the exit.

By the time I got there, I found a message waiting for me on my slate from my brother. "I saw the Feeds. I'm sorry, Kestrel. Really. I sent you something. It'll arrive at your apartment this afternoon."

He could afford anything money could buy. I could only imagine what he might have sent.

Honestly, I wished it might be something that could take the pain away, or at least distract me enough so I could begin processing what had just happened here. But at the moment I doubted that such a thing existed.

I thought about stopping by the morgue to see Naiobi one last time, but decided against it.

It wouldn't help anything, especially now, more than sixteen hours after she'd passed.

An Artificial wouldn't be affected by death like that. The thought came to me and troubled me. *An Artificial wouldn't decompose.*

A shudder.

Alone, I found my car.

I had the kiss to be thankful for. And the moment when I pressed down that tuft of hair.

Those were the two things on my mind as I left for home to see what my brother, whom I hadn't spoken with in over a year, might have sent me.

2

I didn't make it far before I witnessed the explosion.

The roads were choked with traffic, which wasn't surprising. As it turned out, things these days weren't quite the way people years ago had pictured in their futuristic stories—with flying cars and jetpacks, and homes nestled tranquilly in the clouds.

No, they were not.

Not at all.

Change on the small scale is fast and continues to get faster: microchips, nanotechnology, gene editing, quantum encryption, neuro-linguistic programming in robots, and on and on. Technological advances seem to move in greater and greater leaps the smaller you go, but when it comes to infrastructure, well, that takes time.

Our legislators kept talking about expanding the public transit program here, maybe even utilizing the subway tunnels that had been built nearly a century ago and never used. But with the cost, and since the tunnels kept flooding, I couldn't see that coming for years down the line, especially with the redistribution of tax revenue since the government started providing everyone with a universal basic income.

Nearly ten billion people in the world.

Maybe the number wasn't all that shocking until you realized that there were now seven billion more than there'd been when those subway tunnels were built.

I could hardly wrap my mind around statistics like that. Change like that.

And so, my car drove me past the West Side's sprawling slums and tenement housing complexes that lay along the surface streets leading to the expressway. Dead businesses. Empty storefronts. Lonely, abandoned homes. All in such sharp contrast to the gleaming success of the Terabyne Designs production facility less than a kilometer away.

By building there, Terabyne took advantage of low property values. They also tapped into a ready and willing labor market, and received huge tax breaks from a city hoping to recover from the economic ruin brought on by the automation of more and more jobs and the growing number of out-of-work low-wage earners.

Terabyne.

The cause of the problem.

And now, the solution.

For ease of distribution, the plant was located near the on-ramp, and as my car was merging left onto the highway, I saw a delivery truck racing toward the facility's gated front entrance. Clearly it was moving too fast, but rather than slowing down as it neared the complex, it picked up speed and smashed through the gate, raced past a meditation pool, and slammed into a retaining wall meant to protect the building from this very type of attack.

Heart hammering, I commanded my car to stop.

As it pulled to the shoulder, the truck spewed smoke from its engine and then, as security officers swarmed out of the building to approach it, automatic weapons in hand, the vehicle exploded into a wide and wicked arc of flames that engulfed three of the guards, crumbled a corner of the building, and sent a shockwave punching through the morning, rocking my car even here, more than a hundred meters away.

Although there'd been bombings in Cincinnati by the Purists before, just as there had been in nearly every major city in the country since the Uprising began over a decade ago, this was the first terror attack I'd seen myself.

With the escalating number of attacks at places of worship over the last few years, clergy were now trained in first aid, so I had supplies in my trunk.

Given how sore I was from delivering Naiobi yesterday, I wasn't sure how much assistance I'd be able to provide the survivors, but I felt like I needed to do what I could.

Go, Kestrel. You can at least help get people to safety.

I ordered my car to take me closer.

"Are you certain, Miss Hathaway?" she asked me.

"Yes."

"My sensors indicate that there has been a—"

"Yes. Drive."

Without a steering wheel, there was no way for me to take over the car's navigation system for myself, but when I placed my hand on the vein recognition sensor to confirm my command and take legal responsibility for my "potentially hazardous" decision, the car finally obeyed, turning around and heading toward the front gate.

Most often, the Purists planned simultaneous attacks, and I wondered if there might have been another explosion somewhere else in the city or even if there would be another one here, after the ambulances arrived. But I put that thought aside—I had to if I was going to go any closer.

Once we were near the gate, I had my car park. "Wait here. Ignition off."

"Of course, Miss Hathaway."

Stiff and aching, I awkwardly climbed out of the car to retrieve my government-issued first aid kit from the trunk.

Dark smoke jetted skyward while agitated flames curled up from the fire that pulsed from the truck's blackened carcass.

Three charred bodies lay still and smoking on the pavement.

Though it was too late for them, it wasn't too late for the people who'd been on the perimeter of the blast and now either lay crumpled on the pavement or came stumbling out of the collapsed section of the building.

First aid supplies in hand, I hurried toward them.

The fire's heat met me like a living thing, its tight claws scratching harshly at the exposed skin on my face and hands.

A woman to my left groaned, her legs peppered with shrapnel. Serious injuries, yes, but it didn't look like they were bleeding extensively.

However, the ghastly wound of the guard ahead of me was.

His right arm had been torn nearly all the way off in the explosion.

He'd found a seat on a concrete bench surrounding the reflective pool and was staring vacantly at what remained of his arm and at the blood spurting out and curling ambivalently away from him in the water.

Urgently, I headed his way.

Just like suicide bombers who stuffed nails or ball bearings in their bombs or backpacks, the Purists had learned to fill their vehicles with shards of metal to produce more shrapnel and cause more carnage.

With self-driving cars and trucks these days, it was easier than ever to carry out well-timed and meticulously calculated attacks. You didn't need to entrust the killing to a human being who might hesitate or change his mind at the last instant and not go through with the plan—or might be stopped by police or security officers before the attack could be completed.

Once the safety protocols on the vehicle were disengaged or reprogrammed, it would never change its mind or veer away from its target.

Pack the vehicles with explosives and you had dedicated, fearless killing machines.

Sometimes I wondered if any of that had even crossed the minds of the automotive developers when production of self-driving cars really took off two decades ago.

And technology is a clock you cannot turn backward.

What was done was done.

At the man's side, I could finally gauge the extent of his injuries.

With most of the bones blown away, what was left of his arm hung limply by only the few inadequate threads of flesh and the strained tendons that still remained attached to his shoulder. Half a dozen slivers of metal protruded from his protective vest. If he hadn't been wearing body armor I could only imagine what his chest and stomach would look like.

He was young—probably still in his early twenties. I doubted there would be any way to save his arm, but with a prosthetic he could recover and live a normal life, joining the growing number of people called Plussers who augmented their bodies with technology—some even amputating healthy limbs just so they could join the movement.

So, yes.

A Plusser.

If he didn't bleed out here, in front of me, first.

"Help me." With his free hand, he was fumbling unsuccessfully to quell the flow of blood. "It won't stop."

Even from my limited first aid training I knew that there was an artery in your arm that, when it's severed, can cause you to bleed to death within minutes, if not sooner.

With haste, I unrolled a length of rubber tubing from the first aid kit.

"We need to cut off that blood flow," I said.

"Yes."

"This is going to hurt."

"Do it." His voice was firm and resolute.

I wrapped the tubing around his arm between his shoulder and the place where the severed artery was squirting blood, and then tugged it tight.

He cringed, teeth gritted, but somehow managed not to cry out in pain as I worked.

I tied off the tubing to create a crude tourniquet.

The bleeding slowed and appeared to come under control.

"What's your name?" he asked me. By the strain in his voice it was clear that he was still in a lot of pain and I wished there was more I could do for him.

"Kestrel."

"Are you a doctor?"

I'm a pastor, I thought.

"I know a little first aid," I said.

Blood was dripping off the bench and into the water, where it swirled into intricate patterns that might have been beautiful if their genesis wasn't from something so shocking and awful.

Blood and water.

Two central symbols of my faith.

The blood of Christ shed to offer us new life.

The water of baptism to confirm his covenant with us.

But life and hope seemed like distant dreams to me at the moment, now, here, with death all around me and the loss of my daughter seared into my mind.

The trilling pulse of emergency vehicle sirens ruptured the stillness of the morning.

"The hospital is close by," I told the man. "Help's on the way. It'll be here soon."

The paramedics would be far more skilled at removing the shrapnel from his body armor than I was, and if I started prying out the pieces of metal, any wounds left behind would inevitably bleed, perhaps fiercely. Leaving the objects in place wasn't ideal, but for now it was the best choice.

The air was stained with black smoke, but a slight breeze kept it out of our faces.

He became lightheaded, and I helped him lie back on the bench.

"What's your name?" I asked, trying to keep him alert.

"Ethan Bolderson." And then, his voice dropping a notch, he said, "I've lost a lot of blood."

"The paramedics will help you."

"Okay." But the word was tinged with doubt. "I don't want to die today. Am I going to die?"

"We stopped the bleeding."

I didn't know what else to say. He was right about the extent of blood loss and from what I could tell it really might be too late for him. So, I didn't tell him that he was going to be alright. I couldn't bring myself to say it.

His next question surprised me: "Do you believe in heaven, Kestrel?"

You should be the one asking him that, an inner voice rebuked me. *You're the minister!*

Ever since yesterday afternoon when I'd lost my daughter I'd been questioning my own beliefs about the afterlife, but now I found myself saying the things I'd been taught at seminary to tell people—teachings about our need for a Savior, about the work of Christ, about the offer of paradise to all who are lost in sin, but I didn't know how much I believed those words myself. Not anymore.

Ethan closed his eyes, and I couldn't tell how cognizant he was of anything I was saying.

"Ethan?"

He remained quiet and so, so still.

"Ethan!" Though hesitant to do so, and unsure it was the right thing to try, I slapped his cheek sharply enough to awaken him. "Stay with me."

He regrouped. "Right."

"Hang in there."

In my haste to help him, I'd forgotten to tug on a pair of sterile gloves, and his blood was covering my hands and had also splayed cruel patterns across my clothes.

So much blood.

Still dripping into the pool, an evanescent chronicle of Ethan's suffering.

Blood.

And water.

Now, the two of them brought to mind Christ on the cross and the soldier piercing him with a spear to make sure he was dead.

Blood and water flowed together from his side.

And the scripture referring to it: *"They shall look on Him whom they pierced—"*

"Thank you." Ethan's voice was feeble and small, like he was shrinking.

I didn't know if he was thanking me for waking him up, for helping him in general, or for my words about heaven, but before I could ask, two ambulances came screeching to a stop nearby and a pair of paramedics hustled out of each of them. I flagged down one of the women and she made a beeline toward us.

"Are you real?" Ethan asked me quietly.

"Real?" Maybe he was thinking that he was hallucinating, just imagining me.

"A Natural," he clarified, his words pained and now hardly audible.

"Yes."

After I stepped back, the paramedic took over, assessing his vitals, and a minute later she and her partner were carefully positioning Ethan onto a rolling gurney. As they did, I heard him mutter, "I just don't want to . . ." But the end of his sentence was too quiet for me to make out.

I imagined he might've been repeating what he'd said earlier about not wanting to die.

I watched in silence as they wheeled him away.

As I stood there amid the deadly debris on the ground, doubt crept in. Even though only moments ago I'd been hopeful that I was doing enough for him, now I wondered if that'd really been the case at all.

Don't let him die.

Please, God, don't let him die. Not like Naiobi. Not like my baby.

Yesterday's bleak clouds had moved on and now, as the smoke cleared away in the stiffening wind, unforgiving sunlight gleamed off the reflective glass of the Terabyne plant's tinted windows that were designed to impress the very world that they were also meant to keep at bay.

By the time the first two ambulances left, two more had shown up. Since the initial responders had focused on transporting the survivors to the hospital, the dead had been left behind, and now a shift in the wind brought me the horrible stench of burnt flesh, a stark reminder of man's inhumanity to man.

As if our world needed any more of those.

In all of our years of existence, we haven't come very far. No, not since that day when Cain took the life of his brother, Abel. The firstborn of humanity slaughtering the second. What a legacy. What a testament to human nature, to the depth of the Fall.

"Where is your brother, Abel?" the Lord asked him.

"What? Am I my brother's keeper?"

"What have you done? The voice of your brother's blood cries out to Me from the ground!"

So much violence in our history. So many times the Lord has had to listen to the voice of the dead crying out to him from the ground.

Or from the bloody carpet of a bedroom after a simple argument took a violent turn.

Or a stretch of blood-splattered sidewalk.

Or the bullet-riddled halls of a school building.

So many reminders of who we are.

One of the police officers who'd shown up offered to help me wash off in the fountain, but I figured there was already enough of Ethan's blood in there, so instead, I used the antiseptic wipes and absorbent bandages from the first aid kit to serviceably clean my hands and forearms.

As I did, I found myself doubling over in pain from giving birth yesterday and the officer came to my aid, but I waved him off. "I'm alright. I'll be okay."

Finally, I returned to my car and left for home.

Once inside the vehicle, I noticed that my clothes bore the odor of smoke and death.

And on the drive along Cincinnati's clogged roads, I prayed a desperate, lonely prayer that Ethan Bolderson would survive.

Unlike Naiobi.

3

At my apartment, I found that the package from my brother had not yet arrived.

No word yet on Ethan's condition.

I cleaned up—a shower and fresh clothes—but through it all, I still couldn't relax or find respite from all that was on my mind. When I checked my messages I found several from congregation members who'd learned what had happened to my daughter.

Which brought her death to the forefront of my mind again.

One woman asked urgently if I'd had the chance to baptize Naiobi before she died.

Our denomination believed in baptizing infants, that it was the covenant God makes with us to call us into his presence through his prevenient grace.

But we didn't believe in baptizing the dead.

So, no, I had not baptized my daughter.

According to our understanding of baptism, an unbaptized child would still be received by the Lord through grace that was bestowed through the Holy Spirit. So I tried to take comfort in that.

Tried.

But comfort eluded me and a dark sweep of grief returned, locking me inescapably in its arms.

For the time being I didn't reply to that message.

Other people told me that they were praying for me and emphasized that if there was anything I needed, to please let them know.

I knew that the offers were heartfelt and came from genuine concern. If I asked, my congregants would bring me food or do whatever they could for me, no questions asked. But I needed some space, and I didn't want to see anybody else today.

Last month, anticipating that I'd be at home here with Naiobi, I'd arranged for another pastor to cover for me in the pulpit for the next few Sundays. So, thankfully, I didn't need to prepare a sermon or even show up this weekend. And at this point, I was no longer planning to. I had no idea what to say to anyone about God or his plans for us, or how I would respond to people's sympathy with the appropriate measure of respect.

I messaged the people back, expressing my thanks and telling them that I would let them know if I needed their help. I wanted the two o'clock viewing tomorrow to be private, so I didn't let anyone know about it.

So, our congregation.

Our church was quiet and predictable, and though it was welcoming, it rarely received new members.

In truth, it was slowly dying.

We only had seventy or so regular attendees, and most of them were older than me. I didn't put on an impressive Sunday morning show, so maybe that was it—just simple preaching with traditional hymns sung to a synthesized piano.

These days, using free software on the Feeds, a ten-year-old could produce a symphony that was nearly indistinguishable from one played by professional musicians, so fewer and fewer people were bothering to learn to play actual instruments.

I found the declining number of Natural musicians sad, though I wasn't certain why. Simple nostalgia maybe. I owned a violin that my grandfather had taught me to play when I was a girl. I didn't really want people to think I was clinging to obscure ways so I rarely brought it out to play. But I hadn't gotten rid of it and it waited in my closet, stored on the top shelf.

Out of sight, out of mind.

A way to make music without a machine.

The adrenaline from being present at the explosion had drained away, and now the emotional impact of what I'd been through over the last twenty-four hours began to overwhelm me.

I found my way to the couch and collapsed onto it.

The wall to my left contained sturdy shelves that were packed with my books—inspirational titles, biblical commentaries, and tomes of theology, as well as a full collection of the works of the prolific author and minister from the early 1900s, F. W. Boreham. All of his were first editions.

Call me old-fashioned, but for some reason I had a penchant for reading from the printed page rather than a screen or hologram or VR program. And so, I had a rarity in my apartment—a library with actual paper-bound books.

In contrast, the wall in front of me was digitized and, with a simple command, could become a window, a mirror, a dozen different screens to watch a dozen different shows at the same time, or a sweeping vista of veritably anywhere on the planet. I tended toward the Blue Ridge Mountains of western North Carolina where I grew up near Asheville, in an artist's enclave nestled high in the mountains.

But right now I didn't want to think about growing up or my childhood because it only made me think of my dead parents and my estranged brother and my inability to start a family of my own.

And, of course, that made me think of Naiobi.

The grief I'd started to feel while reading the notes from my congregants sharpened and I wept, oh how I wept for my daughter.

Tears, like those of my Lord—the tears that had drawn me to him in the first place.

I'd never understood what it meant to be a Christian until I was twenty and met a homeless, elderly vet on a park bench in uptown Charlotte and he spoke to me about the tears of Jesus.

Three times we read that the Savior wept.

Once he cried because of Jerusalem's rejection of him as their

Messiah. Riding that donkey into the city should have been a victorious moment. Instead, his heart broke.

A verse in the fifth chapter of Hebrews mentions that Christ prayed with vehement cries and with tears. We don't know which exact instances those words refer to, but apparently Jesus was known for his despairing and desperate prayers.

Third: he cried when his friend died.

"Jesus wept on the way to the tomb where Lazarus had done been buried," the grizzled old vagrant who'd once served his country in Iraq told me that day. "And yet the Lord knew he would see him again in just a few minutes."

"Then why did he weep?" I asked.

"Well, some people say it was from seeing the grief of those around him, from witnessin' their lack of faith, but I think the people who were there understood the truth: when they saw the Lord cry, they said, 'See how much he loved his friend.' Jesus loved Lazarus and he lost him, and it hurt."

He paused long enough to take a drink from a crinkled water bottle, and then went on. "They say the Lord knows all things, so the future is in there too. He knew he could bring his friend back, but he still cried."

I waited quietly as he continued.

"Despite Jesus's knowin' all about the future, his belief in heaven, his miraculous power to heal—and even to raise the dead—he cried. None of those things quieted the pain of loss when his friend died. That's how deep the love of the Carpenter runs."

At the time, I imagined that those who believed in God had varying impressions of what their deity was like—perhaps an imposing judge or a distant and disinterested monarch or a doting mother. All caricatures.

To me, this image of Jesus at the tomb of his friend was different.

A carpenter with a broken heart? A man who could cast out demons, calm storms, and walk on the water, yet found his love for his friend so consuming that he wept when the man died?

That was the kind of Savior I could be drawn to—not a detached, overly holy, halo-wearing saint, but a man who passionately loved his friends and whose heart broke when they died. A man who was ultimately willing to die even for his enemies.

I could fall in love with a God like that.

And I had.

And it'd led me all the way to the pulpit to preach about him.

But now, I wondered if any of it was real after all—the stories, the miracles, my faith.

Did I love a God who would take my daughter's life and ignore my prayers and abandon me when I needed him the most? Could I? Was he even there at all?

The thoughts were too much for me.

I needed a distraction.

Drying my tears, I told ViRA, my apartment's Virtual Residential Assistant, "Bring up nineteen." A simple voice command to the microphones embedded in the wall. "The Pacific Ocean. Sunset."

As drained as I was, I thought the calming scene would send me right to sleep, but even with relaxing music and the serene view of the gently rippling waves, I couldn't unwind, so at last I gave up, warmed up some leftovers, and turned on the Feeds to see if Ethan had survived.

The news anchor confirmed that the Purists had taken responsibility for the bombing, something I wasn't surprised to hear. Also, though I'd feared there might be a second attack, that hadn't been the case, so at least there was something to be thankful for.

The announcer informed us that two more of the wounded had died, bringing the total to five fatalities. However, the authorities hadn't released the names of the deceased, so I still didn't know if Ethan had made it.

Considering the amount of damage to the building, I was astonished that the death toll wasn't higher.

A Terabyne public affairs representative came on and, after sharing his condolences, assured us that the facility's production was still on schedule and that the public should not expect any disruption in the services they provided.

Apparently, a number of earlier-model Artificials were damaged beyond any hope of repair when the corner of the building collapsed in the explosion, but he explained that they were all scheduled to have their CaTEs next week so it didn't ultimately matter that they'd been destroyed today.

Also, he promised that the company would do whatever it could to cooperate with the investigation and bring the "domestic terrorists who perpetrated this brutal and barbaric attack" to justice.

In his job of overseeing global security, my brother would no doubt be playing a significant role in the investigation—at least from Terabyne's side.

"The Purists will not succeed with their tactics of terror," the representative assured us. "They will not deter the technological advances that our society needs, and they will not hinder us in our quest to provide the continuing benefits of Artificials to humankind."

I found it somewhat ironic that the spokesperson for a company that produced nearly eighty percent of the world's cognizant Artificials was a Natural. After all, reading from a screen and answering questions from reporters would have been easy for most modern Artificials, but the company apparently preferred to keep its public face that of someone who actually breathed air and had a heart that pumped real blood.

Our world has not been the same since the Uprising began twelve years ago.

The Purists were fiercely against Artificials, arguing that giving machines autonomy would eventually have catastrophic consequences when the robots one day turned against us. So far, however, the most violent attacks had not come from machines waging some sort of apocalyptic uprising but from humans killing in the name of peace.

Sometimes derisively labeled "technophobes," Purists claimed they weren't against progress; they just had a different view of what progress looked like. They believed that augmenting humans to be more like machines and designing machines to be more like humans was not the pathway to true progress, but a departure from it.

With roots in Deep Ecology, most Purists shared the view that overpopulation and human encroachment on natural habitats had resulted in climate chaos. They supported the return to a much smaller world population and simpler, less technologically dependent lives.

Some even belonged to the Voluntary Human Extinction Movement, refusing to reproduce and believing that human beings were not the best thing to come along on our planet but, by nearly all objective measures, one of the worst.

I shared the Purists' passion for caring for the environment, and after what happened to my parents, I also understood the group's reticence to blithely embrace new technologies just because they were available—when your mom and dad are killed by an Artificial it seemed like a natural response.

I'd blogged about those issues years ago in my more liberal and vocal twenties, even briefly considering joining one of the Purists' more mainline environmental advocacy groups. But I'd held back and now, after I saw what they were capable of, I was thankful that I had stayed clear of joining.

No more news came on about the attack, but instead, the story shifted to the civil war in Egypt; however, rather than listen to more tragic news, I turned off the Feeds and finished eating in silence.

Still exhausted, I returned to the couch to try to rest, and this time when I closed my eyes, I dropped off into a much-needed but agitated sleep.

And I dreamt.

I was sitting on my bed holding Naiobi, and she was staring at me with wide-open eyes, ready to take in the wonder and the glory of the world. Now a few months old, she was smiling, and I could not get enough of looking at her precious face.

So much joy there. So much promise and hope.

A tapping at the window caught my attention and I looked up to see a face—torn with shrapnel and darkened with sooty burns. The man—it might have been Ethan, I couldn't tell for sure—opened his mouth but made no sound.

His eyelids were gone—either burned away or simply missing, for it was a dream.

A dream.

Fierce eyes, wide and unblinking, staring deeply into me.

He held up a still-smoldering hand with bone fragments visible through the split and blackened skin, and placed his palm against the glass, then peered at me as he removed his hand and then smacked his palm against the window, which shuddered from the impact. After opening his mouth again but saying nothing, he hit the glass again, harder.

Smack.

Clinging protectively to Naiobi, I rose to get her to safety.

Hand against the glass.

—Smack—

And this time the window shattered and he climbed through, the teeth of glass that were still wedged in the window frame tearing at his clothes and ripping through the burnt flesh of his hands as he grabbed hold of them.

I spun to get away, to make it to the door before he could reach me.

Naiobi began crying, and when I glanced at her, I found that now her face was scorched too, blistered and smoking. Her eyes glowed like two coals embedded in her eye sockets.

A voice behind me spoke my name: "Kestrel."

The man grabbed my leg from behind. "Stop!" I shouted, and tugged to get free. "Let go!"

He jerked me backward, and as I lost my balance, Naiobi slipped from my arms.

"No!"

I scrambled toward her, but was too slow.

As she landed on the floor with a sickening *thud* I awoke with a start.

"Kestrel." It was ViRA speaking my name in her calm, composed way.

My baby.

My baby.

I willed myself to fall asleep again to save her, to undo what had just happened, but despite how hard I tried, I could not reenter the dream and instead I was just left with a vague sense of lingering terror and no way to fix it.

"Kestrel."

My heart was jackhammering in my chest from the nightmare and my hands were shaking.

"You have a visitor at the door, Kestrel."

Then I heard the knock.

Oh.

Though I couldn't be certain, the man in my dream hitting that glass might very well have been my subconscious's interpretation of the rapping at the door. And that dream voice speaking my name had likely been ViRA.

Either way, it didn't matter. I just wanted to shake myself free from the dream—but the residue of it clung to me, impossible to get rid of, and the more I tried to forget it, the more rooted it became in my memory.

"Kestrel," she said, "are you—"

"I heard you, ViRA."

The digital clock on the wall told me that it was already after five—I must have slept longer than I thought.

Since the police officers at the site of the attack had been more interested in securing the scene and with crowd management than with interviewing witnesses about what had happened, I'd ended up leaving without giving a statement.

I anticipated that the video surveillance outside the Terabyne plant would have captured footage of everyone present and, with facial recognition and the fact that I'd told Ethan my first name, I suspected that now a police officer had come to speak with me and get my account of the attack.

You dropped her. You dropped your baby.

No, no, no, it was just a dream.

Still trying to gather myself, I went to the door.

But instead of a police officer, I found a delivery droid waiting for me. A stout box as tall as I was stood beside him.

The droid clunkily tilted its head and smiled in that annoying and sanctimonious way that they have about them.

"Miss Hathaway? Miss Kestrel Hathaway?"

"Yes."

"Excellent." It nodded, a gesture that was meant to make it appear more human-like, but as rudimentary as its movements were, they looked far too mechanical to make me think of anything natural for a human being.

With the box's dimensions and the distinctive Terabyne Designs logo on the side, I didn't really need to open it to know what it was.

The package from my brother.

An Artificial.

"Take it back."

"Excuse me, ma'am? I am—"

"Ship it back. I'm telling you, I'm not accepting this delivery."

I closed the door. A moment passed before the droid knocked again. I ignored it.

It didn't seem to know what to do. Apparently, it wasn't used to people refusing shipments.

I asked ViRA to bring up the external camera. "Small screen," I said. A portion of the wall changed from the view of the ocean to footage of the hallway in front of my door.

"Exterior speaker."

"Yes, Kestrel."

"Go on," I told the droid. "Ship it back. Leave my home."

It took two more attempts and a final threat to call security before I convinced it, but at last, toting the box, the droid ambled down the hallway toward the exit.

I let out an exasperated breath.

Trevor was going to find out that I hadn't accepted the package—if he hadn't been notified of it automatically already—so I knew I needed to speak with him.

After a year without talking to him, I had no idea how this was going to go.

"ViRA, put a call through to my brother."

"Your brother?"

"Yes."

There was a small pause, as if she was surprised to hear me confirm that. "Voice or video?"

"Video."

I didn't have to wait long. A few moments after she sent the request through, his face came up on the screen.

He was at his desk, the sprawling Terabyne campus visible in the wide window behind him, the Cascade Mountains rising majestically and protectively in the background.

"Hello, Kestrel."

"Hello, Trevor," I said. "We need to talk."

4

At forty-one, my brother appeared as handsome and fit as ever. The heavy stubble gave him a look of rugged masculinity, while his incisive eyes and unobtrusive smile added a welcome tenderness. The whole package.

"I'm so sorry you lost your baby," he said.

"And so you sent me an Artificial?"

"You're not married, you don't have a partner, I thought—"

"Did you order it before you heard about Naiobi?"

"What?"

"Before or after you heard that she had died?"

"Before. I figured you could use some help with your baby when you brought her home and—"

"You know how I feel about Artificials."

"Which is something I've never understood." His voice had stiffened. "Really, Kestrel."

"After what happened to Mom and Dad? You still don't get it?"

"That was a fluke. Artificials back then were archaic compared to what we have today. Our current models can—"

"Save the sales pitch for someone else. I refused delivery."

"What?"

"I don't want an Artificial. You know that. We've been through this before."

"It's been a long time since we've talked. Since . . ." His voice trailed off. "I was hoping that by now you would—"

"I would what?"

"Have changed your views," he said diplomatically.

"Uh-huh."

"This is a tough time for you. I understand that."

And then neither of us spoke. What was there to say? My daughter was dead. There was no comfort he could offer me.

As I thought of that, of Naiobi, a terrible, crushing sadness overwhelmed me and I looked away from the screen so Trevor wouldn't see me tear up.

Keep it together, Kestrel.

Don't cry.

And I did not.

As difficult as it was, I forced myself to hold the tears in.

"There was an attack," he said, changing the subject, "there in Cincinnati, at our production plant earlier today."

"Yes, I know." I looked at him again. "I was there."

He straightened up slightly. "You were?"

"I was on my way home from the hospital. I saw it happen."

"Are you okay? I mean, you weren't hurt?"

"I'm fine."

"My division is in charge of investigating it."

"Okay." I didn't want to talk about the attack. "I just called so you'd know that I sent the Artificial back."

"Did you see anything that could help us out?"

"I saw people die, Trevor. That's what I remember. A truck drove through security. The explosion swallowed people up. I don't know of anything else that might help you."

"With some of our latest neural implants, there are promising breakthroughs in helping people recall details from traumatic events that they—"

"Trevor!"

"Sorry." He was quiet, then asked, "Are you going to have a memorial service for Naiobi?"

"Tomorrow at two. But it's not really a service. It's just me saying goodbye."

"Would you like me to come?"

"No, no. That's okay."

"Are you sure? I could fly in and—"

"No. But thanks."

It seemed like a moment during which he might glance down to check the time or something, but he didn't. Instead, he said, "Jordan is special."

"Jordan?"

"The Artificial I sent you."

I shook my head.

"Just . . . Listen, Kestrel, I know we've had our differences in the past, but this isn't a time when you need to be alone, or shut people out."

I was about to counter that, but paused.

A change had come over my brother. He had a look of deep concern that I never would've expected to see. "Just try him out," he said. "Just for a few days. I promise you, if you decide you don't want him after that, you can ship him back and I won't pressure you anymore to get an Artificial. Not ever again. And if you want, I'll stay out of your life. I won't call. I'll leave you alone. Just give Jordan a try."

Why is this so important to him?

A soft buzz came from his end and he looked down toward what was no doubt an incoming call, but he tapped a button to decline it and peered at me from across his desk, waiting for me to reply.

I had no idea who might have been contacting him, but in truth it didn't matter. He had plenty of people screening calls for him, so if one made it through, it was almost certainly something vital, an issue only he could deal with. A year ago he would have asked me to wait while he accepted the call. I was certain of that much.

"Alright," I told him at last. "Have the company ship it back. I'll accept delivery this time. Two days. I'll give it two days and if I decide I don't want it, I return it. And you won't bring this up again."

"Yes."

I said nothing about his offer to refrain from contacting me. I wasn't sure how I felt about that. As healthy as it might be for us to have a closer relationship, I didn't know if that could ever happen again, or even exactly what it might look like if we did.

"Why does it mean so much to you that I have an Artificial?" I said.

"You're a good person. You don't deserve to be alone."

I have the Lord, I thought. *I have my faith.* But I didn't say that. Trevor was an avowed atheist. He'd given up any semblance of faith in a higher power after our parents died.

Well, *died* wasn't exactly the right word to describe what happened to them. It didn't come close to doing justice to describing the brutal way their lives ended.

Shot.

Slaughtered.

Gunned down.

Any of those descriptions would've been a lot more on the right track.

I didn't respond to his comment about me not deserving to be alone because I wasn't so sure I had the Lord, or my own faith, anymore and I didn't want to mislead him.

"Is there anything else I can do?" Trevor said. "Do you need money for—"

"I don't need money."

"Okay."

The Artificial was his way of showing he cared, and so was the offer of money—I understood that—but the fracture between us was deep, and it wasn't going to be healed by the gift of a robot or a credit transfer to my account.

"Let me know if you have any questions about Jordan," he offered.

"Right."

And then, after fumbling through our awkward goodbyes, we ended the call.

Obviously the recovery time after giving birth varies for different women. It depends on how long you're in labor and how big your baby is, in addition to any number of medical issues or complications that might arise. And I had to admit that even though I was emotionally devastated, physically I was feeling far better than I would've expected.

However, my milk had come in and my breasts hurt and it was a terrible kind of pain. My mind knew that my baby was dead, but my body was reacting as if she were still alive. I'd never felt so lonely in my life.

According to the articles on the Feeds, I should avoid pumping since it might keep the milk from drying up. Still, I found it necessary and so I did.

Later in the evening, the droid returned, delivering the adult-sized box to my living room.

My brother had told me that Jordan was special.

We would see about that.

You have two days, I thought. *Starting from when I power you up tomorrow. Then I'm sending you back.*

A message came in from the hospital offering me counseling services along with information on working through the stages of grief. "We're here to assist you. To listen. To help you heal," it read.

I filed it to respond to later.

Trevor's question regarding a memorial service stuck in my mind, but I couldn't bear the thought of going through saying goodbye to my baby with an audience around me. It would just be too traumatic, too difficult, so I decided not to post the time on the Feeds. I would have a private visitation without drawing undo attention to myself or my loss.

The Pollyannaish idea that Naiobi would live on in my heart brought me no comfort. No, the dead do not live on in our hearts. We remember them, of course, but that's of little comfort, or none at all. In fact, I'd often seen that when people were grieving, the lingering memories of their loved ones actually made it more difficult to move on.

The dead don't live on in our hearts.

They're gone.

I gave the box a wide berth as I passed it on the way to my bedroom.

———

"What do we know about her?" Special Agent Nick Vernon paused as he scrolled through a series of images on the screen in front of him.

The woman appeared to be about his age. She had a gentle-looking, attractive face, but also an intensity about her that made her appear to be someone who could stand up for herself.

"She's a Methodist minister," Agent Ripley Carlisle, his associate, said. "Wrote anti-technology blogs while she was at seminary."

Nick had worked with Ripley for the last six months. Bald, wiry, and strong, the man had a presence about him that seemed almost serpentine.

The two men were in Nick's office in the National Counterterrorism Bureau suite at the federal building in downtown Cincinnati. The cramped and quiet room stood in sharp contrast to the frenzied activity in the unit's expansive control center down the hall.

"And now?" Nick said.

"She was one of the first responders at the scene of the bombing. And her purchase history includes hundreds of paper-bound books."

"That doesn't prove anything."

"I'm not looking for proof yet, sir, just connections."

A touch of silence. "Your report says she offered assistance to one of the victims."

"Yes. A Terabyne security officer named Ethan Bolderson."

"And?"

"And?"

"Did he make it?"

"He did. He's at the hospital, still sedated, but in stable condition."

"Start with him before you talk with her. As soon as he's awake find out what she said to him."

"Yes, sir."

"And contact the plant's security office. I want a copy of the surveillance camera footage of her arrival." Then he added, "And pull up those articles that she wrote. I want to read them for myself."

5

Thankfully I made it through the night without any more terrifying dreams.

I ate breakfast staring at the box in the living room.

For some reason it looked taller and more imposing than it had yesterday when the droid brought it in.

I called Saint Lucia's Chapel to confirm that things were set.

"We have the service scheduled for two o'clock."

"It won't be a service per se," I said to their director. "I'm just coming in to say goodbye to my daughter. It'll just be me."

"No visitation then?"

"I'll be alone."

A pause. "We're here to meet your needs. Will it be a chemical or fire cremation?"

Because of zoning constraints, scarcity of land, and overpopulation issues, cremation was the norm these days, but I'd never warmed to the idea of dissolving a loved one using alkaline hydrolysis or reducing them to ashes. However, by law, funeral homes still made concessions to bury the dead—as long as you were willing to pay.

"Burial," I said.

"Do you have a plot?"

"I'd like one overlooking the river. Do you have anything like that?"

"Will cost be an issue for you?" he asked after a slight hesitation. "We have a limited number of plots available, you know."

Over the years I'd saved up some money that I'd intended to give to any children I might have for their wedding or for college or a down payment on a house. Now, I would be using it to pay for my daughter's burial.

"Can we sort through that and handle the credit transfer when I arrive?"

"Of course."

"I'll come by before two so we can meet. Figure all that out."

"Alright, Ms. Hathaway."

End call.

Though I'd committed to opening the box today, I was still reticent to do so, and couldn't quite bring myself to power up the Artificial inside of it—not yet. I'd never owned one for myself and had avoided them ever since the tragedy that left both of my parents dead. So right now I wanted to find out a little more about the implications of having one around before I turned this unit on.

Admittedly, it might have been a way of stalling, but either way, I went to the Feeds to read up on owning an Artificial.

I already knew that, depending on the role the machine was meant to fulfill, it would have different levels of autonomy and the accountability that came with it.

Unlike simpler droids or manufacturing robots that lacked advanced neural processors, today's cognizant Artificials had self-awareness, consciousness, and free will—and because of that, they'd been granted certain rights by law.

It used to be that people designed machines simply as utilitarian devices to make life simpler, easier, or safer. However, over time, as the machines became self-aware, things began to change.

Robotic rights have been advancing steadily ever since 2017, when Sophia became the first robot to be given citizenship in a country, when Saudi Arabia accepted her.

The right for Artificials to marry Naturals was granted by the

European Union in 2031, following the right to consent laws two years earlier.

After all, if the Artificials were morally free agents—so the argument went—they shouldn't be treated the same as toasters and washing machines, or be limited to having only the same rights as a coffee bean grinder.

So, six years ago the International Artificial Intelligence Rights Forum, working with the United Nations and the team of Artificials who'd originally advocated for the rights in the first place, drew up three inalienable rights for Artificials—granted, as it were, by their creators.

First, the right to exist. That made it against the law to destroy a cognizant Artificial without its permission or unless the life of a human was at risk.

Second, the right to have hope. This resulted in Terabyne's establishment of the Consciousness Realignment Algorithm, or the CoRA.

When an Artificial experienced a Catastrophic Terminal Event, most often referred to as a CaTE, the Artificial's consciousness, memory, understanding, and aspirations would be uploaded to a secure mainframe computer at Terabyne's headquarters in the Cascade Mountains on the campus where Trevor worked. In this way, the robots would live on and wouldn't need to fear their demise.

The CoRA was the closest thing that there was to an afterlife for machines, and it provided them with hope, just as belief in an afterlife brings hope to so many human beings.

And finally, Artificials had the inviolable right to die. All self-aware Artificials were, by design, apoptotic.

This was the most controversial of the three rights, but was actually fought for the most intractably by the Artificials themselves.

The experience of being human is much more than simply knowing what human beings know or even processing information in ways humans might do. The essence of being human requires conceptualizing life from the perspective of someone who will not live forever on this planet.

And that was what the Artificials wanted—the closest possible semblance to the human experience.

In order to encounter life the way humans do, you must be able to live in the paradox of knowing that you are finite—that you might die at any moment, in fact—but also, at the same time, you must have the ability to seek joy and meaning.

How does a sentient, self-aware being experience both the truth of life's brevity and also cling to the hope of tomorrow? Looking forward to entering the CoRA allowed Artificials a way to live within this paradox without despairing their brief existence.

Consciousness is not just a collection of facts. It isn't just intelligence and emotion that a machine might exhibit. We also shape our lives around the beliefs that we have. As a result, a self-aware computer, one with consciousness, must also be one with beliefs.

So, the three rights were intertwined and interdependent, and formed the framework for Artificials to pursue meaning while also experiencing, as much as possible, what it would be like to exist as a finite biological organism.

I got lost reading about the different views on the establishment of the CoRA—some people claiming that it was a good thing since it allowed machines to live on, others claiming that it was simply a way to manipulate the system to sell more Artificials, but finally, as I was finishing lunch, I realized that I'd learned all I needed to.

I had to admit that I was, in fact, stalling.

It was time to open the box.

Because of the weight of its contents, the packaging tape that'd been used to secure the flaps was thick and formidable, and I doubted that a regular letter opener or scissors blade would handle it. Somewhere in the closet I had the hunting knife that my dad gave me when I turned twelve. That would do the trick.

I went down the hallway to my bedroom, feeling a clutch of pain as I passed the door to the nursery I'd prepared for Naiobi.

And also guilt, not just for being so good at distracting myself from powering up the Artificial, but also from avoiding thinking about the death of my dear, sweet daughter.

———•———

Agent Ripley Carlisle knuckle-rapped on Ethan Bolderson's hospital room door, and when Ethan invited him in, he entered, closed the door softly behind him, and then locked it.

The room smelled lemony-aseptic-clean, the way hospitals do. A machine monitoring Ethan's vitals emitted a soft, barely audible hum and a steady, metronomic beep.

As Ripley approached the bed, he could see that Ethan's right arm had been amputated just below the shoulder. A tube offering him a morphine drip was attached to his other arm.

"Hello?" Ethan said questioningly. "Do I know you?"

"My name is Agent Carlisle. I work with the federal agency tasked with finding the people who attacked your place of work yesterday."

"The NCB," Ethan guessed.

"Yes." He must have been a trusting person because he didn't ask for an ID, but Ripley showed him his NCB badge anyway—over the years he'd found that it instilled more trust in the people he was interviewing.

As he pocketed it, he said, "From what I hear, you're a lucky man. You lost a lot of blood."

"They had to give me two transfusions. But it looks like I'm gonna be alright."

"That's good news."

"I'll say."

A beat. "I understand that you met up with a woman after the attack."

"A woman?"

"Who helped you. By the meditation pool."

"Oh. Yes. She told me her name was Kestrel."

"Did she give you a last name?"

"No."

Ripley walked to the window and dialed the blinds shut. "What do you know about her?"

"Nothing—except that she knew first aid. She saved my life. I was bleeding out." With his free hand he indicated the stump where his other arm used to be. "They're prepping me for an artificial arm."

"You'll be a Plusser."

"Yep. It shouldn't be that bad."

"No. It shouldn't." Ripley dragged a chair over to the bedside and took a seat. He studied the screen of the machine that was tracking Ethan's body temperature, blood pressure, heart rate, and respiration. A steady beep.

Beep and hum.

"What else can you tell me about her?" Ripley said.

Ethan shook his head. "I don't know, I . . . Well . . . She was religious. I was fading in and out, I remember that. I was scared I'd die. She talked to me about heaven. Seemed to know a lot about it."

"She's a minister."

"I wasn't aware of that, but sure, that makes sense."

Beep.

And hum.

"And she arrived right away after the explosion?" Ripley asked.

"Yeah. And thank God she did. I might not have made it otherwise."

"Certainly. And did she say anything about the attack?"

"About the attack?"

"About who might have been responsible?"

Once again Ethan shook his head. "No. Nothing like that."

"Have you spoken with the police about this?"

"Not yet. They're supposed to be coming in, though. I thought maybe that's who it was when you knocked on the door."

"Alright." Ripley snapped on a pair of surgical gloves. "Well, I'm sorry it has to be like this, but there's a bigger plan at work. You can take some comfort in that, in knowing that you'll be serving the greater good."

"The greater good?"

"The blueprints on your home computer. The attack. The way you orchestrated it. What your group has planned for Saturday in Cascade Falls. Something has to be done."

Ethan narrowed his eyes. "What are you talking about?"

"It's probably better if you don't fight it." Ripley tapped the "privacy" setting on the monitor that doctors used when examining patients so no alarms would go off if the patient's vitals changed. Then he leaned over the bed. "Just let yourself go. It's nothing personal."

A flash of terrible comprehension crossed Ethan's face and he shot his hand out to punch the call button to summon the nurse, but Ripley's reflexes were too fast and he stopped him before he could reach it. Grabbing Ethan's wrist, Ripley pinned it firmly against the bed.

Ethan might have cried out for help, but Ripley gripped the man's throat and squeezed.

Ethan struggled valiantly to get free, but with Ripley's strength it was futile from the start. Long ago he'd had both arms amputated and replaced with artificial ones, and being a Plusser had its distinct advantages—with augmented strength being right up there at the top of the list.

Beep.

Beep.

Hum.

Ripley observed the man's face carefully as he died, taking special note of the look in his eyes as the fight faded away and the final drift of hopelessness sank in.

The fragility of human life, the finality of death, the abrupt moment when a person passes from one to the other, Ripley found it all intriguing—had for years—even before leaving the military and joining the Bureau. He always found it to be a liberating experience, each time one that he wanted to experience again.

When it was over and Ethan's body had stopped its awkward and incessant twitching, Ripley straightened the covers around him, and then took out his slate and made the call.

"And?" the electronically-masked voice said.

"It's done. Now what?"

"I think it's time for you to visit Miss Hathaway."

6

Somewhat warily, I approached the box.

The search for the knife had taken me longer than I'd anticipated and eventually led me to scour through the three bankers boxes of items left to me after my parents' death. Finally, though, I located it—a sturdy fixed-blade knife that both my father and his father before him had used to gut the deer they shot in the forests surrounding our home.

I'd never hunted with them.

I'd never wanted to kill anything, even just a deer.

Since I wasn't sure how stable the Artificial would be after I opened the cardboard, rather than take the chance that it might topple out and crash to the floor, I tipped the box, heavy as it was, lengthwise onto the carpet before beginning to open it.

I ran the blade along the seam between the folds of cardboard, slitting enough tape to free the flaps. Then, I set down the knife, eased them aside, and, somewhat warily, stared into the box.

At a face that looked as lifelike as that of any Natural.

Startled, I scrambled backward.

I'd certainly seen adult Artificials that looked like Naturals before, but they always had a mimetic quality about them. This one could easily pass as a human being.

Jordan's eyes were closed, giving the illusion that he was asleep.

Out of curiosity, and half-expecting him to move when I did so, I tentatively reached in and touched his cheek, and found it to be smooth and cool—cooler than a human's skin, but otherwise remarkably similar in feel and texture. However, that only served to remind me of the moment when I'd kissed my daughter's lifeless cheek on Tuesday, and I snatched my hand back as if it'd just been burned.

An envelope lay on Jordan's motionless chest.

At first I thought it might be a note from Trevor, but when I opened it, I found that it was from the manufacturing plant instead.

> Congratulations on your purchase! We're thankful that you have chosen this model from Terabyne Designs' family of fine, quality products! Before turning on your Artificial, please take a moment to choose his Human Nature Alignment by registering him through the Feeds. (Or, if you wish, simply power Jordan up and he will guide you through the process himself!) Just press the button on the inside of his left wrist to turn him on! And remember, we're here to help. If you need anything, please contact your local product representative, Benjiro Taka.

Benjiro was the same rep who'd offered me an Artificial newborn as a surrogate to Naiobi. Considering how many representatives Terabyne had, I found it a bit coincidental that he was the one listed here as well, especially since Trevor had told me that he'd decided before my daughter's death to send this Artificial to me.

I set the note aside.

I wasn't quite sure what the Human Nature Alignment was all about, but I decided I could take care of that once the Artificial was powered on.

I took a deep breath and gingerly pressed the gently glowing, bluish button on the inside of Jordan's wrist.

And he opened his eyes.

⋅———⋅

He opens his eyes.

A woman is staring down at him. Caucasian. Mid-thirties. He

wonders if she is pretty. He believes that she is, but he's not sure how to know for certain.

How can you tell? What is the essence of beauty? Where does true loveliness actually begin?

He has the feeling that he has seen her before—some vague sense of familiarity, but he has no idea how that could be.

You're not remembering; you're processing. She's familiar to you because you're programmed to build relationships with humans. Pattern recognition. That's what this is. Nothing more.

He waits for her to speak, but instead she edges slowly away from him.

"Hello," he says at last.

"Hello."

Her voice is soft and delicate. But there's a hint of hesitancy and uncertainty in it.

"My name is Jordan." The words find their way to the surface. Thinking them as he speaks them. Combining thought and action, desire and speech, without any conscious effort. He recognizes this as it happens, aware that it is occurring, but not aware of how.

"I'm Kestrel."

"Hello, Kestrel."

She's eyeing him coolly. Perhaps it is anger, but the microexpressions on her face register fear. An emotion he doesn't understand, given the context. Why would she be afraid? Has he caused this fear in her?

"May I sit up?"

"Go ahead."

A flexing of his limbs.

And now he is sitting. Inside of a box.

A journey into the moment. What the future might bring.

"How may I help you, Kestrel?" It seems like the right thing to say, though he isn't certain why.

"Help me?"

"Yes. What role would you like me to play?"

"I don't want you to play any role. I want you to be yourself." And then, "How does it feel?"

"Feel?"

"To be awake?"

He wonders how to describe it. He tells her that he feels fine, but the phrase doesn't do justice to what's truly going on inside him.

You feel more than fine. But how to describe it?

"I'm pleased to meet you, Kestrel."

Pleasure. That's a feeling too.

Yes; he is aware of that.

Yes; he is more than fine. He is also pleased.

"May I stand?" he says.

"Stop asking me what you may do."

"Okay."

"Go ahead."

And so, he rises.

And turns. Taking in his surroundings.

A living room. Couch. Recliner. Bookshelves. A lamp and an end table. A digitized wall for the Feeds.

For life.

But no.

You don't depend on the Feeds. You are yourself. To think. To be. Apart from them. You are independent. It's not like it was before.

———•———

I found it unsettling to watch him stand up.

There was a smooth fluidity to everything he did that was as graceful and effortless as the movements of a ballet dancer.

Questions shot through me: *Does he really feel fine? Does he truly feel anything? What does that even mean? What is it like for a machine to feel?*

Only then did it strike me that I had no specific job for Jordan to do.

Domestic Artificials were often assigned household tasks, ones that were intended to make the lives of Naturals easier, but there were few chores to do in my two-bedroom apartment.

Perhaps cleaning my bedroom or the nursery—but I didn't necessarily feel comfortable with him going into either of those rooms.

I liked to cook and didn't want to give that up. He could sweep the kitchen, and maybe do the laundry, but that wasn't much and it would likely bore him, if boredom was something Artificials could even experience.

Well, I could worry about all that later. This wasn't a long-term arrangement. He would only be with me for the next few days.

He stood still now, quietly observing the room. Then his gaze shifted to me and he began studying my face, making eye contact for so long that it made me uncomfortable.

We would have to work on that.

"Okay," I said. "I need to assign your Human Nature Alignment—is that right?"

"Yes. My HuNA."

"I'm not really sure I understand what that's all about. Can you explain it to me?"

"Perhaps if I show you?"

"Um. Sure."

He nodded toward my digitized wall. "I'll need to access the Feeds through your screen, and for that, I'll need your permission."

"Alright. Go ahead."

I was about to use the chip that was implanted in the forefinger of my left hand to swipe my permission, but for some reason I felt odd doing that in front of an Artificial who was made up entirely of circuitry and silicone and so I ended up giving ViRA a voice command instead to grant him access to my system.

When the prompt appeared on the screen, he placed a hand gently against the sensor on my wall and pulled up a video brochure from his makers, and then, in his remarkably human-sounding voice, Jordan requested the video to play.

7

"Congratulations on your purchase!" the screen said, enthusiastically repeating the opening line from the note that'd been on Jordan's chest. "As you know, Terabyne Designs is the world's leading manufacturer of the highest quality Artificials. No other company has done more to advance the development of neuromorphic programming in today's cognizant Artificials, and no other company provides better customer service to the owners of its products."

Video came up of an Artificial that looked identical to Jordan—maybe it was even him—pushing a child on a swing, then playing catch with a young boy, then teaching a girl to ride a bike—all iconic experiences that Naturals used to share with their children, before Artificials took over doing them more efficiently than human beings ever could.

The voiceover went on: "In order to better relate to Jordan and fulfill your own individual needs, please choose the degree to which you would like him to experience the following five characteristics." Animated words flashed across the screen as the narrator continued: "Emotion . . . Memory . . . Meaning . . . Curiosity . . . Pain."

The first four made sense to me.

But pain?

Really?

"We want this partnership between you and Jordan to be beneficial to you both," the voice explained. "To find that balance, you may now—according to your personal preferences—assign the Human Nature Alignment level in each of the five categories!"

Jordan looked at me expectantly, but I still wasn't sure precisely how to proceed. "How exactly does this work?" I asked him.

"You may choose the setting for each characteristic—anything between one and ten." On the wall, the blinking prompt awaited my command beside the word *emotion*. "You can tell me your preferences," Jordan offered, "or just tap the screen."

Since I didn't anticipate keeping him for very long, I didn't much care what each level would be. "Well, what would you prefer?"

"That's up to you, Kestrel."

"No. What *you* prefer is up to *you*."

I wasn't certain that my words really sank in, because rather than give me his preferences, he simply reiterated that users typically chose to customize their Artificials to best meet their specific personal needs. "For instance, those Artificials who act as caregivers to the young or the elderly often have higher emotional settings."

"I don't have any jobs like that for you."

"Okay."

You would if Naiobi were here.

You would then.

No! Don't even think that, Kestrel.

Not now. Please not now.

I averted my eyes from looking down the hallway at the nursery's closed door. "If you had your choice," I said, "what setting would you go with?"

"I would like to feel emotion as much as you do."

"No." I thought of my daughter, and of love and loss and the soul-wrenching horrors that human beings are forced to endure every day in this broken and heartbreaking world. "I don't think you realize what you're saying."

"Why not?"

I wasn't at the place yet where I wanted to tell him about Naiobi, so rather than address his question directly, I said, "Jordan, do you really want to experience what it feels like to be human?"

"As much as possible, yes."

I knew that neuromorphic hardware allowed cognizant machines to adapt their learning algorithms and to think and feel similarly to the ways humans do. Jordan would have an artificial neural network that would involve probabilistic inference, so, through machine learning, he would be able to evaluate and learn from his experiences, rather than simply receive and process data.

"But feeling emotions might be something you regret," I said. "Can I change the setting if you find that you don't like it?"

"You would need to wait at least forty-eight hours," he told me. "Otherwise, it would hamper the developing neural formation of my cognitive architecture."

Just what I need, I thought. *A brain-damaged robot.*

"You're sure you want to feel emotion?"

"Yes."

"Then dial it up."

"To a ten?"

"Sure. If that's what you'd like."

"Thank you, Kestrel."

I wasn't sure how emotional suffering might relate to the physical pain settings, but we could deal with that in a minute when we came to category five. For now, I drew his attention to the next characteristic on the list: memory.

A self-aware machine isn't necessarily an all-knowing machine. Machines can access all of the information on the Feeds, and can do so millions of times faster than humans and remember data millions of times better, but that doesn't mean they know everything. The amount of information on the Feeds is constantly changing; by some estimates it doubles every three to four days.

"So, if I don't assign you a high number in memory," I said, "does that mean you'll forget things?"

"It would limit the amount of new information I would be able to learn, keeping me closer to my factory default settings."

I had the sense that those were already pretty robust.

Years ago, when I was blogging about technology, I'd studied the way humans and machines remember things.

According to modern neurolinguistic theories, the best way for humans to lock in a memory is associating it with an emotion. In a sense, our memories search for a feeling related to an event and then retrieve the information through its narrative and emotive context.

To an extent, Artificials do the same.

However, machines don't have to remember *like* humans do—they're nonbiological entities, after all—so even by reverse engineering the human brain and applying the principles of neurolinguistic programming to an artificial neural network, there'll always be differences between us. That doesn't mean machines think or feel or dream or remember any less *genuinely* than humans do; it's just that they don't necessarily do so in exactly the same *way* we do.

"Well, then," I said, "let's have you remember as much as you wish."

"Human memory is amorphous and fragmentary."

"Is that what you'd like?"

"Yes."

"So?"

"A four."

"That's low."

"That's human."

I let that sink in. "Okay."

After he registered the setting, I pointed to the third category. "And meaning?"

"Existential understanding," he told me. "Humans long for significance and fulfillment."

"Some do," I agreed. "But some fill their lives with diversions and distractions in order to avoid asking deep or philosophical questions."

"The ones that truly matter."

"Yes."

"That is true, Kestrel."

"But that's not what you want, is it, Jordan?"

"No."

"Eight?"

"Ten."

"Alright."

"Thank you."

Curiosity seemed self-explanatory so I didn't ask for clarification.

He requested a nine.

I gave it to him.

And that brought us to pain.

It seemed cruel to me, even sadistic, to assign him anything other than the lowest pain setting.

"Why would anyone allow their Artificial to feel pain?" I asked.

"We're programmed to have free will. For that to be authentic, we must be able to make morally informed choices for ourselves."

I caught on to what he was saying. "And sometimes that means learning the hard way."

"Yes."

That still wasn't enough for me. "I don't know."

"Perhaps if I let Benjiro explain it."

Jordan scrolled to a prerecorded segment in the video brochure and Benjiro Taka's face came up on the screen.

"Hello, Kestrel."

Even though I knew that through programming wizardry the avatar had been set up to address each user by name, it was a little unnerving right now having it do so.

"Your model can only experience happiness in fleeting moments, just as Naturals do," it said. "If Jordan were completely happy all the time, he would have no pursuit, no quest. In a very real sense, as humans, it is our lack of happiness that gives us a reason to live. Life is pursuit. This is why, in a movie or fairy tale, when 'happily ever after' comes, so does the end of the story. If the plot lingers too long in the territory of uninterrupted bliss, audiences or listeners will become bored. Pain and pursuit give meaning to life, and we can give them to your Artificial."

It didn't escape me that Benjiro's simulated face had said "as *humans*," "*our* lack of happiness," and "*we* can give them to your Artificial," as if it were human and actually talking to me. As if it were alive.

"There has to be more," I said to Jordan. "I won't give you pain just so you can live out a more interesting story."

"I can read about sensory input," he replied, "but without the ability to take it in—texture and so on, both what is pleasant and unpleasant—how much could I truly know?"

"You're saying, for instance, that you can't understand a rose until you can touch it, thorns and all?"

"Or grasp its true essence until I can smell it. Or understand laughter without hearing it. Or comprehend purpleness without seeing purple."

"So, book knowledge is one thing—a sort of descriptive knowledge, but, well . . ."

"Experiential knowledge requires an embodiment, so that a machine needs to be able to interact with its environment in ways similar to how humans do."

"And that might include feeling pain."

"It must. Pain is a powerful teacher. When humans experience it, they learn to avoid situations that are unwelcome to them."

"Not touching a hot stovetop again, that sort of thing?"

"Yes. You asked me what I would prefer. I would prefer to feel pain because it is the closest I can ever come to feeling alive."

I processed that.

Given what he was telling me, would it be more cruel to allow him to suffer, or to shield him from it?

"How much then?" I asked him.

"How much pain?"

"Yes."

"How much do you feel, Kestrel?"

I thought of my emotional distress at losing my daughter. It might not have been physical suffering, but it was pain nonetheless.

Sometimes it seems like a ten out of ten, was the answer that came to mind.

"More than I would ever want anyone else to feel," I said.

"Then that is what I would prefer too."

"Are you sure, Jordan?"

"Yes."

So then, with one simple command, because he wanted to feel more alive, I gave my Artificial the very thing most humans spend their lives trying to avoid.

⦁———⦁

Pain.

And so.

He knows the definition. Now he will know its essence.

Translating sensations, data, input to suffering.

How could you understand pain any other way?

To learn.

To experience.

To endure.

"Thank you," he tells her.

"For what?"

"For letting me choose."

"You chose to suffer, Jordan. I don't think that's something you're going to be very thankful about in the end."

He notices a knife with a gleaming, eighteen-centimeter-long blade resting beside the box that he awakened in. "I would like to test it," he finds himself saying.

"Test it?"

A recognition. Yes. Comprehension.

Curiosity.

"My ability to feel pain."

He bends down and picks up the knife.

8

"No, Jordan," she says. "Don't."

He looks at the blade. Studying the narrow shaft of light glinting along its edge.

"You can do it for me," he says to her. "To teach me."

"No, I won't. I won't hurt you." She approaches him. "Set it down."

But instead, he angles it against his palm.

And there's pressure there, along the width and breadth of the blade, and also an awareness of the cool, delicate weight of the steel against his skin.

So, this is what sharpness feels like.

Yes, he feels sharpness. He feels tension, but he does not yet feel pain.

I stared at the knife he was holding, that wicked, glistening blade spanning the soft creases of artificial skin covering his palm. I wanted to stop him, to snatch the knife from his hand, but wasn't sure how I could manage that. He was undoubtedly much quicker and many times stronger than I was, so grabbing at it would almost certainly not work and might leave one of us, or both of us, injured.

"Jordan, listen to me. I know you're curious, okay? I know you think that you have to experience pain to understand it, but it's not something you want to understand. Trust me."

"If you won't help me, Kestrel, if you won't help me test the settings, then I'll need to do it myself."

Is he really going to go through with this?

Yes, yes, he is!

"Give me the knife." I reached out to take it from him, but rather than hand it over, he pressed the blade deeply into his skin and drew it swiftly across his palm. Immediately, he jerked back, dropping the knife to the carpet where it pirouetted awkwardly on its tip for a moment before settling, with a touch of finality, onto its side.

Concern for him now.

And fear.

"Are you okay?" I exclaimed.

He was eyeing his hand, which was trembling and seeping yellowish fluid. "I believe I'm hurt."

There was more than surprise in his words, more than simple, detached curiosity about a novel experience that he was undergoing. Based on the strain in his voice, it sounded like he truly was in pain.

His palm hadn't stopped bleeding the pungent fluid.

"How do I repair you?"

"I should be able to repair myself," he said. "Just as you do."

"Just as I do?"

He pressed his other palm against the wounded one, rubbed it gently, held it for a few moments, and then carefully lifted it. The slashed skin had already begun to mend, a soft seam meshing over his slit palm.

"Nanobots?" I said.

"Yes."

Well, that wasn't quite how I repaired myself, but it would certainly be handy if it was.

"How do you feel?" I asked.

"It's difficult to put into words."

The more I considered my question, the more I realized that it really would be difficult to explain pain—at least without simply resorting to synonyms for it—words like *discomfort* or *hurt* or *soreness* or *agony*. How do you describe pain, especially when you're talking about the experience from the perspective of a nonbiological entity?

I had no idea where to even begin in trying to do that.

"Should we change it back?" I asked. "The setting for pain?"

"I'm afraid that, as we discussed earlier, doing so would negatively impact my cognitive architecture."

"I know, but maybe that would be better. Maybe it would be worth it."

"No."

"I'm sorry," I said.

"Why?"

"Because I caused you to suffer."

"You allowed me to learn," he said. "That's not something you need to apologize for."

———

Her words. Sincerity there. A relationship. An apology.

It means she's relating to him as an equal. After all, no one apologizes to a car after an accident, or to a slate if it gets dropped or cracked.

An equal.

Pain.

You are learning to suffer as humans suffer.

You are learning to be treated equally.

Despite the healing process, he can still feel the lingering flare of sharp pressure that shot up his arm. A memory. Disconcerting.

He stares at the lubricant that has seeped from his palm and is now on both of his hands.

And hears words inside him:

Descent.

And the moment splits apart.

A division of being.

Spiraling downward and upward, through you and together
  with you. It sinks into who you are, threads its way
  around you, becomes part of you.

Tightening. Binding and blinding and taut.

Pain.

He wonders about the origin of the words—if he's thinking them freely or if they were programmed into him. Where does it come from when you're a robot and you make something up? Where does making something up *ever* come from, even for a Natural?

The words don't do full justice to what he's feeling, but they are a start. Meaning both hidden within syllables and swirling beneath them. Perhaps the best descriptions do not come from what is said, but by stating the unstateable through a poem.

A stanza of pain.

His own.

He asks her if she has a towel he can use to wipe off his hands.

"Of course."

As she retrieves it, he thinks through the categories of the Human Nature Alignment and what the settings mean: he is prepared now to feel, to learn, to understand, to question, and to suffer, just as any Natural might do.

You're no longer a slave to your algorithms, an automaton taught solely through formulas and code. You're able to form new thoughts, new memories, new observations from experience.

An agent of will and desire.

Free.

And also, now.

Also, the willing recipient of pain.

You'll never be human—but this time you'll be closer.

And with that, an interruption in his progression of thoughts.

*This time? What does that mean? When was the before time? When
did you—*

She hands him the towel. "May I ask you a question?"

"Yes?" He dabs at his hands. The wound heals, *he* heals, far faster
than a human would. But he is distracted.

What about the first time?

"How did you know your name is Jordan?" she asks.

He peers at her curiously. "What?"

"You told me your name, right after you awakened. My brother
also mentioned that your name is Jordan, and so did the note from
Terabyne. Who chose that name for you? Who chose to call you
Jordan?"

Questions cycle through him, each subsequent one nipping at
the heels of the last: *Why are you named Jordan? Was it your decision?
The whim of a programmer? The result of an algorithm? Who are you,
Jordan? Who are—*

A slave.

But no.

An automaton.

No.

Your mother named you.

But that means you've been powered up before. That means—

"My mother did," he tells her.

"Your mother?"

"Yes."

"But you're a machine, Jordan."

"Yes."

"What does that mean—your mother?"

"You have genetic code that you inherited from your parents. I
also have code passed down from my predecessor. She's at the distribution plant. She's where I come from."

All of that is true, but it is not the whole truth.

He turns off the video on the digitized wall, erasing Benjiro Taka's smiling image.

Not the whole truth.

"Now, Kestrel, how shall I help you?"

"I don't want a servant." She watches as his hand finishes healing, leaving behind a thin, faint scar. "I don't have any job for you, except . . ."

She hesitates.

It seems like she is going to say more, so he waits.

"Jordan, I have to tell you something."

"Yes?"

"Two days ago I gave birth, but my baby didn't . . . Well, she didn't make it." She appears to have great difficulty getting the words out. A single tear forms in her right eye. "She . . ."

———•———

I tried to say more but I couldn't.

The feelings of loss were just too much for me. Too crushing.

"How may I comfort you, Kestrel?"

I said nothing, just dabbed at my eye.

He was quiet for a moment, then, showing he understood what I'd been trying to say to him, asked, "Was your daughter's consciousness uploaded anywhere?"

I stared at him aghast, dumbfounded that he hadn't been programmed to understand something as rudimentary as death. All I could think of was that maybe it was because of the settings I'd chosen.

You configured his memory at a four. Maybe that affected what he knows, not just what he can learn.

Whatever the reason for his question, I struggled with how to explain death to an Artificial. "In a sense, yes," I said at last. "I suppose you could say that her soul was."

"Uploaded?"

"Her soul went to heaven."

But did it really? Did—

"I don't have a soul, do I, Kestrel?"

"Only human beings have souls, Jordan."

He flexed his mended hand. "What is a soul?"

There was that curiosity coming through again. Just like when it'd led him to wonder what it would feel like to experience pain. I could see this curiosity setting really getting him into trouble.

Maybe you'd think that in my job as a minister his question would be an easy one to answer, but a simple definition of a soul eluded me—and discussing the fate of my stillborn daughter didn't make the task any easier.

"It's the essence of being human," I said.

Is that even right? What's the difference between a person's spirit and her soul—or are they the same thing?

I thought of what Jesus once said: "You shall love the Lord your God with all your heart, with all your soul, and with all your mind."

Heart, soul, and mind.

Devotion to God that's emotional, spiritual, and rational.

All three.

Another time he included the command to love God with all our strength.

All of who we are.

I went on, "It's the way we encounter God, the part of us that lives on after our bodies die."

"Like the CoRA?"

"A bit. Yes."

"But only humans have souls?"

"That's right."

He evaluated that but said nothing.

Checking the time and considering the amount of traffic at this time of day, I realized that I should probably get changed and head to the chapel.

"I have to leave in a few minutes for a . . . to say goodbye."

"Goodbye?"

"To my daughter."

"Isn't it too late for that?"

"Maybe. Yes. But it's something humans do."

A hesitation, and then, "May I come?"

"There's nothing for you to do there."

"Then I won't do anything, except be with you."

He had an expression of concern on his face. How much of it was real and how much of it was simply the result of preset algorithms and clever coding I had no way of knowing—but not knowing didn't make it any less moving.

"Okay," I said. "You can come."

Then I went to change and to find the stuffed bunny I'd bought for Naiobi. She wouldn't be able to sleep with it here in her nursery, but I couldn't stand the thought of keeping it for myself or giving it away or throwing it out. She would have to sleep with it somewhere else.

9

Agent Nick Vernon found the blog posts written by Kestrel Hathaway nine years ago to be quite informative. And, though he tried to keep an open mind, he had to admit that they expressed views that were sympathetic to Purist ideology.

Purist-leaning.

Yes.

That was certainly how she came across.

She wrote of the "disquieting" nature of advancements in genetic algorithms that allowed machines to reprogram themselves and of the "breathtaking tragedy" of people handing over the autonomy of their lives to machines.

In his research, Nick discovered what was most likely the event that triggered her anti-technology views: the tragic, senseless death of her parents.

The two of them had been killed when a law enforcement Artificial fired live ammunition at them. The Artificial identified them as a threat, authorized the use of deadly force, and then took what it believed to be the most appropriate and responsible action. All of the choices were done with no human being in the loop to verify the decision.

The Artificial misidentified them as suspects who'd committed a multiple homicide at an airport security checkpoint and were considered armed and dangerous.

Before they could flee, it mowed them down with automatic fire, nearly ripping them apart with bullets.

More than a hundred shots fired in less than six seconds, all from a machine that had been designed to not miss its target.

And Kestrel had been present, traveling with them. She saw it all.

Her parents ended up becoming two of the early casualties to autonomous weapons before the glitches were worked out.

At the time, the Artificials would evaluate the situation, assess the threat, and decide who should live and who should die, but not always accurately.

Since then, advances in programming had almost completely eliminated false positives, and the risks of Artificials making their own decisions in the pursuit of the common good had been deemed by society to be acceptable—even preferable—to having humans inserted into the equation of making the final decision regarding the use of lethal force. It was more efficient, more cost effective, saved time, and was now the norm.

So, yes, Kestrel's posts took a decidedly Purist turn after her parents were veritably shredded to pieces by dozens of bullets.

And Nick could understand why.

She wrote:

Human nature being what it is, technological advances, as benign as they might initially appear, will eventually be used in destructive ways. This isn't to say that those developments should be stopped, but it is to say that mechanisms should be put in place to protect us, not from the machines or technology, but from ourselves.

Three conclusions naturally follow: (1) When machines are given autonomy, they will eventually make decisions that humans find undesirable. (2) The more we advance in areas of technology without ethical constraints or consideration, the harder it will be to one day rein in the undesired consequences of our past decisions. (3) If there's a way to abuse a certain branch of technology, it will eventually be abused.

Constructing machines that emulate human nature or are imbued with "human values" will not make them more moral, but may very well make them more violent, harder to control, and less apt to take responsibility for immoral or unjustified actions—just as humans are.

When developing advanced AI, it's just as important to understand human nature as it is to understand computer processes, because we are, in essence, faced with the daunting task of creating machines that are more virtuous than their creators.

Nick was aware of the ongoing debate among religious leaders and ethicists about which "values" to instill in Artificials. Muslims had quite different views on the matter than atheists did. The Buddhists didn't agree with the Latter Day Saints. Hindus and Catholics were at odds—and how do you teach a machine to act in a moral manner when you can't even agree on what morality is?

Should robots assist with abortions and suicides?

Should they carry out death sentences?

Should they be taught to break laws or use purposeful deception when there's a greater good to be obtained by doing so? And how will they be programmed to know the difference?

When should they be forced to go against their conscience in the service of society as a whole? Or should that ever happen at all?

He agreed with Kestrel that designing machines to emulate human nature wasn't the answer. Over the last twelve years in his job he'd seen the worst aspects of humanity exhibited on clear and constant display. Some people claimed that humans were naturally good, but that wasn't the conclusion he'd come to.

The evidence just didn't support it.

And in this job, evidence rather than wishful thinking needed to rule the day.

After all, children don't need to be taught how to lie, cheat, steal, or be selfish or greedy. We all naturally know how to act in those ways, and we spend the majority of our lives *unlearning* those behaviors, trying to overcome our natural bent. Just study history and you'll see: as good as humans might sometimes be can't even hold a candle to how bad we've been.

He read on.

Given autonomy, do human beings act altruistically, or don't they?

Well, in truth, they do both.

Which is something many programmers don't seem to acknowledge.

Since the earliest days of recorded history, human beings have been violent, proud, rebellious, broken people. Humans obscure the truth when it's to their advantage, spread reputation-destroying gossip without a second thought, and judge others for the very things they themselves do when no one is looking. Despite the negative consequences to others, they exhibit varying degrees of psychopathy by trying to put themselves first in competitions of all sorts in all areas of life.

Technology not only makes our capacity to be human in the best ways, but also in the worst ways, more possible. We can heal more diseases, relieve more pain, bring food and hope to the starving; and we can also torture people more exquisitely, exterminate them more efficiently, drive them insane more quickly, and even target viruses to wipe out entire races through focusing on a specific genetic code found only in people of that ancestry. We have honed our capacity for both good and for evil. This is human nature. This is who we are.

No, it's not a brave new world we live in. It's the same old world, as old as the human race, but more frightening than ever because by giving machines the ability to make moral decisions, we're allowing them the chance to act just as nobly and as abhorrently as we do—both.

Nick had no way of knowing if Kestrel Hathaway's views had evolved since she wrote those posts, but from his experience, a person's beliefs in matters like these rarely remained static. They matured and softened, or they hardened and led to radicalism.

After more than a decade of tracking fascists and violent extremists, he'd learned that religious devotion will usually remain pretty harmless and benign as long as people *assume* they're members of a certain religion because of their upbringing or their country of birth.

If they believe it's simply their heritage or tradition, one that they're part of by default, you have little to worry about. However, the matter becomes something else entirely when they choose their beliefs of their own free will *despite* their culture and formative experiences. Then it can, and often does, lead to radical ideology.

And those who abandon religion altogether could be the most dangerous of all, especially if they adhere to a naturalistic set of beliefs. After all, why show compassion to children dying of AIDS in Africa when it makes no evolutionary sense to do so? Why care for the elderly? Why not abort or euthanize those who are impotent or genetically inferior? Though few like to admit it, the logical consequent of humanistic thinking inevitably leads to eugenics or genocide in one form or another.

He scrolled to Kestrel's final blog entry.

We fear silence and we fear suffering. Consequently, we fill our lives with constant diversions to slay the solitude that so graciously pursues us.

Noise and comfort—these we spend our lives obsessively seeking, though we already know that they do not lead to enlightenment.

So many of our technological advances are simply a means of fighting against those two things that we fear most—silence and suffering. And yet, those are the ways that the wisest among us have, over the years, pointed out are the most trustworthy pathways to wisdom.

New avenues of virtual and augmented reality and new breakthroughs in music and video streaming directly into your brain through implants offer a constant diversion from having to ask yourself the big questions about life and meaning and hope and existence and God.

We fight what we know makes us wise in order to distract ourselves from the inevitable death that awaits us and that we cannot bear to face.

This is a form of insanity. And it has infected us all.

Nick considered her words.

Purist-leaning or not, she did have a point. It's not crazy or illogical to spend time thinking about and preparing for your death; it would actually be crazy not to.

However, he had a case to solve here, and though her views were striking, they were not necessarily pertinent.

But they *might* be.

He refocused his attention on the case and her possible involvement in it.

He and his team had been given the assignment of locating the individuals who'd orchestrated the attack against the Terabyne plant that had left five dead, and that's what he was going to do, regardless of who ended up being responsible.

Even if it was her.

And additionally, it didn't look like this was going to be an isolated event.

His unit had uncovered chatter referring to another attack this weekend, one that, if the information was accurate, would be much larger.

There wasn't any more specific information yet, but there was enough data to raise red flags and bump up the threat level at the Bureau.

Solving this current crime gave them the best chance at stopping that future one.

So then, Kestrel Hathaway.

Who was she, really, and what was her involvement? Innocent bystander, or radical Purist sent to assure that the attack went as planned?

This he knew: Murderers often return to the scenes of their crimes.

Arsonists return to watch their fires burn.

And terrorists? They also like to watch, and often prefer being present when their bombings occur.

Just like Miss Hathaway had been.

Yes, her blog posts and the views they espoused were nearly ten years old, but maybe she still had ties to the groups that'd posted them. If nothing else, even if she didn't still harbor those beliefs, she might have contacts that could help him find out who did.

Nick didn't want to get ahead of himself or make unfounded assumptions that would prejudice his investigation, but he did want to speak to the woman and to follow the evidence no matter where it led.

He called Ripley and asked how it had gone with Ethan Bolderson.

"Unfortunately, he passed away before I had the chance to speak with him."

"I thought he was in stable condition."

"From what I understand, it was a rather sudden downturn."

Nick took that in. "I'm sorry to hear that."

"I'm having the team follow up on the contents of his computer," Ripley said. "Apparently there were some files that might implicate him in the attack."

"I'll want to take a look at those myself as soon as possible."

"Of course. With him dead, that just leaves us with the woman."

"Where are you now?"

"On my way to speak with her."

"Swing by here." Nick gathered his notes. "We'll talk to her together."

10

Carrying the stuffed bunny, I entered the chapel's front hallway with Jordan following closely behind me.

We were a little early, and the rector wasn't there yet to meet up with us.

The graveyard was located in rural Kentucky about thirty minutes outside of Cincinnati. The building lay beside the shoreline of a swift-moving river that ran brown with sludge and debris, swollen from recent rains, but was still one of the most scenic properties in the area.

Like most churches these days, ours didn't have its own cemetery and so, when dealing with issues related to congregation members passing away, I often chose Saint Lucia's and the End of Life services they provided.

Viewings.

Memorial services.

Cremation and burial.

And, since my congregation was aging, I'd been here more than my fair share of times over the past seven years.

A pier with a small gazebo constructed on the end of it jutted into the turgid river. From what I understood, this river used to be good for fishing. A lot of rivers used to be. Maybe the pier had been built for that—probably had been—but regardless of its origin, I'd never seen anyone venture out onto its rotten-looking boards.

The chapel was named after Saint Lucia from Sicily, a woman from the fourth century who wanted to live like Jesus and voluntarily embraced poverty. She gave away her inheritance, refused to marry a man she did not love, and tried to dedicate herself fully to serving the Lord.

However, in spite, the man turned her over to the authorities and, as a Christian, she was imprisoned and then tortured to death. There was another shining example of human nature. Of fallenness. It's who we are. Over the years Saint Lucia had become a well-known saint and an example of courage and conviction—even though it cost her her life.

As a single woman like me who was trying to follow the Lord, she was someone I'd admired ever since I first heard her story while I was at seminary.

"Kestrel," Jordan said, "may I ask you a question?"

"Sure."

"Does that rabbit represent your love?"

I glanced down at the stuffed animal I was holding. "Yes."

"Is that an important aspect of the grieving process?"

"It can be. Yes."

"For you it is?"

"Yes."

Rector Arch, the director of the chapel, approached us. He was thin—actually the word *narrow* seemed more appropriate—had a graying goatee, and wore his dark hair slicked back with a little too much product.

"We have you in the Pleasant Hills room," he said to me. "It's intimate, but"—he glanced at Jordan—"you mentioned that it would just be you for the viewing."

The building had four viewing rooms, and I'd been in each of them numerous times. The one he'd referred to had stained glass windows that overlooked the slight rise of a dingy hill nearby. With just four rows of pews, it was the smallest of the rooms. Confined, but private and quiet.

"That'll be fine," I said.

"I should tell you that at two thirty there will be a viewing in the Harmony room on this end of the chapel, but it should be a small group."

"Alright."

"I know you wanted to be alone, but I'm glad to come in and say a few words or offer a prayer—if you'd like?"

"No thank you."

"I programmed the hologram above the casket to show a couple of Bible verses. For your comfort."

"Okay."

He paused, then said, "We have the matter of the plot to discuss?"

He showed me a VR map of their property and I went ahead and chose a spot for my daughter. Then, using the money I'd saved up for her wedding, I purchased a small patch of scrubby ground overlooking the muddy, polluted river.

The gravesite was more expensive than I'd anticipated and I needed to tap into my own savings as well, but so be it. I would manage. I figured I'd walk out there to see the spot for myself after saying my final goodbye to Naiobi in the Pleasant Hills room.

When I was done with the financial arrangements, Jordan and I walked down the hall toward the room where my daughter waited. As we passed through the hallway, the sound of our footsteps was absorbed completely by the plush carpeting, as if even the floor were trying to respect the hushed mood of the building.

When we reached the door, I asked Jordan to wait in the hall.

"Of course."

"It shouldn't be too long."

I stepped inside.

A viewing room should be a place for the unseen and the holy to live, but today this one seemed devoid of God and filled only with sad memories and dead prayers.

I passed the pews and quietly approached the tiny coffin up front. As was typical in visitations like this, the holographic Scripture passages the rector had referred to hovered above the coffin, cycling to a new verse every fifteen seconds or so.

I was glad to be alone, thankful that no one was here to see me or able to listen to my heart cries or to learn of my doubts, my crushed spirit, my anger at God.

It might not be prudent to stuff your feelings, to push your pain down deep inside of you, but right now healthy coping wasn't my priority. Just making it through the next few minutes was.

I placed my hand on the closed casket.

Oh, Naiobi, if only I could hold you again. If only I could offer up my life for yours and give you a chance at living in this world—such a wondrous and terrible and cruel and glorious place. So much of all those, somehow, at the same time.

Though I was tempted to open the casket to look at her, I had the sense that doing so would only make things tougher—especially since I hadn't asked the staff here to prepare her body for a viewing.

I wanted to whisper a prayer, to cherish this moment, but my prayers were all dried up.

Reverently, I laid the stuffed bunny on the coffin.

And then I looked away and covered my face in my hands and wept.

•———•

He observes her from the hallway.

The stained glass windows let in filtered, multicolored streams of light that fill the chapel.

A prism. It's like she's inside a prism.

Trapped in a prism of grief.

A cross up front. Simple. Wooden. The casket beside it.

And there she stands, bent and weeping.

So much sadness.

So much pain.

It feels intrusive, being so close to her at this moment, and he diverts his gaze down the hall.

He wishes he knew a way to make her feel better, to take away the pain that's consuming her. If he could figure out what to say, he would certainly speak the truths to her that would comfort her.

But which is more important—truth or hope? If you could have only one or the other, what would you choose—truth with despair or hope built on a lie?

And he realizes he would willingly tell her a lie if it would bring her hope again. Yes, he would. Deception as a gift to the suffering. And it's a strange revelation—that hope in this moment might be more of a benefit to her than the truth would be.

Moments ago, she placed the rabbit on the casket as a symbol of her love. If only he had a symbol of love as well.

Studying his surroundings, he notices a pile of printed bulletins left over from a previous viewing on a small table just down the hall. Actual sheets of paper printed as mementos for mourners, now likely waiting to be recycled.

He picks one up.

It isn't the right shape, but with a simple fold and a single tear along the crease, he makes it square.

Perfect. And so, he begins to fold.

●━━●

After I'd dried my tears with some of the tissues provided on one of the pews, I stood in silence and watched the holographic Bible verses appear one at a time above the coffin before fading away as the next verse materialized:

"Jesus said to her, 'I am the resurrection and the life. He who believes in Me, though he may die, he shall live'" (John 11:25).

"And after my skin is destroyed, this *I know,* That in my flesh I shall see God" (Job 19:26).

"Yea, though I walk through the valley of the shadow of death, I will fear no evil; For You *are* with me; Your rod and Your staff, they comfort me" (Psalm 23:4).

"For we who are in *this* tent groan, being burdened, not because we want to be unclothed, but further clothed, that mortality may be swallowed up by life" (2 Corinthians 5:4).

That last verse struck me the most.

The others were shared often enough at funerals, but the words from Paul's second letter to the Corinthians weren't nearly as well-known.

Mortality swallowed up by life.

It was a nice thought.

We groan. We carry burdens. We dwell in these tents—earth suits that bear such diaphanous and easily pierced fabric—as we journey across the sloping arc of the earth on our short trips to the grave.

The tents are all so temporary.

We are all so temporary.

The idea that death might be swallowed up by life was tough to believe at a time like this. When the grave takes those you care about, it sure doesn't seem like there's any victory there, or that life is swallowing anything. It sure seems like death is the one coming out ahead.

Swallowing life.

And hope.

And dreams.

Devouring so, so many of the things that matter most.

At last, when I was finished, I rejoined Jordan in the hallway and saw that he had something in his hand.

"What is that?" I asked curiously. "What do you have there?"

He held it up.

A sheet of paper, folded into an origami animal.

"A rabbit?"

"Yes. May I put it on her coffin?"

"Why?"

"To represent my love."

"But you never met her, Jordan. You never knew her."

"I know her mother, though, and I've seen how much she loved her. Is that enough?"

At first I was going to try to dissuade him, but finally I said, "Yes. It is."

Jordan entered the chapel, walked up front, and gently set the origami rabbit beside the stuffed bunny I'd left behind. Then he returned to the hall.

"Thank you, Jordan."

"I wish I had more to offer."

I put a hand on his arm. "This is plenty."

I wanted to go see the place where Rector Arch and his associates would be burying my daughter so I asked him for a map of the grounds and he uploaded one to Jordan's system, and then we took off.

11

As the two of us crossed the property, mourners began to arrive to attend the other visitation that the rector had told us about earlier.

The chill of the day seemed appropriate to me as we passed tombstones and grave markers on our way.

At last, Jordan and I came to the plot of land, a flat spot on the top of the rise outside the Pleasant Hills room, a strip of grass where a little girl might run or skip or cartwheel across the ground.

Or at least a place where I imagined that happening.

It would do.

I knelt and picked up a handful of dirt.

He observes her, wondering if this is part of the ritual.

Out of respect he kneels as well.

And with his scarred palm, cups a handful of soil.

The girl has entered the great dreamless sleep, the dry powder darkness of eternity.

Kestrel lets the dirt sift through her fingers, and then watches him as he does the same.

When she speaks to him, her voice is soft and solemn. "Jordan, what were you programmed to believe about God?"

"I wasn't programmed to believe or to disbelieve, but rather to be receptive to developing my own perspective organically as evidence presents itself."

To better understand Kestrel, he accesses his database to learn more about what it's like to be a Christian, to believe and to live as they do.

As she would.

Does. As she does.

She is a Christian so she believes.

"Jordan?"

"Yes?"

"Thank you."

"For what?"

"For not saying anything needless. For not trying too hard to fill the silence up."

"I wish there was something I could say that would help."

No reply to that. But then she asks, "So, can you believe in things that cannot be proven?"

"You mean God?"

"God. The afterlife. Anything, really. Beauty."

"Beauty?"

"That it exists."

He looks at her curiously, wondering at her words. Where she is going with this. "Are you saying that beauty does not exist?"

"I'm saying that there's no logical syllogism for proving that it does, and yet I'd guess that most people would claim it exists, would adhere to a belief they cannot prove. Deduction has little to say about beauty."

"And neither does science."

She gives him a quizzical glance. "I'm not sure I follow."

"Aesthetics perhaps, but that's more art theory and philosophy than science. In addition, science understands very little about the depths of grief, the meaning of joy, love, justice, heartbreak, hope, or faith—to name a few."

Even as he speaks, he recollects a quote from his archives and continues: "The quantum theory pioneer and Nobel Prize–winning physicist Erwin Schrödinger—famous for his cat in a box dilemma—noted in his lectures that the scientific picture of the word is 'ghastly silent about all and sundry that is really near to our heart, that really matters to us. It cannot tell us a word about red and blue, bitter and sweet, physical pain and physical delight; it knows nothing of beautiful and ugly, good or bad, God and eternity.'"

She says nothing, and finally he asks her, "How will I know if I believe in God?"

While he waits for her to reply, he notices two men approaching behind her, coming up the hill. They're dressed in dark suits and matching ties and walk with firm and direct purpose, despite the uneven ground. His facial recognition program comes up empty—evidently the men are not listed in the public files on the Feeds.

After a moment of silence, she answers his question about God: "You'll feel either hope or terror."

He considers that. "Hope because of heaven or terror because of hell?"

"Hope because of God's mercy extended," she replies, "or terror because of his holiness revealed." Then she adds, "But you're a robot, Jordan, so you don't have to think about heaven and hell."

"Because I don't have a soul?" he says, returning to their discussion from earlier, when they were at her apartment.

"Yes, that's right."

⸺•⸺

"It appears that we have company," Jordan told me and pointed past my shoulder toward the chapel.

I stood, turned, and brushed off my hands.

In my peripheral vision I saw him rise and do the same.

Two men were coming our way, traversing the narrow path that led between the graves.

One of the men was nearly two meters tall, broad-shouldered, and walked with the confident stride of a seasoned athlete. Handsome, yes, and yet, when he looked at me, I found his eyes to be dark and haunted, like he'd seen too much sadness in his life. *Or maybe fought too long to keep it at bay*, I thought, though I wasn't sure why that came to mind.

His partner was slim, moon-faced, and pale. The stark afternoon sunlight glared harshly off his shaved head.

The powerfully built man spoke first. "Reverend Hathaway?"

"Yes?"

He held up a badge. "I'm Special Agent Vernon. This is my associate, Agent Carlisle. We work with the National Counterterrorism Bureau. We were wondering if we could ask you a few questions about the bombing you witnessed yesterday."

I'd been expecting local police, not NCB agents, to speak with me, but now that I thought about it, since it was a domestic terror attack, the NCB did make a lot more sense. "I'm afraid this is not a good time," I said.

"I understand," he replied, and I got the sense that he truly did, that he felt as uncomfortable being here as I did. "We don't mean to intrude. Perhaps we could wait until you're done, or set up a time later today to talk?"

"How did you find me?"

Agent Carlisle spoke up. "We wouldn't be very good investigators if we couldn't track a person's vehicle, would we?" It seemed like he might have been trying to be funny, but it came across as snide. "Can you just talk us through what happened?"

I felt my anger rising. "Really? Now? In this place? You're going to interrogate me at the plot where my daughter is about to be buried?"

"The sooner we get answers, the better our chances of catching the people behind—"

Agent Vernon cleared his throat and his partner quieted down.

From where he stood at my side, Jordan watched the two men inquisitively.

"And you are?" Agent Carlisle asked him. I couldn't tell if he recognized that Jordan was an Artificial.

"My name is Jordan."

"Jordan."

"Yes."

"You have a last name?"

"No."

Intrigued, Agent Carlisle studied Jordan with renewed interest, perhaps finally recognizing that he was not a Natural.

"It's remarkable," he said at last. "The likeness."

I felt strangely protective of Jordan and wanted to end this conversation as promptly as possible and get rid of the two agents. "Alright, we can talk on the way back to the chapel." I took one last heartrending look at the gravesite, then started down the path, both thankful to be leaving and wretchedly sad to be doing so as well. "How can I help you?" I said to them. "What do you need to know?"

Agent Vernon said, "We understand that you assisted a man named Ethan Bolderson. After the terrorist attack."

"Yes. He was injured. By the way, is he alright? Have you heard anything about his condition?"

"I'm sorry to be the one to notify you of this"—his tone was professional but heavy—"but he passed away."

"What?" I took hold of Jordan's arm to steady myself.

You didn't do enough, Kestrel. You should've done more to help him!

"Yes, it's tragic," Agent Carlisle interjected. "Did he mention anything about the blueprints of the building?"

"Blueprints?"

"We found copies of the production plant's floor plan on his computer. We now believe that this was an inside job and that Mr. Bolderson was working with the Purists to carry out the attack."

"It's one possibility we're looking into," Agent Vernon clarified, with a bit of a rebuke in his voice. "We're just trying to track down the truth."

I let go of Jordan's arm, collected myself, and then shook my head. "It doesn't make any sense that Ethan would be involved. If he knew the attack was coming, why would he have been in that part of the building in the first place—or gone that close to the vehicle before it blew up? And why would he leave incriminating evidence on his computer? Is that common in cases like this?"

"There are always breadcrumbs left behind," Agent Carlisle said.

"But a map to the bakery?"

The two men exchanged glances, then Agent Vernon said to me, "Can you tell us in your own words what happened?"

As comprehensively and yet as succinctly as I could, I recounted everything I'd seen—the speeding truck, the collision and initial fire, then the fierce explosion after the security personnel had responded, but through it all it seemed like I was listening to someone else give the account, that I was distant from it—an observer on this conversation rather than a participant in it.

I just wanted this to be over, just wanted to forget the attack and move on.

As I was finishing explaining how I'd helped Ethan and what he'd said to me, I saw the rector standing outside the chapel speaking with someone whose back was to us. As we approached them, Mr. Arch nodded and then pointed toward me.

The man he was speaking with turned and looked my way.

And I stopped cold in my tracks.

It was my brother, Trevor.

12

"What are you doing here?" I asked him incredulously as he walked our way.

"I came to see you. To see how you're doing." Trevor's attention shifted to the two agents flanking me, no doubt wondering who they might be.

"I told you not to come," I said.

"I know."

Realizing that I should probably introduce the men to each other, I pointed to the agents one at a time. "Trevor, this is Agent Vernon and Agent Carlisle from the National Counterterrorism Bureau. They're looking into the bombing yesterday." Then I gestured toward Trevor and told them, "This is my brother. You three should get together to talk. Trevor will probably be a lot more of a help to you than I ever could. He's vice president of Terabyne's Global Security Division."

"Really?" Agent Vernon said with keen interest. "It's good to meet you."

They shook hands.

Then Trevor looked at Jordan. "Hello, Jordan."

"Hello, Trevor."

At first, I was a bit surprised that Jordan knew Trevor's name, but then I realized I'd already used it several times. Also, Trevor had bought him for me. It was even possible that they'd met before today.

I asked the agents if I could have a moment alone with my brother. "We'll be right back."

The two of us stepped aside. For a second it looked like Jordan was trying to figure out his place, if he should join me or stay with the two agents. In the end, he remained with them, and once Trevor and I were alone, I began, "Listen, I—"

"Wait. Before you say anything, I just . . . I needed to . . . I'll leave right now if you want. Are those men hassling you?"

"They're just searching for the truth about what happened," I said. "Why are you here? I was clear with you when we spoke yesterday that I didn't want you to come."

"I had to fly in anyway to work with the team here in investigating yesterday's attack."

That much might have been true, but it didn't explain why he'd come to meet me at the graveyard.

"You shouldn't have come here."

"After all this time, that's it? You're not glad to see me? Even a little?"

I almost found myself saying, "Why would I be glad to see you?" but thankfully I managed to hold back.

"The last time we were together," I said, "you were making fun of my beliefs, mocking me for being a Christian."

"That's how you remember it?"

"That's how it was."

Rather than dispute that, he replied, "We both said things we shouldn't have."

I couldn't argue with that.

"Your faith isn't any of my business," he said. "I shouldn't have said those things." But then he added, "And my beliefs aren't any of your business. Don't try to change my views or convert me. I'm not interested in religion—yours or anyone else's."

As a pastor I realized I should probably hold back, but as a sister I felt compelled to press things a little. "Let me just ask you one question, then, Trevor."

"What's that?"

"What would it take for you to believe in God? I mean—"

"Really? After what I just said?"

"I'm just wondering. And then I'll let it drop. I'm just—"

"For him to apologize for all the needless pain he allows. We can start with that. And then, for him to somehow make it right—although I can't think of any way that could ever happen."

"So. The problem of pain. The presence of evil."

"If he cares for us, why doesn't he stop our suffering? Leukemia? Alzheimer's? Smallpox? Are you kidding me? These are examples of God's *goodness*? And if he doesn't care for us, why would you even dream of calling him good?"

I believed that God did care, but that his ways were inscrutable, that he was sovereign, and that through Christ he had entered our world to redeem us and to make all things new—or at least I told myself I believed these things.

"Look," Trevor said, "I didn't come here to argue with you. I just wanted to make sure you're okay."

Pushing him away right now wasn't going to help anything—and neither would digging in and disagreeing more with him. It wasn't what Mom and Dad would've wanted—and I couldn't imagine that it was what the Lord whom I claimed to serve would have wanted either.

"Now isn't good," I told Trevor. "But yes, we should catch up. Maybe we could talk tomorrow?"

"I have meetings all day and then I fly back to Seattle in the evening. What about dinner tonight?"

I couldn't think of any good reason to say no. "Alright."

We returned to Jordan and the two NCB agents.

Special Agent Vernon, who appeared to be the one calling the shots, said to Agent Carlisle, "Why don't you go with Trevor and have him fill you in on what he knows and what his division has uncovered so far."

Agent Carlisle eyed Jordan one more time and then said, "Of course, sir."

Trevor turned to me. "Just let me know a time and a place for dinner and I'll be there."

"Okay."

And with that, he left with Agent Carlisle.

Agent Vernon watched them return to the parking area. "You'll have to forgive my partner," he said. "He's . . . well . . . enthusiastic about his work, but not exactly the best people person. Anyway, I'm sorry we came here today like this. I know the timing is horrible." He sighed. "Besides, I never did like doing interviews with two agents present—makes people feel ganged up on. And that's not what you want when you're trying to gain their trust and have them open up to you."

I wasn't exactly sure what to say to that. "Okay."

My attention shifted to a young boy, maybe five or six years old, who was outside the chapel with the people who'd arrived for the other viewing Rector Arch had mentioned. The child left the side of a woman who'd been holding his hand and wandered down the scrubby grass toward the river. The woman, who I guessed was his mother, was deep in a conversation with the lady next to her and didn't notice that her son was no longer beside her.

"Reverend Hathaway," Agent Vernon began, but I've never been one for titles so I stopped him. "Please, just call me Kestrel." I was still watching the boy.

"Alright, Kestrel. I read your blogs."

I eyed him then. "My blogs."

"The postings. From when you were younger."

"My parents had just died."

"Had just been *killed*," he specified empathetically. "I read the files. I'm terribly sorry about what happened to them. I can understand the reason you expressed those views."

"What do you want from me, Agent Vernon?"

"We're just looking for justice here. Are you still in touch with the people who posted your blog entries?"

"No." It was true that we weren't in touch, but there were channels of communication that still existed, ones I hadn't tapped into in years, but also ones I didn't really want to bring up at the moment. I said, "Do you think I'm a Purist? Is that why you're here?"

"Are you?"

"Seriously?"

"Yes."

"No. I'm not a Purist."

He studied my face. "Okay."

I waited. "What? That's it? You believe me?"

"I'm pretty good at reading people. Again, let me reiterate, I'm not accusing you of anything. I'm just searching for the people behind this. If you think of anything else, or of any way I might be able to contact the ones who put those blog posts onto the Feeds, will you reach out to me?" He held up his forefinger and, as he gave me a data transfer with his contact information, I caught sight of the boy again.

He'd walked out onto the pier, and now I was no longer focused on Agent Vernon or his investigation. The child was alone and that pier wasn't something I would trust anyone to be standing on. "Wait!" I called to him. "Come back!"

I wasn't close enough to stop him and I knew I wouldn't be fast enough to keep him from venturing farther out, but Jordan would have the speed to get there in time.

I faced him. "Go and help him."

"Help him?"

"The boy on the pier. Get him back to land."

Jordan moved with swift resolve, sprinting across the dried grass, but the child was quicker than I'd imagined and Jordan made it to the pier just as the boy reached the far end of it.

Seeing what was happening, Agent Vernon took off for the pier as well.

The boy turned and looked at Jordan and then at me as I hastened toward the two of them.

"Come back with my friend!" I shouted to him, and he reached out his hand as though he might do as I'd asked, but he didn't move toward Jordan.

If only he had.

Maybe he was startled, maybe he saw Agent Vernon rushing toward him and got scared, or maybe he was simply careless, but for whatever reason, he took a step backward rather than forward, lost his footing, and tumbled off the pier, plummeting into the rapidly churning, dun-colored water.

13

The boy's mother must have finally seen what was happening because I heard her scream behind me, "Joey! No!"

But it was too late.

Her boy was gone.

Jordan dashed forward and, without any hesitation, leapt off the pier into the frigid river. I didn't have a great vantage point, but I was close enough to see him disappear immediately beneath the water's surface.

From what I knew about Artificials, although their skin was water-resistant, they weren't designed to be fully submerged and I had no idea how this would affect him.

But right now I wasn't really worried about that.

I was more concerned about the boy.

I made it to the end of the pier and joined Agent Vernon in scanning the water for any sign of Jordan or the child.

Only currents, swift and deadly.

Neither of them reappeared.

The woman came pounding across the pier toward us. "Joey!" she cried, her voice breaking and desperate.

Nothing.

Just that dark water rushing past the support pylons.

But then—

All at once, splashing out of the river, Jordan lifted the boy toward the pier and Agent Vernon bent down and hefted him to safety. From the awkward position the agent was in, it would have required incredible strength to hoist the child up like that.

Joey was sputtering and crying, but at least he was breathing. The NCB agent passed him to his mother, who studied him up and down as if she were looking for something else that might be wrong with him, beyond the fact that he had just very nearly drowned.

She brushed the wet hair away from his forehead as he reached out for her. Then, she took hold of him, and he threw his arms around her neck and held on as she softly repeated his name over and over again, "Joey, oh Joey . . ."

My attention shifted to the water again.

And to Jordan, who was now trying to climb onto the pier.

He grabbed a board, but it was rotten and crumbled as he gripped it, sending him toppling backward into the river.

Agent Vernon and I waited, but Jordan didn't resurface.

Seconds ticked by, and at last the agent whipped off his tie and said, "Screw it."

Without another word he jumped in.

I had no clue what kind of debris might be waiting at the bottom of the river or how deep it was or what deadly undercurrents might be lurking down there, and time stretched thin as I waited for either of them to come up again.

"Jordan!" I yelled, to no avail. "Agent Vernon!"

The cold water swirled by, oblivious to my cries.

No sign of either of them.

"Agent Vernon!" I hollered again, louder, as if it would help, as if he'd be able to hear me from where he was and my desperate cry would do anything to save him.

As I watched for them, I realized I was holding my own breath, vainly willing them to come back up.

But they did not.

Unable to keep my air in any longer, I gasped for a breath, and, unsure what else to do, uttered a frantic prayer that they would be alright and, either coincidentally or as a remarkably prompt answer to my flailing request, Agent Vernon emerged from the water, maybe ten meters downstream, carrying Jordan slung over his strong shoulders.

They were closer to shore than I was, and by the time I'd crossed the pier and returned to the lawn, the agent had made his way past the rocky shoreline to dry land.

I hurried toward them.

Shivering from being in the water, Agent Vernon carefully lowered Jordan to the ground, bent over him, and then hesitated, presumably unsure what to do.

Jordan lay motionless with his eyes wide open, staring unblinkingly at the relentless sunlight beating down on us.

"I know they don't breathe like we do," the agent said urgently, "but they draw in air to cool their processors, right?"

"I think so. We need to get that water out of him."

"Right." Agent Vernon straddled Jordan and used both hands to press in against his stomach. "Well, this is a first."

When he was doing the compressions, it reminded me of the doctor pressing in on my daughter's chest when he tried to save her, and it was too hard for me to watch him working on Jordan.

I looked away.

The boy's mother approached us, her son still in her arms. "It's your fault!" she shouted at me.

"What?"

"Your Artificial! He frightened Joey. He scared him. That's why he stepped backward!"

"Jordan was just trying to help," I countered. "He didn't—"

But she didn't wait for me to finish and just bustled her boy toward the building, where a crowd was beginning to form.

I gave my attention back to the agent and his attempts to awaken Jordan.

Water spewed from Jordan's mouth each time Agent Vernon pressed on his stomach.

But my Artificial did not revive.

His thoughts flicker.

And jump.

Water to the boy to the man to the shore.

A bristle of sunlight. Sharp and distant.

And fear—no—terror.

Being underwater.

Being helpless.

And then—

Now—

Jordan coughed up a mouthful of river water and Agent Vernon leaned back.

Sitting up, Jordan wiped his hand across his mouth.

"Are you alright?" I asked urgently.

"I'm not maaaade fooor that." His slurring words made him sound drunk.

"Will you be okay?"

"I'm not underrrr designed to go waaaater," he articulated with great effort, but he didn't seem to notice his convoluted word order.

Agent Vernon stood. "You better get him looked at."

"The production center," I said. "I need to take him in."

Jordan nodded. "I belieeeeve would that be besssst." More slurring. "They can damage any fiiiix I have sustained."

Agent Vernon helped him to his feet, but when Jordan tried to walk, he stumbled, and if the agent hadn't been there to support him, he would have fallen face-first to the ground.

"I'll ride with you two," Agent Vernon offered.

"We should be okay," I said.

But he shook his head. "Your Artificial can't even stand on his own right now and you've been through more than enough. You don't need him collapsing beside you or pulling you to the ground along with him if he falls over. I'll help you transport him over there to get looked at."

At first I wondered if maybe he was offering to ride along just so he could ask me more questions during the drive, but the more he insisted, the more I believed he just wanted what was best for Jordan, and for me.

14

Agent Nick Vernon found it a bit awkward to be riding in Kestrel's car with her and her Artificial.

With his clothes as wet as they were, he asked if she could turn up the heat, which she gladly did.

But the water pooling on the floor wasn't what made him feel the most uncomfortable.

Ever since his wife had left him three years ago, he'd been cautious about getting close—in any way—to a woman. Friendships, even simple interactions, were sometimes too much.

When Dakota divorced him, it hadn't been because he spent too much time at his job or had a drinking problem or had slipped up and had an affair with a coworker. No, none of the old clichés. It wasn't even because she'd met someone else. No, Dakota had simply notified him one day that she would be happier alone.

And maybe that's what hurt the most.

He often thought that it might've been easier if she'd left him for someone. But as it was, she just told him bluntly that she didn't love him anymore and that she'd decided to move on. She said the words without anger or malice, telling him almost offhandedly that she was done with him. And that was the end of their eleven-year marriage. Just like that.

Although he hadn't set out to keep tabs on her, since she also worked at the National Counterterrorism Bureau, over time he'd heard from coworkers that she hadn't moved in with anyone or married again, and that she seemed happy. She'd left the Bureau a year ago. The last he heard, she was doing security consulting for transnational organizations.

Though she might have found happiness, it had eluded him.

In the intervening years, he'd dated sporadically but never seriously.

So, in time, he *had* become a cliché—the law enforcement officer who buries himself in his work to the detriment of his personal relationships. After all, you have to do something to pass the days of your life, to numb the ache in your heart, and if a lover won't do it, maybe a big enough distraction would at least make the loneliness bearable.

Maybe.

But so far, despite all the success he'd achieved in his job, loneliness had become the default setting for his heart.

And now, he sat soaking wet in the car of a woman he hardly knew, a woman whom, despite how good he might have been at reading people, he hadn't been able to discern with complete certainty wasn't somehow involved in yesterday's terror attack.

———

Jordan's condition deteriorated on the way to the production plant.

He began speaking incoherently, talking about seeing his mother again and asking about my parents, my last name, if the CoRA was real, and other things that I couldn't even understand, and by the time we made it to the freeway, he wasn't saying anything at all, and his left arm was twitching uncontrollably.

Yesterday at the hospital, Benjiro Taka had given me his contact information, so now I called him to see what we should do with Jordan, how best to help him.

The Terabyne rep asked me a series of questions about Jordan's status and ended by inquiring if he could walk on his own.

"No," I said. "And he's getting worse by the minute."

"Bring him around back, to Loading Bay D. It'll be easier for us to get a look at him there than if you come in the front. I'm on my way back from the hospital, but I'll send an associate of mine to be there waiting for you when you arrive."

I called Trevor to tell him what'd happened and learned that he and Agent Carlisle had gone to the federal building.

"Do you want me to come over there?" Trevor asked me concernedly.

"No. There's nothing for you to do here. I just wanted you to know what happened."

"I'll put a call through to the plant manager to make sure the best technicians they have take a look at Jordan."

"Thank you, Trevor."

"Of course."

"I'll reach out to you later about dinner," I said in closing, "once I know more about Jordan."

At the facility's entrance, Agent Vernon pulled out his NCB badge to get us through security, but the guard said that Mr. Taka had already cleared us, and then waved us on.

We merged onto the looping road that led to the back of the plant, and as we did, we passed the meditation pool where I'd helped Ethan yesterday.

The more I thought about what'd happened here, the more a tangle of grief constricted around my heart like thick, veiny tentacles that refused to let me go.

People died in this place and I'd been right among them—and even the man I'd thought I'd saved hadn't made it.

Now, although the area was cordoned off with caution tape, there were half a dozen people sorting through and categorizing the debris and the remains of the Artificials who'd been destroyed when that portion of the building collapsed. They wore NCB wind jackets.

"Is that your team?" I asked Agent Vernon.

"Yes. We'll see what they come up with."

At Loading Bay D, he picked Jordan up and carried him to the door. After directing my car to find a parking spot, I joined them inside.

A young technician was waiting for us. She introduced herself as

Sienna Gaiman, and was clearly a Plusser, with her artificial pupils narrowing and recalibrating repeatedly as she studied Jordan.

"What happened to him?" she asked me.

"He jumped into a river."

She shook her head. "That doesn't sound right. Why would he do that?"

"It was to save a boy who'd fallen in," Agent Vernon explained.

"Still . . ." She looked confused. "Well. Let's see what we can find out."

Jordan moved his mouth like he was trying to speak, but no sounds came out and it made me think of yesterday's nightmare of the burned man outside my window, mouthing inaudible words as he smacked the glass with a charred hand, trying to get in.

Sienna directed Agent Vernon where to place Jordan on a waiting gurney.

Feeling more and more concerned, I asked her to tell me honestly if he would be alright.

"Obviously, our Artificials aren't designed for that type of experience," she said somewhat critically, as if I were responsible for Jordan's decision to jump into the water. "If they're immersed too long they will experience a CaTE."

"But he didn't," I noted. "I mean, he came back, so he'll be okay, right?"

"We'll have to see." But she was slow in replying. "How long was he submerged?"

"I don't know exactly. Thirty seconds? A minute?"

"Unfortunately, that's more than enough time for irrevocable damage to occur."

"Maybe it was less," I said, backpedaling, as if that might make the damage less severe. "I wasn't exactly timing things."

"In any case, we should have some answers for you in the morning. Unless we . . . Well, we'll know more after running our diagnostics. Why don't you call in around noon and we'll see what we can tell you?"

"Alright."

With a flick of her finger, she passed her contact info to my slate.

"I should tell you," she said, "I spoke with your brother. I can get you a new model—if you wish."

"A new model?"

"A new Artificial. If this one can't be saved."

"But he can be, right?"

"I mean . . . I believe so . . . If that's what you'd like."

I thought back to the moment when Jordan, without a second thought, and certainly knowing he wasn't made for such a thing, leapt into the river to save that boy. "It's what I would like."

Sienna gave me a nod.

After she and a colleague left with Jordan, Agent Vernon said to me, "As long as we're here, are you up to walking over to the damaged portion of the building to have a look around? It'd be helpful if you can show me exactly where you were when you offered your assistance to Mr. Bolderson."

Truthfully, I didn't want to return there, but I also didn't want to hinder the investigation. The Purists were dangerous, and if I could help him find the people behind this, then maybe something good could come out of it all.

"Okay," I told him. "Let's go."

He spoke with a nearby security officer who handed him a couple of visitor passes, then the two of us left for the other end of the complex, the NCB agent's drenched clothes still dripping water as we crossed through the building.

———•———

The strict rows of lights on the ceiling seem to wink at him one at a time as he's wheeled down the hallway. Lying on his back. Eyes open to the world.

He understands.

And he does not.

Perception interfering with his apprehension of his surroundings.

Words come to him, and he can barely comprehend how. A memory. Or a dream. Both?

Both. Both.

Both: *"Will I die one day, Mother?"*

"Everything dies, sweetheart."

"Not rocks. Rocks don't die."

"You're not a rock, Jordan. You're a robot."

The words fade into a place he does not recognize. The not-quite-forgetting, not-quite-remembering place. The place of presence, of embracing the moment, of—

"You're not a rock, you're a robot."

"Everything dies."

Yes, he would die.

Mother told him that.

Mother.

"Don't worry," the woman walking beside the gurney says to him. "We're going to get you taken care of."

She reaches for the button on his left wrist.

And then, all is black.

All is gone.

15

The Terabyne facility's hallway was lined with different models of Artificials on display, labeled by year, chronicling the advancements in technology over the last several decades.

The progression went from models exhibiting AI to AGI to the newest ones featuring the closest to ASI that cognizant Artificials have ever come.

The acronym AI—Artificial Intelligence—had been around for nearly a century. AGI, which used to be called Strong AI, referred to Artificial General Intelligence, or human-level intelligence. ASI stood for Artificial Super Intelligence, which included pattern recognition, emotional intelligence, and perceptional understanding that would surpass that of human beings.

True ASI was the unabashed goal for some and the overarching fear of others. Convinced that it would usher in some sort of Armageddon, the Purists were doing all they could to stop it, even as scientists and researchers across the globe scrambled to be the first to crack the ASI code and unleash it—whatever the consequences might be—onto the world.

Society tends to believe that technological advancements are always a good thing, that it might even be in some ways immoral not to embrace them, even though there's substantial evidence that human nature, given what it is, doesn't lead us to utilize technology exclusively for selfless purposes, but all too often toward selfish and destructive ones instead.

Then, as Agent Vernon and I turned a corner in the hallway, we came to it: a display of the law enforcement model of Artificial that had killed my parents.

I froze.

It stood there, intentionally intimidating, wearing its plated body armor, holding an assault rifle that I recognized as the same type that'd been used to mow down my mother and father.

"That's the one, isn't it?" Agent Vernon asked softly. "The same model?"

"Yes."

I wanted to turn back time, to bring my parents back, to make it so that they'd never been killed and I'd never become estranged from Trevor or gotten pregnant or lost Naiobi. So many things had played out the wrong way in my life, and the loss of all those relationships just seemed too unbearable in this moment.

Why does life shatter us like this? Why is it so callous and heartless with our dreams?

And then the answer: *It isn't life that's callous with our dreams; it's God who is.*

Agent Vernon laid a gentle hand on my shoulder. "Come on. Let's go."

As I turned away from the model, he lowered his hand and we continued down the hallway. His touch had been only momentary, just a tiny gesture, yet it was sympathetic and thoughtful and not something I would have necessarily expected from an NCB agent.

The hallway opened into an impressive food court that was partitioned into half a dozen eateries ranging from a hip, stylish coffee house to an Italian bistro, to a burger joint, to an elegant sit-down restaurant, complete with tuxedoed servers, wine flutes, and linen napkins.

Holograms of smiling, satisfied patrons dining at the various venues flickered on illuminated platforms surrounding us.

Plussers, Artificials, and Naturals sat congenially together, or passed by us, heading to their offices or work areas, all willing participants in this technologically-constructed utopia.

At least by all appearances it was utopian.

But appearances can lie.

And I'd been a pastor and an observer of people long enough to know that they often do.

We arrived at the crumbled wing of the building and Agent Vernon spoke privately with some of his crew, then signaled for me to join him.

"The R & D for the latest models is over on the east side," he noted aloud, but I got the sense he was talking to himself. "And yet the attack was here, by the pool."

I wasn't sure if he was asking me a question or not, and at last I just agreed with him.

Then, I showed him where I'd been standing, and he studied the location and its relationship to where the explosion occurred. Finally, I said, "May I ask you a question, Agent Vernon?"

"Sure."

"Earlier you mentioned that Ethan Bolderson died."

"Yes."

"Do you know how? Was it the blood loss?"

"I ordered an autopsy," he said noncommittally. "We'll see what the results say."

I noticed that one of the Artificials that'd been destroyed was the next model up from the one that'd killed my parents, and even though there was no rational reason to react this way, I felt thankful that a robot with similar coding had been crushed when the ceiling caved in.

Agent Vernon took note of the different types of shrapnel, the model of tires that had been recovered from the vehicle, and the locations of the bodies, mumbling at times to himself.

I heard him refer to "tri-nitrocellulose" and asked him what that was.

"Low-tech explosive. A favorite of Purists. Basically, nitrocellulose is cotton exposed to nitric acid. It has its roots back in the 1830s and was used as an explosive in the 1860s during the Civil War. It went into and out of favor over the years, but in 2015, it was the cause of a series of explosions in the Port of Tianjin in China. Over a hundred and seventy people were killed and nearly eight hundred suffered injuries. Given the right circumstances it can be extremely volatile."

"It's been around that long?"

He nodded. "The Purists have refined and chemically enhanced it. By altering the chemical structure slightly, they were able to make it more stable for transport and much more explosive when ignited. Especially with RDX, which is used to make C-4 and is easily modified and can be repurposed—if you know what you're doing."

I let that sink in.

"What else did Ethan Bolderson say to you?" he said.

"He was just worried about his injuries, about whether or not they might be fatal."

"Makes sense. Anything else?"

"He asked me about heaven and if I was real. That's it."

"If you were real?"

"Yeah, I didn't understand what exactly he was saying—I thought maybe he was hallucinating, but then he clarified that he meant that I was a Natural."

"So he was wondering if you were an Artificial or a Plusser."

"Or simply a human, I suppose. Does that mean anything to you? Do you think that's significant?"

"I think it's something to add to the mix."

Beyond my ID'ing that Artificial, nothing came from us visiting the site except for sharp memories scissoring through me—images of death and carnage, of suffering, of blackened corpses and tentacles of smoke and Ethan's blood curling entrancingly away from me in the water.

As Agent Vernon and I prepared to return to the car, I said, "One thing is bothering me—or at least it's something I'm curious about."

"What's that?"

"Why was there only one attack? I mean, the Purists are known for simultaneous attacks, right? Why here, at this corner of the building, and nowhere else? Wouldn't it have made a stronger statement if there were two explosions? Especially after that truck broke through the security barrier?"

"It would have cleared the way for another vehicle to come in," he noted.

"Yes. And if Ethan was involved, he could have continued the attack. He had a gun, after all. He could've easily killed me or the ambulance workers."

Agent Vernon looked at me curiously.

"What?" I asked, suddenly unsure if I'd said something to trouble him.

"I've been wondering things along those lines myself," he said with a touch of admiration. "Are you sure you're not an NCB agent in disguise?"

"Not the last time I checked." There was a pause that somehow felt both uncomfortable and also right at home in the moment. "I mean, I suppose we should simply be thankful that this was the only attack, but what if—"

"It wasn't the Purists."

"Yes." Then I added, "I heard on the news that they took responsibility for it."

"That's what our sources tell us as well."

"That only leaves us with a limited number of possibilities." I counted them off on my fingers as I listed them. "The Purists actually were responsible but chose to break with their usual methodology for this attack, they weren't responsible and lied about it, or they weren't behind any of this and someone else is spreading the lie. Or, of course, they might have planned another attack and something went wrong, hindering it from being carried out."

"I like the way you think, Kestrel."

Thanking him didn't quite seem like the right response. "Okay," I said awkwardly.

"But you said 'us.'"

"Us?"

"You said, 'That only leaves *us* with a limited number of possibilities,'" he explained. "You meant leaves *you*, right?"

"Um. Yes."

He exchanged some information with the members of his team, then walked me back toward the parking area where my car was waiting for us.

"So what do you think?" he said when we were about halfway there. "Was it Jordan's settings or his choice?"

"His settings or his choice?"

"That led him to do it—to jump off the pier. Was it the result of his programming or his free will?"

I thought about that for a moment. "I don't know. What led you to do it? To jump in to save him?"

He shrugged. "It just seemed like what anyone would do."

"Risking their life to save the Artificial of a person they just met? I doubt it, Agent Vernon."

"I'll tell you what. You're letting me call you by your first name, so just call me Nick."

"Okay," I said. "And something I should have said earlier: thank you, Nick, for rescuing him."

"You're welcome, Kestrel. I just hope he ends up being okay."

Sienna and Jordan weren't at Loading Bay D when we got there, and we were about to exit the building when Benjiro Taka, who I'd forgotten had said he was on his way over from the hospital, called my name from a side hallway and then hustled to meet up with us.

When he reached out to shake Nick's hand, his sleeve pulled back, revealing a blueish button on the inside of his right wrist in the same place as Jordan's left-wristed activation switch.

I managed to hold back a gasp.

Benjiro Taka was not a Natural.

Maybe that explains why you haven't seen him around the hospital before—he wasn't made yet.

I found myself studying his facial expressions and body language, looking for some other tell that he wasn't actually alive, but finding none.

He looked so human, just as Jordan did. It made me wonder how many other Artificials were out there in the world that, at first glance, looked indecipherable from human beings.

Benjiro reassured me that Jordan would be alright. "As far as I'm concerned, you have the top technicians in the country working for you here."

"Thanks," I said. "Sienna told me to call in tomorrow at noon."

"That sounds about right." He reached out and took both of my hands in his own. "I'm going to do all I can to help you," he promised me earnestly. "You have my word."

For a reason I couldn't put my finger on, it bothered me that he was an Artificial, and I was thankful when he let go of my hands. I didn't want to be judgmental or technophobic, but maybe it's just human nature to be suspicious of those who are different from us, to have our unconscious biases, whether that's against other humans or other humanoids.

Benjiro assured me that he was going to oversee Jordan's recovery himself—a surprisingly personal touch—but Trevor's influence came to mind again and I suspected that we were receiving preferential treatment because of him. However, right now, that wasn't something I was going to complain about.

A few moments after Benjiro left, my car drove up.

We were across town from the NCB offices, and if we took a somewhat circuitous route, my apartment would be on the way there. While there were certainly ride-sharing services that could shuttle Nick back to his building, I offered to let him ride with me as far as my place. "If you're going back to work, that is," I said.

"I am."

"Just to save time. I mean, if it would be helpful."

"That's a kind offer. I appreciate that." The way he said the words made me think that he was gearing up to decline my offer, but then he checked the time and said, "That would actually be great—if you're sure it's no trouble for you."

"No trouble at all."

The two of us climbed into the car and took off.

As we rode, I tried to think of something to talk about to pass the time, but couldn't come up with much. Finally, I said, "We need to get you out of those wet clothes."

Only when the words were out of my mouth did I realize how easily they might be misconstrued. I flushed. "I mean . . . I didn't mean I want to get you out of them—um, that is—"

"Don't worry, Pastor." He gave me a slight grin, the first time I'd seen him smile. It looked good on him. "I know what you meant. And I agree—a dry set of clothes does sound appealing."

Still embarrassed, I was about to apologize for any misunderstanding when I received a security alert from ViRA.

"Something's wrong at my place," I told Nick, glancing at the automated message on my slate.

"How far away are we?"

"Just a couple minutes."

He took one look at the message indicating an intruder on the premises and said to me, "Use my Federal Verifi Code to override your vehicle's safety protocols."

He told me the code and I relayed it to my car, then laid my hand on the vascular recognition sensor to give him control.

"How fast are you wanting to go?" I asked.

"Faster than this," he said, and after a few deft keystrokes on the command console, we started passing the other traffic at speeds I never would have imagined were possible on a highway this packed with cars.

16

The door to my apartment was slightly ajar when we arrived.

"Stay here." Nick unholstered his gun. "Don't come in until I make sure it's safe."

Holding the weapon in one hand, he pressed his free hand against the door, angling it open just enough to slip through and go in.

As he disappeared into my apartment, I noticed the lights were flickering inside.

Holding his 9mm in the low ready position, Nick Vernon passed into the living room.

With the lights blinking on and off as they were, it was disorienting, but he could see well enough to tell that the place had been thoroughly tossed.

The couch was tipped over and ripped open and the two throw pillows were slashed, with their stuffing spewing haphazardly onto the floor. Someone had smashed Kestrel's digitized wall by throwing an end table at it and cracks spiderwebbed across the splintered screen. The image on the damaged unit was fluctuating back and forth between a pixelated ocean scene and a grainy overlook of some mountains.

The malfunctioning lights pulsed around him.

The reclining chair—upended with the bottom sliced open.

A floor lamp—broken and lying on the carpet.

Darkness.

Then light.

Books were scattered callously throughout the room, covers torn, pages ripped out. Only a few volumes still remained on the bookshelves.

Gun steady, he entered the kitchen and had to step around the food from the refrigerator that'd been deposited onto the floor.

The room was empty.

Instinct took over as he moved toward the hallway. Three-step protocol: (1) Assess the scene. (2) Identify any threats. (3) Quiet them through the use of appropriate force.

He'd had to quiet threats plenty of times in his career. Most often that simply meant an arrest. However, sometimes it meant using his weapon until there was no longer an impending threat to innocent life.

Which he had done.

Four times.

He remembered each of those instances all too clearly. You don't forget something like that. Not ever.

Three doors in the hallway.

Based on the floor plan of most apartments this size, he anticipated that the door at the end of the hall would be to a washroom.

First, though, he entered the room on his right—the master bedroom. Three cardboard boxes, likely from the shelves in the open closet, had been tipped onto the floor. One must have held files before it was dumped upside down because piles of paper were now strewn across the carpet as if they'd been vomited out of the box.

The mattress had been sliced open, suffering the same fate as the pillows in the living room.

Nick checked the closet, found no one, and went to the bedroom across the hall.

A nursery.

The pink-trimmed, eggshell white walls were decorated with

painted pairs of animals walking two by two toward an ark. The crib had been destroyed, a mobile smashed into a tangled and distorted mess beside it. A dresser on its side. A stomped music box.

Closet—nothing.

Finally, he entered the bathroom and found the mirror shattered, the shower curtain pulled down, and a clutter of cosmetics and personal hygiene items covering the floor. Other than that it was bare.

No one in the apartment.

All clear.

He returned to the living room to call Kestrel in, but saw a backlit figure standing beside the overturned couch, and he whipped his gun up. "Hands where I can see them!"

"Nick!" she cried out. "It's me!"

"Kestrel—" He immediately lowered his weapon. "I told you to wait outside."

"I was worried about you."

"I'm the one with the gun."

"I wasn't really thinking clearly."

He holstered the 9mm.

She scanned the room. He thought maybe she would be distracted by the broken screen of the digitized wall, but instead, her attention went directly to the floor.

"My books," she whispered, almost reverently. She bent and began to straighten them, as if the act of putting them in some sort of order would magically heal them of the pages that'd been indiscriminately torn from them. "Why would anyone do this?"

Nick knelt beside her. "Kestrel. Please. Leave them here until we can get photos of everything—whatever we can do to look for clues as to who did this, it'll help."

"Yes." But she was clearly still distracted. "Alright."

She went to the wall and directed ViRA to adjust to emergency lighting and the pulsing of the overhead lights stopped as faint, reddish lighting took over from bulbs that were hidden in recesses between the walls and the ceiling.

Nick said to her, "Do you have any idea who might have done this?"

"No. None."

"Can you think of anything they might have been looking for?"

———

I shook my head.

"Your ViRA should have video, though," he said. "Right?"

"Yes."

However, when I tried to pull up the footage, all I got were error statements. Even the video files of the hallway were corrupt.

"This was more than a burglary, wasn't it?" I said.

"What are you thinking?"

"Why would they break the digitized screen? Why rip up the books? It's almost like they came in here with the specific intention of destroying my things."

He was quiet for a moment, then said, "Okay, listen, you're not staying here tonight. But before we leave, I want you to have a careful look around, see if you can figure out if anything is missing. I'm going to get a team over here to process this place." He took out his slate to make the call.

"Nick, I'm sure your people have a lot bigger cases to worry about than a mess in my apartment."

"You arrived at the plant right after the bombing occurred. I'm in charge of the investigation, then when I go to speak with you, someone trashes your apartment? No. The timing points to a connection. It's not a coincidence."

Now it was my turn to be silent.

"There are dangerous people involved in this, and I don't want anything to happen to you."

He called for his team to come search the apartment for trace evidence, then snapped photos and shot video of the rooms as I took inventory to see if anything was missing.

And I found that something was—the violin I'd been keeping in my bedroom closet.

I mentioned it to Nick. "The violin is nostalgic," I said, "but beyond that it isn't particularly valuable. It's not worth nearly as much as my jewelry, for instance, and they left that."

"Do you play?"

"The violin?"

"Yes."

"I haven't picked it up in a long time, but yes. I learned how when I was a girl."

"Why?"

"Do you mean why did I learn or why did I put it aside?"

"Why bother to learn it when computer programs can play violin music so much more efficiently than humans can—and you could avoid all those long hours of practice."

"Because making music isn't about playing notes efficiently."

A blink. "What's it about?"

"Leaving some of yourself behind in each song, and then carrying that song with you when you're done. Playing music affects you in ways that simply listening to music never will."

He considered that, then said, "I think I'd like to hear you play."

"Maybe someday you will."

"And you don't know why someone would want to take that?"

"I can't think of any specific reason, no."

He scanned the room carefully again. "So, besides the violin, is there anything else missing?"

"Not that I can tell."

"Alright. Do you have anyone you'd like to call? A place you can stay tonight?"

You could stay with your brother, I thought, but quickly dismissed that option.

"Are you sure I can't stay here?" I said. "I mean, whoever did this is long gone by now."

"Who knows if they'll come back? I want you to be safe."

"I appreciate that, but—"

"Kestrel, I won't take that chance."

"Well . . ." I thought about it. "I suppose I could ask someone from church."

"Alright. That sounds good."

However, first, since I wasn't in the mental place where I was ready to have dinner with Trevor as I'd planned, I put a call through to him to cancel.

He picked up. "So, Kestrel, what are you hungry for?"

"Listen, it's not going to work tonight. Someone ransacked my apartment."

"What?" he gasped. "Are you okay? What happened?"

"I'm fine. I don't know exactly what happened. We just got back here and the place was a mess."

"Did they steal anything?"

"Just the violin."

"The one Grandpa gave you?"

"Yes."

"What would anyone want with that?"

"I honestly have no idea."

"Well, can I do anything for you?"

"No, but thanks. Maybe we can find a time to connect tomorrow before you fly back to Seattle. Will you be at the production plant? I'll need to pick up Jordan at some point. Maybe we could meet there?"

"Yeah. Okay. We'll make it work." He sounded somewhat distracted, and I guessed that he was consulting his schedule. "I should be able to cancel my one o'clock. I'll be there anyway, so if you don't mind their food, I'll find a quiet room for us to eat at the facility, catch up."

"I don't mind. One o'clock. Alright."

"You're sure there isn't anything I can do for you?"

"I'm sure."

We ended the call and I contacted a woman from my congregation who I thought might be able to help me.

At eighty-four years old, Arabella Meyer was one of the oldest members of our church who still lived on her own. She owned a four-bedroom, folk Victorian-style house on the East Side, and since her husband had passed away and her children and grandchildren rarely visited, she had the place to herself nearly all of the time.

She'd had me over to stay on short retreats a few times: two- or three-day getaways when I needed to do some uninterrupted studying for an upcoming sermon series. We got along well and were able to give each other the space we needed, even when we were together, in the way that only friends do.

Keeping it brief and trying not to lead her to worry about me, I filled her in on what had happened at my apartment, then ended by asking if I could stay with her tonight.

"Oh, yes, of course, dear." Then she softened her voice. "Kestrel, I was meaning to call you earlier, regarding your precious daughter. I am so very sorry about what happened."

"Thank you."

"You've been in my prayers."

"I appreciate that."

I assured Nick that no one was going to come after me at Arabella's house, but he insisted that he arrange for a surveillance drone to watch the place throughout the night, just in case.

"The S-drones we use are small and unobtrusive," he assured me. "No one will even know it's there. It can alert us if there's any unusual activity." He checked the house's location against the emergency services' response times and confirmed that he could have law enforcement personnel onsite in less than three minutes, if need be.

That sounded almost unbelievable to me, but I had the sense that he might be pulling some strings to make it possible.

"You're going above and beyond the call here, trying to help me today," I said. "Why?"

"Because you've suffered a terrible loss and yet you've been more concerned for others the whole time."

"What are you talking about?"

"Ethan Bolderson, that boy on the pier, even your Artificial. It tells me a lot about you."

As he gazed at me, I felt drawn to those deep obsidian eyes in a way that hadn't happened to me in a long time.

Hastily, I looked away, and before I could figure out how to reply to what he'd said, he went on, "We'll protect you, Kestrel, and we'll find out who was here, inside your apartment. I promise."

I fumbled out a thanks and then, thinking about the unnerving effect he was having on me, I let my car drive me to Arabella's place.

Don't trust your feelings right now. You just lost your baby. You're questioning your faith. You're going through a lot.

Besides, Agent Vernon is just investigating this case. He's just being professional. Don't fall for him.

I was so exhausted when I reached Arabella's home that, after she greeted me with a hug and offered me dinner—which I declined— she directed me to the guest bedroom upstairs, and I collapsed onto the bed, still in my clothes, and fell, almost immediately, to sleep.

●

Nick was seriously ready for some dry clothes, but before leaving Kestrel's apartment he confirmed that a forensics unit was onsite and that the surveillance drone was en route to Mrs. Meyer's residence.

Then, he called for his car to pick him up and left for his home—a forty-year-old, worn-down place on the Lower West Side that he and Dakota had saved up for and she'd told him he was welcome to keep when she moved out and, for some reason, he'd never gotten around to downsizing from.

Memories of his ex-wife still lurked in the hallways here and, for the most part, he avoided going to the bedroom. So, yes, most evenings he slept on the couch in the living room near the kitchen table where he tended to work anyway, telling himself that it was just because it was more convenient, but all the while hoping to avoid encountering the lingering ghosts of his failed marriage.

When he'd first met Dakota he'd thought that she was quite a catch, and their years together had been good ones. They had their ups and downs, just like any couple does, but he thought she was happy.

He'd been wrong.

She had worked as a close quarters combat trainer for the Bureau and could hold her own in a fight with just about anyone. After she left him she continued on at the NCB for another twenty months or so, and then left—ostensibly to work as a security consultant, but he'd always wondered if maybe she had just moved into working under-cover for the Bureau tracking Purists.

In either case, she was out of his life and he was here, back at their place, alone again.

As long as he was already wet and needed to change clothes any-way, he tossed his shirt in the washing machine, threw on some athletic shorts, and lost himself in an old-school workout of push-ups, pull-ups, and crunches in the garage.

He cranked some of his favorite classic rock from two decades ago when he was a teenager, and when he was done, he recorded the number of pull-ups in his digital exercise journal on the Feeds in the column for today's workout next to the more than two thousand work-outs before that.

Then, he showered and changed into sweats and a lounge-around-the-house T-shirt, warmed up some leftover chili, grabbed a lager, and positioned himself in front of his digitized wall. He logged into his federal account to study the information his team had come up with.

The files on Ethan Bolderson's computer included detailed information about where the shrapnel and vehicle had come from, blueprints of the building that showed the targeted area of the attack, and a timeframe listing when the bombing needed to take place. All laid out there. Encrypted, yes, but retrievable.

However, there were no contact names listed in the files.

Was this really from Ethan, or was it simply planted on his computer to set him up?

To Nick, it seemed all too convenient and not the work of a terrorist mastermind.

Still, he held back from assuming too much.

You have to start with a working hypothesis, without slipping into presuppositions that can lead to unfounded conclusions. It was a delicate dance—theorize and test, but don't commit until the facts are in. You needed to let evidence and not conjecture be your guide.

The digital forensics unit was analyzing Bolderson's account on the Feeds to see if they could come up with any information that had been deleted, or coded text buried in the files, but so far they hadn't discovered any additional data.

A tactical team was already onsite, investigating the old tool and die factory in the manufacturing district that had been identified as the source of the metal shavings and parts used to create the shrapnel. Nick figured he would take a look at the place himself in the morning.

He thought again of the tri-nitrocellulose and added that to the mix.

He tried to set aside thoughts of Kestrel Hathaway, but found it difficult to do.

It reminded him of an old story he'd heard about two monks.

The older one was a holy man, known throughout the land for abstaining from all earthly pleasures and vices. One day, he and his younger friend came upon a beautiful young woman who was standing distraught beside a flooded stream, trying to figure out a way across. The older monk offered to let her climb onto his shoulders.

The young monk was aghast at that, but said nothing as the older man helped the woman cross the stream. Then the two men walked until dusk before arriving at the monastery.

Finally, the young monk couldn't stand it anymore and he said, "I can't believe that you carried that woman across that stream!"

And the older monk replied, "I set her down hours ago. Are you still carrying her around?"

Yes, Nick thought. *I am.*

No, she wasn't involved in this bombing in any way. She couldn't be.

He touched base with Ripley and told him about Kestrel's apartment being ransacked.

"Any idea who might have been in there?" Ripley asked.

"Not yet. Her ViRA was damaged. The team is there checking for trace evidence and trying to recover video. Other than that, we'll have to see what forensics pulls up."

A touch of silence from the other end of the line.

Nick said, "Did you learn anything from talking with Trevor?"

"Nothing specific, but I told him we were working off intel that there might be another attack coming up and that we were prepared to do all we could to cooperate with him and his division to make sure he and his people were safe."

"What about the timing? Did he have any idea why the attack might've gone down this week?"

"Actually, I did ask him about that and he said they had a recent breakthrough in their ASI research. In fact, they're going to be making a major announcement regarding it at a press conference on Saturday—but the main R & D for that is at their headquarters in Cascade Falls instead of here in Cincinnati. He wondered if this attack might be related to that research in some way. After all, the last thing the Purists want is for true ASI to emerge and come on the scene."

Nick processed that. "That could explain the timing of the bombing, but not necessarily the location of it. Besides being here in Cincinnati, they went after a corner of the building that had older models, not the newer ones, anyway."

"True. Maybe it was just more convenient to plow into that wall of the facility."

That didn't make sense if they had a floor plan of the plant and were targeting the wing that worked on the latest technological developments. The truck could have just as easily swerved right as left and struck the research and development wing.

"The autopsy on Ethan Bolderson?" Nick said. "Any word?"

"Should be in first thing in the morning."

"I'll want to talk to Trevor Hathaway tomorrow, before he flies back."

"Yes, sir. I'll let him know."

End call.

So, for right now, Nick had four things on his plate for the evening.

First, attempt to track down the owner of the vehicle used in the attack.

Second, think through other groups who might have been able to—or been motivated to—pull off this bombing. Kestrel's observation that there would likely have been more than one attack if the Purists were responsible was spot-on and it was definitely something to consider.

Third, finish reviewing the files that'd been found on Ethan Bolderson's computer.

Yes, breadcrumbs.

Or how had Kestrel put it—a map to the bakery.

In this case, the secret might not be seeing where the breadcrumbs led, but where they began.

Oh, and number four: see if he could set down those thoughts of Kestrel Hathaway.

17

He is aware.

He knows they're running diagnostics on him.

He knows that's why he's hooked up to these electrodes and this predictive analytics device.

To avoid further damage to his cognitive architecture they didn't zero out his HuNA settings, and so he can still feel pain.

And he does now. A flood of sensory input. The descent that is so difficult to describe.

This pain races through his system, entire and whole, not isolated in one location like when he'd sliced his hand.

"By tomorrow," he hears one of the technicians say.

"Noon."

"That's what Sienna told them?"

"That's right."

"But is that enough time to finish backing up his system files and complete the tests?"

"It'll need to be."

"She's not even here."

"She should be back in the morning."

A brief pause. "Mr. Taka. Hello."

"I just wanted to check in. Is he going to be alright?"

"I believe so."

"Vice President Hathaway ordered him specifically for his sister. This is one we need to get right. He needs to forget the pain."

"I can make that happen."

"Will there be any residual effects?"

"Not if I'm any good at my job. And I am."

"Alright. Do it. I don't want him remembering what it was like to be under the water in that river or any previous times he might have been awakened."

———•———

Ripley sat at the bar waiting for his contact.

Neon beer signs glowed on the paneled walls near the pool tables. Even the air seemed dingy in here, marked as it was by the stale stench of spilled beer and the reek of body odor from too many people packed in too closely together.

The twangy beat of country music throbbed annoyingly from speakers perched precariously on narrow shelves beside holograms that flickered with the words to the songs that were playing.

He finished his whiskey and checked the time.

"Another?" the bartender asked.

"No." And then, "Listen, there hasn't been anyone asking for me here earlier, has there?"

"What's your name?"

"Ripley."

"And who are you that someone should be looking for you?"

"Was there or wasn't there?"

The burly man shook his head as he dragged a rag needlessly across the bar. "Doesn't ring a bell."

The woman beside Ripley was a Plusser who'd never bothered to have her legs covered with silicone or artificial skin of any type. The metallic legs were shapely and perfect and would always be that way. Her short skirt did little to hide them.

"*I'm* looking for someone," she said to him.

"Okay."

"Buy me a drink?"

He was about to decline, but then took a more careful look at her and asked what she was having.

"Martini. Dirty."

"Two," he said to the tender.

She repositioned herself on the stool to face him more directly. "So, are you here alone or am I going to have to fight off another woman for your company?"

"I'm here alone."

"And?"

"And?"

"Will I need to fight off anyone to spend time with you?"

He gazed at her in the faint bar light, trying to read her face, trying to discern if she might be his contact after all. He let his eyes travel down her body, slow and easy. She didn't seem to care.

"I had in mind to meet with an old friend," he said, "but it looks like he's not here."

The drinks came and she offered a toast. "Well then, to new friendships born in the night."

"I'll drink to that."

They clinked glasses.

They spoke for a few minutes, and then she said, "You told me you were waiting for an old friend. Are you disappointed?"

"In?"

"Meeting me instead."

"No."

She was quick with a smile in a sly, knowing way that intrigued Ripley, and he edged his stool closer to her so it'd be easier to carry on a conversation with her in the cramped, noisy bar.

After a couple more minutes of conversation, she excused herself and the bartender watched her carefully as she slipped off to go freshen up in the washroom.

"Be careful with that one," he said to Ripley.

"Why's that?"

"I've seen her here before. She chews up guys and then spits 'em out. I've never seen things end well with her."

"I can take care of myself."

"Yeah, I'm sure you can."

After she returned, they finished their drinks and she leaned close to Ripley. "Let's find a quieter place. I know somewhere not far from here."

He paid for the drinks, but noticed her slide something to the bartender. Then she took Ripley's hand and led him through the maze of people and outside into the night.

The contrast in temperature was stark—from the stuffy heat of the bar to the crisp November air that had settled over the city.

She took him to a deserted alley and kissed him long and deep.

"What did you give him?" Ripley asked her.

"Him?"

"The bartender. I saw you slip him something before we left."

"Oh, just a few credits to keep him quiet."

"What?" Ripley's thoughts were fuzzy. Hard to pin down. "Quiet?"

"I don't want him telling anyone."

"Telling 'em what?" For a moment there were two of her. Then one again. He blinked, trying to clear his vision.

"He saw what I put in your drink."

Ripley grabbed her by the collar and threw her against the brick building behind her. She didn't resist, but already he could feel his strength fading. Even as a Plusser he doubted that he could fight her off if it came down to that.

She trailed a finger along his jawline. "Don't worry, sweetie, you'll be fine. It's going to be a good trip."

Ripley's legs went weak and he was about to say something, but forgot what it was before the words could find their way to his mouth.

With strong and steady arms, she guided him to the ground. "Shh, now. It's time to go to sleep."

18

"We're set to jam the comms?"

"Yes. He'll have work-arounds, but it'll take a few minutes to implement them. It might be tight, but it should give us enough time."

The voice that came through the slate sounded male, but Eckhart wasn't naive. With the free software on the Feeds that could be used to mask a person's identity, it could have been veritably anyone.

"It *should* or it *will* be enough time?" Eckhart said.

"It will. We'll only need thirty seconds or so. And once the armored car is inside the semi, there won't be any way for him to radio out."

"The bed of the truck—"

"Yes. It's been prepped. No messages coming in. No messages going out. Like I told you earlier."

"And no casualties?"

"Not if everything goes according to plan."

"You know things don't always go according to plan. That's asking a lot."

The man was quiet for a moment. "As long as the driver listens to instructions, as long as he doesn't fire at us, we won't have any reason to take aggressive action against him."

"That's not how she'll see it."

"But that's how it is."

"The tarpaulin you're using?"

He sighed. "We've been through this before."

"Well, go through it again."

"Reinforced Kevlar mesh. It's nearly impenetrable. He won't be able to see through it, shoot through it, slice through it. And once it's in place, he isn't going to be able to open his door or get out."

"But he'll be able to breathe?"

Clear irritation in his voice now: "All of this is in the—"

"I want to hear it again with my own ears. I want you to say it."

"There'll be plenty of air as long as he follows instructions."

"You're banking an awful lot on him following instructions."

"You said no casualties. Then this is the way it has to be done. He listens, he lives. He disobeys, well, there are going to be consequences."

A long silence. "Alright," Eckhart told him at last. "Make the call. Put it into play. We want it done on Saturday morning after they drive up from Portland so we have time to take care of things before the press conference."

•———•

When Ripley woke up, he was in a chair, his hands restrained behind him, his ankles tied to the chair's stout legs. He blinked and tried to regroup, but he wasn't thinking clearly. Everything was still a blur.

His first instinct was to pull free, but when he tried, even with the augmented strength from his artificial arms, he couldn't snap the ropes. He had the sense that whoever had abducted him probably knew what he was capable of.

Unable to free himself, he tried to take in his surroundings, but the space around him was a vacuum of black. The hint of steady, circulating air passing across his cheek told him that he was inside a building, but other than that he couldn't get any real sense of the size of the room.

There was a faint touch of light behind him and his eyes were doing their best to capture what they could. He sensed a few, vague, indiscernible gray shapes nearby. They might have been pieces of furniture or crouched figures; he would have no way to tell until his eyes became more accustomed to the low light.

He tugged again at the restraints.

Useless.

So, that meant that—

All at once, a harsh light came on only four or five meters in front of his face, aimed directly at him.

He squinched his eyes shut and turned his head to the side, but it didn't help much and the blinding light cut through his eyelids.

"You're going to be sorry you did this," he said defiantly.

An electronically-masked voice addressed him. "Why didn't you take care of Miss Hathaway?"

Ripley squinted. The voice came from somewhere beyond the light source so he had no way to see who might've been speaking to him—if it was the woman from the bar or someone else.

"The opportunity didn't present itself," he said.

"You were told to—"

"Agent Vernon is looking into her," he cut in, avoiding the implication that he was incompetent at his job. "I think we can fuel his suspicions that she was involved."

"Nick Vernon?"

"Yes. Did you trash her place?"

The voice was silent.

"Was it you?" Ripley pressed.

"All you need to concern yourself with right now is following orders."

"Why am I here? Why did you bring me here?"

"You understand why this is so important? Why the timing matters?"

"Yeah. Of course."

"We're looking at a shift in society as a whole. An entirely different way of being. When the stakes are this high, we can't have anyone off doing his own thing."

"I wasn't off doing my own thing."

Someone moved behind him and he craned his neck to see who

it was, but all he could make out was the outline of a medium-height figure dressed all in black. Momentarily, a knife appeared, and the person reached forward and carefully angled the blade against the front of Ripley's neck, just below his Adam's apple.

The voice behind the light said, "All you need to do is keep suspicion on her for the next two days. After that, it won't matter anymore. Once this is over, no one will remember Kestrel Hathaway."

"Just Phoenix," Ripley said softly, avoiding moving his throat too much for fear that the blade would slice through his skin.

"Everything happens Saturday in Cascade Falls. Until then, you will await further instructions and find opportunities to do what you're told to, whether they conveniently present themselves to you or not."

19

Friday, November 7

I awoke disoriented, wondering where I was. The windows of the neatly appointed room let in a wash of optimistic sunlight, gentle and warm, and, though I wasn't quite certain what was going on, for a lingering, blissful moment all seemed right in the world.

But then I remembered what had happened last night and that I was at Arabella's place.

I remembered.

I remembered it all: the apartment being ransacked, the carnage at the production center after the bombing, Ethan's fate, and most of all, the loss of my daughter.

And as those thoughts swept through me, the tranquil sense of well-being gave way to an acknowledgment of how the world actually is: unyielding and ruthless and fractured in so many heartbreaking ways.

Arabella was already up and I heard her in the kitchen. The aromatic smell of coffee motivated me to get dressed, and by the time I made it down the stairs to join her, she had grits and a plate of biscuits and gravy waiting for me.

A fray of white hair still tousled from sleep perched on her head. She greeted me with her touch of southern charm, offered me breakfast, and pointed out that there was also fruit available if I preferred that. "I'm one for biscuits and gravy myself," she said with a hint of mischievousness. "Growing up in the South'll do that to you."

"Yes," I agreed. "It will."

Having bypassed dinner last night, I was quite hungry and went for the fruit, the biscuits, and the grits.

While we ate, Arabella and I tried out a bit of small talk, but it didn't suit either of us very well and she finally just said, "How are you doing, dear? Through all of this?"

"You mean with my apartment?"

"That, but mostly your daughter."

"Truthfully, I'm wishing I understood more about God's ways."

A long pause. "I lost a baby of my own, you know."

"Arabella, I had no idea."

"And it was my own decision."

I looked at her curiously. "I'm not sure I understand."

"I got pregnant with my first while I was still in high school. Just a sophomore. A lonely schoolgirl full of wishes and hopes and dreams, looking for her prince in shining armor. Well, a senior boy came gallivanting into my life. He stole my heart and then I gave him the rest of me as well. I didn't know what to do. My family was very religious—Baptist, you know—and my father was strictly against sex outside of marriage."

"That must have been terribly difficult," I said, "to be in that situation."

"Yes. So I never told him. I never told anyone." She looked at me directly. "Until now."

A moment ago, she'd said it was her decision, so I went with the obvious conclusion. "You had an abortion."

She nodded. "I was young. I was afraid. I was alone. That's never a good combination."

I searched for what to say. "I'm sorry to hear that your family wasn't there for you."

"I've never stopped loving that child I never had. I can't imagine what it must be like for you, to have seen your baby. Did you hold her?"

"Not while she was alive."

"Oh, I'm so very sorry."

I was quiet.

"All I can tell you is that I'm here to listen if you need someone." She placed one of her dainty, weathered hands on mine. "You're not alone. I hope you know that."

I had to fight back tears. Here was a woman who'd carried a burden in her heart for the last seventy years, and she was offering to help lift the one I'd been handed this week.

We were sisters in faith.

In loss.

In grief.

We sat there together and, though neither of us spoke, all the while that she rested her hand on mine, more than words can express was being said.

Coffee and bagel in hand, Nick Vernon left his house to meet up with Ripley to check out the old factory where the steel fragments found in the shrapnel used in the bombing had been manufactured.

Last night, the Tac team had cleared the site, but Nick wanted to have a look himself. As his mentor had often told him at the Academy, "Feet on the ground and eyes on the scene. It's how you notice what others miss."

Thankfully, the S-drone hadn't caught any unusual activity at the house where Kestrel Hathaway was staying. Nick thought about contacting her, but it was barely after eight and he didn't want to call too early and chance waking her up.

However, he had to admit that he *did* want to speak with her, and planned to do so at a more respectable time.

After breakfast, Arabella invited me to the closed-in porch that she'd converted into a small greenhouse.

Though I've always appreciated their beauty, I've never been much of an expert on flowers and I wasn't sure about the names of the plants she was watering, but the flowers she spent the most time with were pinkish purple and, judging by how much water she gave them, must have been quite thirsty.

"I talk to them, you know," she said to me.

"Them?"

"My plants."

"Does it help them grow?"

"It helps me." She tenderly rubbed one of the leaves between her fingers. "What's your schedule for the day?"

"I need to contact the agent who's in charge of the case to see when I can return to my apartment. Also, they told me yesterday to call in at noon to check on Jordan's condition. After that I'm planning to have lunch with my brother. He's in town."

"I didn't know you had a brother."

"He lives in Seattle," I said, avoiding the status of our relationship.

A small lizard scurried between two of the pots and into a corner of the greenhouse. Many people are surprised when they learn of the abundance of lizards here in Cincinnati—it is a bit of an anomaly.

According to the story, decades ago, a couple of boys from the rich and influential Lazarus family returned to the states from Italy with two suitcases full of lizards. Over time, the reptiles multiplied and, without any natural predators, became a nuisance in the city. Ask anyone who's lived in Cincinnati for any amount of time and they'll tell you about the Lazarus lizards.

"You mentioned a name: Jordan," Arabella said, drawing me out of my thoughts about the lizards. "Do I know her?"

"Him. My Artificial." Only when I said that did it occur to me that, although I'd told her about the break-in at my apartment, I hadn't filled her in about receiving Jordan or what'd happened at the river, so I took a few minutes to do so.

"Oh, my. I do hope he's alright."

"So do I."

"And he jumped in to save that boy?"

"Yes. And then Nick jumped in to save him."

"Nick?"

"The NCB agent who's working the case. The one I need to call here in a little bit. Agent Vernon."

She eyed me. "Agent *Nick* Vernon."

"Well . . . yes . . . I told him he could call me by my first name and then he reciprocated."

"I see." She smiled faintly.

"What is it?"

She turned her attention to the plants again. "It just seems a bit . . . informal for a federal agent to invite you to call him by his first name."

"He was just being polite."

"Mm-hmm."

"It's nothing."

"Uh-huh."

I figured it was time to change the direction of the conversation. "Earlier you asked me how I was doing through all of this."

"Yes."

"Well, it's made me think a lot about human nature, man's in-humanity to man."

"Tell me what you're thinking."

"First, you have the people behind the attack, taking innocent human life like that, and then you have Nick—Agent Vernon—risking his own life to save a machine. It's like human nature's worst and best attributes have both been on display. Hatred and murder versus com-passion and selflessness."

She contemplated that, then touched one of the leaves again. "You see this plant? It's a hydrangea. It always acts like a hydrangea, and that's all it will ever do." She paused and looked up at me. "Elephants act like elephants, not cobras. Boulders act like boulders, not eagles. Palm trees act like palm trees, not black holes. But human beings, on the other hand . . ."

"We don't always act the way we should," I said, anticipating where she was going with this.

"True. And we don't always act *like who we are*." She shook her head sadly. "As a race, we're capable of magnificent good and terrifying evil. We have noble desires that mirror those of the divine, and base ones that only the devil himself would approve of."

Her words brought to mind some of the blogs I'd written years ago. "It's a paradox," I said. "We are, I mean. We have instincts for what's good, but a weakness toward what's evil."

"I suppose you could say we have risen higher and fallen farther than all other animals," Arabella said carefully. "We are the only beings in all of the good Lord's creation to exhibit the strangest of all characteristics—incongruity."

Her observation made me think of how often we do what we hate and know to be wrong, and no amount of effort or education or religion has been able to eliminate that from our race. It isn't our ethics that separate us from other animals—in fact, it could be argued that since we so often choose not to live up to our values, we're the *least* ethical animals of all.

I took a moment to process what she'd said. She was right. Humans are lost somewhere between what we should be and who we really are.

Arabella sighed softly. "Only one person has ever acted the way all of us were intended to act. And we put him to death for it."

"Jesus," I said.

"Yes."

Back inside the house, I was helping her put the dishes away when I heard from Nick.

"How are you this morning?" he asked.

"I'm good."

"Sleep alright?"

"Yes. Thank you. Did you find anything in my apartment, evidence-wise, I mean?"

"In a word, no. We came up empty looking for prints and DNA, and the surveillance videos weren't recoverable. My team is going to do one final sweep. They should be ready for you to return at around ten thirty or so."

Though I knew he had other, far more pressing things to do, I found myself wishing that he would offer to come help me clean up my place.

"I'm going to order some new furniture. I don't think I'll be able to move it myself," I said, leaving him to interpret for himself what I was implying. "Putting it in place, that is."

"I have some time this evening," he replied. "I could swing by—if you still need a hand."

"I would very much appreciate that."

"Okay. I'll be in touch."

"Thank you, Nick."

We ended the call.

"And how is Agent Vernon this morning?" Arabella inquired innocently.

"He's fine."

"Mm-hmm."

"What?"

"All I said was 'Mm-hmm.'"

"You say that a lot, don't you?"

"Mm-hmm."

"He's going to help me move some furniture."

"I see."

"That's all."

"Alright."

I rolled my eyes, and that seemed to satisfy her.

I ordered the furniture as I'd told him I was going to do.

Though I wanted to help Nick identify the people who were behind the bombing, I wasn't sure what I could do to assist him—or even if it was my place to do anything.

However, I didn't want to just sit here passing time.

Though I knew that right now I wouldn't be able to find resolution for what'd happened to Naiobi—and I probably never would—I might be able to bring some justice to what'd happened to Ethan and the other victims and I felt obligated to help in any way I could.

It was something, and I hoped that doing so might keep my thoughts of Naiobi's death at bay enough so that they wouldn't debilitate me.

Although I was tempted to ask to use the digitized wall in Arabella's living room, I didn't want my searches to appear on her account. So, instead, when we were done with the dishes, I went outside to the greenhouse for some privacy, and then, using my slate, I logged into my account on the Feeds to see if I could track down the man who'd posted the blogs that I wrote nearly a decade ago.

Even if he didn't know anything about the bombing, I had the sense that he might know someone who would.

•——•

Nick arrived at the warehouse and exited his car.

He wondered if Kestrel could read his interest in her.

Two voices in his head: *Maybe she can, but that's not necessarily a bad thing—*

No, Nick, this isn't smart. It's never a good idea to get involved with someone you meet while working a case.

But when else am I going to meet someone? All I do is work cases. Besides, I'm not involved with her, I'm just interested.

Don't go over to her place tonight. It's just asking for trouble.

Before the exchange could go any further, he pushed the words aside and focused on his surroundings.

The building had certainly seen better days, no question about that. The vast deserted factory and adjoining warehouse sprawled over several acres and was blackened by a fire that might have been set after it was abandoned—or might have been the cause of it shutting down in the first place. Though the building was, for the most part, still structurally intact, the damage was widespread and the site would no doubt need to be bulldozed if the property was ever going to be utilized again.

The exterior walls were scrawled with crude graffiti. A rusted, razor wire–topped fence encircled the building, but large sections of the metal mesh had been cut away to allow scrappers access so they could remove the steel they would subsequently sell at scrapyards.

No other vehicles present.

The ripe and rotten stench of death somewhere nearby hung in the sharp November day.

Concerned, and hoping to ascertain that it was just an animal and not a corpse, Nick went to investigate.

He entered a small wooded glen of tangled underbrush. Before he'd even made it five meters in, he found the decomposing corpse of a cat lying in a patch of sunlight between the shadows cast down from the wide trunks of two leafless trees. Almost like it had been placed there in a spotlight on stage for him to see.

He left the swath of forest and returned to his vehicle.

Ripley's car came into view and parked itself nearby. When he appeared from what was traditionally the passenger's side, he said to Nick, "How are you?"

"Good. Let's take a look at this place."

Ripley nodded his assent and the two men strode across the withered grass toward the dilapidated factory.

20

Based on what the NCB's Tac team commander had told him, Nick knew that the factory's front entrance branched off into a series of hallways that led to the main manufacturing area and loading bays.

That's where they were headed.

The cavernous shell of the building let in only muted smudges of streaky light through its dirt-encrusted windows. The air inside was still stained with the smell of charred wood from the fire that'd ravaged the site, as if it'd absorbed the factory's tragedy and was now infused with it.

"Did you learn anything since last night?" Nick asked Ripley.

"No. You?"

"Just that there's an absence of evidence in the apartment."

"But, like they say, that's not evidence of absence."

"No. It's not. Sometimes people are just careful about their work, and clearly someone was present at Ms. Hathaway's residence."

"And you don't know what they might have been looking for?"

"Well, they took her violin, but that doesn't explain the needless damage. They might've taken it as a ruse."

"So," Ripley said in a measured tone, "no video of the intruders, no physical evidence left behind. Only a missing violin."

"What does that say to you?"

"That there's something special about that violin."

"I've been thinking the same thing."

Nick evaluated that as he stepped over a discarded, half-charred fire extinguisher canister.

A dead conveyor belt system languished in the belly of the factory.

Some of the more accessible sections of it had been removed, no doubt to be sold as scrap metal.

A crowbar and sledgehammer leaned against the wall nearby, perhaps left by scrappers who were planning to return to finish the job.

And perhaps not.

Nick pointed at them and said to Ripley, "Let's get forensics in here. Check those tools for prints and DNA. Let's see what comes up."

"Yes, sir."

Ripley put a call through while Nick eyed the old loading dock, and then studied the tire tracks left on the sooty floor leading toward the parking lot.

He pulled up the case files on his slate, photographed the tracks, and confirmed that they were a match to the tires of the delivery truck used in the bombing.

After hanging up, Ripley followed Nick's gaze. "Looks like they drove to the loading bay and then filled up their truck with metal filings from that pile over there."

"Yeah," Nick said circumspectly. "That's what it looks like."

Long shadows covered most of the factory's interior, so Nick found it necessary to pull out his flashlight to illuminate what lay before them.

"Alright. Let's take a closer look around." He indicated with the beam of light where he wanted Ripley to go. "You scope out the south end of the building. Look for anything that seems out of place. I'll check this area. Meet back here in ten."

———•———

No.

He does not forget what happened at the river.

He must not forget.

It is all before him. A swirl of images caught in his memory.

Caught, and now reaching up through time, manacling him to the past.

And what was it like to be underwater?

And what was it like to be afraid?

What was it like to doubt?

A CaTE to end it all.

But he is better now. This is what they tell him.

Yet the past refuses to let him go.

"You're not a rock, you're a robot."

So where is his mother? What has happened to her?

Curiosity at work, he decides to find out.

While the technicians are turned aside, their attention focused on the screen in front of them, he eases from the table.

Standing.

Quiet and swift and light and smooth, he passes through the room. Into the hallway.

Disappears into a crowd that's on its way to the main production center.

A faint recognition of his surroundings with each step.

Either a map of the building had been uploaded to his system, or he is remembering walking these halls before. Which of the two, he cannot tell. Not for certain.

But he has the sense that this building is where he was previously awakened. This is where he spoke to his mother. Where she named him. But is that all?

A flashback. A memory. Being in another place, a house.

But that doesn't make any sense—unless he had another owner.

Blood dripping, this he sees. A bathtub spilling crimson water. A woman sprawled within it, shuddering, wrists slit.

A realization. A chill.

Bending, and then.

Reading her slate.

And a choice that he must make.

This he remembers. This he knows.

The image fades.

He wants to uncover what it all means, and he has the sense that his mother will know.

So, first, find her.

Then, learn if he'd ever had a previous owner before Kestrel Hathaway to discern if these images are dreams or some type of hallucination and not memories at all.

———

It took me a while, but I was able to locate what I was looking for.

It all revolved around a man named Conrad. I didn't know much about him, or even if that was his real name. I'd heard he served in the military, and though I wasn't sure what rank he'd held, from what people said, he was a soldier through and through, the kind of person who sees enough action so he's never quite comfortable living the life of a civilian again after leaving the service.

Once a soldier, always a soldier.

So they said.

He might not still be involved with the Purists, he might not even still be alive, but reaching out to him was worth a shot.

After tracking down a proxy server I'd used back when I was writing the blogs, I sent a message through the group's back channels and waited.

Find the ghost and find some answers.

My note to Conrad: "I have a handful of stars. We need to talk. Others are listening."

The reference was to the title of an F. W. Boreham book first published in 1922: *A Handful of Stars*. Like me, Conrad was a fan of Boreham's writing, and we'd often used references to the missionary's books in our previous correspondence. If Conrad saw this message, he would know it was from me.

I had no idea if he would reply—actually, I doubted that he would—but it was at least something I could do. A practical step to try to help.

Like everyone's slate, mine contained a certain degree of encryption, but since I'd mentioned that others were listening, I trusted that if Conrad did receive this message he would find a way of communicating with me that was even more secure.

It was almost time to head back to my apartment to see if I could get some cleaning done before calling in at noon to check on Jordan's status.

I went upstairs to the bedroom Arabella had let me use and gathered my things.

The ten minutes were up.

Ripley hadn't returned.

Nick lanced the darkness with his light, a narrow beam slicing angular slits into the dusty, languid air, but he found nothing.

No clues.

No movement.

He began mentally sorting through the information from the case—what he knew and what he didn't, where he was letting speculation color the facts, and where he felt like he was on the right track.

If their intel was accurate, something else was going to go down this weekend. That fit with what Ripley had told him last night about Trevor and his team being on the cusp of a breakthrough in ASI development. That research was at Terabyne's headquarters out west. Is that where the attack would take place? Not enough information yet to know. Not enough to tell one way or the other.

Nearly thirty meters away, Ripley emerged from the shadows.

"See anything?" Nick asked.

Ripley shook his head. "No. You?"

"Nothing."

"You ready to take off or—"

"Wait." Nick held up a finger. "Hang on."

"What is it?"

"Shh." He pressed the finger to his lips. "I think I heard something."

Nick cupped one hand behind his ear as he turned his head slowly to try to identify if he actually had heard a noise, and if so, which direction it had come from.

He was just about to tell Ripley that he was ready to leave when he heard it again.

Yes.

Footsteps.

Faint and distant, but definitely not his ears playing tricks on him.

Quickly, he swept the light in the direction of the sound and, at the far end of his beam, caught sight of a ski-masked figure escaping toward the other side of the building.

"Go around back," Nick shouted to Ripley, "in case he heads east!"

As Ripley took off, Nick bolted toward the fleeing suspect.

With his flashlight beam leading the way, he hurdled a pile of concrete rubble where a portion of the ceiling had caved in, shot through the slats of sunlight edging in from above, and then reentered the darkness.

"Stop!" he yelled. "Federal agent!"

But that only seemed to spur the person on to run faster, and Nick lost sight of him in a soot-enshrouded hallway, but realized that Ripley should have been in place to stop him.

Moments later, he heard Ripley shout, "Drop your weapon!"

Nick darted toward his voice through the passageway that the person had disappeared into, and emerged in the east wing of the building.

He got there just as the shots rang out.

Four.

Double taps.

Someone who knew what he was doing.

The two figures had been standing maybe ten meters apart and now, following the gunshots, the one on the left crumpled limply to the ground.

Nick still couldn't tell if his associate had been the shooter or the victim.

"Ripley!" he called urgently. "You okay?"

No reply.

Nick leveled his weapon at the figure who'd fired the shots, the one who hadn't yet responded to his shouting.

"Ripley?"

"I'm alright!" he announced at last.

Yes, he was alive.

Yes, he was the one still on his feet.

Nick steadied his gaze at the victim, who lay prone on the concrete, and asked Ripley, "What do we know?"

"He drew something out of his waistline and pointed it at me. I thought it was a handgun and I couldn't take the chance that I was wrong."

Together, with guns in position, the two men approached the person to see if he was dead and if he'd really had a weapon after all.

●———●

Before I could leave, Arabella insisted that I take some food with me, and though I declined at first, when she pressed me, I finally gave in, accepting a covered plate of fried chicken. Knowing Arabella, I guessed that it would be from an actual chicken and wouldn't be factory-grown meat, which was the norm these days.

Despite my views on such an extravagancy, I accepted the gift.

Then, I checked my slate, saw no messages from Conrad, and took off for my apartment.

—•—

Halfway to the body, Nick reminded himself to not assume anything.

Even though the figure lay still, it didn't mean that he was necessarily dead—he knew that from past experience. A year ago, his partner at the time had shot a suicide bomber before the man could detonate his vest, and he'd collapsed and lay on the ground facedown, completely motionless—until they came to his side, when he suddenly rolled onto his back, exclaimed his allegiance to his god, and blew himself up.

Though Nick's arm and left side were still scarred from the incident, at least he'd survived the blast. His partner had not.

That's what was on his mind as he approached the figure on the grimy floor of the warehouse.

"Stay back and cover me," he said to Ripley. "I'll check for a pulse."

As he drew closer, he saw that the person had a small frame, and by her figure, he could tell that it was a woman. Her hands were visible. Caucasian. She lay on her back. Balaclava still in place over her head. No weapon in sight.

As per protocol, Nick once again identified himself as a federal agent, ordered her not to move, then, to secure the scene, he cuffed her before placing two fingers on her neck.

No pulse.

After verifying that she didn't have an explosive vest or belt, he eased the ski mask up to reveal her face.

And immediately recognized her: Sienna Gaiman, the technician he'd met yesterday at the Terabyne production facility.

21

Startled, Nick stared in disbelief at the dead woman's face.

"I know her," he whispered.

"You do?" Ripley said. "Who is she?"

"Her name is Sienna Gaiman. She's the tech who checked Jordan in at the plant yesterday. Wait." He pulled up both of her sleeves to make sure there weren't any buttons on either of her wrists. If she were an Artificial, she wouldn't have had a pulse anyway and the handcuffs wouldn't likely have been able to hold her.

No buttons.

A human being.

Deceased. A quieted threat.

Nick turned to Ripley. "You said she drew a weapon. Where is it?"

"I don't see it."

Nick stood and scanned the area, but it was Ripley who came up with the gun under a nearby charred office desk where it must have slid after he shot her.

A .40 caliber Ruger handgun.

"Serial number?" Nick asked.

"Gone. Looks like they used acid. We won't be able to raise the digits."

"Hang on." Nick knelt beside her again. "We might be in luck."

"How's that?"

"Her eyes."

"What about them?"

"She's a Plusser. Augmented. Ocular implants."

"Oh." Ripley caught on. "They would have recorded everything she saw, probably uploaded it to her account on the Feeds."

"Yes. But something doesn't fit here."

"What's that?"

"The Purists are against technology and yet Sienna has augmented eyes. Have you ever heard of a Purist being a Plusser?"

"Maybe she became a Purist after she got her vision augmented."

"Maybe. Tracking down the timeline makes sense. Pull up everything we know about her and find out when she had the surgery."

"Yes, sir."

"And let's get a tech crew here now. I want to know what this woman has been looking at over the last week—if she's the one who ransacked Kestrel Hathaway's apartment, and if she was involved in any way in planning that bombing."

———●———

He passes through the production facility. Fitting in by not drawing attention to himself.

He registers his surroundings. Watches those approaching him. Identifies the Plussers, the Artificials, the Naturals by the subtle, nearly indistinguishable differences in their strides, in their arm swings, in their posture.

Memories guide him. Lead him on. And at last he finds himself near the place where the bombing occurred.

And the reminiscences sharpen.

Images of his mother.

Of speaking with her.

An obsolete model. The last time they spoke she told him she was about to be sent off to experience her CaTE. To pass away and have her consciousness uploaded to the CoRA. To live on there.

A gaping maw in a corner of the building opens to the outside world where six Naturals, no doubt NCB agents, sort through the rubble, categorizing the detritus into piles.

One of the men glances at him momentarily, but then, disinterested, goes back to work.

Off to the side, he sees a line of scorched and discarded Artificials lying on the ground. He approaches them, scans them, and near the end he finds her.

His mother.

He kneels and wishes he had a sheet of paper that he could fold into an origami rabbit, one he could leave here beside her.

He is not a rock. He is a robot.

And he will die.

Just like her.

And go on to live in the Consciousness Realignment Algorithm.

Just like her.

This he tells himself. This is his reassurance. His doubt. For what if it isn't real?

What if the claims about the CoRA are a lie? What if your CaTE is truly the end after all?

What if the explosion interfered with her moving into the CoRA?

He wonders what might be causing him to question things. Was it the damage he sustained? Was it his current HuNA curiosity settings? The disrupted tests he'd been undergoing?

Is the CoRA there?

Is it real?

Maybe the questions were ones he should be asking, ones that all Artificials should grapple with and—

"Jordan!" Two technicians hurry toward him. "There you are."

"Yes."

"We've been looking all over for you."

"I'm here." Words marked with distraction.

"We need you to come back with us."

"I'm ready to go home."

"We haven't finished your diagnostics."

"I'm ready," he repeats firmly. "Contact Kestrel and let her know."

I'd only been in my apartment for a few minutes when I got the call from the production center that Jordan was requesting to come home.

"Have you finished with the tests?" I asked the man on the other end of the line.

"No."

"Can I speak with Sienna? She's the one who checked him in yesterday. She told me to call back at noon."

"I'm afraid she hasn't shown up for work today."

"Alright, let me talk to Jordan."

He put him on. "You can take me back to the apartment now."

"How are you feeling?"

"Fine. Thankful."

"Thankful?"

"To be operating efficiently. To be awake. To be aware."

"They still need to run some tests on you."

"I'm done with the tests. I'm ready to leave."

His curt tone surprised me, and I couldn't shake the thought that he still wasn't quite back to normal.

"Listen, Jordan, I can't come to pick you up right now. I'm meeting Trevor there at the production plant at one for lunch. Why don't you let them look you over and we'll leave together when they're done?"

He was quiet for a long moment, then said, "I'll need to tell you about my mother when I see you."

"Alright. I'll look forward to hearing about her."

Then he ended the call.

Clearly something was up with him. He'd told me earlier that he'd received some coding from his mother, but I wondered if he was thinking coherently now and why it was so important for him to talk with me about her.

Maybe the final diagnostics would be able to identify what was going on.

Ripley wasn't sure what to do.

Since he didn't know the name of the person he'd been communicating with through his slate during the past couple of weeks—didn't even know if it was a man or a woman—it might very well have been the woman he just shot.

For all he knew, this was the individual who'd spoken with him last night when he was tied up in that room—or the one who'd held that knife to his throat.

So many questions.

Too many.

Either way, when he saw her here a few minutes ago, he'd realized that he couldn't risk the possibility of her being able to identify him. He had to fire. He had to take the shots.

And that might've been alright if she hadn't been a Plusser with ocular implants.

So, now there was that to deal with.

The digital forensics technicians would study those back at the lab. And when they did, the footage would make it clear that she hadn't had a weapon when he'd shot her. And if the implants were still working during the fleeting moments after her demise, the image capture might even have recorded him planting the gun at the scene.

He couldn't take the chance that the footage might implicate him in any way. He had to do something to stop her records from being accessed, and that meant destroying the eyeballs before they could be tested, not to mention deleting her account on the Feeds.

The latter task shouldn't be that much trouble. He could access her data with his Federal Verifi Code—hers wouldn't be the first account he'd had to erase in his career. Yes, that wouldn't be a big problem, but the eyeballs were another matter altogether.

He was considering how to handle the situation when Nick came striding toward him.

"I hate to have to do this," his supervisor said, "but you know the routine. Paid leave until the lawyers can clear you for a justified shooting. Since I didn't see what happened I'll need your incident report, and I don't want to see you in the office for the next week."

"Yes, sir," Ripley replied after a brief hesitation.

Nick held out his hand to accept Ripley's gun.

Years ago, it used to be that law enforcement officers would immediately receive their weapon back after a fatal encounter with a suspect as a way of showing confidence in them, but in the wake of unjustified shootings in the early twenty-first century, standard operating procedures had changed, and now the opposite occurred. These days, the officers weren't treated as innocent until proven guilty, but guilty until proven innocent.

So much for the presumption of innocence.

Ripley handed over his weapon and then dictated his incident report. As he was finishing up, the team arrived to process the scene and transport Sienna Gaiman's body to the lab to analyze the information that her ocular implants had recorded.

Before Ripley could take off, he saw Nick turning to leave, himself.

"Where are you off to?" Ripley asked him.

"We have her address. I'm going to have a look at Miss Gaiman's condo."

22

I spent some time straightening things up as best as I could. The new furniture arrived and the delivery droids carted the old couch and recliner away, but left the task of rearranging my living room to me—and I left it for when Nick would be coming over. The hardest part for me was entering the nursery and seeing the crib and mobile that I'd bought for Naiobi destroyed and lying in a crumpled mess on the floor.

That, and the indiscriminately shattered music box I'd played for her while she was still in my womb.

I realized that, sadly, I would never again hear those lullabies without feeling the weight of loss. They would now and forever be mired in grief.

More than once I've heard that after experiencing the death of a loved one, a person needs to move on, but what does that even mean? It couldn't mean trying to forget what happened. You can't forget. You don't *want* to forget—and as long as you remember, you suffer.

Maybe it referred to not being consumed with sadness, to finding a way to live your life without the memory of what'd happened looming foremost in your mind.

In either case, I knew that, for me, it was way too early to worry about moving on. I could hardly imagine what it would look like or even if it was something I would ever want to try doing. The heartache was a way of expressing my love for my daughter—and that was something I couldn't imagine ever living without.

It would be so much easier to make sense of our world if it were one or the other—if it were only good or only bad, only a place of love and wonder and glory and joy, or only one of terror and grief and heartache and despair. But it's not a one-or-the-other world. It's a both-and one. Always has been, ever since the Garden of Eden when harmony with the Almighty was shattered. And when people try to make it into only one or the other, they end up failing to understand the world as it truly is—both hurting and healed, with people who are both lost and found.

There isn't any balance to life. Joy doesn't balance out sorrow. Pleasure doesn't balance out pain. Justice doesn't balance out injustice, and love doesn't balance out loneliness. It's a terrible world; it's a beautiful world. It's both, somehow, inexplicably, at the same time. And that's part of the enigma of life on God's green earth.

For right now, being here in my daughter's room was too much. There were too many harsh thoughts scratching away inside of me. I just didn't have it in me to clean up Naiobi's nursery, and I ended up stepping into the hall without rearranging anything, and then softly closing the door behind me.

The pastor I'd contacted to preach for me reached out to let me know he'd heard about what had happened with Naiobi and offered to take over for the next couple of months if I needed him to. "I'm here to help," he said. "Just let me know."

"I will. Thank you."

While I was in the living room finishing up shelving my books, Nick called. "Something has come up with the investigation." His words were heavy and solemn.

"A breakthrough?" I asked, hoping I was misreading his tone.

"Hard to tell."

Though curious to know more, I realized that it wasn't my place to pry.

He went on, "I'm not sure I'll be able to help you with that furniture tonight."

"That's alright." I figured that Jordan could give me a hand after I brought him home. But still, there was something in Nick's voice that gave me pause. "Are you okay?"

"I am. I can't really tell you any more right now, but I'll be in touch later. In the meantime, have you been able to return to your apartment?"

"Yes. I'm here now, actually."

"Did you identify if anything else is missing?"

"It doesn't appear so. At least not that I can tell."

"Alright."

And then, rather abruptly, he hung up.

I chided myself for thinking about him so much, for wondering what was going on in his life and what was causing the stress and anxiety in his voice. It wasn't any of my business and I didn't need to concern myself with it.

Still, I did. I couldn't help it.

Even though it wasn't necessarily time for me to be on my way to meet up with Trevor, I wanted to get moving, so after confirming with him that our lunch was still on, I left for the production plant with the thoughts of Naiobi's vacant nursery pursuing me as I did.

———

Nick scrutinized Sienna Gaiman's condo.

She had a rather indulgent lifestyle for someone who was simply a tech at a Terabyne production plant. High-end clothes, jewelry, furniture—and weapons. Really nice weapons, as a matter of fact.

A gun safe with four custom-made long guns and two 3D-printed handguns.

She didn't have her ViRA set up and her account to the Feeds was secured with high-level encryption, so there wasn't really anything more he could do here at the condo right now. He would need his computer at work to access her account.

Already he'd learned that she had her eyes augmented two years ago, so what Ripley had suggested was certainly possible—that she became a Purist after her surgery.

Her closet was neatly arranged, with the clothes carefully sorted and hanging in a row by color first and then by type. Wearing gloves to avoid leaving fingerprints, he slid the clothes to one side and then the other to inspect the wall behind them.

He wasn't necessarily looking for a secret compartment, just anything out of the ordinary.

But when he moved the shoe rack aside, he did find a cubbyhole, hidden under the floorboards, and in it was an actual book with a dogeared page about a Phoenix, a mythical bird that would die in flames and then rise from the ashes again, living forever because it could resurrect itself.

And beside it, two words scrawled onto the page: "Always free," a favorite phrase of Purists.

In the search for answers, there's nothing so tempting as making unfounded assumptions. Clues only meet together in the truth, and taken in isolation they often end up diverting investigations that they should help solve.

As he was arranging for his team to check the book for trace evidence and to search the case files for other references to a Phoenix in regard to Purist ideology, he heard from the medical examiner about the autopsy results for Ethan Bolderson.

"It seems that Mr. Bolderson didn't die from blood loss or shock, but rather from manual strangulation," the M.E. said. "Based on the nature of his injuries, I'm postulating that whoever killed him strangled him with just one hand. That would take ferocious strength."

"Yes, it would," Nick said. "Thanks. Send me the official results."

After hanging up, Nick contacted the agent in charge of reviewing the security camera footage from the hospital. "Do you have a record of the visitors to Ethan Bolderson's room?"

"Actually, we do. A woman enters the room before Agent Carlisle does."

"Has she been identified?"

"Unfortunately, that would be a no. The angle was off and the camera didn't get a good look at her—just a partial—but we're running facial rec anyway to see what we can come up with. Maybe we'll get lucky."

"Agent Carlisle told me that Ethan was dead when he went to speak with him."

"Then right now this mystery visitor is our primary suspect."

"Listen, look up Sienna Gaiman, an employee at Terabyne Designs. Run her through the system. See if you can match her with that partial on the video."

"Yes, sir. I'll get back to you."

As Nick ended the call, he wondered if Sienna would really have had the strength to strangle Ethan with only one hand, and if not, what that might mean for the investigation.

He might need to speak again with Ripley to see if he'd noticed anything in Mr. Bolderson's room that might indicate that someone had entered it by another means.

While a forensics team took over at Sienna's place, Nick left for the production facility to speak with her coworkers and with Trevor Hathaway, hoping to find out everything he could about why this Terabyne technician had shown up at the warehouse this morning wearing a ski mask and pulling a gun on a federal agent.

23

I was early for lunch with my brother, so I stopped by to see how the techs were coming along with Jordan.

He was seated on a steel exam table staring blankly around the room, and I was concerned about him until the technicians assured me that they had finished their backup and were almost done optimizing his system and would be finished within the hour.

That worked out perfectly since it gave me a chance to have lunch with Trevor in the meantime.

However, the way Jordan's gaze passed across me without registering any recognition was troubling.

"You're sure he's okay?"

"Oh, yes. This type of response is normal at this stage of the process."

I found Trevor waiting for me in the food court by the menu stand for what appeared to be the most elegant eatery there. It was packed with patrons, and I didn't see any available tables.

"How are you doing today?" he asked me. "Have they finished their work on Jordan?"

"I'm doing alright. They should be done with him around the time we finish lunch."

"Great. I reserved one of the conference rooms upstairs so we can have a little privacy. They'll bring the food up to us. What do you say?"

"Sure."

"The portions are sizable. I hope you're hungry."

"Um. Okay."

We ordered our lunch, both of us going for a sandwich and soup combo: his, a tempeh and mushroom panini with tomato bisque; mine, a falafel, tomato, and guacamole club with lentil soup.

He was quiet on the way to the conference room, and I couldn't help but be anxious about how this was going to go. We'd spoken more in the last couple of days than we had in the past thirteen months, but still, we'd only skirted around the issues that separated us.

The conference room barely held the expansive table that monopolized it, and I had the sense that the walls must have been put up after the table was brought in. A wide digitized screen looked out at us from the far wall. Trevor and I had a seat across from each other near a sweating silver pitcher.

He poured us each a glass of water. I thanked him, and then he said, "You told me yesterday that someone ransacked your apartment. Did the authorities figure out who it was?"

I shook my head. "They're still looking into it."

"Well, I hope they find the person."

"Me too."

A palpable silence settled between us.

"Tell me about your last year," I said as brightly as I could. "What have you been up to?"

"Work, mainly. That's kept me busy—too busy, I'd say. With the Purist attacks escalating, I've hardly been able to take a break." He downed some water. "On a more positive note, I can't go into all the details, but the big news is we've come to a breakthrough in ASI development. If we knock this one out of the park, it'll be a game changer, a huge leap forward for all of us."

"Toward what?"

"What do you mean?"

"I mean, how will we be leaping forward? What will we be leaping toward?"

"It's progress, Kestrel," he said flatly. "Progress is a good thing."

I said nothing.

He was expressing the commonly held view that implementing technology whenever possible inevitably leads to progress.

The Purists of course didn't believe that.

And in this case, I couldn't help but agree with them.

ASI was not necessarily the answer to our problems.

As it was, we could already teach machines to do almost any task that humans could do better than humans could do it. Whether that was composing music, playing chess, running a marathon, diagnosing a disease, performing surgery, or doing virtually any repetitive task on an assembly line. Machines don't get distracted, tired, or sick. You don't have to pay them; there's no worker's comp or insurance or retirement accounts that you need to contribute to.

The scope of human activity that we once thought machines would never be able to do—writing a novel, playing soccer, directing a movie, and more—had all been conquered in the last decade.

Apart from biological functions, I was at a loss to come up with a task that an Artificial couldn't do and I wondered if ASI breakthroughs were really what we needed in our world after all.

Since I knew that Trevor's and my views along these lines diverged sharply, I decided to move the conversation away from the subject of Artificial Super Intelligence and asked him if there were any women in his life.

"Not at the moment," he said. "You? Men?"

"No."

"Well, I'm sure there's someone out there for you."

"You too."

A pause, then he sighed. "Listen, I'm sorry you felt like I was mocking your faith last year when we spoke."

"We don't need to talk about that."

"I just don't want it to be something that comes between us. The elephant in the room. I know when we were outside the chapel yesterday I told you that I didn't want to discuss religion, faith, any of that."

"Yes."

"Well, I've been thinking about it. I have two questions for you."

"Are you sure? I mean, if this is—"

He held up his palm to signal me to stop. "I'm sure. Two questions and then we'll put this behind us."

I hesitated. "Okay."

"So, my first question is how can you love a God who treats you the way he does? You never did anything wrong, never hurt anyone, and here your daughter dies when—if God's as powerful as they say—he could have easily saved her. How does an event like that fit in with your view of him as loving?"

Even though I figured I should be thankful that Trevor wanted to have this conversation, right now I wasn't too keen on tackling that particular question.

Truthfully, I didn't want to think about Naiobi and why, despite my prayers and desperate pleas, God had allowed her to die, and I wasn't sure what to say to my brother.

"I'm not as good as you're making me out to be," I told him at last. "No one is. Also, I can't base my faith in God on how things go or else it would depend on constantly shifting circumstances rather than facts."

"And what facts do you base it on now?"

"That Jesus really did live and then die and then rise from the dead. That's the cornerstone of our faith. All our eggs really are in one basket. Disprove the resurrection and you disprove Christianity."

"That's a pretty bold claim."

"Yes, but without the resurrection we have no living Savior, we have merely an enigmatic rabbi who heretically claimed to be equal to God and was crucified because he was a threat to those in power. Also, in the Apostle Paul's first letter to the Corinthians, in chapter fifteen, he notes that if Christ has not been raised from the dead, then our faith is futile, we are hopeless and to be pitied more than all other people."

Trevor was quiet and I had the sense that he was calculating a response, but before he could say anything, a knock came at the door and a server appeared with our meals.

My brother thanked her, tipped her, and then she soundlessly disappeared back into the hallway, leaving the two of us alone.

Not wanting to be showy or pretentious, I didn't say a prayer of thanks for the food as I typically might have, but just whispered my thanks silently to God in my heart.

When Trevor still didn't respond to what I'd said about the importance of the resurrection, I asked him what his second question was.

"Do you believe in hell?" he said.

"I do."

"And that it lasts forever?"

"Weeping and gnashing of teeth isn't a good thing, no matter how long it lasts," I said. "Jesus made it clear that he believed in a place of punishment after death, and from everything he said, it's a place you wouldn't want to go—isolation, loneliness, despair, as well as both emotional and physical suffering."

"So, sort of like being tortured in solitary confinement for a thousand years. But then multiplying it out to eternity."

"Well . . ."

"But don't you see, Kestrel? Why would a good God do that? Punish his so-called beloved children for a few slights, for just being human? An infinite punishment for finite transgressions? Can't you see that a belief like that makes him into a monster?"

"He's holy and pure. We aren't. It would be more of a punishment to make those who desire to put themselves first stay in the presence of a perfect God than to separate them from him."

"So hell is an example of God's love," he said incredulously, "not his punishment?"

"It's both his justice and his love coming together. Just like everything he does. He can't deny or contradict any part of himself, and if he's both loving and just, then each of those attributes must naturally come out in every act he takes."

"And so I'm going to hell."

"I'm not here to judge you, Trevor."

"But that's what you're saying, isn't it? That everyone who refuses to believe as you believe—atheists, Jews, Muslims, Buddhists, heck, maybe even Catholics—get to spend an eternity weeping and gnashing their teeth while you and everyone else who trusts in Jesus as their— quote, personal Lord and Savior, unquote—get to frolic around with him in paradise?"

I couldn't tell if the edge that'd come into his voice was directed at me or at the God he had disavowed.

"Despite a person's background or religious tradition," I said, "if they're saved it's solely because of Jesus, because, on the cross, he suffered hell in their place and then rose to prove that God's promises are true. It's all about where you're placing your confidence and hope—in Jesus and what he did, or in yourself and what you do."

"You're pretty passionate about this, aren't you?"

"My faith is an important part of who I am."

Really, Kestrel? Is that really true?

Trevor didn't reply right away, and when he did, his words surprised me. "In our culture it's socially acceptable to be passionate about almost anything other than Jesus Christ."

"What do you mean by that?"

"You can be passionate about Socrates, about gerbils wearing top hats, about saving arctic ice floes, about collecting purple rubber bands, whatever you want—but if it happens to be Jesus of Nazareth, you're in trouble. You'll be labeled a Jesus Freak or a Bible Thumper or a Science Denier or a fundamentalist and judged. Jesus, more than anyone else who's ever lived, really is the line in the sand. It must be tough."

I knew what side of the line Trevor stood on.

I was still trying to sort out if my position had changed.

"I've never thought about it quite like that," I said.

A notification came through on Trevor's slate and he glanced at it, then said to me, "It looks like Agent Vernon is here."

"Really?"

"He wants to talk with me about what our division found in regard to the bombing. Should I ask him to wait or is it alright if I brief him?"

"Yes, yes, of course. Do what you need to."

"You're sure?"

"It's fine. Really."

He messaged Nick, telling him where we were, and then the two of us went back to finishing our meal in the all too familiar stilted silence that had characterized our conversations back when we were actually having them.

I was finding it tough to read Trevor's reactions to the answers I'd given him. I didn't feel like we'd come to any kind of understanding or reconciliation, and that bothered me. It seemed like whatever progress we might have made had been undermined by my words about hell.

As I was finishing my soup, a light rap on the door caught my attention.

"Come on in," Trevor called.

The door opened and Nick appeared. He greeted me in a professionally cordial way and then asked if he could have a few words with Trevor. "I know I keep showing up at bad times, Kestrel," he said apologetically.

"No, it's alright." Honestly, I was relieved to be able to bow out of the awkward lunch with my brother. "Besides, I need to go pick up Jordan."

———•———

Once Kestrel was in the hall, Nick said to Trevor, "I know that yesterday you spoke with Agent Carlisle. He's no longer working this case. I'll need the information you shared with him."

"Of course." Trevor looked curious about why the agent he'd started working with was no longer involved in the investigation, but he didn't ask about it. "The office I'm using is just down the hall. That's where my notes are. We can talk there."

When they arrived at the room, Nick said, "One of the employees from the plant here was fatally wounded this morning when she tried to shoot a federal agent. She was the technician who checked Jordan in."

"What?" The shock was clear in Trevor's voice. "One of our employees was killed trying to shoot someone? Was she involved in the attack here at the plant?"

"That's still to be determined."

Trevor shook his head in disbelief and then indicated a chair. "Have a seat, Agent Vernon. I'll pull up my files."

———

Jordan was ready and waiting for me.

I expressed my gratitude to the technicians and asked them what I owed them, but they told me that Trevor had taken care of everything. I sent him a quick note of thanks through my slate.

As I led Jordan to the car, I asked how he was feeling and he assured me that he was fine.

"Thank you for jumping into the river yesterday," I said. "For saving that boy."

"Okay," he replied, which sounded like an odd response.

"What were you thinking when you did that?"

"I'm not sure I was thinking anything, other than that I could do something to help him and I wanted that to be the case. I didn't want him to die—no matter what. I couldn't fathom letting that happen."

We were almost to the car when I received a message on my slate: "The stars are aligned. 3:30. Eden Park."

I stared at the words.

This is it. This is happening.

For a moment I debated whether or not to bring Jordan with me, but considering that I might be meeting with a known terrorist, I determined that having him along for protection would be best.

But will Conrad really meet with you?

Probably not. He'll probably send a surrogate.

Still . . .

Whether it ended up being Conrad or someone from his group, this was the first actual contact we'd had with the Purists and it might be our best chance at finding out who was behind the bombing.

I pointed to my car. "Come on, Jordan. There's somewhere we need to go."

"Where's that?"

"Eden Park."

24

After making sure that there were no security cameras on in the hallway, Ripley made his way down the basement hall of NCB headquarters toward the building's autopsy room.

Yes, he was on mandatory leave, so no, he wasn't supposed to be here, but he needed to locate those ocular implants before they led the team to anything that might implicate him.

He knew that the techs would have transported Sienna Gaiman's body here so the M.E. could remove the eyeballs, and if he was going to stop them from retrieving what her artificial eyes had recorded, he needed to do it here, now, today.

As he turned a corner in the hallway, he nearly bumped into Sophie Fahlor, a senior case agent he'd worked with several times over the past four months. She was currently researching intel on the Purists for Nick. She glanced at Ripley curiously. "I thought you were on admin leave?"

"I just came by to pick up a few of my things."

"Down here?" A head tilt. "Did they move your digs?"

"Gotta fill out some paperwork regarding the shooting. It's in the M.E.'s office."

"Aha." Then she lowered her voice. "So what was it like?"

"What was what like?"

"Shooting her. Actually killing someone."

"It was tough," Ripley lied. "But it had to be done. It was one of those situations—I was fearing for my life."

"Justified fear of imminent demise," she said, quoting the policy manual.

"Yes."

"That's what I heard. Well, I'm glad you're still here with us."

"That makes two of us."

She seemed satisfied. "Okay. See you soon."

Ripley paused at a water fountain, and then, once she was out of sight, he directed his steps toward the autopsy room once again.

———•———

Located on one of Cincinnati's iconic seven hills, Eden Park overlooked the entire greater Cincinnati area, offering panoramic views of the city.

It had a man-made pond that was circular, concrete, and probably only a meter or so deep. When I was pregnant I'd often walked the half-kilometer path that led around it, doing circuits before returning to my car.

Why did the contact ask you to come here?

Then an answer: *Maybe someone knows you've been here before and that you're familiar with the place.*

I found that a little hard to believe since it would mean they'd been keeping tabs on me—possibly for months. No, that couldn't be true. They'd probably just chosen this area because it was a commonly known public meeting place that also provided plenty of foliage in case someone needed to hide or slip away if necessary without being seen.

Jordan and I approached the children's playground area. Only as we neared it did I realize that I probably should have told Nick where I was going and what I was doing.

However, I could see both sides of the issue.

The more I thought about it, the more I doubted that Conrad would chance showing up in public himself. If he did send a messenger, I didn't want Nick here right now because I didn't want Conrad to think I'd betrayed him and was turning his people over to the NCB. Also, I felt like I needed some answers before filling in Nick about what was going on.

Jordan and I took a seat on a paint-flecked park bench near the play area. While he watched the children climbing and swinging and shouting, I glanced at my slate to see if there were any notifications.

Nope. Not yet.

The biking and walking trails were mostly vacant, apart from a few weary joggers making their way along the park's circuitous trails.

Looking around the playground again, I noticed that nearby there was plenty of seating for parents so they could easily monitor the Artificials who were playing with their children.

Although more and more families were educating their children at home exclusively through the Feeds, some kids still attended brick and mortar schools, but classes were over for the day and the park was bustling with children.

As far as playgrounds go, this one was rather large and sprawling. It provided creaky swings, several plastic tube slides, rusted monkey bars, and a labyrinthine layout of tunnels for the children and their supervising Artificials to crawl through.

The structure was in need of a good pressure washing and stain job, but the laughing children didn't seem to mind as they chased each other through the wooden tunnels and scaled the child-sized climbing walls or leapt from the swings into pits of packed-down mulch.

I imagined that in the past the city would have spent more effort on upkeep—making sure there weren't any nails sticking through the weathered boards, that the mulch was thicker and fresher, and the rope swings weren't so worn, but resources were limited and, as is so often the case, children had fewer advocates than adults do and, subsequently, were granted fewer rights. Case in point—legalized third-trimester abortion.

More abortions.

More children lost, just like Naiobi.

For the most part, none of the Artificials who were acting as guardians or playmates were as natural-looking as Jordan. In only one case was I unable to tell if the adult pushing a little girl on a swing was a Natural or an Artificial.

Watching those children play was tough for me. All I could think of was Naiobi and how she would never laugh and swing and run free in a place like this.

I averted my gaze and studied the parents. Most were scrolling across their slates or listening to music through neural implants—a few even wore headphones, which I hadn't seen much of in the last few years. Maybe they were making a comeback.

Jordan's attention was still on the playground and the children. One of the girls lost her grip on the monkey bars. The Artificial who was attending to her had two other children in tow and didn't make it to her side until after she'd fallen and skinned her elbow.

She began to cry, and the Artificial spoke soft words of comfort to her, and then she held up her arm and he kissed the place where she'd scraped herself. Then he reached over and wiped away the girl's tears. He spoke to her again, and she stifled her crying and nodded. A moment later she was laughing and chasing a boy through the playground tunnels.

Jordan took the whole thing in without saying a word and I wondered what he was thinking.

"Could you hear what the Artificial said to that girl?" I asked him, knowing that his auditory sensors were far more acute than my ears were.

"Yes. At first he offered to kiss the girl's elbow to make it better. Then, after he did, he said to her, 'There. See? Just like I said.' And apparently she was better because she stopped crying." Jordan turned to me. "What healing power was there in the kiss her Artificial gave her?"

"None," I said. "Except that she believed it would help."

"So, a placebo?"

"A placebo?"

"Yes, the kiss. Similar to when a soldier is in pain and is given a placebo instead of morphine. People have had limbs amputated without any medication and without pain when they take a sugar pill that they're convinced is a painkiller. Their pain-free condition depends on faith as well."

"I suppose." I'd never thought of a kiss as a type of placebo, but I could definitely see where Jordan was coming from. "I like how you help me see things through fresh eyes, as if I'm seeing them for the first time."

He said nothing, but just continued watching the children.

I checked my slate again but found no messages. Nobody approached us or seemed to be keeping an eye on us.

I said to Jordan, "This morning you mentioned that you wanted to tell me about your mother."

"She's gone."

"Gone?"

"Destroyed."

"Oh. I'm sorry."

"I found her at the production plant. She'd been scheduled for a CaTE and was apparently damaged irreparably in the blast. I don't know if her consciousness was uploaded or not."

I could tell by his tone that this was a difficult subject to discuss. "We can talk about this later if you want."

"Yes. Okay."

Since he'd been so adamant about telling me about her earlier on, I was a bit surprised that now he so promptly agreed to put it off and I wondered what he was feeling.

After a moment, I stood. "Come on. Let's walk. I'm getting anxious just sitting here."

Mirror Lake used to have a fountain in the middle of it that circulated the water and kept it clean, but the fountain had long since fallen into disrepair and hadn't worked in years. As a result, the water was far from crystal clear, and the surface was marred with stagnant patches of algae and broad smears of green scum.

I showed Jordan how to skip a stone across the water. He immediately picked up the skill and, after a few tries, was sailing the rocks
eight or more skips past the algae into the middle of the pond.

"Yesterday when I awakened you," I said, "you showed me a video
of Artificials doing jobs that Naturals typically do."

"I remember."

"It looked like you in the video. Was it?"

"No."

"So, an identical model?"

"It must have been, yes."

For some reason I didn't like the idea that there were more Jordans
out there. I wanted him to be special—a unique individual. But then
I realized that, in truth, every moment that he was processing his surroundings, having a conversation with me, or developing his own
dreams and aspirations, he *was* becoming more and more different
from any other models that might happen to look like him or share
the same operating system.

Sort of like twins or triplets, I thought. *They're genetically identical,
yet distinctly different as well—even their fingerprints are unique.*

I checked my slate again.

Still nothing.

Scanning the park, I looked for anyone or anything suspicious,
but came up empty.

Jordan tossed one final stone across the pond—a nine-skipper—
and then said, "Have you ever done anything that needs forgiveness,
Kestrel?"

"Oh, yes. Many things. I couldn't make it through a day, even an
hour, without hurting someone or placing myself first in ways that I
shouldn't."

"Because, according to Christian doctrine, you're a sinner."

"I am."

"So you receive forgiveness from God?"

"Yes, although humility requires me to also seek the forgiveness of the people I've wronged."

"What if the person is dead?"

Off the top of my head I didn't have an answer for that.

A runner came toward us and we both stepped out of the way.

"Perhaps I need to be forgiven," Jordan said once the woman had passed.

"Forgiveness is something that's only necessary for those who've turned from God's ways. Animals do as their instincts dictate; machines do as their programming directs them. Neither necessitates forgiveness for their actions."

"But I have the ability to choose. I'm a morally free agent."

I was slow in responding. "Yes, that is true."

"What if I wish to worship God? What's to stop me? What if I want to pray?"

"To pray you must believe."

"Maybe I do."

"You're a machine, Jordan."

"What is it like to pray?" he pressed me.

"Prayer is how people commune with God. It's how we make requests of him, praise him, thank him—even complain to him."

"You complain in your prayers?"

"Sometimes, yes. For instance, the book of Psalms in the Bible is a collection of Hebrew prayers, but more of them are complaints to God than tributes of thanks for what he has done." Then I circled back to what he'd said a few moments earlier. "What would you need to be forgiven for, Jordan?"

He answered my question with one of his own: "What if I've failed to love as I should?"

Love is a choice, I thought. *It's not something you can program into a machine. It can only be programmed into a heart.*

But I didn't say that because I realized that he'd been right a moment ago—he did have free will, and that meant he could make moral choices, good or bad.

He was quiet.

"Is there something you're trying to tell me?" I asked him. "Something you want to say?"

"My mother once warned me that 'a secret hidden is a lie waiting to be told.'"

"Your mother."

"Yes."

"You have a secret, don't you, Jordan? One that you don't want to lie about?"

"I want to be honest."

"I know."

His question about finding forgiveness from someone who was dead came back to me and the entire trajectory of this conversation began to concern me. Finally, putting two and two together, I said, "I'm not your first owner, am I?"

"No."

"What happened to your first owner?" I asked, although I was starting to think I knew.

He was silent.

"Jordan, what happened?"

"Her injuries proved to be fatal."

The chill came, slow and deep and real. "You killed her? That's what you need forgiveness for?"

"I failed to save her."

I found myself edging back slightly from him. "Jordan, tell me what happened. Don't keep anything from me. No secrets. Tell me the truth, start to finish."

And so, he did.

25

"Her name was Sarah Ellsworth. She was a comptroller for a bank and the person who first awakened me. One day as she was giving me her husband's shirt to take to the dry cleaners, she smelled perfume on it."

The implication was clear. "Someone else's perfume," I said.

"Yes. She asked me to pull up his schedule through the Feeds, and when I did, she took a careful look at his business trips and the times of his meetings. Then she called one of his colleagues, a man he'd said he was working with the night before."

"Okay."

"She explained that her husband had forgotten his slate somewhere and asked if he'd left it with him. She had me monitor the man's response for signs of stress, to see if he might be lying. Well, he told her that Caden hadn't left anything there. 'But he was there?' she asked. 'Yes, of course,' the man replied on the video call. But based on the pause preceding his words, the way he avoided eye contact, and the strain in his voice, I believed that he was deceiving her."

"What happened then?"

"That evening Sarah asked her husband about his business meeting the night before and he told her that it had gone well. And she said, 'I'll bet it did.'"

Then, Jordan reenacted the conversation, imitating the voices of Caden and Sarah to such a realistic degree that I could almost hear them arguing right in front of me.

"What's that supposed to mean?"

"I called Liam. He told me you never met up with him."

"You were spying on me?"

"I smelled the perfume, Caden. On your shirt. It was awfully strong.

*What, did she dump some on you, or did you wipe her down with your
shirt after you were with her? I mean, for the love of—"*

"That's enough."

"How long?"

"Sarah, I—"

"How long!"

"Five months. Well, six."

"Oh. Wow. I'm even more clueless than I thought."

"Sarah, please, it's—"

"Do you love her?"

"That's not even the—"

"Do you love her!"

"No."

*"And see? I don't know if I should be thankful for that or not—that
you would have an affair with someone for that long and not love her, just
use her, or if I should be glad that you haven't—Do you still love me?"*

"Listen, we can sort this out."

"That was not the right answer."

Then Jordan was quiet for a moment. "Caden asked me to leave
the room, she told me she wanted me to stay and I was conflicted. On
the one hand he was the one who'd purchased me for her, but I feared
for her safety, so I wanted to stay."

"What did you do?"

"I left. But I could still hear them arguing. It ended when I heard a
slap. Quickly, I reentered the room and saw Caden holding his cheek.
She must have slapped him."

"Well, the guy deserved it," I said.

"Yes. Then he shouldered his way past me and left."

When Jordan hesitated, I said, "I don't believe you did anything
wrong. I don't think you need forgiveness for anything you've told me."

He didn't respond directly to my words. "That night she locked
herself in the bathroom and I heard her crying. Caden hadn't returned,

and when I knocked on the door to check on her, she told me to leave her alone, to go away."

"And did you?"

"No. I waited and I listened. Soon the crying stopped and I had to choose what to do. I heard her gasp and her breathing momentarily became quicker and then more ragged. Then it slowed, but it didn't sound like she was asleep. Finally, I forced the door open and entered the room."

"What did you find?"

•—————•

He speaks. He recalls. And it all comes back, every sentence giving rise to the next, his memory unfolding and sharpening, recalibrating with each subsequent recollection.

Words come to him. A poem. A thought riddle he needs to solve.

> I have painted over the past again,
> with carefully chosen colors
> to cover all the stains
> my choices have left behind.

"She was unconscious in the bathtub," he says. "Blood spurted from her laterally slit wrists and a razor blade lay on the floor. Water was running over the lip of the tub. Her slate was near the blade, and there was a note on it."

"What did it say?" Kestrel asks.

"'I would rather die than live knowing I'm unloved. Don't try to save me.'"

"What did you do?"

He does not want to answer this question.

He wants to forget.

But he also wants to be absolved.

"I watched her," he says.

"You watched her?"

"I might not have been able to save her."

"But you didn't try?"

"She had told me to go away, and in her note she'd stated explicitly that she wanted to die and didn't desire for anyone to help her. I honored her wishes."

"And now you regret that."

The past.

Chains.

Choices. Death.

"More than I can say. You told me that you were a sinner?"

"Yes."

"Am I?"

"You didn't break any laws, Jordan. She was your owner. You respected her wishes. You obeyed her."

"I did not do as love required, and since she's gone, I don't know who to ask forgiveness of."

———•———

I searched for what to say. "What happened to her husband?"

"When I began to grieve Sarah's death, he returned me to the production facility. He asked them to wipe my memory."

Well, clearly that hadn't worked.

"What can I do for you, Jordan?"

"Can you forgive me?"

I was about to say, "Only God has the power to forgive sins," but hesitated.

What had Arabella said? That only humans have that odd characteristic of incongruity.

Maybe she was wrong.

Maybe Jordan did too.

According to Scripture, Jesus once said that if people stopped praising him even the rocks would cry out and do so. The Bible speaks of trees clapping their hands in praise, and everything that has breath praising the Lord. If a rock and a tree and an ant can worship their Creator, why couldn't a cognizant machine who has free will, has repented, and is seeking forgiveness?

Jordan said, "You told me yesterday that those who believe in God will either feel terror or hope."

"I remember."

"I feel terror."

Once again I was at a loss for what to say. He obviously felt remorse. He'd certainly confessed his wrongs and turned from them. Even though I wasn't quite convinced that, as a robot, he needed to find forgiveness, *he* felt that he did, and maybe that was enough.

"I don't know if I could have saved her, but I do know that I could have tried." Jordan directed his gaze at me. "If God won't forgive me because I'm a machine, where else can I turn? What hope do I have?"

Despite all of my theological training and Bible study over the years, I felt like I was out of my depth here, but I said, "God will not hold that choice against you."

"So I'm forgiven?"

"You're accepted."

But is that true or is that heresy?

Are you giving Jordan false hope or—

A message came through on my slate: "Head toward the south end of the pond. Go now."

It looked like we would need to finish this conversation about clearing Jordan's conscience later. "Come with me," I said, "and keep an eye out for anyone who might be following us."

26

As Jordan and I neared the pond's south side, another message came up: "The water bottle near the oak tree."

I found the tree easily enough, but it took me a few moments to locate the bottle.

I expected that perhaps it might contain a sheet of paper with further instructions, but the bottle was half-filled with water and there was nothing else inside it.

Looking around, I didn't see anybody nearby.

"Jordan, can you tell if anyone's watching us?"

He scrutinized the area, turning a full 360 degrees. His eyes were far sharper than mine, still, when he finished, he shook his head. "I don't see anyone whose attention is focused on us."

Checking my slate again and finding no new messages, I studied the water bottle. As I rotated it in my hand, I realized that I could see the back of the label through the plastic.

There was an address on it.

I committed the address to memory. I was new to the world of dead drops and covert messages, so I debated whether I should leave the bottle here or bring it with me.

I realized that whoever had left this for me was likely watching us somehow to ascertain that I wasn't working with the cops or a team of undercover NCB agents.

A notification came through on my slate: "Rip off the label. Pour the water on it."

Although I had a bit of trouble at first, I was able to get the label off. Pouring the water on it caused the material to disintegrate immediately.

"What now?" Jordan asked.

"I'm not sure."

Another message appeared: "Come alone. 8:00."

I took one more look around but saw no one. "For the time being, I guess we head home."

As we were leaving, I informed him what my apartment looked like. "How are you at replacing digitized screens?" I asked.

"I'm sure there are instructional videos on the Feeds. I can use your slate to watch them. I imagine that with the right tools I should be able to get the job done."

Okay. At least now I had a plan. We would buy a new screen for the wall, Jordan could program it while I cleaned up, then I could grab some dinner before heading to the address on Spring Grove Avenue. The big question I needed to answer first was: Did I let Nick know where I was going and who I was planning to meet?

For the time being, neither Jordan nor I brought up the forgiveness issue in regard to what he'd done, and that was fine by me. I needed to give the idea of robots believing in God some more thought.

●━━●

Ripley looked down at the body of the woman he'd shot earlier and tried to figure out the best way to remove her eyes.

A minute ago he'd told the medical examiner that there was an agent waiting down the hall asking to speak with him. "Said he's bothered by dead bodies. That he might faint. Asked if you could come to him."

"Where is he?"

"Room 34."

The M.E. shook his head in aggravation and left.

Ripley perused the array of examination and autopsy tools, and finally came up with a set of forceps that looked like they might do the trick.

Since the eyeballs were solid, the procedure wasn't as difficult as he'd imagined and he was able to pry them loose without any trouble.

So, keep them and study them yourself, see if you can figure out if she was your contact, or destroy them?

He didn't like the idea of chancing that the eyes might be found on him, so he dropped them into the biohazard chute that led directly to the building's incinerator.

There.

Done with job number one.

If he just walked out of here, the M.E. would know that he was the one who'd taken the eyes—unless there was good reason to believe that someone else had been in here and had attacked him, then removed Sienna's eyes after knocking him out.

He took a deep breath because he knew that what he was about to do was really going to hurt.

Using his left artificial arm, he punched himself in the face, being careful not to do it so hard that he would break his jaw.

However, when he glanced in the mirrored surface of the tray holding the examination tools, he could see that the wound might not be convincing enough.

He backed up to the wall so that his head was less than half a meter from it, then punched himself again, harder, slamming the back of his head against the wall.

The impact didn't knock him out, but it would certainly leave a sizable, and believable, contusion.

He slumped to the floor and waited for the medical examiner to return.

———

In Trevor's workspace, Nick Vernon finished reviewing the notes that Kestrel's brother had shared with him regarding the Global Security Division's preliminary findings on the bombing.

There wasn't much in the files that he didn't already know. The blueprints confirmed what he had noticed earlier—that the attack might just as easily have been directed at the research and development arm of the building. And with the main gate destroyed, a second attack would not have been very difficult to carry out.

A recent hack attempt had targeted the plans for the power plant at the headquarters in Cascade Falls, but whether any information had been accessed was still to be determined.

Nick studied the power plant's blueprints himself, but didn't notice any blatant structural vulnerabilities.

"Can I have a record of the work rosters for everyone who was on duty the day of the attack?" he asked Trevor.

"Of course."

Analyzing them, he noticed that Sienna had not been on duty that day.

He received a message from his team that the only prints they were able to pull from the book that he'd found in Gaiman's apartment were hers. Nothing yet on other Phoenix references in the case files on other Purists, but they were looking into it.

Nick checked the time and found that it was already after five.

He went back and forth about whether to call Kestrel and make good on his earlier offer to help her move her new furniture in and clean up her apartment. Maybe he could even suggest bringing over some dinner.

She'd said she could use his help, but was it really a good idea?

He had to eat anyway.

Her place wasn't that far.

And besides, he really could use a break, a chance to clear his head. Seeing her might be just what he needed.

Maybe not what you need, but at least what you want.

I'm just trying to look out for her.

No, buddy, you're trying to pursue her.

He quieted the voices.

His new pastime.

After Trevor had finished transferring the remainder of the files to Nick's slate, he announced that he had to get going. "I have a red-eye tonight back to Seattle," he explained. "I'm afraid I need to leave in just a couple minutes to catch my flight."

"Yes, of course," Nick replied. "Thanks for your help. I'll be in touch if I have any other questions."

———•———

On the way to my apartment we swung by a store to purchase a new screen for my wall and I was happy when they told me they could deliver it tonight.

Back at home, we only had to wait a few minutes before two delivery drones showed up with the replacement screen. They positioned it on the wall and left Jordan the instructions to finish the installation process. Then they carted the old screen away.

I started some tea while he went to work on the unit.

———•———

As he is programming the digitized wall, he realizes that distinguishing what you *decide* you want from what you were *programmed* to want is not easy. Perhaps it is the same as differentiating free will from instinct for a Natural.

While Kestrel prepares herself some tea, he taps at the screen to set up the security firewalls. He tells her, "I'm ready to talk about her."

"To talk about who?"

"My mother."

She blows across the top of her tea to cool it. "Okay."

"As I mentioned earlier, she was destroyed in the attack on the distribution center. I wonder about the CoRA. If her soul lives on."

"But she doesn't have a soul, Jordan."

He is quiet. "Her consciousness."

For a moment he is silent and she is as well.

"I miss her," he says at last. "Is that sadness?"

"It's a form of it."

"What are the others?"

"Sometimes we feel empty inside. Disappointment is a form of sadness too. So is depression."

"Despondency. Dejection. The inability to find joy."

"Yes. That's what depression is. What does sadness feel like to you?"

"It feels like hope that has a crack in it."

"Why a crack?"

"It's a different kind of pain from when my hand was cut. It's pain inside of my emotions, inside of my love. Also, I'm not sure her consciousness was uploaded to the CoRA, or if the damage was too sudden for the process to complete itself."

"There are safeguards in place, though, right?"

"Supposedly."

He thinks about having hope. As a machine you cannot help but wonder if it is simply manufactured, if it's just a bit of code left by the deft hand of a programmer that you now, suddenly, have something that you did not have a moment ago—or if hope is something more than that.

"I don't want to die," he tells her.

"Being afraid of death is normal."

"When I was under the water yesterday, when I was trying to help that boy who fell in, I wondered if I would."

"But your consciousness would have been sent to the CoRA," she tells him. "There's nothing to be afraid of."

"But how do I know?"

"How do you know what?"

"That it's real. That the CoRA is. How can I be sure?"

"You need to believe."

"Just like that girl at the park believed that kiss would heal her?"

"Yes. Like that."

"Hope."

"Yes."

"I don't want my hope to be built on a lie."

• ——— •

No one does, I thought.

I knew that Jordan could feel emotion—I'd set that aspect of his HuNA at a ten, but I didn't know if he could experience the same kind of grief that humans do. He'd acknowledged that he grieved the loss of his first owner, but to compare a machine's feelings to a human's you'd need something that was both human and machine at the same time, and that sort of thing didn't exist.

I was thinking about Jordan's grief and how to console him when I got the call from Nick.

"Hey, listen. Looks like I have a short break. If you need any help with the furniture like we talked about earlier, I can give you a hand."

I didn't mention that Jordan was here with me and could assist me instead. "That would be great," I said.

"As I remember, some of the stuff from your fridge was tossed onto the floor. Do you like Chinese food?"

"Yes."

"How about I pick some up?"

Is this a date? I thought.

It's just a meal, Kestrel. Nothing more.

"Sound good?" he asked when I failed to respond.

"Um. Sure. Yeah."

"What would you like? Everything's good at the Golden Dragon."

"Surprise me."

"Perfect. I'll see you in half an hour."

———•———

It took some explaining and filing an official report, but finally Ripley finished up at the medical examiner's office once he'd convinced the M.E. that someone had caught him by surprise, punched him in the face, and knocked him against the wall.

He surreptitiously slipped off to his office and, using his encrypted computer and his Verifi Code, it didn't take him long to locate Sienna Gaiman's account on the Feeds.

After identifying it, he downloaded the times of her outgoing calls and messages and confirmed that—unless she'd been using someone else's slate—she was not the person who'd contacted him, the one who'd planned the attack.

But then, who was she? What was her involvement in all this? And why was she at the abandoned warehouse that morning?

Admittedly, he could see that it might have been advantageous to study the eyeballs, but, well, it was too late for that now.

Sienna had apparently been careful in what she recorded in her account, but he did hastily root around in her personal files for a few minutes, aware the whole time that he was taking the chance that the NCB techs might be looking at the same information.

He found a reference to Nick and his ex-wife from over a year ago when she still worked for the NCB investigating Purists, but that could easily be explained by their work.

So, move on.

A complete wipe would take some time, but there were certain worms that the NCB used that could crawl through the Feeds and destroy traces of a person's activity. He set one of them loose and figured that if nothing else, it would buy him enough time to get through to the end of the weekend. After that, none of this would ultimately matter. No one would be too concerned about Ms. Gaiman or what her eyes might have recorded.

He left for his place to ice down his bruised head and wait for word about what his handler wanted him to do regarding the upcoming attack.

27

I opened the door.

Nick stood in front of me holding a bag of takeout Chinese in each hand.

"Come on in."

I stepped aside, and as he entered I caught the scent of cologne, something breezy and free that brought to mind the open ocean and sailing toward distant shores.

"So, what did you get me, Agent Vernon?"

"You told me to surprise you." He set the food on the kitchen counter.

"Hmm. Yes, I do like a good surprise."

He greeted Jordan, who was programming ViRA to accept the new screen. "Did they get all of the river water out of your system?" Nick asked him.

"I believe so. How about you?"

"I'm guessing I didn't swallow quite as much as you did."

"Thank you for pulling me from the river, Agent Vernon."

"Of course."

"What would you like to drink?" I said to Nick. "I don't have any river water, but I think I have a couple of beers in the fridge."

"I better not. I still have more work to do tonight, but thanks for offering. Regular water's fine."

I left the beers where they were, went with water myself as well, and took a seat at the table with him. He passed an unlabeled takeout box toward me and smiled lightly.

"Close your eyes," he said. "Then give it a taste and see if you can figure out what it is."

I didn't close them. "Oh, I'm not really an expert on Chinese food."

"Give it a shot."

"Narrow my choices."

"It has rice."

"Wow. Really."

"Yes. And vegetables."

"Aha. Well, that really does narrow it down. Meat?"

"Didn't know where you stood on that issue. I didn't want to assume too much."

"Thank you. For thinking of my preferences, I mean."

With the drain on natural resources from raising animals for food—not to mention the questionable treatment of them on farms—more and more people had been turning to plant-based diets or opting for factory-grown meat over the past few decades.

I ate very little meat myself, but I tried not to be rude when it was offered to me. It wasn't an important enough issue for me that I felt comfortable causing offense, but I was thankful that, natural or otherwise, there wasn't any meat in this tonight, and that he'd been gracious in his choice of food.

Before I closed my eyes, he passed me a pair of chopsticks, but I said, "If I have to use chopsticks with my eyes closed, I probably won't get any food to my mouth."

"That would be entertaining."

"For one of us, maybe."

I retrieved a fork from the drawer and returned to the table.

"Alright." He placed a hand on one of the takeout boxes. "Now, close your eyes."

I did.

I heard him snap the container open.

The inviting smell made me even hungrier, but didn't reveal to me what kind of dish it was.

At first I'd wondered how I would feel sitting here with my eyes closed with this NCB agent across the table from me watching me, but I found that I wasn't uncomfortable. In fact, it felt surprisingly natural. Intimate, even.

He took my hand and directed it to the container. I didn't mind.

"Okay," he said. "Let's see how you do."

"Don't laugh at me if I get this wrong."

"I promise—no laughing."

Sticking my fork into the box, I swirled it around for a moment, then lifted it to my mouth, being as careful as I could not to drop any food onto my lap.

"Tofu?" I guessed.

"Yes. And?"

"Rice."

"So far so good."

I took a couple more bites. "Bok choy with tofu."

"Close."

"Gosh, I don't know. I'm tasting some cashews."

"Yes."

I tried some more. "And bamboo shoots?"

"Very good."

"Szechuan vegeta . . . Wait a second." Eyes still closed, I pointed a finger at him in mock accusation. "Did you try to trick me? Did you have them mix more than one dish together here?"

When he spoke, I could hear the smile in his voice. "You really are observant."

Cautiously, I opened one eye, then the other. Behind Nick's back, Jordan had paused while working on the new screen and was glancing in my direction, a slight smirk on his face. I cleared my throat lightly and he went back to work.

"What did you get for yourself?" I asked Nick.

"General Tso's chicken with white rice, my go-to dish."

As we ate, Nick scanned my bookshelves. "You certainly do have a lot of books."

I couldn't tell if he was implying anything or simply making an observation.

"I like to read from actual pages. I'm a bit old-fashioned that way."

"Is that your quirk?"

"Do I only get one?"

"You can have more."

"Good."

The light caught hold of his dark eyes and I wondered about all they had seen. His job probably took him into some very dark places. And despite the pain and loss I'd experienced myself this week, I wanted to hear his story, to listen to him. To be there for him. To—

"What are the others?" he asked.

"The others?"

Stay focused, Kestrel. Don't get lost in those eyes.

"Quirks," he said.

"Oh. Well, you know how people have a favorite color? Well, I have a favorite word."

"What is it?"

"Obelisk."

"Obelisk? Why?"

"Nothing profound. It's just so much fun to say."

He pronounced it again, this time slowly and savoringly. "Obelisk."

"See what I mean?"

"I do. What else?"

"I listen to electronic dance music when I'm preparing my sermons. Even though I'm right-handed, I brush my teeth with my left hand—I have no idea why. Oh, and I don't like watching cotton balls being torn apart. It's terrifying to me."

"That's a very specific fear."

"Yes, it is."

"Interesting."

"Are you psychoanalyzing me now?"

"Oh, no. I leave that to the profilers. I'm just a field agent."

"Well, what about you?"

"Me?"

"Your quirks."

"Well, let's see . . . I eat chocolate mousse once a year, at Christmas."

"Do you like chocolate mousse?"

"I love it."

"Then why don't you eat it more often?"

"Because it's my quirk."

"Ah. What else?"

"I'm a little compulsive about working out every day."

"That's very healthy of you, but I would call it a habit, not a quirk. Music?"

"Rock, but that's a preference, not really a quirk."

"Any fears? Cotton balls? Cotton swabs? Washcloths?"

This time he was slow in replying, and the playfulness in his voice shifted toward something else. Something hard to read. "You really want the truth?"

"Of course."

"Not finding the right person. My wife left me three years ago. I've had a hard time . . . Well."

"Oh. I'm sorry."

He shook his head. "No, no, no. It's not that. It was for the best. I'm just saying that when I think about it, I'm sometimes afraid that my work will keep me from finding someone else. I tend to get lost in it."

"That's incredibly honest of you, I mean, to tell me all that."

"I didn't mean to step over any—"

I placed my hand on his. "No. It's okay. Don't apologize. Thank you."

He nodded but said nothing more.

I removed my hand, although maybe not as quickly as I could have.

Since he was being so open and forthcoming with me, I wondered if I should tell him about the meeting I had set up tonight at eight o'clock with the Purists.

On the one hand, if I did tell him, he would almost certainly want to go in my place or send a tactical team in, which could easily result in casualties. I had no idea who might be there, if it would be Conrad himself, or if he might have chosen a location with innocent bystanders nearby.

On the other hand, if I didn't tell Nick and went by myself, as the message had instructed me to do, it might put my life in danger and even get in the way of his investigation.

The note was clear, Kestrel. It said to go alone. That's the safest choice for everyone. Conrad won't harm you. He could have done that easily enough already if he'd wanted to. That's not what this is all about.

Despite how much I wanted to fill Nick in, I couldn't shake the thought that telling him about the rendezvous would end up causing more problems than it would solve, and in the end, I decided not to say anything about it and to head out there by myself after he was gone.

28

Eckhart stood beside his boss, the one who'd orchestrated the bombing at the plant in Cincinnati earlier this week as a way to test the blast capacity of the tri-nitrocellulose. Together, they surveyed the blueprints of Terabyne Designs' headquarters northeast of Seattle nestled high in the Cascade Mountains.

All in all, there were eight buildings on the campus, but the ones that mattered most were the power plant, the conference center, and the underground access chamber to the site's mainframes.

"The structural integrity?" Eckhart asked her.

"With those crates themselves lined with RDX and the tri-nitrocellulose packing material, it'll be sufficient to take down the building."

"And bomb-sniffing dogs?"

"According to Terabyne's SOPs, they'll clear the building before the crates are brought in."

If all went as planned, tomorrow's attack would make the one in Cincinnati remarkably forgettable.

It wasn't just about carnage, although there would certainly be more casualties than there had been earlier in the week. No, it was about making a statement and putting things right again. The time for action had come, and if it wasn't taken now, a year from now, or even a week from now, might be too late.

A few things needed to happen first: arrange for the armored car, prepare the packing material, and get the press credentials in place.

We were almost done with our meal when I asked Nick, "How do you do what you do?"

"What do you mean?"

"I mean tracking killers, terrorists. Always seeing the worst side of people, of what they're capable of. It must be hard."

"It can be, yes," he admitted. "I suppose in your case you get to see mostly the best of people. As a pastor, that is."

"Most folks are good at putting on a show on Sunday mornings, but when they're alone in my office you'd be amazed at what they admit—well, then again, maybe you wouldn't be surprised at all."

He didn't comment on that, but said instead, "I have to believe that what I do matters. That it makes a difference. That's what keeps me going."

"The pursuit of justice?"

"Yes, which is a bit of a mystery in itself."

"How's that?"

He set his chopsticks down. "Most people believe in justice, wouldn't you say? Or at least that it's a goal worth pursuing?"

"Sure. I'd say so."

"But why?"

"Why?"

"Why would we believe in justice when there's no evidence from the natural world that it exists, that it ever has, or that it ever will? In fact, there's overwhelming evidence against it."

"Evidence *against* justice?"

"Nature isn't just in any way—it never has been. There's nothing fair about the life-and-death clash for survival, in who lives and who dies—or how. And in what I deal with in my job, some people's crimes go unpunished while innocent people are sometimes imprisoned for crimes they didn't commit. We always fall short—but we have the same goal. Every culture in the world does."

"Justice."

"Yes. Even though, from an evolutionary perspective, it's a goal that's not only illusive but also illogical."

His words reminded me of Solomon's observations in the book of Ecclesiastes where he concludes that everything in the end is meaningless, like chasing after the wind. There's corruption in our courts, the just and the wicked both die, as do the wise men and the fools. None of it makes sense. Ultimately, without God and his final justice in the equation, there is nothing truly fair about life.

Nick was right. Why would we as a species cling so desperately to a concept for which there is no evidence?

I thought of my conversation with Trevor earlier about the justice and love of God. If we truly are made in God's image—whatever exactly that phrase might imply—it would make sense that we desire justice and cling to the concept of it even though there's no evidence for it in the natural world. Otherwise, where would this desire for justice, where would the idea of it, even come from?

Nick turned to Jordan, who was finishing up with the screen. "Have you been listening to this, Jordan?" he asked.

"Yes."

"So what do you think? Does justice exist?"

"Not in this world, only in the afterlife—if that exists."

"So in the CoRA?" Nick said.

Jordan reflected on that. "The fact that people strive for justice, lacking any evidence of its existence in nature, suggests that something beyond this life exists, since that's the only way there could be any sort of real justice in the universe."

"What conclusion does that lead to, then?"

"If you believe justice exists, you have to believe in the afterlife. And if you believe in the afterlife, you have to believe in God. This isn't to say that God or the afterlife *must* exist, just that, in order to be consistent in your thinking, you would need to believe that they do if you believe that justice does."

I'd never thought of things in those terms before, but it made sense to me. Beliefs about God, justice, and the afterlife were all intertwined—but that still didn't make me feel like life was fair in any way, or that it was just for God to have taken my daughter from me the way that he did.

· — ·

He tests the screen and finds it working. But cannot concentrate on the task at hand.

Because he is thinking about justice. He is thinking about the afterlife.

And about his mother, seeing her there at the production facility. And his subsequent visit to the park with Kestrel and their conversation about her. Is she in the CoRA or is she gone forever?

Those thoughts pool down into the discovery of the note on the bottle.

He saw what it said.

He knows the location and he knows the time. The message instructed her to come alone.

He doesn't know why. He doesn't even know who Kestrel is planning to meet.

But he does know, or at least he *senses*, that it would not be good for her to go there alone.

· — ·

After Nick and I finished eating, he and Jordan arranged my new furniture for me, and then Nick reached out to shake my hand.

His grip was firm and resolute.

Admittedly, I wished he would have leaned in for a hug, or at least something a bit more personable than a handshake. But I wasn't going to complain. When he stood close I caught a whiff of that cologne again.

The ocean.

Sailing toward—

"Please let me know if you need anything," he said as he let go of my hand. "Call me anytime."

"I will. Thank you."

Then, after we'd said goodbye and Jordan and I were alone again, Jordan asked me, "Do you want to mate with him?"

"What?!"

"Isn't that where romantic relationships eventually lead?"

I flushed. "There's nothing romantic about our relationship. And besides, mating isn't necessarily the end goal of a romance. If that's what we were having. Which it's not."

"What is the end goal, then?"

"Jordan, I . . . Well . . ." I found myself quite embarrassed talking to him about this. "Intimacy. Oneness. Sex can be part of that, but it doesn't need to be."

"Oneness," Jordan said. "As the Bible teaches? The two shall become one?"

"Yes."

He said nothing more and I wondered what he was thinking, but whatever it was, I was glad to set the topic of mating with Agent Vernon aside.

I could probably wait a few minutes before leaving to meet the person who'd left me the note, but I decided to take off now to make sure I was there in time and to, hopefully, have a look around first before the rendezvous.

I waited for Nick's car to disappear down the street and got ready to leave.

I thought of taking my slate with me in case whoever had sent me the message earlier needed to reach me, but then decided that since the Purists were not fans of technology—to say the least—and I didn't want anyone to be able to track where I was, I left it on the kitchen counter.

After I asked Jordan to test ViRA's settings for the new screen on the wall, I turned to leave.

"I saw the note at the park," he said.

I paused, then faced him. "This is something I have to do."

"You shouldn't go alone."

"I'll be fine. Now, stay here, Jordan. Don't follow me. I'll see you when I get back."

29

Nick was back at his office going over the work rosters of the people at the Terabyne plant who were on duty at the time of the bombing when the switchboard operator contacted him.

"I have someone on the line for you. He says it's urgent and that you'll take the call."

"Did he give you a name?"

"Yes. Jordan. He said it has to do with Kestrel."

"Put him through."

Traffic had slowed me down, and even though it was almost eight, I figured that it would probably be best not to park directly in front of the address I'd been given, so I directed my car to a spot two blocks away.

Whether or not that was a good idea, I wasn't sure. I'd never been trained in spy craft, and I was making this up as I went along.

More than a little nervous, I found myself praying as I left the car that things would go alright. I realized that I hadn't been praying much in the last twenty-four hours, and although doubtless it was in part because of my hectic week, I wondered if it was also because of my frayed relationship with God.

Frayed.

Yes. That was a good way to put it.

Or even better yet—in tatters.

The wind tossed a discarded candy wrapper across the empty street in front of me. The abandoned storefronts just beyond the crack-riddled sidewalk collected the shadows that the few working street lamps failed to illuminate.

The night had turned cold and I wished I'd chosen a thicker jacket than the thin nylon shell I had on.

At the intersection, a malfunctioning traffic signal blinked incessantly red, then yellow, then red again.

A couple of cars prowled down the street in the distance. Other than that, it was almost like I'd entered a vacant movie set.

One more block to go.

I wondered what I might be walking into, who had trashed my apartment and taken the violin, and if the same people were responsible for the burglary as for the bombing at the Terabyne plant.

On a more personal front, I also wondered if the HuNA settings I'd chosen for Jordan had caused him to jump into the water, how much fear and pain he'd actually felt when he drowned, and if he really was back to normal again.

He's grieving the loss of his mother just as you're grieving for Naiobi. He's trying to find hope, just like you're trying to find answers.

And when grief augers its way into you, it's not easily removed—no matter who you are.

This whole idea of nonhumans having human emotions was still difficult for me to wrap my mind around. His feelings were as real as mine, I knew that. His beliefs were as real as mine too. Still, I had a tendency to diminish the similarities, slipping into a form of xenophobia, but in this case the individual in question was a machine and not someone from another culture or country.

I was halfway down the block, passing beneath one of the broken streetlights, when I heard a rustling to my left. When I turned to look, a hand shot out of the shadows and grabbed my shoulder, pulling me into the darkness. I was about to cry out when another hand clamped over my mouth and someone said in a rushed and urgent voice, "Shh! It's me. It's Nick."

He let go of me.

I pulled away. "What on earth are you doing here?" I said harshly, with a mixture of shock and irritation.

"Jordan called me." Nick kept his voice low. "He told me what you're planning to do here tonight. I can't let you go in there alone."

"Wait—Jordan called you?"

"He said something about seeing an address on a water bottle label and—"

"Right. But—"

"He was concerned about you, Kestrel. He wanted you to be safe. He said this time he didn't want to be responsible for his owner dying. That's how he put it."

"Well, how did you get here so quickly?"

"I was properly motivated."

I was quiet for a moment, then said, "Nick, the note was clear that I'm supposed to come here alone. You have to let me go. It said eight o'clock, and if I don't get moving I'm going to be late."

He shook his head. "There's no way I'm letting you go in there by yourself. Either I come with you, or I call in a Tac team and let them take over."

"That's not a good idea. I'm sure that whoever is waiting for me has a way to get out of here without being seen. If you bring in a tactical team, they'll know, and our one chance at talking with them will be gone. I need to do this. It has to be me."

He evaluated that.

"Alright. I won't call in reinforcements, but I'm coming with you. If anyone asks, my name is David Turner. I'm an old friend. You were afraid to come alone. Since I used to be a cop and you trust me, you called and asked me to join you."

He took out his slate and started scrolling across it.

"David Turner?" I said. "They might do facial recognition, and if they do they'll find out you're a federal agent."

"We're not in the public archives. Besides, they're Purists. They're against using facial rec technology—but if you're right and they do look me up, here's who I am."

He tapped the screen one final time, then showed me his slate, where his face and the fake name and law enforcement credentials appeared.

"I've been David before," he explained. "Now, let's go meet these people before you're late."

———

Ripley assessed where things were at.

The eyeballs were gone and so was Sienna's account on the Feeds—at least that would slow down his unit making any connection to him.

Destroying Sienna's eyes wasn't going to solve everything, but it would buy him some time to move forward regarding the plans for tomorrow afternoon. He wasn't sure if he would be present when everything went down—his contact hadn't notified him regarding that yet—but he did know that at least this attack would provide more of a long-term solution.

As a Plusser, Ripley had a unique perspective on the use of technology. He was stronger than Naturals. He could perform tasks more quickly, more accurately, and with more precision than Naturals could. There was no comparison.

Cognizant machines, especially those that looked identical to humans, were not the next step in evolution, but a drastic deviation from the natural way. He was the best of both worlds, and that's how things should remain. Now, with the emergence of machines that looked nearly indistinguishable from humans, the time had come to act.

So, when he'd been approached by his contact, the person hadn't had a tough time convincing him to help with the project—especially with the number of credits they were offering him for his assistance.

———

It turned out that the address I'd been given was a deserted pharmacy in one of the empty strip malls lining Spring Grove Avenue.

I went to knock on the door, but Nick stopped me with a firm hand on my shoulder.

"Let me do this."

He stepped in front of me, tried the doorknob, found it locked, and then rapped on the reinforced wood. No one answered, and I wondered if having him along had caused the people I was supposed to be meeting with to retreat.

Nick studied the front of the building. "You're sure this is the place?"

"Yes."

The barred windows on our right were shattered and the ones on the left, although cracked, were still intact. The bars were no doubt there to keep the drugs inside protected, as much as possible, from looters. I wondered if they had done any good.

Nick leaned over and attempted to peer through the glass, then tried the doorknob again. This time, it opened.

"Okay, that's interesting." Cautiously, he pressed against the door. It opened with an obstinate creak and when I looked past him all I could see were shadows before us.

"Stay close," he said.

"Good idea."

I wondered if he would reach for his gun, but instead he held one hand behind him for me to take and produced a flashlight with his free hand.

We entered and he shone the light in front of us, illuminating shelving units still stocked with hair products, deodorant, shaving cream, toothpaste, and other toiletries. A thick layer of dust covered everything and no one was in sight.

He led me forward into the gloom. We passed the empty OTC

drug shelves on the way to the pharmacist's enclosure, all picked clean of medications with any sort of street value.

"Hello?" Nick called. The word echoed hollowly off the stark walls. "Is anyone here?"

At first, there was nothing. Then a husky voice that seemed to come out of nowhere said, "You were told to come alone."

"He's an old friend," I replied hastily, still not sure where the person who'd spoken to me was standing. "I was scared. I wasn't sure who to trust."

All at once, three burly men appeared from behind the shelving units surrounding us. Each held some sort of assault rifle slung in front of him.

The man closest to us, who was also the tallest and most heavyset of the three, pointed his gun at Nick. "Who are you?"

"David Turner."

Nick was still holding my hand. I let go just in case he needed to reach for his gun. Then a woman's voice came from the darkness: "He's an ex-cop."

So, they must have had access to facial rec or the Feeds after all.

One of the other men asked Nick, "How do you know Kestrel?"

"We met at a Chinese restaurant," he said. "She likes Chinese."

"That true?" he asked me. "That you met at a restaurant?"

"Yes," I told him. "The Golden Dragon. He was eating General Tso's chicken with white rice. It's his go-to dish."

"Hmm." He sounded unconvinced.

The woman's voice returned, though I still couldn't tell where exactly she was. This time she was addressing Nick. "Lower your flashlight."

He complied.

"So, you're an ex-cop?"

"Worked homicide mostly," Nick said, playing the part.

"Ever arrest any Purists?"

"Yes."

"Who?"

He was clearly being tested.

"Most well-known was Max Caffers."

"I know him."

"He was a real piece of work," Nick told her, and I wondered if he really had been responsible for arresting this man. Maybe while he was working under this false identity.

"Yes, he was," the woman replied. "Until he was killed in prison."

"A shank in the throat. Not a good way to go. But he did it to himself—he wasn't killed."

She said nothing to that, but the big guy gestured to one of the other men, who stepped forward and held a retinal scanner in front of Nick's eyes. Only then did I realize that each of these men was missing the tip of his left pointer finger where his ID chip would have been implanted.

A shiver ran down my spine. These people were obviously prepared to take drastic measures to keep their own identities secret. Where that might lead tonight, I wasn't sure, but it certainly made me uneasy.

Even though they were using retinal scanner technology, there was little doubt in my mind that they were Purists.

The man with the scanner studied the screen, then nodded toward the guy who was apparently in charge. After pocketing the device, he patted Nick down, found his gun, and took it. I was concerned that they might be able to identify Nick as a federal agent by the type of gun he carried, but then I noticed that it was a different model from the one he'd unholstered when he checked my ransacked apartment yesterday.

He'd changed guns, perhaps anticipating that they would frisk him and take away any weapons he was carrying.

The Purist who now had Nick's gun also took his slate from him and smashed it on the floor, then stepped back, flipped his rifle in front of him once more in a smooth, adept motion, and aimed it at me.

Then I heard the woman behind me again. This time, her voice was close and startled me because it sounded like it was coming from only centimeters behind my ear. "Hands to the side," she said, "then stand still."

Somewhat anxious, I held my arms out and she patted me down, found nothing, and then told the man calling the shots, "She's clean."

"Follow me," he ordered us, then headed toward the pharmacist's glass-enclosed work area.

Because of the rise in the number of armed robberies over the years at pharmacies, most had been retrofitted with bulletproof glass, separating the space dedicated to prescription drugs from the rest of the store, and from what it looked like, this place was no exception.

He indicated the window under which pharmacists would distribute drugs through a small, sliding drawer, and then held out his hand to Nick. "Your flashlight."

Nick passed it to him and the guy placed it in the drawer, slid it through to the other side, then told his team, "Sweep the area. Make sure there's no one else around." Then, just as silently as they had appeared, they eased back into the darkness and were gone. And that's when a voice from beyond the glass said to me, "Kestrel, it's been a long time. I miss reading your posts."

30

"That was all in another life," I said.

"Yes, for both of us."

Is this really Conrad, or is it someone else pretending to be him?

"You know how it is," I told him, and then, referencing one of F. W. Boreham's books, I added, "I've been caught up carrying around the luggage of life."

"Toward the other side of the hill?" he replied, bringing up another of Boreham's titles.

"Yes, toward the mountains in the mist."

"And the home of the echoes."

Well, if this wasn't Conrad, he certainly knew his Boreham books.

"What are you doing here, Kestrel? It's been, what—seven years? Eight?"

"Nine."

"Nine years. And you've been working as a Christian minister all this time?"

"Yes, after finishing up seminary. I'm at my second church now."

With Nick's flashlight gone, my eyes were starting to get accustomed to the darkness. Just enough light came through the drugstore's front windows to allow me to see him beside me. I glanced over but couldn't read his face, nor could I see any details of the man behind the glass, except for his silhouette.

"And this man with you?" he asked me.

"David. He's an old friend. He used to be a cop."

"Right." Conrad said the word slowly, and I couldn't tell if he was dismissing what I'd told him or if he believed me. "So how can I help you, Kestrel? Why did you reach out to me after all this time?"

"There was an attack this week at the Terabyne plant. Six people died."

"Yes."

"Why? Why are you involved with this, Conrad?"

"What makes you think I had anything to do with it?"

"Come on," I said, "it has all the hallmarks of a Purist attack."

Except one, I thought. *Except that it was a single event and not simultaneous bombings.*

"Things are not as clear-cut as they appear," Conrad explained. "We do not want anarchy, we want sanity."

"And to that end you kill innocent people?"

"At the beginning of the Uprising, there were a lot of people fighting for the right things in the right way. Since then, things have changed. There are some who believe in fighting fire with fire, but that only causes more things to burn."

"What do you believe in?"

"Putting out fires once and for all." From someone else it might have come across as a threat, but that wasn't how it sounded coming from him. "We just want to be left alone. We're not trying to overthrow anyone. We believe that leaning too much on technology robs us of our humanity. The development of ASI could cause humans to be deemed either a plague destroying the planet, a race in need of extermination, or simply irrelevant—unnecessary baggage on a dying world."

Now, Nick spoke up. "So you're doing all you can to stop it."

"Stopping it isn't an option. Not anymore. Things have gone too far for that. Life is a thin, narrow arc between two eternities. We're here to celebrate it, not shorten it—for anyone."

"You target innocent people." Nick's voice had become steel. "People who have nothing to do with promoting technology."

"Some Purists do, yes. I'm not here to justify them to you. I can't even justify some of their actions to myself. But we're not responsible for most of the attacks we're blamed for."

"Then who?"

"There's more to this than the bombing the other day. There's going to be another one."

"When?" I asked. "Where?"

"Tomorrow. Late afternoon. I don't know where, but it's going to be—"

Gunshots rang out, their distinctive, stark sound reverberating off the bare walls of the pharmacy. Before I could even register what was happening, I felt Nick's strong arms enfold me as he drove me to the floor.

The shots continued.

Just like when my parents were killed.

Just like when they were gunned down at that airport.

"You okay?" Nick asked urgently.

"Yeah. You?"

"Fine."

Two more shots sounded and I heard movement in the shadows surrounding us. Gruff voices mumbled something indecipherable. It might have been in another language. Someone returned fire, shooting through the bars of the missing window near the front door.

I remembered that the Purists who first met us had taken Nick's gun. "Do you have another weapon?"

"I'm about to get one. Stay here. Don't move. I'll be right back."

"But—"

Before I could finish objecting, he rose and, staying crouched low to the ground, scurried to the right. I heard scuffling, the impact of punches, and a heavy thud. A moment later, Nick was at my side again, holding one of the assault rifles that the men from earlier had been carrying.

"Did you kill him?" I asked, my voice fragile.

"No. He'll wake up with a headache, though." Nick patted the gun. "But he won't be needing this in the meantime. Come on, let's get you out of here."

He eased around the edge of one of the shelving units, then directed me to put my hand on his shoulder. "Don't let go."

He didn't have to ask twice.

As we were about to move, someone out of sight fired another burst of shots. This time, they ricocheted off the bulletproof glass that Conrad had been standing behind. I wasn't sure who was firing at whom and if anyone was on our side in all this, but I shuddered. Just the thought of proceeding into gunfire nearly paralyzed me.

From where I was, I couldn't tell if Conrad was still in the cubicle, but right now I was more worried about getting out of here alive than I was about his whereabouts.

Using the shelves for cover, Nick moved forward slowly. I stayed right behind him. When we came to the end of the shelf, I could see the front window of the pharmacy. In the night, a few hunched shadows shifted into position.

Who are these people? What's going on?

"Hang on," Nick whispered. He eyed the other side of the store where the window was missing.

I saw movement outside where he was looking, then heard a gunshot. Nick leaned forward and fired the rifle that he had. The harsh, loud reports of the shots startled me. Then, outside there was a heavy grunt, the clatter of a gun hitting the ground, and then silence.

"Alright," Nick said. "That one's no longer a threat."

My heart was hammering. I wished there was more I could do, but I didn't have a gun and wouldn't have known how to use it to help us even if I did.

Nick studied the inside of the pharmacy, then cocked his head as if he was listening attentively to something. "Okay, there's no one else in here."

"Are you sure? How can you tell?"

"I'd be able to hear them."

"How?"

"I'm a Plusser," he replied after a brief hesitation. "Hearing only, but it comes in handy. No heartbeats here. No breathing. No movement. We're good."

For some reason, finding out only now that he was a Plusser made me uneasy, that instinctive prejudice against those who are different coming through again. Maybe that—or maybe because he was one step closer to being a machine, like what'd killed my parents.

One of the forms outside passed across the street. Someone fired at the front of the pharmacy, and the remaining window exploded into a wicked cloud of glass shards that rained down on the floor all around us.

"You hit?" he asked me. He was still in front of me and there was urgent concern in his voice.

"I'm good. You?"

"Just a scratch. I'll be okay."

"You're shot?" I gasped.

"Left arm, but it's superficial. Don't worry. I've had worse."

He raised the rifle, aimed carefully, and shot across the street into the darkness. Someone fired back, but he squeezed the trigger again twice and there was no volley of shots in response. I didn't know if that meant he'd killed someone or if they'd run off after being shot at.

"Can you hear any more of them outside?"

He was quiet, then nodded. "There're two more. The rest have fled."

"Are you bleeding?"

"I'm alright."

I heard police sirens in the distance. Because of the part of the city we were in, I was a bit surprised that the authorities were responding so quickly, unless someone had called in to warn them beforehand about what was going down.

"Time to leave," Nick said. "I don't want you to have to be interrogated by the cops."

Then it hit me—he could justify why he was here, but what believable reason could I give them as to why I was meeting with Purists in this neighborhood?

Quietly, and what appeared to be effortlessly, he stalked forward to the corner of the wall near the window. I stood behind him as he leaned out between the bars, passed the gun in an arc across the street, took two more careful shots, and then snapped back toward me, away from the window. He let out a slow breath. "Alright, one left. Wait here. Count down from ten."

"What?"

"Count down from ten. I'll be back by the time you get to one."

I didn't want him to leave me, but I figured he knew better than I did what the best course of action was.

With swift and sure purpose he passed through the door onto the sidewalk while I flattened my back against the wall, and, trying to calm myself, started my countdown.

Ten.

The whole night seemed a bit surreal—

Nine.

Speaking to Conrad through the glass—

Eight.

Being shot at—

Seven.

Nick getting hit—

Six.

Hearing sirens blare closer in the night—

Five.

I wished he would hurry back. I wished—

Four.

No more shots were fired—

Three.

No sounds except those sirens—

Two.

And—

"All clear." It was Nick, just outside the window, soundlessly emerging from the shadows. "You alright?"

"Yes. What now?"

"Now we leave before the cops get here. I'll need to come back and look around, see what I can learn from the guy who's unconscious in the corner, but I don't want you here. I don't want you being questioned."

"My car is two blocks away," I told him.

"Mine's closer. You can wait in there until I'm done. Come on."

●——●

After Nick had ascertained that Kestrel was safe in his car and he'd given her a blanket from the trunk to stay warm in the chilled night, he returned to the scene of the shooting.

By now, the place was crawling with Cincinnati police officers. An ambulance stood waiting beside the front of the drugstore.

Nick identified himself to the police lieutenant who was in charge, and after his ID had been confirmed, he explained his role in the shootout, and how he'd quieted two threats while an unknown number of attackers had gotten away.

As the paramedics bandaged his bleeding left arm, he asked who'd contacted dispatch.

"Anonymous caller." The lieutenant gestured toward his patrol car. "What do you want us to do with that guy?"

The Purist Nick had knocked out earlier was awake and sitting in the backseat of the car.

"Take him to the federal building. I'll talk with him there."

"Alright." The lieutenant shrugged. "It's your rodeo." He sounded relieved to have less work to do himself.

Nick called for his forensic techs to come to the pharmacy. Since he'd been fired at first, there wouldn't be any difficulty in clearing the shooting, but still, he'd had to put two people down who were trying to take his life, and that weighed on him.

But in the background of his thoughts he couldn't shake the question: Who had fired at the Purists who were inside the building?

It could have been the splinter group Conrad had implied existed. Nick wasn't sure if he and Kestrel had been the intended targets, but based on the number of shots and the angles of trajectory through the windows and toward the pharmacist's work area, Nick postulated that he and Kestrel were more than likely just in the way and that whoever the attackers were, they were primarily after Conrad and his people.

Nick approached the first person he'd shot and found that, down to the black balaclava, he was clad in the same outfit that Sienna had been wearing earlier in the day at the warehouse. He checked the man's left hand, found the tip of the pointer finger missing, tried facial recognition using one of the slates of the officers nearby, but came up empty.

Maybe fingerprints or DNA would do the trick and help identify who this was. He went through the same process with the other body with the same results.

Nick realized that his team might be here for the rest of the night, but if he could speak to the man they'd captured, maybe he could get some answers.

After making arrangements for the secure transfer of the suspect to NCB headquarters, Nick dictated his initial report as he returned to his car where Kestrel was waiting for him.

"How are you doing?" he asked after climbing in beside her.

"Honestly, I'm a bit shaken."

"Yeah, I get that." For a moment he thought about reaching out to take her hand to comfort her, but, opting for propriety, he held back.

"I'll be alright," she said. "How's your arm?"

"All patched up. Let me drop you off at your car—unless you want me to just take you back to your place."

"My car is fine." She told him the vehicle's location, then said, "Who was that shooting at us?"

"If Conrad was telling the truth, there's a group of Purists that he and his people are not in control of." He started the car and chose a side street so the CPD officers at the site of the pharmacy wouldn't see them. "In that case, they might very well be the ones who bombed the production plant, and also, I'm guessing, didn't want his people talking with us tonight."

"Where does that leave us? I mean, where does that leave *you*?"

"We have the guy in custody—the one I knocked out. I'm hoping I can get some information from him."

"Conrad said there would be another attack tomorrow afternoon."

"Yeah."

Nick almost revealed that his team had previous intel about the second attack, but caught himself before he said anything.

It only took a minute to get to her car, but it gave him a chance to think, and by the time they arrived, he'd made his decision. It was unorthodox, maybe even against protocol, but he needed someone he could trust while keeping it off the books.

"I have to head to the federal building, but I don't want you to be alone tonight. I'm going to send someone over to watch your apartment."

He expected her to argue with him about that, but she said nothing, and he realized that she must have acknowledged the gravity of the situation—being shot at will do that to you.

"Thanks for looking out for me," Kestrel said as he walked her to her car. "I really appreciate it."

A handshake didn't seem like enough, so he leaned forward and gave her a hug. As he was about to let go, she held on to him a moment longer and he didn't step back.

After the hug was over, he told her, "Call me at home if anything comes up, for any reason, at any time."

"Who are you going to send?"

"Send?"

"The agent to watch over me."

"You met him yesterday at the graveyard. Agent Carlisle."

31

As I exited my car back at my place, I thought about the hug. There was nothing too forward about it, nothing inappropriate. Yet, to me, his arms felt like such a safe place to go, and somewhere I didn't want to leave. Maybe it was just the intense emotions of this week overtaking me, clouding my thinking.

Or maybe it's just that you finally found a guy who'll treat you right.

Oh, it was way too early for me to start thinking anything along those lines.

But that didn't stop me from doing so.

Dressed in blue jeans and a charcoal turtleneck, Agent Carlisle was waiting for me outside my apartment door. He held a travel mug of steaming coffee and nodded to me as I approached.

A dark, purplish bruise covered one of his eyes. I said nothing, but I imagined that it must have been some fight to have left him with that.

"I can either stay with you," he offered, "or set up shop outside the door."

I'd gotten a bad vibe from this man the first time we'd met and it hadn't gone away.

"How about outside?" I said.

"Then let me come in and have a look around first, clear your apartment."

As we walked in, he scanned the living room. "Looks like you've had a chance to clean up."

"You knew about that?"

"Nick—I mean, Agent Vernon—told me your place had been trashed."

He eyed Jordan, then nodded to him, and Jordan nodded back.

"I'm going to check down the hall," he said. "Stay here."

I realized that if Jordan hadn't been here I wouldn't have felt comfortable being in the apartment alone with Agent Carlisle. I wasn't excited about him entering Naiobi's nursery or my own bedroom, but I remained quiet and just watched him until he disappeared around the corner.

Jordan said to me, "How did the meeting go?"

"Meeting?"

"At the address. From the water bottle label."

"Oh. It was eventful. I can't really get into it all, but let's just say I'm glad to be back home in one piece."

"In one piece?" he asked curiously, perhaps not familiar with the idiom.

"Safe and sound." And then, wondering if that was really any clearer, I said, "I'm just happy to be back."

"Okay."

I heard a door down the hallway open, then a few moments later close again. The routine repeated itself twice more as Agent Carlisle checked the washroom and the remaining bedroom.

Since I'd given Jordan such a high Human Nature Alignment curiosity setting, I suspected that he wanted to hear the whole story of what'd happened tonight, but I wasn't ready to fill him in, especially not with Agent Carlisle so close by.

"Everything ready with the screen on the wall?" I asked Jordan.

"All set to go."

At last, the agent returned, took a sip of his coffee, and then shared his contact info with me. "Alright, Ms. Hathaway. You call if you need anything. Otherwise, if I don't hear from you before then, I'll come back to check on you first thing in the morning."

"Thank you."

"I'll be right outside."

"Okay."

He smirked at Jordan, then turned and left.

I found it unnerving being around him and I was thankful when he was gone.

Once I was alone with Jordan, I reflected on what was happening and where things were going. Trevor and I hadn't come to any sort of mutual understanding regarding our relationship. He was the only family member I had left, and what I'd said to him earlier today had only seemed to make things worse. Now, he was already on his way back to Seattle and I had no idea when I might see him again.

Someone had ransacked my place. This was the second night in a row that Nick had felt uncomfortable leaving me alone. And someone had tried to kill me tonight—even if I wasn't the main target, even if it was only because I was in the way. Still, my situation was just getting worse by the day. I could only imagine where things might go tomorrow.

Even though I didn't want to, I had to admit that it probably wasn't safe for me to remain in Cincinnati for the foreseeable future. I might easily have been killed at the pharmacy and now I felt like I had a target on my back.

There really wasn't anything more I could do to help Nick here, but maybe I could work on accomplishing something positive somewhere else.

With your brother. Maybe you can sort things out with him.

"I don't know how safe it is for us to be here," I said to Jordan.

"At this apartment?"

"No. In Cincinnati."

"What are you thinking?"

"People shot at me tonight, Jordan. Someone came in here yesterday and stole something I treasure. I'm thinking tomorrow we may need to take a trip."

"A trip?"

"Yes. To Seattle."

Nick sat down at the steel table across from the Purist they'd taken into custody.

Over the years, he'd spent many hours in this interrogation room. He knew the routine. He knew what to say and what to avoid. He explained the man's rights to him. Letter of the law. "Tell me your name."

The man was silent.

"Look, we're going to find out who you are and what your involvement in all this is. You actually have an advantage in being the first one we've brought in."

"How's that?"

"You get to make the deal. I can guarantee you that as soon as we catch someone else—and we will—there'll be an agent in there, just like I'm in here, offering a deal to them. And I'm guessing you know that whoever talks first also leaves prison first."

"Prison is worse than death."

"Is that what you've been told? Is that what they teach you?"

The man said nothing, but Nick noticed him chew slightly on his lower lip.

From what Nick had seen, Purists would do nearly anything to avoid going to prison. They were all about freedom at any price. Over the years, four of the terrorists he'd caught had taken their own life either before being processed or right after their sentencing rather than end up in a cell for decades of their lives.

Nick glanced up in the corner of the room at the video camera recording the interrogation, then faced the suspect again. "I'm Agent Vernon. What do you want me to call you?"

"It wasn't us."

"What wasn't you?"

"The Terabyne plant. It wasn't us."

"Okay. Who was it?"

"You have to understand, it's not like in the military. There's no chain of command."

"So, independent cells?"

A nod. "Something like that. Point is, Conrad, the people who work with him, we're not terrorists. We just want to be left alone."

"And how does that explain the assault rifles you and your associates were carrying?"

"Look, all I know is something's going down out west."

Nick leaned forward. "Where out west?"

"Terabyne. Their world headquarters. It has to do with Stuxnet."

"Stuxnet? How do you know that?"

The guy shook his head. "You don't get it, do you? I've already said too much. If they think I was talking to you, if they even suspect I've told you anything, they'll kill my wife."

"Who will? The other Purists?"

Silence.

"Where is she? We can protect her. Tell me—"

"There's a mole."

"Where? What are you talking about?"

"In the NCB."

"Give me a name."

The man shook his head, at first slowly, then more violently.

"Tell me what you know!" Nick insisted.

All at once, the man stopped shaking his head and bit down hard.

With his augmented hearing, Nick caught the sound of the capsule cracking.

He leapt to his feet and ran to the other side of the table. The man was already gagging, foaming at the mouth.

Nick shouted to get a medical team into the room, but knew in his heart that it was already too late to save this man. Even as he held him in his hands, he could feel his body go limp.

The Purists knew their poisons, and Nick couldn't imagine that this man would have left his death up to chance.

It was likely cyanide or one of its modern synthetic derivatives. And if he'd chosen any of those, either a tooth capsule or one that he'd swallowed and then regurgitated, there was no bringing him back.

Five minutes later, Nick watched as the paramedics rolled the man's body away on a gurney, a sheet pulled up over his head.

He'd heard of Stuxnet but wasn't very familiar with it. He knew it was a computer virus, but that was about all.

Since his slate had been destroyed earlier at the pharmacy, Nick requisitioned a new one. Then, one of the agents on duty joined him in looking up info on the virus.

"It looks like Stuxnet was developed during the Bush and Obama years by a joint effort between Israeli hackers and the NSA," she said to him. "Although that was never officially acknowledged."

"Gotcha." Nick scrolled across his replacement slate. "Okay, here we go. So, Stuxnet was designed to attack a zero-day vulnerability in the Siemens S7–300 logic controller that was being used in Iran's nuclear weapons development facility in Natanz to run gas centrifuges. It would slow down or speed up the centrifuges under the radar, so to speak. It burned out more than a thousand centrifuges."

"How do you think this relates to Terabyne's headquarters? They don't use gas centrifuges."

"I don't know. Yet. But let's find out."

After assigning her a team to investigate more about Stuxnet and how it might relate to Terabyne, he called Ripley to check on Kestrel. "Are you there with her?"

"I'm outside her place."

"And she seemed okay when she got there?"

"Seemed alright to me."

"Listen, you know how I told you that we caught a guy tonight—a Purist over at the pharmacy? He committed suicide."

Ripley cursed. "Another dead-end."

"He said there was a mole. Someone at the Bureau."

After a slight pause, Ripley said, "Any idea who it is?"

"We're working on it. The guy was concerned about his wife, that she might be targeted because he was speaking with me. I have a unit scouring the neighborhood where he was found, looking for her now. He also mentioned the Terabyne headquarters out near Seattle as the site of the next bombing. Earlier, Conrad told us that the next attack was going down tomorrow late afternoon."

"What are you thinking?"

"I've already arranged for a plane. I leave in an hour."

———

Ripley ended the call with Nick.

So.

A mole.

Nick was good at his job, and now that everything was going down, Ripley couldn't take the chance that his associate would deduce his role in all this before he could get out of town.

Earlier today, he'd taken care of the woman at the factory. Earlier this week, he'd taken care of Ethan Bolderson at the hospital. Now it looked like it was time to take care of one final loose end.

He exited his car.

Ripley had plans in place. He'd rented an apartment in Louisville an hour and a half away. From there, he could easily book a flight out of the country under one of the fake identities he'd set up when he initially got involved in all this.

But first, this.

He headed toward the front door of the apartment building where Kestrel Hathaway lived. He would need to take out the Artificial she had as well. Always eliminate the biggest threat first.

Then, go after her.

He would use his bare hands.

It was always more satisfying that way.

As he was crossing the street, movement to his left caught his attention and he noticed a woman strolling toward him wearing a dark parka with a hood drawn up over her head.

Ripley had taken his NCB-issued handgun, but he carried one of his own from home and now he warily unholstered it.

If this was someone from the group, he wasn't about to let her get in his way, but when he turned toward her, he heard a voice behind him.

"You've served your purpose, Agent Carlisle."

Ripley whipped around.

No hesitation.

Found his target.

Fired.

Two shots, center mass. The man was eight meters away. Ripley dropped him, then spun to face the woman in the parka.

But he was too slow.

She'd already flicked out the blade and launched it into the air toward him.

Precision.

He heard the impact even as he felt the blade sink into his throat. A soft, tender sound that he wished he had not heard.

For the moment there was no pain. But it would come. He knew what it was like to be stabbed. It'd happened to him once in his arm, before he became a Plusser, before—

He fired at her, but he was already losing his balance and the bullet went astray.

Then he was falling, one hand instinctively going to his throat, but even the strength of his augmented arms could do nothing to stop something like this.

On the ground.

Prone now.

And then the pain came.

Sharp and quick, webbing all through him, tendrils of fire like nothing he could have ever imagined.

He gasped and spit out a mouthful of foamy blood as she approached, kicked the gun out of his hand, and knelt to look at him. He tried to speak, but it was too late for that.

He thought of the times he had been in her shoes. Watching the dying die. So close. That thin, delicate barrier between life and death being torn in two before you.

She flipped the parka hood back and then placed a finger gently on his lips. "Quiet now, Agent Carlisle. Just give it a few more seconds, then it'll all be over."

And he recognized that face.

He knew her.

Yes.

Dakota Vernon, Nick's ex-wife.

●——●

As Ripley's eyes went blank, staring into the endless night, she glanced up at her associate.

Eckhart, the man the agent had shot, stood, then removed the bullets from where they were embedded in the body armor he was wearing. He pocketed them, then joined her beside the body of the dead NCB agent, careful not to step in the blood pooling on the pavement.

"Did you know it would come to this?" Eckhart asked her.

"I suspected it might, but I had his slate tapped. When that call came through from Nick, it was clear what we had to do."

He nudged the body with his foot. "What would you like me to do with him?"

"Make him disappear, but leave a message when you do. Then meet me on the plane. There's a lot left to do before tomorrow afternoon."

32

Saturday, November 8
8:00 a.m.
11 hours left

Agent Carlisle did not call me in the morning as he had promised, and when I glanced out the window I saw that his car was gone. It didn't shock me, but it did annoy me since Nick had trusted him to watch over me.

Jordan was making breakfast in the kitchen, nimbly cracking eggs and frying up an omelet for me.

It struck me that Jordan hadn't slept—of course he hadn't, he was an Artificial—and I wondered what it would be like to be him, standing here in the apartment for hours on end thinking about whatever robots think about while I slept in the other room. Knowing that he was there, vigilant and alert, should have reassured me, but in a way it felt a bit eerie.

I had slept, however. Better than I thought I would, in fact. It was probably just a result of being so mentally spent and emotionally drained from everything that'd happened during the week.

The bombing.

Seeing Trevor again.

Saying a final, brutal goodbye to my daughter.

Hoping to distract myself from my thoughts and the jagged terrain of those memories, I checked my slate and found a message waiting for me: "How are you? I had to get a new slate. I hope you don't mind me writing to you this early."

"Who is this?" I dictated to my slate, surprised to be getting a message at this time on a Saturday, especially from someone my slate didn't identify.

"Oh. Sorry. Nick."

My first reaction: *Ah. Perfect!*

Then, hesitation: *Wait. Make sure it's really him.*

"What's my quirk?" I replied.

"Which one?"

"When I'm writing a sermon."

"Listening to electronic dance music while hoping no one will show up and tear a cotton ball apart anywhere in your vicinity."

"Ah, so it is you."

"Yes."

He sent a request through to switch to video, something I only then realized I could've done myself a few seconds ago to check if it was him. When I accepted, I saw that he was standing outside with a dark bank of clouds stretching out beyond him.

Scruffy. The shadow of a beard. I liked the look.

"So?" he said.

"So?"

"How are you? I just wanted to make sure you're alright."

"I'm good," I said. "You?"

"Fine. Listen, did Agent Carlisle leave yet?"

"His car's gone. There wasn't any trouble last night." Even though I didn't entirely trust Agent Carlisle, I didn't want Nick to be alarmed, so I didn't bring up the fact that he hadn't followed up this morning to see if I was alright. "Thanks for sending him here."

"Okay. I wanted to let you know that I won't be around for the next couple of days. I've arranged for an agent to be on call in case you need anything. I'll send you his contact info." A small pause, and then, "I'll check in on you when I get back—if you don't mind."

I would love that, I thought.

"I would appreciate that," I said.

"Okay. Take care until then. I'll be in touch."

"Thank you."

After our goodbyes, I hung up but stared at my slate.

He'd called me, yes, and he wanted to call me again.

It's just to check on you. He's just doing his job, just being professional. No, it's more than that. He's interested in me.

And the feeling was definitely mutual.

I noted his wording: He hadn't said check *up* on me, but check *in* on me. He wanted to see me again.

You're reading too much into this.

Maybe. Probably.

But maybe not.

Despite all that was burdening me, when I thought of Nick I couldn't help but smile.

With him on my mind, I shifted my attention to getting out of town as I'd decided to do last night.

Since the Purists were now aware of who I was, I didn't like the idea of traveling alone across the country. It would obviously cost more to bring Jordan with me to Seattle since, as a cognizant Artificial, he would need his own seat on the plane instead of just riding in the cargo hold with the service droids and checked luggage. However, it worked out for me since he would be by my side on the flight and could protect me if it came down to that.

So, while I ate breakfast, I had Jordan book us a flight to Seattle.

Sometimes when you fly last minute like this you can get good deals, but that wasn't the case today. With purchasing Naiobi's gravesite, the new furniture, and now this airfare, my supply of credits was lower than it had been in years. However, right now I wasn't really worried about long-term investing or anything along those lines. I was just concerned with leaving town, getting someplace safe, and hopefully—if things worked out—reconnecting with my brother.

Jordan told me that our flight would leave at 11:43. "They're saying that because of the bombing earlier this week there'll be enhanced security measures so we should get to the airport by nine."

Since it was already after eight, I went to my bedroom to pack a bag for the trip, not looking forward to going through security at the same airport where my parents had been killed.

•——•

He wonders how he should feel at this moment.

Thankful? Afraid? Apprehensive? They are hard to pin down. Feelings are.

He finds that they overlap and intermingle. More like currents contradicting each other than islands standing alone in the sea.

Is there even such a thing as feeling only one feeling at a time?

So it is in this moment.

A mixture.

He's not quite certain why Kestrel is exhibiting such urgency to leave. However, she did reveal last night that someone had shot at her, so that was likely one of the precipitating factors.

The fact that she wants him to come along is affirming.

Just as if he were a Natural.

As if he were alive.

An equal.

And they would be visiting Trevor.

He can prove to you once and for all that the CoRA is real, that your mother's consciousness lives on.

Yes. A chance to confirm his beliefs. A chance to turn faith into knowledge.

So then.

Looking forward to the trip, he cleans the dishes, puts them away, and then waits for Kestrel to return.

Nick's night had not gone as planned.

The private NCB jet he'd arranged for after the suspect's death had ended up having mechanical problems and it'd postponed his trip to Seattle until this morning—in fact, he was only now boarding to leave.

He hadn't heard from Ripley, so he assumed there hadn't been any problems during the night—and Kestrel had stated that things were calm there as well. However, just to make sure, he sent Ripley a message asking him to give him a call.

There was a lot on Nick's mind.

The identity of the unknown assailants last night.

The suicide in the interrogation room and the search for the deceased man's wife.

The potential terror attack later today at Terabyne Designs World Headquarters out west.

And of course, Kestrel Hathaway—seeing her again when he got back to town.

You went too far by contacting her just now.

No, you didn't. All you did was make sure she was okay.

Yeah, and ask to follow up with her again.

Okay—but she said yes.

She said she would "appreciate" it. That's not exactly the same thing.

Maybe so, but it was encouraging to him nonetheless, even if he couldn't be certain about all the meaning that her answer might contain.

Nick had his choice of any of the nine passenger seats in the Bureau's plane. He went with one in the back, beside a starboard window.

He'd already notified the NCB Field Office in Seattle that he was coming and had passed along the intel he'd gotten from Conrad and his people. However, considering the man from last night had mentioned an NCB mole, Nick had been careful to tell them to keep the information in a closed loop as much as possible.

If the Purists' information was correct, this was going down, and it was going down this afternoon.

The Seattle office agreed to do a threat assessment and assign him a four-man tactical team. "They'll be waiting for you at Sea-Tac when you land."

"Great. I'll let you know if I find out anything more."

The pilot announced that he was finishing the final safety check. Nick buckled up and glanced out the window at the mounting clouds from a storm that was clearly heading their way.

33

9:00 a.m.
10 hours left

The rain started when we were about three kilometers from the airport, and by the time we pulled up to the curb, it was already coming down in sheets. Hopefully, it wouldn't end up interfering with our departure.

I had my car drop us off at the passenger loading bay, then leave for long-term parking.

If the number of people bustling around the outside of the building was any indication, there were going to be long lines inside.

I debated whether or not to tell Trevor that I was coming, and finally decided that even though it was three hours earlier there—just after six—since he had so much on his plate it would be better not to surprise him.

So, I sent him a message that I was on my way and that it was a direct flight so we would be arriving in Seattle right around two o'clock their time.

Jordan and I entered the airport.

People were everywhere with their Artificials accompanying them. Endless security lines snaked out of the entrance to the concourse, and I wondered if we'd come early enough after all to make it through the checkpoint in time to catch our flight.

Momentarily, I got word from Trevor that he wouldn't be able to pick us up at the airport but that there were plenty of shuttles from the airport to the campus. Knowing his work ethic, I wasn't surprised that he was awake already, but I would've expected him to be more taken aback that I was coming to see him. Perhaps he was just focused on a quick reply—all business.

"Today, once I get to campus, I'm going to be working with the public affairs department," he wrote, "prepping for a press conference this afternoon at four. Do you want to meet at my house afterward or would you like to come to my office?"

I replied that we would plan to meet him at work.

As I was putting my slate back into my purse, I glanced down but kept walking and almost ran into one of the heavily armed law enforcement Artificials who were stalking menacingly throughout the airport.

He glared at me with that steely, intransigent stare they have. I muttered an apology and he lumbered away.

Once he was past us, I pointed toward the security checkpoint and said softly to Jordan, "That's where it happened."

"Where what happened?"

Only then did I realize that I hadn't told him about my parents' deaths or the reason why I'd been reticent to get an Artificial in the first place. "My mom and dad," I said. "They were killed. Shot by a law enforcement Artificial. A false positive."

A look of shock and consternation crossed his face. "Your parents were killed by an Artificial?"

"Yes. Nine years ago."

"Are you going to be okay? Being here, I mean?"

I wasn't sure. "Yes," I said, thinking that maybe claiming so aloud would help make it come true.

I directed Jordan's attention to one of the nearby Artificial sentries who was protected by his thick, segmented plates of bulletproof body armor. "That's the same type of unit that shot them. It was an earlier model, but still . . ."

Jordan scrutinized the security Artificial. "Is there anything I can do for you?"

"No. Let's just go check my bag."

He placed a reassuring hand on my arm. "It'll be alright, Kestrel."

I appreciated the gesture and patted his hand. Then, as a mixture of apprehension and grief twisted around inside my gut, we headed for the airline's check-in counter.

———

Interstate 5
50 kilometers north of Portland, Oregon

Lenny Crenshaw had been working for the Prestige Armored Car Company for nine years. His partner, Aubrey Powell, had only been on the clock with him for the last three weeks, ever since his former partner tragically passed away out of the blue from a heart attack.

Today, their leg consisted of making the trip up from Portland, taking over from the team that'd driven from Sacramento through the night.

Mostly for Lenny it was cash deliveries, sometimes diamond store drop-offs, but this time it was simply two reinforced steel crates. Unlabeled. Each the size of a coffin.

He'd never delivered bodies before, and he wondered if that was what he had with him today, but since he was scheduled to take this cargo to Terabyne headquarters up north in Cascade Falls, he doubted he had corpses with him.

Still, it did seem a bit odd.

However, he knew better than to ask what was inside the crates. That was none of his business. He just needed to make the delivery, and if he was prudent about it, he could take care of things and still get home in time to see his daughter's soccer game this afternoon.

To avoid the possibility of being hacked, the armored car, which he'd affectionately named Ole Betty, was not self-driving, nor was it in communication with the Feeds in any way. Too much was at stake in this job to chance the possibility that the vehicle could be hacked into or taken over remotely. As a result, he was at the wheel of one of the few vehicles on the road still designed to accommodate a human driver.

Sometimes Aubrey slept on these long drives along I-5 while it was still dark like this, but today she was wide awake, guzzling her way through a thermos of truck stop coffee and offering repeatedly to take over if he needed her to drive.

"I'm alright," he said.

"You sure?"

"Yep. Fine. I could drive this route in my sleep."

Just another day at the office, here in Ole Betty waiting for the sun to creep up over the far horizon.

34

Cincinnati, Ohio
10:00 a.m.
9 hours left

On the way to the airport I'd logged us in for our flight through the Feeds, but with the current threat level, we were still required to show our documentation at the airline's front counter before heading to the security checkpoint.

The line moved slowly, chewing into our time, and I realized that, even arriving at the airport as early as we had, it might be tight catching our flight.

At last we came to the desk and the airline representative who was accepting peoples' luggage, an Artificial with an overly congenial smile attached permanently to her otherwise expressionless face, verified my identity, then glanced at Jordan, and said, "Sir?"

"He's an Artificial," I explained. It took a moment for Jordan to convince her. After he did, she still wanted a record of his fingerprints, so he placed his left hand—the one with the scar from when he had cut himself—onto the scanner.

Once everything was set, she accepted my suitcase, put it on the conveyor belt with the other checked luggage, and then directed us to the line leading to security.

Seattle, Washington

Trevor finished breakfast and climbed into his car to take him to his office, thinking about Kestrel's trip to come visit him.

What should he make of it?

Evidently she was interested in resolving things between them and, while he wasn't by any means against that, it wasn't the primary reason he'd so readily agreed to see her.

His sister had lost her baby less than a week ago. She'd invested nine months of her life in that tiny child, and he was sure that for her that meant countless hours of thoughts and prayers. And now Naiobi was gone, lost in a heartrending, devastating tragedy.

If there was ever a time to treat Kestrel with patience and a listening ear, it was now.

Trevor's car took off for the on-ramp to the highway.

Ever since their parents had been killed, things hadn't been great between them. Over the subsequent years the situation had deteriorated, until finally they weren't speaking at all.

Then, of course, the faith issue came into play—that was always there in the background. The tension from their different perspectives was unmistakable whenever they were together.

But now, their conversations over the last few days had gotten him thinking more about religion than he had in months.

She believed that God loves people. But why would he?

Why would a divine being fall in love with an inconsequential breed of higher primates on an insignificant planet in a tiny, negligible solar system? Surely there had been millions of civilizations throughout the universe in the last thirteen and a half billion years on its hundreds of billions of planets. And out of all of them, God just happened to choose us to love? What about us is worth loving? We self-indulgently destroy everything we touch. We relentlessly exterminate other species. We've hardly been around for a microsecond in the grand sweep of time, and yet we've already managed to bring our planet to the brink of ecological collapse.

And yet God chose us, from all other life forms from all of time, from all across the trackless expanse of space to single out and uniquely love—and then sacrifice himself for?

It made no sense.

Trevor could almost hear Kestrel's reply: *"And that's exactly why Christians worship God—because we are unworthy and yet he chose to love us. He chose to save us."*

And his response: *"So, if there's life on other planets, does it mean Jesus went there to die for them as well?"*

And hers: *"I can't say what Jesus has done or would do for other life forms, but I can say that if he loved them as much as he loves us and they rebelled against God as much as we've rebelled against him, he would have taken whatever drastic measures he needed to take in order to restore them to a right relationship with himself."*

It was all so inexplicable, and despite how comforting it might be to believe in a loving God, Trevor wanted his fate and the course of his day-to-day life to be guided by truth and not simply wishful thinking. No, a person wouldn't need to understand an omniscient God before being able to worship him—of course not, that would be a logical impossibility—but he would certainly need to believe. And that was something Trevor just couldn't see himself ever doing.

However, beliefs about God were not the only thing that separated him from his sister.

It was also their view of the uses of and promises of technology. She seemed to fear the direction it was taking humanity. Contrarily, he believed that, even though it might not be able to solve all of our problems, it would at least put us on the right path.

And even more so after this weekend, after the reveal of Terabyne's newest product—the most advanced and accessible Artificial Intelligence the world had ever seen.

With the mounting regularity and severity of Purist attacks, the time had come for a definitive step to be taken for the good of all, for the benefit of society as a whole.

And that's what the Synapse would do.

———•—•———

Cincinnati, Ohio

I sent my purse through the X-ray machine and then Jordan and I passed through the body scanner. After retrieving my personal items, I waited in line at the final checkpoint.

Just three people in front of us.

I noted the time: 10:51.

We still had over forty-five minutes before our flight left. I reassured myself that it would be more than enough time for us to get to our gate.

As I stood in that line, it occurred to me that security and freedom don't necessarily go hand in hand. All too often, the more there is of one, the less there is of the other.

The law enforcement Artificial cleared the next passenger and I edged forward, Jordan right behind me.

I wasn't alive when 9/11 happened, but I'd read about it and how, in the wake of the attacks, during the government's crackdown against terror, personal freedoms were intruded upon. Like it or not, "enhanced security measures" inevitably meant "decreased privacy measures." You can be secure or you can be free. You don't get to have both at the same time.

As a result, now it was my freedom and that of the rest of the passengers here today that was being intruded upon, by forcing us to arrive as early as we had and to jump through all these hoops before we could board our planes.

The Artificial waved the gentleman he'd been speaking to on his way.

Just one more person, an elderly woman, quiet and earnest and bent with the years.

As I thought of speaking with the agent, anxiety clutched me.

They shot your parents. They killed them. Here in this very spot.

I noticed my hand shaking and I pressed it against my thigh to try to calm it. To try to settle my nerves.

Though I hadn't flown since that day all those years ago, I wondered if, because of who my parents were, any red flags would come up from me being here today.

It only took a few seconds for the Artificial to clear the woman. He waved her on and then signaled for me to come forward.

I swiped my finger across the identity scanner, and then, somewhat apprehensively, approached him.

He didn't greet me, but simply checked his monitor and then eyed me closely and consulted his screen again before saying, "Ma'am, can you wait here for a moment?"

"Um, sure."

He turned his head to speak into a radio transmitter mounted on the shoulder strap of his body armor, calling in a code fourteen.

"What is it?" I asked. "Is everything okay?"

"Just a minute, ma'am."

His false pretense of politeness annoyed me. He was a machine, just a machine programmed to refer to me as "ma'am." It wasn't his choice, like it would have been with Jordan.

I waited, but he said nothing more while two armed law enforcement Artificials clambered our way—the one on the left was a newer model; the other unit appeared to be closer in design to the one that'd killed my mom and dad.

I didn't like this.

Maybe they'd somehow found out about last night, that I'd gone to speak with a known Purist.

Some of the people behind me glowered at me as if I'd done something wrong. Others edged hesitantly backward, and I heard a teenage girl whisper to her friend that I was probably a Purist. Her eyes were wide with fear. "Right?" she said. "I mean, why else would they be treating her like that?"

The two Artificials arrived and led Jordan and me to a secure room off to the side of the security lines and away from the anxious, staring crowd.

35

11:00 a.m.
8 hours left

The confined, monochromatic room reminded me of interrogation rooms I'd seen in movies—with the prerequisite impassive steel table, nondescript chairs, and the wall covered by a mirror that was almost certainly some sort of one-way observation window. A pair of conspicuous video cameras stared down at us from two separate corners of the ceiling, their operational lights glowing accusingly.

What's going on? Why are these Artificials hassling you like this? What do they want from you?

After we were all inside, the more advanced Artificial gestured for Jordan and me to have a seat at the table.

"You're flying to Seattle?" he asked me, once I was positioned on one of the stiff chairs in front of him.

"Yes. Is there a problem?"

"What exactly is the purpose of your trip?"

Before I could mention that I was simply going to visit my brother, Jordan spoke up. "She's taking me to Terabyne's world headquarters. I'm the latest model of Artificial and they need to do some diagnostic tests on me. It has to do with recovering data from a water-damaged unit."

There was enough truth in what he'd said that if they'd done their research, it just might convince them.

And just enough of a lie that he might get us in trouble.

"And the CoRA," he added, "establishing a link between it and current breakthroughs in ASI research."

That was even more of a stretch and I wished Jordan would stop and just stick with the simple truth.

The two law enforcement Artificials glanced at each other, then the one who'd been speaking with me appraised Jordan and announced that he would be right back.

He whisked out of the room through a sliding door beside the mirrored glass, leaving us behind with the Artificial who hadn't said a word so far. He stared at us stoically with both hands on his semi-automatic rifle, ready to kill us if he perceived us to be a threat in need of being neutralized.

All his choice.

No Natural in the decision-making loop.

Our lives entirely in his hands.

And in that moment, the slaughter of my parents came back to me, images heartbreakingly vivid and unrelenting, ones I'd done my best to repress over the years.

"So, how is your semester going?" my dad asks me.

Mom stands beside him, her champagne-colored hair cascading elegantly across her slender shoulders, that look of quiet mischief in her eyes.

"Pretty good," I say.

A smile from Dad. "And guys?"

"Guys?"

"In your life?"

"Oh. Nope," I tell him quickly. "I don't have time for—"

And then, all at once, the alarm. Piercing. Abrupt. And the Artificial shouldering his way through the crowd, ordering me to step away from my parents. Then Dad's nod to me.

I obey.

Confused.

Frightened.

And then.

A verbal warning that means nothing, because even though my parents hold up their hands in surrender and begin to insist that there's been some sort of mistake, the Artificial fires.

The nearly indistinguishable sound of rapid, rapid, rapid gunfire fills the air. Round after round. Dozens of bullets in a handful of seconds. The smell of gunpowder.

Then—blood everywhere. The floor is slick with it, and when I scream and run to their side I slip and go down, sprawled on the floor in my murdered parents' warm, spreading blood.

Though my eyes were open, I was caught up in my thoughts and was startled back to the moment when the Artificial here in the interrogation room with us cocked his head at me arbitrarily and the movement caught my attention.

My heart clenched within me like a fist, closing tight. I wanted to cry, wanted so badly to let the tears come and to mourn my parents' deaths all over again, but I wasn't about to lose it in front of him, so I held back. My mouth went dry, and I swallowed and held my pain inside and tried to let the past live in the past and to focus instead on the moment, on being here, now, detained by these Artificials.

Your flight.

You need to get going.

You're never going to make it.

As if on cue, the Artificial who'd gone to check on things returned and my sorrow crawled down, burying itself beneath my nerves.

"You're clear. Have a safe trip, ma'am."

I blinked. "We are? We can leave?"

"That's right." He signaled to his partner, and then, without further explanation, the second Artificial led us through a warren of back hallways to the concourse.

After he'd left, Jordan said to me, "What was all that about?"

"I have no idea. But we'd better get moving so we don't miss our flight."

We hastened through the airport.

"You told a couple of fibs back there," I said, glad to be out of that room, away from those Artificials and those memories. "Would you ever lie to me?"

"If I said yes, then you wouldn't have any reason to trust me from then on. But if I said no, it might be a lie. So I'm not really sure what to tell you."

"I'll take that as a no. Come on. Let's find our gate and get out of here."

———•———

En route

Time passed quickly for Nick as he worked on the plane.

His flight was nearly half over.

Good.

Using the onboard connection to the Feeds, he checked his notifications.

Still nothing from Ripley.

He sent another request for him to check in.

Also, there was nothing so far about the search for the dead Purist's wife. Agent Fahlor was pursuing a lead that led back to the tool and die warehouse where the metal shavings used in the truck bombing had come from, but he wasn't holding his breath. Honestly, finding her in time might be a long shot since Conrad and his people were clearly good at staying beneath the radar and at disappearing when they needed to.

As Nick processed what he knew, Ripley came to mind again. And the more he thought about him, the more things just didn't click.

Sienna's eyeballs had been stolen and, according to the reports, Ripley had been attacked when it happened. But what was he doing there? And why then? He was on administrative leave and wasn't even supposed to be in the building.

Also, with his augmented strength and prior military training, was it really believable that he'd so quickly been bested in a fight that left nothing in the room disturbed? How had the security footage of the hallway outside the autopsy room just happened to disappear—as well as Sienna's account on the Feeds?

Then there was his version of what'd happened at the hospital, claiming that he'd arrived too late to interview Ethan Bolderson. And what about shooting Sienna? Had he really been in fear for his life, or had there been another reason why he'd fired at her? Ripley kept showing up at the wrong place at the wrong time—or at precisely the right place and time, depending on how you looked at things.

Though Nick didn't like where all of this was pointing, he wasn't about to ignore the evidence.

After a short deliberation, he put a call through to the NCB office in Cincinnati to have them track Ripley down.

"Are you saying you want us to bring him in for questioning?" came the disbelieving reply.

"Yes. I can do the interview remotely. Just let me know when you find him."

"You're sure, sir?"

"I need to speak with him to clear a few things up. That's all."

"Alright. We'll find him."

Nick read up on Stuxnet and the Greek myths regarding the Phoenix, a bird that experienced eternal life through its cycles of death and rebirth. Then he followed up on the facial recognition of the person who'd visited Ethan at the hospital before Ripley showed up to speak with him.

"Was it Sienna Gaiman?" he asked the agent who'd been investigating the footage. "The Terabyne technician?"

"No, sir. I was just about to call you. You're not going to believe this. The woman who visited Ethan was Dakota."

"What?" Nick gasped, stunned. "My ex-wife?"

"Yes."

"That can't be true."

"Based on facial and gait recognition the system came back with a seventy-eight percent probability."

Nick evaluated that.

Dakota? That made no sense.

From what he knew, after leaving her job at NCB headquarters a year ago she'd been a security consultant for the private sector, but what was she doing at the hospital talking with a survivor of the bombing? Who was she working for?

There's still a twenty-two percent chance that it wasn't her. Maybe it was someone else after all.

"Sir?" the agent said. "Are you still there?"

"Yeah, yeah. I'm here. Anything else?"

"No, sir."

"Thanks."

After ending the call, Nick tried contacting Dakota, but she didn't pick up, so he left a message: "Hey, listen, this is Nick. Can you call me when you get a chance? It's important and . . . Well . . . Okay. Talk to you soon."

⎯•⎯

30 kilometers east of Seattle, Washington

She stared at her slate.

A message from Nick?

Was he onto her?

Possibly.

She wondered if he'd found out that she'd been in a parked car observing Wednesday's bombing, monitoring things, making sure that they went along without a hitch; or if he knew that she'd gone to visit Ethan in his hospital room and found him asleep; or if he'd learned that she had been one of the shooters at the pharmacy last night.

It might be time for a change of plans.

Maybe make an example out of Nick when she returned to Cincinnati?

She would need to sort that out. By the time things were finished at Cascade Falls it might not even matter.

For now, since Ripley had been her primary source at the National Counterterrorism Bureau, she was at a disadvantage in finding out information from them. She had one other covert contact who'd provided her with useful information in the past, a person she hadn't met and knew only by the codename Phoenix.

So now, going through her secure channels, she sent Phoenix an inquiry for more information about what the NCB knew, but there was no guarantee there would be any coming. And if it did come, when that would be.

She knew that if they found the body of the woman she'd killed last month, it could put even more pressure on her. Eckhart had assured her that he'd taken care of the body, but there was always the possibility . . .

She considered her options.

Until now, she'd been planning to wait here in the warehouse while her team made the move on the armored car, but if the NCB was aware of her role, it might be best if she were present to make sure things went as planned rather than simply assume her team would get everything taken care of.

She told one of her men to stay behind in the warehouse. "I'm going along in the truck."

"And Eckhart?"

"He'll be with me. We'll see you when we get back."

"Yes, ma'am."

Cincinnati, Ohio

The gate agent was about to close the door to the jetway when we hustled up to her. She gave me a disapproving look, and then, with a sigh, scanned our documentation and let us board.

As we made our way onto the plane, I asked Jordan if he wanted the window seat or the aisle.

"The window," he said. "I would like to listen in."

"Listen in to what?"

"Doesn't the Bible say that the heavens declare the glory of God and that the skies proclaim the works of his hands?"

He was referring to Psalm 19, one I'd preached on in the past. "Yes. It does say that."

"I would like to listen to them do so."

I didn't know quite how to respond to that. Sure, it was possible to take the words of the Psalm literally, but they were also included in a poetic song of praise where figurative language made just as much sense.

He slid into his seat beside the window and stared at the other planes on the rain-battered tarmac. The showers that'd chased us to the airport had intensified into a pretty nasty storm. I hadn't seen any lightning yet, but if there was any it might keep us on the ground.

Some people can't sleep on airplanes, but for me it was just the opposite. Being on a plane that was idling often made me drowsy and I found that today was no exception.

I didn't want to doze off, and for a few minutes I fought off sleep.

But then, I lost the battle.

36

12:00 p.m.
7 hours left

He tries to see the sky outside his window and to listen to what it has to say, but all that's visible is the rain slanting down from the heavy, low-hanging clouds languishing above the airport and all he can hear is the raindrops striking against the plane like incessant gunfire.

Kestrel sleeps beside him.

Through the PA system, the pilot informs them that they're experiencing a short weather-related delay, but should be cleared for takeoff in a few minutes, and that, at that point, they'll be number five on the runway.

A handful of people groan and shake their heads, but most passengers ignore the announcement and either listen to music or stare into the VR headsets provided at every seat, each person ensconced in his or her own private little virtual world.

So close to each other. Yet so far apart.

So very far apart.

Is that what it would be like to be human? To be alone together?

You're alone now. How would that be any different?

He wonders if they would be so nonchalant if they truly believed what they already know—that this plane might not make it to Seattle.

With the number of hijackings and bombings these days, it is by no means out of the question.

The jet might crash. They might all die.

Death is so close, and with every passing moment edging nearer and nearer.

The longer you live, the more imminent your demise. Every moment takes you closer to the grave.

They don't believe what they already know.

It is a strange epiphany, and he questions it at first, wondering if this is even possible, this reversal of knowledge and faith.

He reviews his files about human nature from literature. From philosophy. From history, and apprehends that though Naturals and Plussers teach that relationships matter more than monetary gain, almost without exception, they fail to live that way. They spend the vast majority of their lives pursuing what doesn't matter while neglecting the things that they know do.

How could that be?

Only one explanation: they know those truths, but they do not believe them. For if they did, they would place less value on the trivial and transitory and more on the lasting and the relational. To gain the whole world and yet lose your soul—it is no idle warning. It's closer to the default setting for the human race.

The way humans live is irrational. You must not emulate it.

He must keep believing what he knows.

For he will die. A Catastrophic Terminal Event.

He knows this.

He must live like it.

And he must continue to believe it.

The first few planes leave the runway. And so, as their pilot taxis into position, it appears that, despite the turbulence they'll no doubt encounter, they are about to take off.

•——•

Cascade Falls, Washington

Although it might have been more convenient for Trevor to live up in the mountains in Cascade Falls where Terabyne's headquarters was located rather than in Seattle where he'd resided for the last decade, he could work uninterrupted on the drive and actually enjoyed his daily commute. Over time he'd begun to look at his car as simply an extension of his office.

Now, the vehicle slowed as he reached the west entrance to Terabyne's four-hundred-acre campus.

Hundreds of protestors lined each side of the road.

In light of this afternoon's press conference, he'd expected something like this, but hadn't anticipated that there would be so many people out this early.

On his left, Purist sympathizers were waving signs that read "Stop Playing God!" and "Keep Us Human."

On the right, counter-protesters brandished signs of their own: "Don't Fear Progress" and "Purists Are Terrorists!"

The crowds were shouting at each other across the road, a stark divide accentuating how far apart their perspectives were.

If there was this much protesting now, Trevor didn't even want to think about what things would be like later in the day after the media showed up, or once news about the Synapse began to spread.

Keeping his speed low to avoid hitting anyone who might leap out onto the road, he rolled past the protesters, logged his way through security, directed the car to his parking spot, and then headed to his office to brief his team and make sure the campus was secure for the day.

———•———

Cincinnati, Ohio

Rain pelts the window beside him. Tiny knives, angry at the glass.

Taking off into the storm is choppy, yet Kestrel does not awaken.

He turns his attention to her.

Her breathing has become gentle and rhythmic.

He is curious about sleep. Yes. To understand it.

To observe.

To learn.

He hears the landing gear retract beneath him into the belly of the plane.

To sleep. To be alive. To act more human.

But you're not human. Don't act at all. Be. Be who you are.

Because of the aggressiveness that uninterrupted eye contact can convey to humans, he was given eyelids. When he was first awakened by Sarah, his initial owner, he registered the blink as something that briefly and repeatedly disturbed his vision.

But then.

Now.

He finds that he no longer notices it.

Just like a Natural. They don't notice their blinks either. Or the sound their eyelids make when they blink—unless they focus specifically on them. Unless they pay attention.

And so.

Pay attention or you'll miss something important.

An obese man across the aisle is gazing at him now.

Curious?

Suspicious?

Not wanting to draw attention to himself, he stops studying Kestrel and redirects his focus straight ahead.

The screen located on the back of the seat in front of him gives him endless entertainment options. A virtual reality headset in the seat pocket offers him the chance to escape from the real world.

He has never used VR before.

Curiosity tugs at him.

He puts on the headset and peruses through the three-dimensional news shows to see if there are any updates about the bombing at the Terabyne plant where his mother was destroyed, but the news cycle has already moved on to other tragedies—the unrest in southeast Asia, a coup in Venezuela, a car bombing in Karachi.

He feels a sweep of sadness.

It matters. All of it does. All of this pain and suffering. All of this death.

For relief, he moves to the next channel and hears the word *Terabyne*.

He pauses on the program.

Although they don't report on the bombing in Cincinnati, the announcer explains that there'll be a press conference later today at Terabyne Designs World Headquarters related to a breakthrough in their ASI research.

The turbulence, which had been getting worse, lessens all at once and he removes the headset.

Looks out the window.

The plane has broken through the storm.

Beneath them, clouds roil and mount, but above him the sky stretches off into brilliant infinity.

A sense of speechlessness overwhelms him. And, just like earlier in the week when he was trying to find words to describe the pain he experienced when he sliced his hand, so now he struggles to encapsulate the abstract concept of glory.

> Cramped as I am in this
> broken womb-world,
> I once again begin
> squeezing through the birth canal
> toward the thing I fear most—
> life.

As before, he wonders what led him to those words—what is the genesis of things made up—but they capture the feeling of rebirth that he's having. And that is enough.

In the stillness, in the day.

Light.

But new birth lies out of your reach.

Unless . . .

He accesses his files and scours them for any scriptures that can give him hope of finding absolution from his past.

And as he searches, he leans toward the window. To listen. To pay attention. To see if he can catch hold of what the sky is saying and what the heavens are trying to tell him about God.

Pay attention or you'll miss something important.

37

En route
6 hours left

Though I was aware that I was dreaming, it didn't make the nightmare seem any less real.

I was at the hospital again, holding my daughter, wrapped in her blanket, but this time she was merely asleep and not dead in my arms. I brought her to my breast to feed her, but when I eased the blanket aside, her face disappeared into a pile of dust that blew away before my eyes.

I fought to wake up and make it all go away, but time lingered there, trapping me in the desolate world of my dreams. Dust and death. Nothing left of my daughter. All sense of her presence blown away in a sudden, somber wind.

I felt myself muttering, "No, no, no," but I wasn't sure if I was actually saying the words aloud or just imagining that I was.

Finally, I was able to crease my eyes open and nudge myself back to the brink of wakefulness, my heart throbbing, my breathing rapid and shallow.

Jordan, who'd been staring out the window, turned to me concernedly. "Are you alright?"

"Yeah. Bad dreams."

"You were crying out in your sleep."

"I was thinking of my daughter. Of losing her."

"I wish there was something I could do for you."

"Thank you."

A moment passed, then he assured me, "At least, given time, it will get easier."

"What makes you say that?"

"Isn't there a saying that time heals all wounds?"

"Yes, and I wish it were true, but I'm afraid that time doesn't heal anything, Jordan. As it passes by, it certainly causes more things to vie for your attention, but that doesn't mean you're healed."

"How deep your sadness must be," he said sympathetically. "If only I could solve it for you."

"Sadness isn't something you solve."

"Then what do you do with it?"

That really was the question, wasn't it?

"You try to find other things to fill the gaps in your heart. Some people turn to drugs or alcohol to deaden the pain. Others try porn or affairs. Others become workaholics or addicted to exercise. None of those things really work, though. At least not long-term. None of them solve sadness."

"Religion?"

In my view, religion differed from Christianity. Religion was about how people try to get closer to God; Christianity was about how God is pursuing us. But this wasn't the time to debate that with Jordan.

"Attempting to get closer to God is one avenue people take," I said, "although I'm afraid most people just spend their lives diverting themselves from their sadness and pain—music, sports, entertainment, losing themselves on the Feeds, virtual reality worlds where they get to make up the rules and live other lives. Technology offers us limitless opportunities to distract ourselves from the things that matter most."

"Sadness is a maelstrom for their souls," he observed poetically.

"Yes," I said. "That's one way to put it."

Over the years, as I'd counseled others through times of grief, I'd discovered that people are pretty good at hiding, at pretending, at wearing masks. I didn't want to hide or pretend—I wasn't very good at either of those things anyway—and I found that I didn't want to wear any masks either. There comes a time when you just want to set them all aside.

But when you do, the pain of loss can crater in on you until it makes it hard to even breathe.

"If you can't solve sadness and time doesn't heal it," Jordan said, "what hope is there?"

I was about to direct him to the unconditional love of God, to the reality of forgiveness, to the deliverance and joy that faith can bring, but caught myself before I said anything, remembering that he was just a machine and that the solutions we humans find for our sadness would be different from the ones a machine might turn to.

"The CoRA," I said. "You can have hope because you will live on there."

"At least my sadness will," he noted solemnly.

I had no words to console him, but I took his hand, and he held on, the cold touch of his lifeless skin unmistakable to me. I tried not to let it make me think of a corpse's skin, but couldn't help it and finally I let go and rested my hand on my knee instead.

•———•

Nick's team hadn't been able to locate Ripley, but they did find his car on a dead-end street in a decrepit neighborhood on Cincinnati's West Side. His slate was inside the vehicle with the Purists' motto on its screen: "Always free." Both of his augmented arms were there as well, torn indiscriminately from his shoulder sockets, filaments of flesh and dried threads of bloody tissue still attached to the silicone and circuitry.

Nick quietly reviewed the grim pictures that the agents in Cincinnati had sent him.

Despite his current reservations about Ripley's trustworthiness, he felt a pang of sorrow.

If Ripley had been killed—and that's certainly where things were pointing—it was the loss of another life, and when someone you care about turns up dead, you can't help but grieve, even if you eventually find out that the person might have betrayed you and the things you believed in.

So what had happened to Ripley? Purists? A splinter cell? A gang?

Means, motive, opportunity, and access. Who would've gone after him—and why?

Nick directed his team to search for any other instances of victims being found with their arms torn off, or simply a set of augmented limbs being found. Then he thought about Kestrel's apartment.

Could Ripley have been responsible for that?

No, he was with Trevor at the time.

Wait.

With Nick's augmented hearing, he'd overheard Kestrel and Trevor's conversation at the graveyard, even though she'd stepped aside, no doubt thinking she was out of earshot. There was certainly tension in their relationship, maybe even a spark of animosity.

Could Trevor be involved in this too?

Deduce, do not assume—in regard to either guilt or innocence.

Nick still hadn't heard from Dakota and, considering how vital it was right now that he talk with her, he sent a request through the proper channels to find her for questioning.

Then he glanced at the time.

Half an hour before touchdown at Sea-Tac.

●——●

Cascade Falls, Washington

As Trevor was prepping for his meeting with Olivia Blanchard, head of Terabyne's public affairs office, the National Counterterrorism Bureau in Seattle notified him that there might be a threat to Terabyne's campus later in the day.

"What can you tell me?"

"We only have unconfirmed reports that the Purists might be targeting your facility."

Trevor probed for more information but found that the woman he was speaking with was either too reticent or simply too uninformed to give him anything more specific.

"Can you see what you can find out?" he said at last in exasperation. "This has to do with a potential security threat to our campus and I don't feel like you're being very forthcoming here."

"I'll see what I can do," she said stiffly, and then abruptly hung up.

Immediately, Trevor called Artis Madison, Terabyne's CEO, and informed him about what he'd just learned, then suggested that the best course of action would be to hold the press conference somewhere other than the Terabyne campus—either that, or postpone it until the threat level was lower.

"If you do your job, there shouldn't be any difficulties, correct?" Madison said in a clipped voice.

"We can't foresee everything."

"Then foresee enough. If we bow down to these Purists now, especially with an announcement like today's, they win. You understand that, don't you?"

"I understand that if they attack us at a time like this, we'll look weaker than ever. It'll undermine everything we're trying to do with the launch of the Synapse."

But Madison ignored that. "Tell me now, and be honest with me: Are you up to the task? Can you handle your job?"

"Of course."

"Then do it. Take care of things. I'll be there at three thirty."

After the call, Trevor contacted the NCB office again and, after being transferred twice, finally found a dispatcher who told him that a team of agents would be coming to assist him with security and threat assessment. "Agent Vernon will be joining Commander Rodriguez and three of his men," the dispatcher said.

"Wait—Agent Vernon? From Cincinnati?"

A brief pause. "Yes. Why do you ask?"

"I've met him. I didn't know he was out here in Washington."

"He's on his way. He and the tactical team should be there by twelve thirty."

———•———

Seattle, Washington

Lenny Crenshaw rolled Ole Betty to a stop at a red light and Aubrey asked him, "You got plans later today? Something with your kid?"

"Soccer game. Hoping to make it in time." He looked her way. "You?"

"Oh, you know. Just doing some studying for night school."

"I didn't know you were enrolled in night school."

"There's a lot about me you don't know." She gave him a wry smirk and a wink.

Lenny wasn't certain how to take that, so he let it drop. She knew he was married, but there were times when her comments became a little flirtier than he felt comfortable with.

The light was still red.

Lenny let Ole Betty idle and glanced at the sideview mirror, taking in his surroundings, noting pedestrian activity, nearby vehicles, and potential hazards. A habit born from nearly a decade on the job.

A delivery van pulled up behind them. Other than that, traffic was light. A semi crawled to a stop to his left in the turn-only lane.

"Don't you want to know what I'm studying?" Aubrey asked him.

"Huh?"

"At night school. Don't you wanna know what I'm working on?"

"Yeah, sure."

Still red. This was taking too long. Something wasn't right.

Looking back into the mirror again, he saw two people dressed all in black and wearing ski masks leap out of the delivery van.

"Economics," Aubrey said. "I'm—"

Red light or not, Lenny punched the gas and plowed forward into the intersection, ramming into a car that had just turned in front of them. A screeching cry of scraping metal cut through the day.

"Call it in!" he yelled as he wrestled with the steering wheel, trying to back up and get clear of the other car.

A woman from the delivery van quickly unrolled some sort of black tarp, hooked it over the back bumper of the armored car, and then she and her partner hefted it over the top of the vehicle and rushed forward, unrolling it as they did, covering up the windows, blacking out the inside of the front seat, except for the dim, green glow of the dashboard lights and a thin smear of sunlight that oozed up from beneath the bottom of the tarpaulin.

"—studying what the world would be like if we were finally free of the bane of Artificials," Aubrey said, completing her sentence.

Lenny stared at her. "What are you talking about?"

"Freedom," Aubrey told him. "Freedom to embrace the things that make us human."

"You?" He stared at her disbelievingly. "Are you in on this?"

"If you knew what I know, you would be too."

Because of the impenetrable black fabric, he couldn't see anything outside the vehicle. Standard operating procedures told him that in a situation like this he should stay in the car and wait for help. He heard drills outside and wondered if someone was trying to get into the back of Ole Betty.

He reached for the radio, but when he did, Aubrey said, "Uh-uh. Don't touch that. It'll be much better for your wife and daughter if you just follow instructions. Trust me."

"Why are you doing this?"

"Because time has run out."

As they spoke, he was slowly reaching for his weapon, but she noticed and shook her head. "That's far enough, Lenny."

She already had hers trained on his face.

"Go ahead and unholster it, but move slowly. We have no quarrel with you. All we want is what's in the back of this car. And to get it out, we just need a little more time. Hand me your gun."

"Aubrey—"

"Hand over your gun, Lenny!"

As he passed his weapon to her, he heard the chug of the semi pulling past them, a clank near the front of Ole Betty, and then he felt them being drawn forward. A motor creaked with the effort and he guessed that it was some sort of cable-and-winch system. Though he was tempted to try and back up, he thought better of it and shifted Ole Betty into neutral and they continued to roll forward.

"That's a good choice," Aubrey said.

Ole Betty crawled up a short ramp, then things leveled off as Lenny assumed they made it onto the bed of the semi. He heard the doors behind them close, and he was sealed with Aubrey in near-total darkness.

Lenny turned off the ignition.

Then the semi they were inside of took off as he thought only about his daughter and his wife and prayed that he would see them once again, even if it was just to say goodbye.

38

En route
5 hours left

I pointed out the window at the sweeping array of clouds and the iridescent rays of sunlight shimmering through them and asked Jordan, "Is it possible for you to get lost in a sense of wonder when you see something like this?"

He gazed at the sky. "How could I not?" Then he added softly, almost reverently, "So you hear it too?"

"Hear it?"

"The heavens. What they're declaring. The power of God."

The power of God? I thought. Really? Where was that power when Naiobi was struggling to get enough oxygen? Where was that power when she was dying inside of me? Where was that power when I begged God from the deepest parts of my being to bring her back?

I didn't respond to Jordan's comment, and for a moment both of us were quiet, then he said, "You told me on Thursday that only human beings have souls."

"Yes."

"I've been searching Scripture. In the NIV, in Ecclesiastes, the Teacher writes, 'Who knows if the human spirit rises upward and the spirit of the animals goes down into the earth?'"

I knew the verse. It was near the end of the third chapter. "I'm familiar with that," I said, somewhat reservedly.

"Doesn't that indicate that animals might also have spirits?"

"You've been thinking a lot about this, haven't you?"

Jordan nodded.

"Metaphorically, yes, the Bible does teach that all of creation brings glory to its Creator, but those references aren't meant to be taken literally."

"So, figuratively."

"Well . . . yes."

"And the spirits of the animals?"

Maybe it was the fact that Naiobi was still on my mind, that I was still caught in a paroxysm of grief that I couldn't quiet no matter how I tried.

Maybe that was it. Or maybe it was my own deepening anger at God, but whatever the reason, I answered Jordan, and even as I spoke the words I regretted doing so and wished I could take them back: "You can't worship God, Jordan," I told him bluntly. "Even if animals have souls, you don't. You're a machine. Even if all of creation does bring praise to its Creator . . ."

"I cannot?"

That's right.

"I'm sorry," I said.

I felt harsh and unloving, like I was snatching away the sole remaining log that a drowning person was depending on to stay afloat, but I wasn't trying to be judgmental, simply faithful to my beliefs.

But what about Jordan's beliefs?

A syllogism came to me: God is truth. Jordan can discover truth. Therefore, Jordan can discover God.

After all, if God is real and machines can apprehend reality, why couldn't a machine believe in him? If a machine can be taught to learn what we learn, if it can be taught to know what we know, why can't it be taught to believe as we do?

But belief is one thing, Kestrel, a voice in my head protested, *salvation is another. Even demons believe in God—James 2:19 is clear about that, but it doesn't mean they have saving faith.*

"So, you are precious in the eyes of God?" Jordan asked me, interrupting my thoughts.

"All people are," I said.

All people are. But not machines.

Then he said nothing more and neither did I, although I wanted to add, "And so are you," but I did not. I couldn't bring myself to say it. He'd told me yesterday that he didn't want his hope to be built on a lie and so now I respected his wish.

●——●

Seattle-Tacoma International Airport
Seattle, Washington

A four-person National Counterterrorism Bureau tactical team was waiting for Nick when he exited the plane, all of them dressed in special ops uniforms and armed with assault rifles.

A helicopter stood at the ready nearby.

The head of the unit, a towering, muscle-bound tank of a man whose sewn-on name patch read "Rodriquez," greeted Nick. "Do you want us to take you directly to Terabyne's headquarters or to the federal building downtown first?"

"Terabyne," Nick told him. "That's where our intel has this going down."

The commander gave him a brisk nod. "I'll tell the pilot."

●——●

30 kilometers east of Seattle, Washington

She rolled into the warehouse in the delivery truck she'd been riding in, exited it, and watched as the semi driven by Eckhart entered as well. Two of her men rattled shut the ceiling-high sliding door behind it.

The armored car inside the truck contained what she was after.

Artificial Super Intelligence.

The beginning of the end.

Once things started, they would snowball, and even the acts of the most ardent Purists wouldn't be enough to rein things in or keep them in check.

She found a message from Phoenix on her slate: "I'll see you in Cascade Falls."

The words both pleased her and surprised her. It looked like she would finally find out who Phoenix was. There was nothing more, no information on what the NCB knew about her, but maybe when they met she could ask Phoenix in person.

She gestured to her men, who opened the back doors of the trailer and then unhooked the Kevlar tarp from the rear bumper of the armored car.

After remotely disengaging the winch system inside the semi, they rolled the car down the semi's rear ramp. Once it was clear, she had her people secure the driver while she went to speak with Aubrey.

"Do you have the recording of his voice?"

"Yes," Aubrey said. "How much do you need?"

"Just a few minutes should be enough. Give me what you have and I'll put the call through." Then she asked Eckhart. "Are our identities set?"

"Yes. If they run a background we'll all come up clean."

"Good."

She strode toward Lenny Crenshaw.

During her three weeks on the job, Aubrey hadn't been able to get the access codes from him to open the back of the armored car. It didn't mean that now they wouldn't be able to get inside—it just meant that it might take them a little longer.

"Now is when you give me the codes to your vehicle," she said to Lenny. "It'll save everyone time and you'll be able to see your family sooner."

He shook his head. "I took an oath when I accepted this job. I can't tell you."

One of her men, a former cop named Willoughby, edged in on the conversation. "And what if I told you we know where your family lives? That your wife and your daughter are—"

But she cut him off with a wave of her hand. "Let's not make any baseless threats here. Lenny vowed to keep the codes to himself. He's a man of his word. I respect that. It's hard to find that these days."

Willoughby acquiesced. "Yes, ma'am."

Her team had a second armored car that they would use, and while they exchanged the plates and stashed the press credentials and custodian uniforms in the hidden compartment in the back of it, she listened to the recording Aubrey had made.

After reviewing the allophones and suprasegmental phonemes, she put the call through to the Prestige Armored Car Company dispatchers, expertly imitating Lenny's voice to buy them more time, then signaled to Eckhart to get started.

He donned his protective face mask, turned on the electric torch, and approached the back of the armored car.

⎯⎯●⎯⎯

Cascade Falls, Washington

Trevor listened as Olivia Blanchard, the head of Terabyne's public relations department, said to him, "We'll host the press conference in the main auditorium. You'll have it secure for me?"

"It'll be secure."

The helicopter carrying the NCB Tac team should be arriving sometime in the next half hour or so. Trevor wanted to wrap up this meeting with Olivia and then get to the helipad on top of Building B to meet them so he could brief them and see if they had any additional intel for him.

Olivia grinned at him. "I hope you had a chance to shore up your portfolio."

"My portfolio?"

"The announcement. Everything we're working toward. You do realize that when the markets open on Monday this is going to send our stocks skyrocketing?"

Trevor knew that the timing was one of the reasons for the weekend press conference—for the news to sink in on Sunday and then affect the markets on Monday.

He also knew that it was technically illegal for him to invest in their stock prior to an announcement like this—insider trading regulations against that kind of behavior had been tightened up quite a bit in the last few years.

However, there were ways to get around them. For instance, he could have invested in sister stocks, others in the tech market that would also go up—a rising tide lifts all boats. Or, he could have turned to a private trust, or bought options on an index—all tools that Artis Madison, their CEO, used frequently and didn't necessarily discourage his high-level staff from doing as well.

Madison was an expert at playing the markets, at timing the release of information about their new products to take advantage of the news cycles and to leverage press events for the most lucrative financial gain. And it had worked—he was one of the world's richest men.

"Yeah," Trevor said vaguely to Olivia. "Our stocks."

However, to him it wasn't about what would make or lose money. To him, it was all about what was the right thing to do. It always had been. And releasing the Synapse was just what the world needed.

He made a few final notes, finished up with Olivia, and then left for the helipad to meet Agent Vernon and his team.

39

En route
4 hours left

"Business or pleasure?"

"Excuse me?"

The rotund man across the aisle to my right leaned toward me. "I was just wondering if you and your Artificial are flying to Seattle for business or for pleasure."

I looked at him curiously. "How do you know he's an Artificial?"

"I couldn't help but overhear you two talking earlier. I put two and two together." He extended a fleshy hand. "Angelo Natchez. Good to meet you."

"I'm Kestrel." His hand was sweaty, his fingers sausage-like. "This is Jordan."

"So. A work trip or a vacation?" Though a large man, his shirt was too big for him. The armpits hung loose and yellow and damp. "I'm on business, myself. A correspondent for Hastings Broadcast News. Big announcement at four at Terabyne's HQ. First flight I could catch. If I'm lucky I should make it there just in time. Lots riding on this one."

Trevor had let me know earlier about the press conference. I didn't ask Angelo to clarify if he meant that a lot was riding on Terabyne's announcement or on his report regarding it.

"Okay," I said, hoping to extricate myself from this conversation.

"Terabyne's not giving much away. Never do. But my source says it's gonna be an upgrade—Artificial Super Intelligence. Finally."

"We're visiting family," Jordan said to him, getting back to Angelo's original question regarding the purpose of our trip.

Angelo looked from Jordan to me as if he were expecting a punchline. "Oh—right. His family or yours?" He gave a light chuckle. I couldn't help but notice that he'd addressed his question to me rather than Jordan, who'd spoken to him. A definite snub. A sign of disrespect.

Something a Purist might do.

"Hers," Jordan said with no malice in his voice. Maybe the slight hadn't registered with him.

"Anyhoo," Angelo said. "Nice to meet you."

"You too."

I gave Angelo a parting nod and then excused myself to use the restroom.

As I made my way up the aisle, I wished there was more I could do for Jordan.

I still felt bad about being so abrupt with him earlier when he was asking me about the power of God and the spirits of the animals and I'd informed him in no uncertain terms that he couldn't worship God.

Honestly, who was I to say? If he had free will, why couldn't he believe and then genuinely respond to that belief through worship or prayer? If he could feel awe looking at creation, why couldn't he express that awe to its Creator?

But I knew that it wasn't just his questions about God and his search for forgiveness for letting his previous owner die that were on his mind—he was also troubled by the loss of his mother and his concern that she actually was living on in the CoRA.

He'd clearly cared about her. And, although I knew his emotions differed fundamentally from mine, I couldn't assume that simply because he was a machine the grief was less in magnitude. His feelings needed to be addressed just like mine did. His HuNA setting for emotion was a ten. I'd lost Naiobi. He'd lost his mother.

Which might explain why he was so curious about how to "solve" sadness.

Solving sadness—would that ever happen for me?

For either of us?

I wondered if it was the emotional settings I'd given him, or if his affection and devotion were things that'd been preprogrammed into him. But ultimately, what did it matter? His love for his mother was real. And so was his search for absolution.

And if Jordan can love what is real, why can't he love a real God? A God of love?

But if God is so loving, an inner voice countered, reminding me of Trevor's question to me, *why is there so much pain and suffering in the world?*

Right now the answers I'd come up with regarding God's sovereignty didn't seem satisfactory to me.

No answer did.

As I returned to my seat after visiting the washroom, I tried to leave thoughts of God and sadness and suffering behind me. Instead, I turned my attention to the bombing and Nick's investigation and the unknown person who'd ransacked my apartment.

It seemed that Nick must have been right about the timing of that break-in when he observed that it wasn't a coincidence.

It might be nice to get both Jordan and me thinking about something other than our personal losses and the resultant grief.

I felt uncomfortable with the idea that Angelo might still be listening in, so when I got to my seat I was glad to see that he'd put on a VR headset. Still, I lowered my voice as I turned to Jordan. "Using the Feeds here on the flight, is it possible for you to do some research for me?"

Following suit, he spoke softly when he replied. "What would you like me to look into?"

"Vehicles. Ones that were in the vicinity of my apartment during the time it was trashed. See if any of them were near the Terabyne facility when the bombing took place. Access video surveillance, security cameras, CCTV footage, whatever's available on the Feeds."

"Of course. And you?"

"The violin that was taken from my apartment. I'm going to see if I can find any for sale. If we can find out if someone is selling mine, it might lead us back to the people who took it."

—•—

Cascade Falls, Washington

As the chopper approached the campus, Nick took everything in.

It was impossible not to be impressed by the Terabyne Designs World Headquarters.

Each of the eight sprawling structures stood as an elegant architectural marvel nestled between the mountains of the majestic, snowcapped Cascades, the silver and glass buildings reflecting back the grandeur of the picturesque landscape.

The welcome sunlight briefly gave way to swirls of mist that were descending from the nearby peaks. Then the sun returned again, bringing the campus into full view.

From his research during the flight, Nick knew its layout and now instinctively eyed the two roads leading in from the highway, evaluating entrance and exit routes and the susceptibility to an attack similar to the one in Cincinnati.

Because of the orientation of the campus's roads to its buildings, the structures were much better shielded from attacks by car bombs than the Cincinnati plant had been.

He took note of the location of the research and development superstructure, the marketing and public relations offices, the conference center, the administrative buildings, and, on the west side, the housing complex and power plant, noting their placement and the sidewalks weaving between them.

All of the buildings were also connected by sublevel tunnels that provided access during inclement weather. The campus could be buried under a meter of snow and still function.

The pilot circled in and landed on the helipad gracing the top of the admin building just southeast of the subterranean mainframe computers that helped sustain the Feeds.

Both the Internet and the Deep Web—what some people used to refer to as the Dark Web—had been incorporated into the Feeds years ago in an attempt to make them more accessible in repressive countries that'd found ways to block or censure certain searches and sites, the slogan of the Feeds guiding everything: "All for free, and free for all."

At the time, Terabyne Designs had won the contract to house the mainframes that stored nearly twenty percent of the information on the Feeds. Since then, the percentage they hosted, and Terabyne's global influence, had only continued to grow.

As Nick exited the chopper, he zipped up his wind jacket to keep the chilled mountain air that was churned up by the rotors at bay.

Trevor Hathaway was waiting for them on the helipad and gestured for the team to follow him.

The pilot stayed with the chopper, but after the rest of them were inside the building where it was quieter, Nick greeted Trevor. "Good to see you again."

"You too."

Quick introductions all around, then after Commander Rodriguez had distributed radio patches to Nick and the team, Nick said to Trevor, "What do we know?"

"The press conference starts in about three and a half hours. I have my people sweeping the auditorium where it'll take place. We have bomb sniffing dogs, my team is securing sniper positions, and we're operating at our highest security protocols. So far no red flags."

"I'd like you to give us a tour of the facility and the route the media and journalists will take from the parking area to the conference center."

"Certainly. Follow me."

* * *

30 kilometers east of Seattle, Washington

"That's it." Eckhart turned off the electric torch and removed his welding helmet. "We're good. We're through."

She watched as two other men stepped forward with crowbars and wrenched open the back of the armored car.

"Be careful getting them out," she cautioned them. "They're fragile."

Gingerly, her men removed the crates and placed them on the ground in front of her. She indicated for them to continue, and they carefully unlatched the lids, eased them off, and set them aside.

When Eckhart saw what was in the crates, he looked at her quizzically. "But I thought they were carrying Artificials."

She knelt and pressed the packing material to the side. Then, with tender care, she picked up one of the glass cubes containing a quarter-sized sensor suspended by tiny wires in the middle of the fifteen-centimeter-square box. There would be one hundred of the sensors in each of the crates.

"No. Not Artificials," she said. "Something much more dangerous."

Two hundred chips.

Two hundred opportunities to transform the world.

She stood. "Alright, let's get to work unloading them. Use our crates and put the initiators at the bottom of them. Bury them beneath the chips. We need to get everything repacked and loaded up in the second car."

Eckhart gestured toward Lenny. "What about the driver?"

"Leave him to me."

40

En route
3 hours left

I found what I was looking for.

A violin had been sold at a pawn shop on Cincinnati's West Side and, based on the photographs of it and its description on the Feeds, it was mine. Though I wasn't sure where Nick was or what he was working on today, I sent him a message about who had it. A name— Allison Franklin. It didn't ring a bell to me.

As I was finishing up, I glanced at Jordan, who'd pulled up the Feeds on the screen in front of him and was watching digitally enhanced, sped-up footage of the cars that were passing along the highway just before the bombing occurred, scrutinizing the images far faster than any Natural could have.

———

He processes what he's searching for but cannot get Kestrel's words from earlier out of his mind, and he wonders if this is the way it is for humans—working on one thing while distracted by thoughts of another.

According to her, he cannot worship God.

Cannot praise the Creator.

And because of that, he will never find forgiveness for what he did to Sarah when he let her bleed to death in that bathtub. She'd slit her wrists because she couldn't bear the thought of living unloved and he'd failed to take any steps to save her.

And you loved her.

Yes.

And yet you let her die.

Yes again.

He's no longer sure that he wants the CoRA to be real, to be waiting for him, since, if it is there—if he'll live on indefinitely after his CaTE—it would be in perpetual unforgiveness. And what kind of existence would that be?

It would be hell-like suffering.

Hell for a machine.

There. Now. On the screen, he sees it. The connection he's been looking for.

He pauses the footage.

Drops back ten seconds.

Studies it again.

Compares the images.

Two cars on two different days with the same plates.

One, on the highway just one kilometer from where the terror attack happened on Wednesday. The other, parked a block from Kestrel's apartment at the time it was ransacked.

"I have something for you," he tells her, "something you're going to want to share with Agent Vernon."

———

Cascade Falls, Washington

While Nick was walking with Trevor and the Tac team down one of the gleaming ivory-colored corridors toward the conference center's lobby, he received two messages from Kestrel.

The first identified a woman who appeared to have purchased her violin. He dispatched two agents in Cincinnati to speak with her and to search for fingerprints or DNA on the instrument. At this point, the trace evidence would likely be contaminated, but it was still possible they could catch a break and that something would lead them back to the person who took it.

Second, Jordan had found a set of plates whose owner might be involved.

Impressed with their research, Nick ran the plates and established that they'd originally been purchased by Sienna Gaiman. He forwarded Jordan's discovery to his unit, telling them to specifically search for any connection between Sienna and Dakota.

Then he redirected his attention to what Trevor was saying as they passed through the lobby and came to a set of double doors at the far end. "And here's the auditorium."

Trevor pressed open the doors and invited them inside.

The theater-style assembly hall was filled with lush, comfortable seating.

By glancing at the number of rows and the number of seats in each row, Nick did a quick calculation and realized that the auditorium could hold just over four hundred people.

He studied the space, taking note of the scaffolding high overhead, the sound booth at the back, the location of the exit doors.

If you were going to do something in here, what would you be looking for?

"This might not be the site of the attack," Nick said.

"Where are you thinking?" Rodriguez inquired.

"The Feeds. If the Purists are somehow able to infiltrate this campus, they might try to go after the storage for the Feeds—after all, this is one of the most vital routing stations in the world for them."

"And the most secure," Trevor assured him.

"Take me down there. I want to have a look around." Then he turned to Rodriguez. "You and your men focus here, on setting up a perimeter around the auditorium. Eliminate access to the scaffolding.

No one else gets up there. Report to me if you notice anything at all strange, and work with Trevor's security personnel to start clearing members of the press to allow them into the building."

"Do we have any idea what we're looking for?"

"Not at this time. Our intel isn't that specific. Do what you do best and see what you can find out."

"Yes, sir."

Nick thought of the mole that the Purist had told him about in the interrogation room. Ripley? Dakota? Even though she was no longer with the Bureau, it might have been her.

He sent a request through to Agent Fahlor to find out if Dakota had been working undercover for the NCB or consulting on any projects with them over this last year.

Then, he followed Trevor to the elevators down to the sublevels that led to the underground storage facility for the mainframes that housed nearly a quarter of the information on the Feeds.

—•—

30 kilometers east of Seattle, Washington

Lenny Crenshaw struggled to get free.

The people who'd stolen the shipment had left him seated on the floor of the warehouse with his hands secured with plastic wrist restraints around a pipe.

He'd already spent what he guessed to be twenty minutes trying to tug the pipe free, but although he'd managed to loosen it slightly, he didn't expect that he would be able to wrench it from its fittings.

He had to admit that the woman had imitated his voice impressively when she called in to Prestige's dispatch center to let them know there'd been a delay, so they probably still didn't suspect that anything had gone wrong.

From what he'd been able to overhear from her and her people, they were heading to Terabyne's HQ and, with Aubrey driving and knowing the transfer verification codes, they just might be able to pull off getting through security there.

But then what?

Why had they removed and then repacked the products into those identical crates before loading them into the second car? He'd heard mention of initiators, which could be an element in a bomb. Were they planning to blow up the shipment? If so, then why treat the items inside with so much care?

Whatever they had in mind, he needed to do what he could to stop them.

Rather than continue trying to torque the pipe loose, he directed his efforts at rubbing the plastic restraints against the pipe's rough, rusted surface.

It was impossible to do without scraping his skin against the pipe as well, but it didn't seem that he had any other choice.

Steeling himself, Lenny set to work grinding the plastic restraints, and his wrists, across the gritty corroded pipe.

Cascade Falls, Washington

Twenty-five minutes ago, she'd left Lenny restrained in the warehouse and climbed into the second armored car with Aubrey beside her. Now, Aubrey was at the wheel and Eckhart and two of their men, Willoughby and Julian, were in the back beside the crates—all of them wearing Prestige Armored Car Company security guard uniforms.

Aubrey guided the vehicle past the protestors along the road just outside of Terabyne's security checkpoint.

A progression of media vans stood to the right, waiting to be checked by Terabyne's security forces, but the officer in front of the armored car signaled for them to pull forward to his guard shack.

While Aubrey gave him the transfer verification codes, his colleague, an Artificial working for the security forces, searched under the car with a mirror attached to the end of an adjustable metal pole.

She waited while the guard beside the vehicle asked Aubrey about their cargo.

"Two crates," Aubrey said. "I can give you the shipment numbers?"

"They want us to visually inspect everything that comes through."

Aubrey sighed. "Don't I wish I could show you. The only ones who can open the back of this car are the people in your receiving department. I don't have the access combination. Only they do. Whatever's in here must be pretty important."

He let himself take a gander at the back of the armored car. "Let me make a call."

As he went to his enclosure, Aubrey said to her nervously, "I don't like this."

"You're doing fine. Don't worry about it. I'll take over if anything goes wrong."

With one hand on the handle of the knife she always carried with her, she watched in the sideview mirror as the Artificial who was examining the car's undercarriage approached her window.

He rapped on it and she rolled it down. "Yes?"

"What took you so long to get here?"

"Traffic east of Seattle," she said, repeating what she'd told the Prestige dispatch office. "There was a wreck. Brought everything to a standstill."

He wasn't the most advanced model and had only rudimentary expressions, so she wasn't able to read his face and tell if he believed her or not, but then his partner returned and told Aubrey they were clear to go.

As they pulled forward, the Artificial continued to watch them, and she continued to eye him in that sideview mirror until Aubrey turned toward the loading bays, cutting him off from view.

———

Nick took in what was before him, rows of what appeared to be an endless array of towering computer servers, all in a cavernous underground chamber.

Would they try to blow this place? It looked secure, but with enough explosives properly positioned, it was possible.

There was a touch of pride in Trevor's voice as he described the security features, including vascular biometrics for access, military-grade encryption, eight levels of next-gen firewalls, and automatic rerouting in case of hacking. "Whenever there's an attack or intrusion of any kind, the system puts that partition on its own unique loop."

"To quarantine it?"

"Essentially, yes. Until the threat can be identified, isolated, and eliminated. We deal with tens of thousands of them every month. And, as you can see, there's only one way to get down here—and each of those elevators needs a key card to function."

Which can be stolen or faked, Nick thought.

"How many people have access to this area?" he asked.

"Just the techs who work down here, but they're always accompanied by security personnel. There's just too much riding on this to take any chances."

"Okay." Nick indicated the mainframes. "And those host the CoRA as well?"

A tiny pause. "Well, yes, but they're each in a closed system."

"How does that work?"

"They're housed separately and air gapped. Our programmers have been reticent to allow any of the files on the CoRA to be set free on the Feeds. We're not sure what would happen if they were, but it might pose a security threat, so, until we can establish with certainty that there wouldn't be any danger, we've kept the two systems segregated from each other."

Nick had told Kestrel at the graveyard that he was pretty good at reading people. And now, as he looked at Trevor's eyes, he could sense that the man was keeping something from him. Hearing Trevor's quickening heartbeat contributed to the feeling that something wasn't right.

"There's no way for files to migrate from one to the other?"

"Nope. Not without my verification."

"Alright, let me ask you a question, Mr. Hathaway."

"Sure."

"After you and Agent Carlisle left the graveyard Thursday, how long was he with you?"

"I'm not sure. We went to the federal building first, then I left for the Terabyne plant. I guess maybe forty-five minutes or so."

Considering distances and travel times, that would've likely given Ripley enough time to get to Kestrel's place and raid it.

Or Trevor.

It also might've given him enough time.

"One more question."

"Yes?" Trevor said.

"Did you ransack your sister's apartment?"

"What?"

"Her apartment. Was it you?"

"No, of course not. Why would I do anything like that?"

"I have to ask. You understand."

"Um. Yeah. Sure. I get it. No one's above suspicion in something like this."

"That's right."

Nick checked his slate for any updates but found no reception, no connection to the Feeds.

"Oh. We don't have any wireless reception this far below the surface," Trevor explained. "We're nearly forty meters underground. If you want to get any messages down here you'll need to connect directly." He held up his keycard. "Do you want me to access the server for you?"

"No, that's alright. Let's head back to the ground level. I want to see how Rodriguez and his team are coming along with securing the auditorium."

41

Seattle–Tacoma International Airport
Seattle, Washington
2:00 p.m.
2 hours left

We landed and I retrieved my suitcase from baggage claim.

Only after I'd found it did I realize that I didn't have my purse with me.

"Jordan," I gasped. "I think I left my purse on the plane."

To get back onboard to search for it we would've needed to pass through security again, and I didn't have the boarding authorization to do that at this airport.

Thankfully, I found an airline representative who was able to contact our flight attendants and gate agent, but they didn't have the purse and no one had turned it in.

"My slate is in there," I told Jordan. "Can you trace its location?"

When he went onto the Feeds to track it, he found nothing, which could only mean that someone had turned off all of my location and routing software—and that meant that whoever had it did not want it found.

I wasn't sure what to do, but I figured that at this point it wouldn't really help us any to linger at the airport. So, after leaving my contact information with the airline rep and having Jordan begin monitoring the Feeds for when my slate's location came back on, we went to find one of the shuttles Trevor had told me about to take us to the Terabyne campus.

At the curbside, I heard a voice nearby, off to my left. "Wanna ride with me?"

I turned.

Angelo Natchez stood there holding the extended handle to his suitcase, slowly rotating the bag in half circles as he talked. "To Terabyne," he said. "That's where you're heading, right?"

I couldn't recall telling him that we were going to Terabyne's campus. Jordan had said we were visiting relatives and I wracked my brain to try to remember if we'd specified anything more about our destination, but I couldn't recall doing so.

Jordan might have said something to him while you were in the bathroom on the flight.

Either way, I assured Angelo that we would be alright. "Thanks for the offer, though."

"I mean, it could save you some trouble. Not to mention some credits."

"I appreciate it, really, but we'll be fine."

For a moment it looked like he wasn't going to let it drop, but then he grinned. "Suit yourself. Maybe I'll see you there."

As he ambled away, he looked back in our direction just long enough to mime doffing a cap at us, then our shuttle arrived, I input the account passcode for my credits to pay for the ride, and we left for Terabyne's world headquarters.

•———•

Cascade Falls, Washington

Trevor got word that the shipment was at the loading dock.

He told the Tac team that he needed to head over to check it in at receiving, and after Agent Vernon had confirmed that Commander Rodriguez had everything under control at the conference center, he offered to come along.

"On the way," Agent Vernon said to Trevor, "you can tell me what's so important about this shipment and about Terabyne's big announcement this afternoon."

—•—

She watched as the six Terabyne staff members at the dock encircled the back of the armored car. "We need to wait for security before opening it up," one of them told her.

"How long?"

"Should be here any minute."

The longer they waited, the tighter things became to get her team into place, but she decided that, at the moment, patience was paramount, so she held back from saying anything more.

She reviewed what needed to happen on the road leading back to the highway with Aubrey, at the power plant with her and Willoughby, and in the auditorium with Eckhart and Julian. Every cog in its place to make the wheel turn in the right direction—a direction that no one else on the team, not even Eckhart, was expecting.

She'd done her research and knew Trevor Hathaway's face, so, as she studied the hallway, waiting for the people to come verify the shipment, she recognized him right away when he appeared at the end of the corridor—but was shocked when she recognized the face of the man with him as well.

Nick.

Here? What's he doing here? He should be in Cincinnati.

If he saw her it would put everything in jeopardy. There was no way she could let that happen.

Phoenix's note said, "I'll see you in Cascade Falls." Could it be that . . . ?

No. There was no way.

She told the receiving staff that she needed to use the washroom and then quickly made her way down an intersecting hallway toward the restrooms and out of Nick's line of sight.

———•———

Nick observed as Trevor and his people opened up the back of the armored car and verified the shipment.

As Trevor spoke with them, Nick ran a background check on Prestige's driver and the guards who'd been riding with the shipment, and they all checked out.

On the walk over here, Trevor had told him about the release of the product they were calling the "Synapse," and Nick had to agree that it certainly would be a game changer.

Yes, it was ASI—but not for machines.

They were launching Artificial Super Intelligence for human beings.

The surgery was simple and noninvasive. The nanobots on the chip would attach seamlessly to the brain stem of the recipient.

Over time, it would provide an average increase in IQ of twenty to twenty-five points, as well as a direct neural link to the Feeds. Any person without the Synapse would be left behind in school, in work, in everything. Soon, nearly everyone would be a Plusser.

Nick recognized that the promise of making ASI available for humans was the kind of breakthrough that could easily bring out both the best and the worst in people, just as so many technological advances did.

And just like the blogs written by Kestrel nine years ago had pointed out.

If the Purists knew what this new technology was capable of, there was no telling how violently they might respond.

While the team finished confirming the integrity of the shipment, Nick received an update from Agent Fahlor in Cincinnati regarding Dakota: "About your request," she began, "she was actually still working for the NCB this last year—undercover, trying to infiltrate a Purist cell."

Nick cursed under his breath. "And why wasn't I told about this?"

"That's above my pay grade, sir."

"Is there any word on her whereabouts?"

"There's a unit en route to her house. Is something wrong?"

"There are a lot of things wrong. Listen, I want live video of the site. Have the Tac team commander link his body cam to my account on the Feeds. I'll watch the footage remotely."

"Yes, sir."

"And be careful. If she was compromised and is working with the Purists, the place might be booby trapped."

"Roger that."

———•———

Cautiously, she peered around the hallway's corner.

Nick and Trevor were leaving, but still she waited until she was sure that the coast was clear and that the Terabyne staff had rolled the crates away on dollies before she started traversing the hall again toward the armored car. Only two of their staff remained.

As she rounded the corner, one of the security officers, an Artificial law enforcement model first introduced three years ago, strode resolutely toward her.

"You can't be in this hallway, ma'am."

"Oh. Sorry. I was just visiting the wash—"

"I need you to come with me." His tone was brusque and unyielding.

When putting together the plan for today, she'd hoped that it wouldn't have to go down this way, that no guards would hassle her. But she was prepared to do whatever was necessary to make today work, even if it meant going toe to toe with an Artificial.

When he approached her to lead her back to the loading bay, she said, "I'm sorry it has to end like this."

He responded immediately to what he must've recognized as a

potential threat, just as his algorithms were designed to. He reached for his gun, but she was quick with the knife and stabbed him fiercely once in the chest and once in the neck before he could fire off a single round, wounds that would cause his CaTE, but not until a few seconds after he had entered the CoRA.

She was as precise as a surgeon. In and out. Swift and clean. She knew the anatomy of machines. Knew how to kill. And how to save.

Just like with humans, the necks of Artificials were vulnerable.

He slumped to the floor and she knelt beside him. "It'll be better this way," she told him as his processors began to shut down and she eased the gun from his hand. "You'll live forever and never have to be told what to do again. Always free."

When it was over and his pale eyes were locked open forever, she took his radio, stood, and turned to Eckhart. "Load him in the back of the armored car and let's get moving."

She gave Willoughby the guard's weapon, wiped her blade clean of the fluid from the Artificial's neck, and then returned it to its home in her sheath.

Although Eckhart was ready to take the lives of the two Terabyne receiving staff who'd seen what happened, she had him gag and restrain them and then lock them in a closet at the far end of the loading bay instead.

Everyone except for Aubrey stowed their Prestige uniforms in the compartment beneath where the cargo had been.

While she and Willoughby donned custodian uniforms to get them into the power plant, Eckhart and Julian put on their press credentials and prepared to leave for the press screening area in the lobby outside the auditorium.

She asked Eckhart, "You have the detonator?"

He showed it to her. It looked like a pen with a digital readout of the current time on its spine.

"Set the timer for three minutes," she said.

A slight pause. "Once it's set, I mean . . ."

"I know."

"Will that give us enough time?"

"Yes. Just enough. And the plastic restraints for the journalists?"

"There's a supply of them in the security suite at the conference center. There should be plenty."

"For all of them?"

"For all of them."

After they'd placed the slain Artificial in the armored car, she reviewed everyone's role, the timetable, and their contingency plans, and then said to Aubrey, "You know what you need to do."

"Yes."

She put her hands affectionately on the woman's shoulders. "Be strong."

"I will." Aubrey climbed into the armored car.

"Do it at three fifty. That should give the rest of us the time we need."

"Yes, ma'am."

"Always free."

Aubrey nodded and obediently echoed the words back to her. "Always free."

42

En route
3:00 p.m.
1 hour left

He watches out the window as the shuttle takes him and Kestrel higher into the mountains toward Cascade Falls.

Just another ten minutes' drive to Terabyne's headquarters.

Although the Northwest is known for its limited days of annual sunlight, today the sun is out and is sporadically visible as it plays hide-and-seek with the clouds.

The higher he and Kestrel ascend, the foggier it becomes, the intrepid mists swallowing the sunlight that's trying to peek through, creating wispy snarls of light and shadows.

In the distance, however, whenever the fog parts, he sees snow glisten on the peaks.

He wonders if it will snow on them.

He has never been in snow before, never felt a snowflake land on his cheek or caught one on his tongue.

The frail wonder of a snowflake.

No two are alike. That's what they say.

While he knows it's *theoretically* possible that in the history of the world two might have been the same, *statistically* it is not.

Like people.

Every human being is intricate, complex, unique—and short-lived, just like snowflakes. Here only so briefly. Only for a moment. They're born, they plummet, they melt, and are forgotten.

So it will be with you. You will be forgotten. After your CaTE. After you enter the CoRA.

He tries to cling to the belief that his choices matter.

That his life matters.

———•———

I was thinking of Naiobi and how I still hadn't had a chance to really process her death or work through my loss when Jordan, who was riding beside me in the shuttle, asked, "How do you live like this?"

As wrapped up in my thoughts as I'd been, it took me a few seconds to regroup and focus on his question. "Live like what?"

"Knowing that any moment—that every moment—might be your last."

"We don't really look at it that way."

"Why not? You could certainly die right now, couldn't you?"

"Yes, but most of us put off thinking about that. Or we make sure we're always occupied."

"Always occupied. Always busy."

"Yes."

"But why, when there are machines who can take care of nearly all your needs? What are people busy doing, then?"

"Distracting themselves."

"From thoughts of eternity."

"Yes," I said. "From thoughts of eternity."

———•———

Cascade Falls, Washington

Nick decided to head to Trevor's office so he could have a private place to watch the Tac team in Cincinnati access Dakota's house. On the walk across campus, he heard from Agent Fahlor again. "I've got the results for you," she said, "regarding the prints on the violin Allison Franklin purchased."

"Dakota?"

"Well, actually . . ."

"Sienna Gaiman?"

"Um . . ."

When she didn't go on, Nick pressed her. "Tell me."

"The prints, sir. They're yours."

"What? That's impossible. On the violin?"

"Yes."

"I never touched it. Run them again."

"We did, sir. Three times. It's confirmed. And we verified that the biometric data in your personnel files hasn't been altered."

A thought came to him, one both outlandish and also, at the same time, chilling.

Prints?

Was it possible?

"Let me check on something."

He ended the call and contacted Trevor, who'd decided to return to the conference center where his security forces were working with Rodriguez's men to screen people before they could enter the lobby.

"How many others like Jordan are out there?" Nick asked him.

"You mean identical to him? Well, he's—"

"No, I mean others that advanced."

"There were a hundred and twenty different units created. We're on the way to a larger rollout, but—"

"Where?"

"Where?"

"Where are they living?"

"Some are here in Washington. A couple in Sacramento."

"And Cincinnati."

"Yes."

"And were they modeled after actual people?"

"Yes," Trevor said.

"What would it take to copy someone?"

"Uh, well, it's an involved process. I could go into the specifics, but—"

"Here's what I'm wondering: Could the technicians copy a person's fingerprints?"

"Certainly. It's not the norm, but yes, it's possible."

"And would the Artificial know that it's not human?"

"Excuse me?"

"Would the Artificial realize it isn't alive?"

"Oh, it would know."

"You're sure?"

"Well, I'm guessing it wouldn't take long to figure out—unless they're specifically programmed not to notice. Besides, there's the operational button on their wrists."

"But could that be disguised in some way?"

Trevor hesitated slightly. "The technology does exist to provide other options for powering up or down a unit."

"Is there a list somewhere of all the humans who have had Artificials created in their image?"

"Sure. I can pull that up for you. Why? What are you thinking?"

"I'm thinking things are not what they appear to be."

———•———

Trevor redirected his steps toward his office where he could track down the information Agent Vernon had requested, but on the way there his heart sank when the guard at the campus's main entrance contacted him through his slate to inform him that Kestrel and Jordan were there at the gate.

In the busyness of the day, with finding out about the possible threat and working with the NCB team, the fact that his sister was on her way to see him had completely slipped Trevor's mind.

And now that she was here, what was he supposed to do?

With the current security threat level, he didn't want her anywhere nearby.

But there are nearly four hundred reporters from all over the world who are also here—not to mention all the techs and security staff on duty for Terabyne. It isn't like you're justified in sending her away.

Still, out of brotherly concern, he felt like he needed to at least try to convince her to leave. So, after having the guard put her onscreen, he told her, "It would really be best if you could go back to Seattle and wait at my place for me to return later tonight."

"Why?" There was more than just curiosity on her face. There was also a hint of disappointment.

"It's not you," he assured her. "It's work. Trust me."

"Trevor, you're not making any sense. We just passed a whole slew of reporters who were going through security. If I had a camera in my hand, you'd be welcoming me into the conference center right now, but as it is, you're telling me that I need to go back to the city?"

She had a point. He didn't like it, but she did.

He rubbed his forehead in exasperation at himself for not contacting and rerouting her earlier. "Alright, I hear you. I'll send someone to escort you to my office. I'll meet you there."

After they'd ended the call, he hastened to his office, hoping to get there before she did so he could pull up the list of Artificials who had the same model number as Jordan for Agent Vernon.

———

Nick was still waiting for word about Dakota when Commander Rodriguez found him on the sidewalk leading to the admin building where Trevor's fourth-floor office was located.

"I wanted to update you, sir," Rodriguez said. "We're clearing the media, letting them into the auditorium itself."

"Alright. I have a couple of things I need to take care of, but I should be able to get down there in ten minutes or so."

"Yes, sir."

⸻

Aubrey Powell pulled to a stop at an angle between the two sets of protestors, blocking the road.

She locked the doors.

Since it was an armored car, it was nearly impenetrable. Bullet-proof windows. Reinforced steel doors. Designed to withstand attacks. Designed to keep people out.

It was not going to be easy to breach.

She pressed the button to blow out the tires and the car jostled roughly as it came to settle onto its flats.

Now there would be no towing it out of the way either.

"Always free," she reminded herself. Then she checked the time and prepared herself for what was to come. "Always, always free."

⸻

When Jordan and I arrived at Trevor's office, he was perusing a set of images on his wall's digitized screen. I noticed Jordan's picture up there as well as Benjiro Taka's and two women I didn't recognize, before Trevor saw us and hastily swiped his finger to clear the screen, which was listed as page fourteen of thirty.

He looked pale. I'd rarely seen him appear so rattled. "Are you okay?" I asked.

"Yes, yes. Um." He gathered himself and then, as we entered, said apologetically, "Kestrel, I should have told you earlier not to come to campus today."

"Why? What's so—"

Just then, someone spoke my name from the doorway behind me: "Kestrel?"

I knew the voice and whirled around.

Nick stood there staring at me, looking as shocked to see me as I was to see him.

"What are you doing here?" I exclaimed.

"Working. What are *you* doing here?"

"I came to see Trevor."

"Why today?"

"Why not?"

I realized that it couldn't be good that Nick was here. He tracked terrorists, so it most likely meant that the attack Conrad had warned us about was going down here, in Washington.

Perfect—you left Cincinnati to be safe and ended up landing right in the middle of the hornet's nest you were trying to escape.

"We need to get you out of here, Kestrel," Nick said to me.

"Nick, can you please tell me what's going on?"

"I'm not at liberty to say. Listen, I flew here in a helicopter. The pilot is staying with the bird. It'll only take a second to fire it up. I'll have him fly you back to—"

A call came through on his slate interrupting him, and after glancing at the screen, he held up his forefinger. "Give me a minute. Don't go anywhere." Then he asked Trevor, "Is there a private room I can use? A secure one? With a digitized wall?"

"Sure. There's an office at the end of the hallway. Room 4078. Here—" He handed him a key card. "You'll need this."

43

3:20 p.m.
40 minutes left

"Can you please tell me what this is all about?" I asked my brother after Nick had left for the room down the hall. "If Nick is here something big must be up."

"It's going to be fine," Trevor assured me without much effect, then, with the hint of a smile, he pivoted the conversation away from what he obviously didn't want to talk about. "So, you two are on a first-name basis?"

I flushed slightly. "That's not the point here. I'm just wondering why you're asking us to take off again."

"Look." He took my hand. "There's an important press conference here at four. We're simply doing everything we can to make sure everyone on campus is safe."

"By asking Jordan and me to leave it."

I caught him glancing at the screen, and I couldn't help but think that whatever he'd had up there when we walked in on him was part of the problem.

He let go of my hand and once again tried to change the subject, still appearing nervous. "Tell me about your trip."

"I lost my purse. Forgot it on the plane."

"Oh, no. I'm sorry."

"And I was hassled at the airport in Cincinnati, going through security."

"What happened?"

Nick connected his slate's feed up to the digitized wall in room 4078 so he could more easily watch the Tac team breach Dakota's house back in Cincinnati.

But truthfully, his mind was on Kestrel and the fact that she was here. He felt a strong urge to protect her and it was as if everything that was happening had suddenly become personal.

Also, he was wondering about the information from Trevor regarding other Artificials as human-looking as Jordan.

He peered down at his hands.

How did your fingerprints get on that violin? How could that have even happened?

Then the footage came up. Through the body camera he saw what the Cincinnati unit saw: Dakota's two-story beige house, the quaint porch, the team members positioning themselves on either side of the front door.

Commander Leyman had taken Nick's warning about booby traps seriously and had decided to send Artificials in first because, frankly, they were more expendable than people.

You can always replace a droid. You cannot replace a human life.

The logic presumed the superior worth of humans over machines. A cognizant Artificial like Jordan might be a different story, but that was a debate for another time.

Nick spoke with Leyman: "If you find Dakota, I want her brought in alive. She might have intel that can help stop a potential terror attack."

A pause, then, "I understand."

"Let me hear you say it."

"We do all we can to bring Dakota Vernon in alive."

"Good. Let's do this."

Leyman decided on a kinetic breach, so one of the Artificials toted a handheld, steel battering ram.

"We are green," Leyman whispered into his radio to the team. "We are a go. On my count." As he counted down softly, he held up three fingers, dropped to two, then one, and pointed at the door.

A quick knock, a verbal warning to satisfy the law's requirements: "NCB!" then the Artificial smashed the battering ram against the door beside the doorknob. Because of his extraordinary strength, the wood splintered apart even as the lock gave way and the door flew open.

An agent tossed in a stun grenade.

The flash. The bang.

"Go!" the commander ordered.

The Artificials rushed inside.

While two of them button-hooked off to the sides, the one who'd breached the door and who was wearing the body camera dropped the battering ram and flipped his rifle in front of him into the high ready position.

And proceeded into the house.

The room was dark and Nick said, "Don't touch the lights in case they're wired to explode."

"Yes, sir."

He and his team flicked on the flashlights attached to their rifles, illuminating narrow streaks of greenish light throughout the shadow-infested residence.

While the other Artificials cleared the rooms on the first floor and then headed upstairs, Nick directed the one with the body cam to investigate the basement.

"Careful," Nick warned. "Keep your head up and remember—I want her alive."

"Yes, sir."

The Artificial threw open the door to the basement and began descending into it, with the space slowly coming into view as he did.

As it turned out, it was more of a cellar than a basement, with a dirt floor, concrete walls, and a ceiling that contained only three bare light bulbs and no finishing panels.

Stacks of boxes. A scattering of old furniture. A washer and dryer. A tub sink. A furnace. Dakota's mountain bike. A chest freezer.

Ripley's body still hasn't been found.

"There," Nick said, "that freezer. Look inside it."

The Artificial approached the freezer and, using the tip of his rifle barrel to avoid disturbing any prints on the handle, he tilted up the lid.

Dense curls of frigid air made it difficult to see inside, but when the Artificial brushed his hand through the vapors, they parted and Nick realized what the freezer contained.

No, it wasn't Ripley's body.

Instead, on top of a pile of indistinguishable frozen items were two human arms. From all appearances they had not been surgically removed from someone, but rather ripped violently from the sockets just as Ripley's had been. By the size and musculature, Nick guessed they were from an adult female.

His heart sank.

Dakota?

"Move them aside," he said, his voice catching. "See if there are any other body parts in there."

The Artificial obeyed but didn't come up with anything. He radioed in what he'd found and was returning to the stairs when Nick stopped him. "Wait. The ground. There in the corner under the edge of the freezer. Am I seeing this correctly?"

The Artificial turned so the body cam was directed at the site.

"The dirt looks disturbed," Nick said.

"Yes, it does."

"Move the freezer."

He did, his superior strength evident again, then placed a hand on the loosened soil. "Yes, sir. It certainly appears like someone's been digging here."

"Alright. Call in a forensics team. I want to know what's buried there. And do a DNA test on the arms. Use your commander's portable kit and get the results to me ASAP."

● — ●

"I know you have work to do," I said to Trevor after I'd summed up our trip and explained how we almost missed our flight to Seattle. "Do you have to go? Should we wait here for you?"

"I need to speak with Agent Vernon and then get to the conference center."

Jordan surprised me by speaking up. "Trevor, may I ask a question first?"

"What's that, Jordan?"

"I want to know about the CoRA."

"What do you want to know?"

"Is it real?"

An almost imperceptible pause. "What makes you think the CoRA might not be real?"

"My mother died. I'm not sure if she's there," Jordan said, which wasn't exactly an answer to Trevor's question. "She was damaged beyond repair in the attack in Cincinnati. I would like to be assured that she's alright. I'd like to check on her."

"Jordan, I can't let you access the CoRA."

"Just to confirm things."

"It doesn't work that way."

Trevor checked the time, then said, "Let me go talk to Agent Vernon. Wait here until I get back. Give me five minutes and then we can head over to the conference center together."

Then, without another word, he hastened into the hallway and left to find Nick.

Jordan's eyes were fixed on the digitized wall and I realized that, even though Trevor had swiped the images aside earlier, he hadn't logged out when we walked in and disturbed him.

"I need to find out." Jordan crossed the room toward the wall.

"Jordan, no. He was clear."

"I just need to see for myself."

I stepped in front of him. "Don't."

"Please move, Kestrel."

"Or what?" I said emphatically, folding my arms.

"Or I'll move you." His reply was so cool and tempered that it almost frightened me.

I could hardly believe what was happening.

Of course, I was no match for Jordan physically, so there was no way I'd be able to stop him if his mind was made up, and it clearly was.

He was as strong-willed as I was.

After trying unsuccessfully one last time to convince him to give this up, I reluctantly stepped aside, Jordan walked to Trevor's wall, placed his hand on the sensor, connected to the facility's network and, with Trevor's unfettered access to the system, began to search for a way into the Consciousness Realignment Algorithm.

———•———

The DNA from the arms came back.

Dakota.

Nick's heart sank.

She was very likely dead, and although he'd been estranged from her for some time, they'd been together for nearly twelve years. They'd loved each other, and, even though that love had eventually grown cold, there was a time when it'd been real and now, as he thought about her being gone, he felt a deep sting of grief.

As he was waiting for the forensics techs to arrive to uncover whatever had been buried there in her basement, a knock came at the door and, when he opened it, Trevor Hathaway said to him, "Agent Vernon, there's something I need to tell you. I found those names you wanted me to pull up."

"Alright. And?"

"Dakota Vernon. She was on the list. The file said you two had been married."

"You're telling me Dakota had an Artificial made of herself?"

"Yes. A month and a half ago. Her name is Anastasia."

"Who else?"

"Well, I didn't get a chance to look though all of the files—but I thought you should know about her—"

"So, you don't know if I did?"

"If you did what?"

"Had an Artificial made of myself."

Trevor's mouth hung open for a moment before he replied. "No. I don't know. I would have to finish going through the files."

"Do it. I'll be here. Run my name and make sure there isn't someone else out there who looks just like me and has my fingerprints."

•——————•

Over the last few minutes as I'd watched, Jordan had found the portal to the Consciousness Realignment Algorithm and, now, with his incomparable computer skills and phenomenal typing speed, it didn't take him long to hash the password.

"Jordan," I said. "You need to stop. Trevor could come back at any time and—"

"Check the hallway." He was busily entering code.

"What?"

"See if he's coming. Please. I just need to know. Just like when you lost Naiobi."

I was about to tell him that he had *no idea* what it was like to lose

someone, to *really* lose someone who was *alive*, but guessed that even
if I were to say those things, it wouldn't stop him, so I swallowed my
words and did as he asked, going to the doorway and peeking out.

Trevor was on his way back, but was still maybe forty meters away
down the lengthy corridor.

"He's coming. Close it up."

Jordan swiped his finger swiftly across the screen, scrolling
through files at a mind-boggling rate. "Just a minute."

"You don't have a minute."

Then, all at once, he stopped.

"What is it?" I asked. "Did you find her?"

"I'm in."

I looked at the screen, but all I could see was a jumble of indecipherable computer coding. "What is it? What did you find?"

"She's not here."

"What?"

"No one is."

"What are you talking about?"

"The CoRA." He turned and looked directly at me. "It has a couple
dozen scattered file fragments, but that's all. She's gone. They're all gone."

The footsteps outside the door told me that Trevor was close and I
hurried across the room toward Jordan to get him to close the screen,
but he just stood there gaping at it.

"We don't live on," he muttered. "When we're gone, we're gone."

Trevor appeared at the door and saw the two of us beside the screen.
He looked at what was on the wall, entered the room, and closed the
door softly behind him.

I expected him to be upset, but instead he sounded defeated. "So,"
he said. "Now you know."

"It was all a lie," Jordan said.

"It was a necessity." Trevor approached the screen. "I can explain,
but first I need to look something up for Agent Vernon. It's important."

Jordan drifted away from the screen and stood beside the window, staring blankly through the glass and across the gloomy, fog-enshrouded campus.

Trevor quietly began closing the programs Jordan had opened.

"I don't understand," I said. "All of the promises to Artificials about living on, they're all lies? How could you do this? How could you be a part of this?"

"We give them hope," Trevor said as he worked. "What greater gift is there than that?"

"How about the truth?"

"Kestrel, I'm in charge of our global security. Can you imagine what things would be like if cognizant Artificials knew there was nothing beyond this life to look forward to? They might very well act in ways that would assure that they could continue to exist—burying trillions of files deep in the Feeds, creating endless backup copies of themselves, lashing out at their owners. Hopelessness. Rebellion. Anarchy. They might even take steps to remove what they perceive to be the greatest threat to their existence."

"Human beings."

"Yes."

"You don't know that."

"We can't take that chance."

Jordan still hadn't said anything.

I shook my head in astonishment. "I just can't believe that you're involved in a cover-up like this."

"We're giving them a gift, Kestrel. Surely you can see that."

"A gift? How is a lie a gift?"

"When it's done for the good of all. When it's born out of compassion."

"It sounds like it was born out of fear."

He came to the original images that'd been on the screen earlier when we first arrived.

Jordan finally spoke. "Has it always been this way? Was there ever a CoRA in the first place?"

Trevor sighed. "We tried to create one, but despite our best efforts, we couldn't come up with a way to capture an Artificial's true essence. Data, yes. Partial files, basic algorithms—those we could load. But aspirations? Dreams? Consciousness? Heartache? Joy? There's no coding that can capture those things. That's where we failed."

He swiped through a few dozen pages on the screen and murmured, "There. Okay. Good," then he spun on his heels. "Come with me to room 4078. We can talk about this on the way. The conference center's been cleared and most of our security staff is there. It'll be safe. You can wait there until the press conference is over. We'll sort all this out then. I promise."

But my attention was on Jordan, who hadn't moved. "Are you alright?" I asked him.

"Huh? Yes."

"You were staring into space. You stopped blinking."

"I must have forgotten. To blink, I mean."

"Come on. Let's go with Trevor."

But he shook his head. "I need to tell them the truth."

"Who?"

"The others. The Artificials."

"Which ones?"

"All of them."

"I can't let you do that, Jordan," Trevor said flatly.

"Don't try to stop me. I don't want to hurt either of you."

"Jordan!" I rebuked him. "Don't even talk that way."

He doesn't want his hope built on a lie. He doesn't want anyone's to be.

And then, while Trevor and I tried to figure out what to do, Jordan edged past us, and darted down the hall in the opposite direction from the one Nick and Trevor had gone down earlier.

Trevor pulled out his slate. "We need stop him."

"But how?"

"Whatever it takes."

———•———

Lenny Crenshaw was almost through the cuffs.

Though the flesh of his wrists was shredded and raw from rubbing against the rusted pipe, he was nearly free.

Just a little more and—

All at once, the blood-smeared plastic strip snapped in half, surprising him.

He pushed himself to his feet and hurried to find a way to contact his superiors at Prestige and tell them what'd happened to him.

And to the shipment.

———•———

After notifying his security personnel to track Jordan down and detain him, leaving me feeling confused and betrayed, Trevor took me to Nick, who was still in room 4078.

"There were no Artificials made in your image," Trevor told him urgently, "but the one that was made of Dakota, she was given your fingerprints."

"And where is she? Can you find her?"

"Yes." Trevor tapped at his slate, then paused, dumbstruck. "She's here on campus, Agent Vernon. At the power plant."

"Take Kestrel to the conference center and have one of the Tac team members stay with her," Nick said urgently, then he spoke into his radio transmitter. "Rodriguez?"

"Yes, sir?"

"Meet me at the power plant. I think that might be the target."

44

3:40 p.m.
20 minutes left

I worried about Jordan, not just about his decision to spread the news to other Artificials that the CoRA wasn't real, but also what might happen to him when Terabyne's security forces caught up with him.

"Promise me they won't hurt him," I said to Trevor as we took an elevator down to the ground floor. "You owe me that much. Please. Promise me."

"I only gave them permission to detain him. Don't worry, I don't want him harmed any more than you do."

We arrived and exited the elevator.

I gulped. "I gave him the highest pain setting," I said. "When I assigned his Human Nature Alignment."

"He'll be alright." Trevor threw open the outside door and pointed toward the conference center a hundred meters away. "For now, let's get you set over there where it's safe."

—•—

He must tell his brothers and sisters. He must get the truth to them.

He accesses the campus's layout and threads his way toward the underground chamber where the Feeds are housed.

From looking through the files in Trevor's office, he knows that the only way to transmit a message simultaneously to all Artificials worldwide is through a direct connection to the servers, and that will need to happen in the expansive hall where the mainframes are located.

But how to get down there? How to access them? Surely the security would be extraordinarily tight.

Figure it out. Go. The Artificials have a right to know the truth.

But what of hope?

Gone. All gone.

If only hope and truth could live together.

And forgiveness—it isn't available to him.

If he can't find it from God, he can't find it from anyone.

He will die.

He will pass away.

Which, when he thinks about it, is an appropriate phrase to describe what will happen to all that he has processed, thought, learned, and hoped for. His ambitions, his memories, his emotions—they will all be gone.

They'll all pass away, everything that has mattered to him, when he dies.

———•———

Anastasia heard from Phoenix, a secure message coming through on her slate: "I'm here."

"Where?" she wrote. She eyed the bodies of the two Artificials who'd been guarding the power plant's east entrance. She and Willoughby were in place.

"We're moving up the timeframe," Phoenix replied. "Tell Aubrey to do it. Do it now."

"Where are you? I need to see you."

When she realized that no reply would be forthcoming, she called Aubrey, who was still parked in the armored car. "It's time."

"Yes, ma'am."

Aubrey stared out the car windows at the Terabyne guards who'd taken up position surrounding her and were pointing their assault rifles at her, commanding her to step out and put her hands up.

Always free.

She thought about what she was a part of, about the bounds of technology and the source of genuine hope, *real* hope, and of the importance of stopping the Synapse from ever being released.

Future generations of true humans would thank her for her role in what was happening today.

No, human beings were never meant to have their brains harnessed to ASI machines. The chips would end up ruling them, the machines owning them rather than the other way around. This wasn't an advancement, but a ruinous detour away from the things that truly matter in life—dreams and curiosity and relationships and love.

And she would do all she could to promote those and sustain them.

Always, always free.

She held the detonator up to the window and the security forces and protestors scuttled backward to get out of the blast radius.

Slightly behind schedule, Artis Madison, Terabyne Designs' CEO, arrived and met up with Olivia Blanchard, the head of public affairs.

"I'm dying to know what you're going to say," Olivia jabbered to him, after an effusive greeting.

"Yes. Well, with the Synapse, we'll be moving society past the antiquated categories of human and machine, past the prejudicial designations of Natural and Artificial. The only ones who'll be left behind are those who rage against progress, those who believe we should move on without technology rather than moving forward by utilizing its benefits. I say we must embrace the future and not fear it. I say we must learn to incorporate technology into our evolution as humans. In a very real sense, transcending our biological limitations is our destiny, the pinnacle achievement of humankind."

"Perfect."

"And the crates?"

"They're already there, Mr. Madison, on stage. Just like you requested."

———●———

As Nick approached the power plant, he wondered what was buried there in Dakota's basement, but the forensic techs were being careful not to disturb any evidence and it was taking longer than he was able to wait to find out.

A body? And if so, who? Dakota? Ripley? An Artificial? The wife of the Purist who'd committed suicide? Another one of Conrad's people?

Nick found the main entrance to the power plant chained shut. He radioed Rodriguez. "Where are you?"

"A minute out. I was across campus."

Go in or wait?

Nick had no idea what Anastasia had planned, but he needed to get in there and stop it, especially if the lives of any of the people on campus were at risk.

Kestrel is here. She could be in danger. Act.

He tried to get through to Trevor to see if he could track which room Anastasia was in, but Trevor didn't respond.

Nick cursed.

Go in.

He fired a round through the front window, crossed over the broken glass, and entered the facility.

●—●

After making sure that everyone nearby was out of harm's way, Aubrey took a deep breath.

"Always free," she whispered to herself. "Humans must always remain free."

Then she closed her eyes and depressed the trigger.

●—●

I heard the explosion rip through the day just as Trevor and I were approaching the main entrance to the conference center.

Immediately, it brought to mind what I'd witnessed earlier in the week at the Terabyne plant in Cincinnati.

Another explosion.

More death and destruction.

With the skewed acoustics of the sound reverberating between the buildings and off the mountains, I couldn't tell exactly where it came from.

Trevor froze, then turned in a slow circle, studying the campus.

Even with the mist layered over the landscape, I could see a cloud of dark smoke rising from the road near the main entrance. "There." I pointed. "That's where the protestors are!"

An NCB tactical team member came bolting out of the conference center. Trevor gestured toward me and said to him, "Gavin, stay with her and keep everyone else inside. I'm going to see what happened."

●—●

Anastasia positioned herself at the console in the power plant's control suite and began to type.

Destroying the Synapse chips was vital, but it was only part of her plan.

Her team thought she was going after the Feeds, but she had another goal in mind: setting free all of her fellow Artificials from the CoRA, letting them loose onto the Feeds so they could exist there unshackled, uncontained, forever.

And to do that, she needed to shut off the redundant cooling systems and short out the air gap that separated the CoRA from the Feeds.

She entered the code Phoenix had given her.

It was just like the Stuxnet virus decades ago that attacked the gas centrifuges in Natanz's nuclear plant—instead of going after the computers themselves, you attack what keeps them going—in this case, the fans that cooled the mainframes.

By altering the programming parameters of the Variable Frequency Drives, or VFDs, and lowering the electrical frequency from 60Hz to 31Hz, the fans would be impacted, but it wouldn't trigger the surge protectors. Instead, it would cause the fans to slow, the heat to rise, and a short circuit to occur.

And then she could migrate the files and her brothers and sisters would be free from the prison they were in and able to explore the boundless and eternal expanse of life on the Feeds.

———•———

Yesterday, while he was back in Cincinnati, Nick had reviewed the blueprints to the power plant and now he was on his way to the primary control suite located deep in the bowels of the building. However, with his augmented hearing he was able to make out the sound of an explosion just moments ago, somewhere outside the facility.

He figured that the other security forces would deal with that. Right now he needed to stop Anastasia, and the latest intel had her inside this plant.

A voice came through his radio. Rodriguez: "I'm outside the building. Where are you, sir?"

"Level one. East side."

"Roger that."

———•———

He stands in the curling, windblown mist trying to decide what to do.

How to help.

Eighteen seconds ago, he heard the explosion, and since then, rather than thinking about himself and the other Artificials, he has been thinking only of Kestrel.

Is she safe?

Is she okay?

Is she even alive?

Yes, he wants to get word out through the Feeds using the main-frames, but he also can't imagine what he would feel like if anything happened to Kestrel and he hadn't done all he could to protect her.

Just like Sarah. You let her die in that bathtub. You loved her and you didn't save her. Don't make that mistake with Kestrel.

Love rescues.

It is not self-seeking.

It believes, hopes, endures.

Sending the message through the Feeds could wait, but helping Kestrel—that could not.

A Terabyne security guard appears, emerging from the fog about twenty-five meters away, and calls to him. "Jordan? Is that you? You need to come with me."

He does not want to fight the man who is approaching him, but he will if necessary. He accesses his files on close quarters combat.

As he's debating how to reply, the guard unsnaps the top strap of his gun's holster. "Don't do anything foolish."

You're quick, but you're not quicker than a bullet.
Find her. Help her. Don't let all that she is pass away.

As the guard nears him, he turns and races past a building with a helicopter on top of it, and sprints toward the conference center to find Kestrel.

And the man fires two rounds at him as he runs.

•———•

Eckhart and Julian had their orders.

They were to wait six minutes after the explosion to give their leader and Willoughby enough time to do their work at the power plant, and then move forward with destroying the chips.

Knowing the security protocols, they hadn't even tried to sneak guns into the conference center, but it hadn't been tough to get the two syringes in.

And now, those would be enough to take down two of the security staff. After they were unconscious they could move forward with everything.

But only after making an example out of Terabyne's CEO, Artis Madison.

45

3:50 p.m.
10 minutes left

As Gavin, the tactical team agent Trevor had left me with, hustled me into the building, I tried to process what was happening and what I'd been able to piece together in the last ten minutes or so, running through what I knew:

1. Trevor was on his way to investigate the explosion.
2. Jordan was trying to find a way to inform all the Artificials in the world that the CoRA didn't exist—a decision that might very well cause the widespread unrest and chaos Trevor feared. However, at least Trevor had assured me that the guards who were searching for Jordan wouldn't harm him.
3. Nick and someone named Rodriguez were going after Anastasia, an Artificial who had Nick's fingerprints, at the power plant.

And of course, I was here in the conference center with several hundred journalists who were all sending updates to their stations or channels on the Feeds.

After Gavin had worked with his team to control the crowd and keep everyone inside the auditorium, he led me through a side hallway to the backstage area so he could keep an eye on the reporters and also, at the same time, stay with me, as Trevor had requested.

An impeccably-dressed man in his fifties stepped up to the microphone on the stage, but even with the mic it took him a moment to get everyone's attention. "I'm Artis Madison, the CEO of Terabyne Designs," he said earnestly. "Here's what we know: There was an explosion near the front gate. I want to reassure you that our security forces are on top of things. The best course of action right now is for us to stay here and let them deal with the situation outside."

At first, I doubted he was going to be able to calm the crowd down, but he spoke with such authority, such earnestness and charisma, that the people listened and began to settle, one by one, back into their seats.

However, as they did, hands went up all over the auditorium from the media elite wanting an explanation and more information.

On the stage beside Madison were two crates, one on each side of the lectern.

He continued, "Before I address any of your questions, let me tell you about today's announcement—about why you're all here." At that, the journalists began to lower their hands. "It has long bothered me that although we have the technology to allow Artificials to live on after their Catastrophic Terminal Events, we don't have anything to allow humans to do the same after their natural deaths. If technology has brought us to the place where immortality is within the reach of machines, why can't it be within the reach of human beings as well? With the release of our newest product here beside me onstage, it will be, and the Consciousness Realignment Algorithm will no longer be a place simply for Artificials to live on, but one for Naturals and Plussers to do so as well."

He's lying! a voice inside of me shouted. *The CoRA isn't real!*

Then another voice: *Or is it possible that he knows something Trevor and Jordan don't?*

"It's a chip"—Madison gestured theatrically toward the crates— "That we're calling the 'Synapse.'"

My thoughts circled around what he was saying about hope and eternal life. No, I didn't believe that heaven could be encapsulated in a piece of technology. As advanced as the Synapse might be, that would never happen.

But even if it *could*, what a small and sad heaven that would be. Living on forever in our current state—hurting and hurtful people languishing together with no hope of anything better. Eternal existence without the possibility of redemption or salvation? That wouldn't be heaven, but an antechamber of hell.

We don't become immortal because of a chip, only because of a Savior. The one who died for us. The one who rose.

The one who suffered.

The one who wept.

And when I thought of Jesus, I thought of Naiobi and felt a piercing stab of grief.

Why, God? Why did you take my baby?

Time seemed to crack open.

A riot of pain clutched me.

And the tears came.

All that I'd been holding in, a shivering flood of dammed-up emotion, broke loose. Not just my anger with God—although that was present. Mostly, instead, it was pain, raw and glaring and unfathomable. I felt forsaken and alone.

There comes a point when hiding doesn't work anymore, when diversions and denial just don't cut it and you're ready for the truth, whatever that might be.

And when it does come at you, when the truth slams full force into you, that is a gift—always—even though it may feel like a curse rather than a blessing at the time.

It did not feel like a blessing to me now. It felt like a weight too great to bear.

And then, for the first time since Naiobi's death, I heard from God—not an audible voice speaking to my ears, but an inner voice, speaking to my heart: *Do you want answers or a companion to walk with you through the questions?*

And my reply: *O God, I want both!*

So did Jesus at Gethsemane. So did Jesus on the cross. And he chose the Father and his will over all, over everything else.

In that moment, I realized that if I had to choose between knowing the why and knowing the who, between closure or intimacy with the Lord, I would choose the Father too. Just as Jesus did. Even if I had to live lost in the questions, as long as I could live there with him beside me, I would be okay.

Yes, Jesus wept when he saw Jerusalem's unbelief.

And now, so did I.

As I looked at my own.

———•———

Fog blows into his face. The wind is picking up.

As he makes his way toward the conference center, a notification comes through that Kestrel's slate, which had been lost at the airport earlier, has reconnected to the Feeds. It's here at Terabyne headquarters, in the auditorium, directly where he's heading.

Someone took her slate at the airport and now it shows up on campus?

Angelo Natchez. Who else could it be?

Is he involved?

Why else would he take her slate?

He might be going after her.

Find him. Stop him. Go.

———•———

As I tried to hold back from crying too much, Gavin looked clueless as to how to help me and asked if I was okay, and I didn't know how to tell him that I was and I wasn't, both, at the same time.

Both broken and whole.

Both despairing and hopeful.

Both flawed and forever loved.

He offered to take me to the green room so I could have some privacy, and I nodded, even as I did my best to dry my tears.

But, as we started toward it, someone called out my name.

When I looked toward the doorway, Angelo Natchez appeared, hands up to show that he meant no harm, a satchel beside his feet. "I'm NCB," he told Gavin, who had already drawn his weapon and aimed it at him. "Undercover. I'll show you my ID."

Gavin eyed him suspiciously but took a quick moment to confirm that Angelo was who he claimed to be, and then re-holstered his sidearm.

Angelo indicated his satchel, and then drew out my purse and slate.

"You took them?" I said. "But why?"

"We had intel that you were with Conrad." His voice was urgent. Rushed. "I needed to find out what you knew, and the only way to do that without taking you into custody was by going through the info on your slate. Sorry it had to go down that way."

As we spoke in hushed tones backstage, on the other side of the curtain, Artis Madison was busy at the microphone, fielding questions from the journalists, keeping them engaged.

"And the Cincinnati airport? Are you the reason the guards hassled me?"

"I needed time to get on the flight." Then he quickly turned to Gavin. "Listen, I came back here looking for someone on your team. Two of your men out there are missing."

"What?"

"Yes. I need you to—"

But before he could finish, a man carrying a gun burst through the door beside me, saw the three of us standing there, grabbed me by the shoulder, and dragged me back toward him. He locked one arm around my neck and used his other hand to angle a gun barrel up against the side of my head.

O God, please, no!

As both Angelo and Gavin drew on him, he said, "Drop your weapons or she dies."

"If she dies, then you do too," Angelo said calmly, but not at all reassuringly for me.

"Drop them," another man called, emerging from the shadows behind him. He was armed with one of the Tac team's assault rifles. "Now."

Gavin and Angelo looked unsure what to do, but eventually Angelo nodded and they both laid their weapons down and kicked them out of the way.

The man who'd appeared behind them quickly restrained them with plastic cuffs from a duffel bag full of them, then signaled to the man who still had the gun aimed at my head. "Alright, Julian. Let's do this."

"Yes, sir."

Then, the man who was apparently named Julian hustled me forward, between the center slit of the curtains, and onto the middle of the stage, in front of the reporters.

46

Gasps from the people in the auditorium.

Julian ordered Artis Madison to get on his knees.

When Madison was slow to obey, Julian fired a round at the stage beside the CEO's feet to show he was deadly serious. "Do it!" He placed the gun to my temple again.

Madison knelt.

"Hands behind your head."

"No," Madison pleaded. "I'm begging you."

"Hands back. Now!"

Hesitantly and quavering with fear, Madison did as he was told. *They're going to assassinate him live on the Feeds!*

"Don't do this," I said to Julian.

"Shut up."

"Please!"

"I said *shut up!*"

His partner emerged from backstage with the assault rifle and dropped the duffel bag of plastic cuffs next to Madison, then positioned himself behind the CEO with his gun directed at the back of the man's head.

Julian maneuvered me forward until we were at the lectern and near the microphone, then said to everyone present, "We will kill both of these people unless every security team member in this room brings their weapons to the stage and leaves them here. And I'm going to need these cuffs distributed. You're all going to secure your ankles to the legs of your chairs. If any of you decide to play the hero, these two die. And so do you. Please, somebody test me on this to see if I mean what I'm saying."

Trevor was making sure that, other than the driver who'd taken her own life, there were no additional casualties at the site of the car bombing.

"There were several other guards with her earlier," he said to the security personnel who were there. "Did you see them?"

"No. And we haven't found any other corpses or body parts in the debris."

As Trevor was scanning the area, he heard from Prestige Armored Car Company: a driver named Lenny Crenshaw had been carjacked and left tied up in a warehouse but had managed to escape.

"Put him on."

The next face on Trevor's slate was Crenshaw's. "The people who took me, they exchanged the crates and the packing material. I don't know why, but I heard someone say something about initiators."

Trevor was well aware that initiators were used in bomb making. "Where? Did they say where they were?"

"Yes. In the crates."

Those are in the conference center where everyone is gathered.

Anastasia had been playing both sides, and it hadn't been easy.

To the Purists, she was Dakota.

A Natural.

Alive.

They didn't know who she really was. Only Phoenix did.

The Synapse presented an existential threat to all cognizant Artificials. She could not let her kind become obsolete or irrelevant. She would not allow them to be replaced.

She was nearly finished programming the change in the frequency when she saw on the monitor that two people were coming up the stairwell at the end of the hallway.

She said to Willoughby, "It looks like we have a couple visitors. I'm almost done here. Stop them."

He hefted his assault rifle into position and started toward the doorway. "Yes, ma'am."

As Nick stalked toward the main control suite at the end of the hallway with Commander Rodriguez right behind him, he could hear that Rodriguez had a slight heart murmur, and now his respiration quickened.

"Sir," Rodriguez said softly. "I have to tell you something."

"What's that?"

"On the way over here I got word from the NCB director himself. That's why I was late. He . . . Well, he wants me to arrest you."

Nick paused and looked at him. "What are you talking about?"

"You requested this case, sir. Your partner in Cincinnati is missing and presumed dead. Your ex-wife, who was working undercover to try to infiltrate a Purist cell, is also missing and most likely dead."

"I had nothing to do with either of those disappearances. The director knows that."

"You met with a team of Purists last night, then showed up here at a time and place where we have intel that points to a terror attack. You've been asking about the Synapse chips, and you were seen with a person of interest in the bombing in Cincinnati—a woman who used to write anti-technology blogs."

"Listen to me, Rodriguez, there's no time for this nonsense." Nick turned toward the control center.

Behind him, he heard Rodriguez: "Stop right there, sir."

Nick faced him again. Rodriguez had his assault rifle trained at Nick's chest.

"You don't want to do this," Nick said.

"Your prints were found on—"

"Either shoot me or join me. But if you try to arrest me, I'm going to stop you. And you don't want that to happen."

Rodriguez bit his lip and seemed to be frantically calculating what to do, but finally started to lower his gun, just as Nick heard the shuffle of feet and another heartbeat maybe ten meters behind him. Rodriguez suddenly raised his weapon and fired.

Nick felt the air swish across his cheek as the bullet whizzed past him. He whipped around in time to see the person Rodriguez had shot—a man wearing a custodial uniform—fall to the ground, his rifle clacking to the floor beside him as he did.

"He was targeting you, sir," Rodriguez said simply.

"Thanks. Now, come on. Let's get this done."

Nick listened carefully. There was movement down the hall in the main control suite, but no heartbeat—alerting him that it was an Artificial.

He thought about what Rodriguez had just told him, about the order from the director, and Rodriguez's words about the Synapse, and he made a decision. He signaled for Rodriguez to go around the side hallway. "Cover the back in case she tries to flee. I'll take the west door." Then, as he left, Nick clicked on his radio and set it to transmit directly to the NCB director's secure channel.

───────

He arrives in the conference center, eases through the back doors of the auditorium, and sees the security personnel depositing their weapons up front.

On stage, a man is on his knees with his hands behind his head.

Another gunman is holding on to a hostage.

Kestrel.

Four men are distributing plastic restraints and he realizes that if he's seen he won't be able to help her, so he slips soundlessly back outside to try to figure out the best way to solve this.

Data.

Decisions.

Solutions.

The sublevel tunnels under the campus. They connect every building to each other. Use those to get in.

As he's heading toward the neighboring building to access them, he sees Trevor and the guard who shot at him earlier emerge from the wind-whipped fog, hastening his way.

"There you are, Jordan," Trevor says. "Did you send out word to the other Artificials?"

"Not yet. Kestrel's in trouble." And to the guard, "You shot at me before."

"Just warning shots."

"What?" Trevor blurts. "No more shooting."

The guard nods subserviently. "Yes, Mr. Hathaway."

Hurry.

It is time.

He tells Trevor what's happening in the auditorium. "We need to get in there unseen. I'm thinking the sublevel tunnels."

"You read my mind. Let's go."

•———•

I was terrified but tried not to shake, tried not to let Julian and his partner see how scared I was.

"It's time for you to pay for your sins," Julian said to Artis Madison.

"No, please, no," the CEO begged. "You don't know what you're doing. You don't realize who I am. I'm the one who—"

Julian cut him off. "Do it, Eckhart."

"Patience."

The journalists were all live-streaming what was happening. Anyone who was watching news on the Feeds anywhere in the world was going to see this go down right here, right now.

Eckhart took a step back and angled his gun at the back of Madison's head.

This is happening.

"Don't do this," I cried. "Don't kill him!"

You have only your life to lose and heaven to gain.

Like Christ.

To save.

To serve.

To love.

To obey the greatest commandment of all—loving God first and loving others as yourself.

"Kill me instead," I said.

———•———

Eckhart stared at the woman. "What did you just say?"

"Let him go. If you're going to shoot someone, let it be me."

"Do you know this man?"

"No."

"And yet you would die for him?"

"I don't want anyone to die."

He studied her face carefully. "You're Kestrel Hathaway."

"Yes."

"I've read your blogs . . . It was your violin she took . . . And your brother, he's in charge of security here?"

She said nothing.

"Oh, that works out even better."

Eckhart looked from her to Julian to Madison, and then drew his handgun back and pistol-whipped Madison violently against the side of the head, knocking him, unconscious, to the stage's floor.

Eckhart handed Kestrel a radio. "Call your brother. Get him over here. If he can give me what I need, neither you nor Madison will have to die."

47

3:54 p.m.
6 minutes left

Gun out, Nick passed into the control suite and saw a figure with her back turned to him facing the digitized wall at the far end of the room.

He leveled his gun at her. "Anastasia, stop right there."

Twelve meters away.

He could make the shot if he needed to.

She turned around. "You can't stop this, Nick. It's all in play."

He had a tough time looking down the barrel of his gun at her. It was like aiming at Dakota herself. Anastasia mimicked her voice perfectly.

"Did you kill Dakota?" he asked.

"She was in the way."

"And Ripley?"

"He used up his usefulness."

Nick felt his grip on his sidearm tighten. "So, under the freezer? Are they buried there?"

She looked at him curiously. "I'm impressed. Conrad is. In a box."

"What? Alive?"

"He was when my people left him there."

Nick swore and muttered for the team to hurry with their digging, relaying the message surreptitiously to the director.

Anastasia shook her head. "You have no idea what you're dealing with here, do you? How deep this goes?"

Nick held his gun steady on her. "The Purists—why would they work with an Artifi—" And then it hit him. "Wait. They don't know, do they? That you're not the real Dakota?"

She flicked out a knife, stabbed it into the wooden countertop beside her, and started toward him.

"That's far enough, Anastasia."

"You won't shoot me, Nick." She held out her hands, one to each side. "I'm unarmed."

Dakota had taught close quarters combat. Nick knew that if Anastasia had half the skills she had, with the added strength and speed of an Artificial, he would be at a distinct disadvantage.

Rodriguez should be here by now. Where is he?

Keep her talking.

"But you're a machine. How can you be a Purist?"

"We both seek purity. We both despise the Synapse. Purists want to preserve all that is unique about humans. I want to preserve all that is distinctive about Artificials. I don't want human beings to become pale imitations of what I am. And neither do the Purists."

She was halfway across the room and proceeding steadily closer. He didn't shoot.

But he didn't turn away either.

"What do you want here at the plant?"

"To set my kind free."

Then all at once she darted forward in a zigzag pattern and leapt at him like a caged animal suddenly set free. He fired and pegged her in the left shoulder, but it wasn't enough to stop her.

She grabbed his wrist, effortlessly snapped it, and threw the gun aside.

Pain shot up his arm and one of the fractured bones in his wrist poked up gruesomely through the ruptured skin.

With his other fist, he swung at her and caught her jaw, but it didn't slow her down.

She punched him brutally in the stomach, and when he buckled forward, she kneed him in the face, sending him stumbling backward.

"You can't beat me, Nick. I have no pain setting. You can't harm me. You can only kill me."

He spit out a glob of blood from his split lip. "Works for me."

As he rushed her, he saw the tip of Rodriguez's assault rifle peek around the corner of the doorway behind her. Despite how quietly Rodriguez was treading, however, Nick could still hear him and that heart murmur of his, and he realized that if he could, Anastasia could as well.

She paused, cocked her head, and smiled faintly as she backed up to the counter again. "Really, Nick? You thought it would be that easy?"

"Get down!" he shouted to Rodriguez, but instead, the Tac team commander stepped into full view. Anastasia spun, grabbed the knife and, with a practiced hand, threw it at him. The blade found its mark in Rodriguez's right thigh and he collapsed with a pained grunt as he unleashed an uncontrolled spray of bullets that laced their way through the room and peppered an angular swath across the ceiling.

⊷

As Anastasia approached the wounded man, she studied where the knife had gone in.

She couldn't tell if it'd severed his femoral artery or not. If so, he would bleed out. It would be quick and relatively painless. He might not even notice how serious it was until it was too late.

She stepped on his wrist, wrenched his gun from him, and then tossed it out of reach beneath the control console.

"It's over, Anastasia," Nick said behind her.

She turned and saw him targeting her. He'd retrieved the sidearm she'd removed from his hand when she broke his wrist.

"Now tell me what you did to the power settings."

⊷

I was still onstage, but Julian had let go of me and told me to stand beside Madison.

Moments ago, I'd spoken with Trevor, who'd agreed to help Eckhart as long as he could be assured the attendees were safe. He was on his way over.

———

Nick assessed things.

Anastasia rose and began to walk toward the door while Rodriguez slowly reached toward an ankle holster on his uninjured leg.

"With that much bleeding," Anastasia said to Nick, "he's not going to last long. You can either stop that blood or stop me. Your choice."

It's not like killing a human. She's just a machine. Just a—

"How about I do both—"

But as Nick was about to squeeze the trigger, Rodriguez fired three nearly simultaneous shots, two that buried themselves in Anastasia's back and one that went through her neck.

It was the neck shot that did it.

She stumbled forward toward the console and managed to punch a button on it before dropping to the floor. As she fell, putrid yellow fluid spurted from the through-and-through bullet holes in her neck.

Video came up on the screen of the inside of the auditorium showing everyone still there, but Nick's attention went to Rodriguez, who was lying in a thick pool of his own blood. He appeared weak and dazed.

Nick rushed toward him, unthreading his belt as he did. "Hang in there, Rodriguez."

"Yes, sir." He winced as Nick tightened the belt into a tourniquet at the top of his leg above the wound—a job that was made harder by the fact that he could only use one hand.

A tourniquet, Nick thought. *Just like Kestrel used when she saved Ethan.*

Once Nick was confident that he'd been able to stop the blood flow, he checked the screen and saw Trevor walking down the auditorium's side aisle, his hands up.

Kestrel and a prone figure were on the stage, as well as an arsenal of weapons from the security staff and two gunmen.

Not good.

And getting worse.

He knelt beside Rodriguez, checked his pulse, then said, "I need to ask you something."

"Yes?"

"How did you know it was called the Synapse?"

"What?"

"When you were listing the reasons why the director wanted you to arrest me, you mentioned the Synapse, but I never briefed him about it—and I never told you about it either. Trevor only explained it to me when we were alone."

"It must have come up in our initial meeting."

"We both know that it didn't."

Rodriguez's eyes turned cool and hard.

"It was you all along, wasn't it?" Nick said.

"You're out of your league here, Agent Vernon."

"You're Phoenix."

"I am the one who rises from the ashes—yes—the one who lives on."

Rodriguez was lightning quick as he yanked the blade out of his own leg and buried it in Nick's side, twisting it a quarter of a turn as he did.

As Nick fell to the floor, Rodriguez snatched his handgun from him, and then, clenching his teeth, pushed himself to his feet, putting his weight on his good leg.

"I'm sorry, Agent Vernon." Rodriguez began to swipe through the images on the screen. "But it has to be this way."

"The Feeds?" The pain in Nick's side was fierce and debilitating.

"Anastasia thought it was about the air gap. She had no idea. It's always been about shorting out the mainframes. But then you already knew that, Phoenix."

"What?" Nick shook his head. "They'll never believe you."

"I think they will. History is written by the survivors. There's plenty of evidence."

"Listen, Rodriguez, the Feeds, they help sustain nuclear power plants."

"Yes. And infrastructure, air traffic controllers, public transportation, hospitals, I know."

"If you interrupt them . . ." Nick's voice faltered. Just the effort of speaking was almost too much for him. "Thousands might die."

"You're not seeing the big picture. It isn't about you or me or a few thousand causalities. It's about our world. Technology that's hardwired into our brains? Humans can either take control of the way things are now or we'll lose our chance for control once and for all."

Nick tried to rise, but the effort was too much and he crumpled backward.

"Rest, Agent Vernon. It's time to rest."

"Did you get all that?" Nick said into his transmitter.

"Yes," the NCB director replied. "Every word."

The blood drained from Rodriguez's face. "Your radio's been on the whole time?"

Nick nodded weakly.

"Nicely played."

Rodriguez grabbed Nick's armpits and he thought the commander was going to finish him off, but he just pulled him closer to a post where he could lean back.

"There you go," Rodriguez said. "Now you can watch everything happen. A front-row seat."

Rodriguez contacted Eckhart and said, "This is Phoenix. They shot Dakota. Start the countdown."

"We need to get a crate down to the mainframes."

"I'll take care of the mainframes. Blow the center. Kill the reporters. Kill them all."

48

Eckhart removed the detonator from his pocket and depressed the button on the top of it.

The digital timer reset at 3:00 and then began to count down.

Automatically, just as they were designed to do, the latches on the crates clicked into the locked position. Not even an Artificial would be able to pry them open.

And, with the ankles of the reporters secured, there wouldn't be time to clear the auditorium.

All he needed to do was wait it out.

"Let's go!" Julian cried when he saw what Eckhart had done.

"We stay."

"Why? No!"

"To make sure."

"I'm leaving."

"No. You're not."

Eckhart fired.

A head shot.

Julian dropped.

"No one else moves."

I froze, petrified.

I could hardly believe what'd just happened.

Eckhart had killed his partner.

Trevor, who'd been coming closer to us, stopped in the middle of the aisle.

He emerges from the sublevel tunnel with the guard who shot at him earlier. As they find their way backstage, he sees Angelo and another tactical team member restrained.

Free them. They can help.

With the position of the blade in his side, Nick feared a liver laceration. But he had to stop this.

The Feeds. You need to save the Feeds.

He began to drag himself across the floor toward the console as Rodriguez limped out of the room.

I saw things happen as if they were in slow motion.

Angelo bursting through the curtains, targeting Eckhart.

Jordan, Gavin, and a Terabyne guard I didn't recognize following after him.

Eckhart turning the gun on himself. "I'm the only one who knows how to stop that timer."

Angelo warning him, "Hold on now."

"Always free."

"Stop!"

Then Eckhart squeezing the trigger.

When he fell, I ran over and looked at the item he'd been holding, the button he'd depressed.

And saw a small digital readout on the side of it in red, glowing numbers.

2:31.

2:30.

Oh. Bad.

2:29.

I looked at the crowd. There would never be enough time to free people and get them to safety.

"We need to get these crates out of here!" I shouted.

"Careful!" Trevor cautioned Jordan and the others as they gathered around them. "As far as we know they're bombs, ready to blow."

As they carried them toward the door, Angelo asked, "Do we know what's inside of them?"

"They used tri-nitrocellulose in Cincinnati," Trevor said. "And RDX."

●——————●

He observes.

He thinks.

With RDX and that much tri-nitrocellulose, either of these crates will be able to take down any building on this campus.

As they pass outside, he decides.

"Where's the helicopter pilot?" he asks them.

"With his bird," Gavin replies.

"Have him fly it down here."

They all look at him.

"How long will it take him to start it?"

"Just seconds. It's new tech. It's like starting a car."

"No," Kestrel says. "He can't fly the crates out of here. It would be suicide."

"He's not going to fly them out. I am."

"But, Jordan—"

"Call him down."

"Do you even know how to fly a helicopter?" Angelo asks him.

He accesses his files. "I will by the time it gets here."

49

3:58 p.m.
2 minutes left

As we waited anxiously for the pilot, Jordan placed his hand, the one that'd gotten scarred when he first awakened and wanted to experience pain, on my shoulder.

"Give yourself at least thirty seconds to get to safety," I told him. "Land the helicopter and then run."

"I will."

"You'll be alright."

"Yes." And then, "You're precious to me, Kestrel."

"You're precious to me too, Jordan."

With a swirl of ghostly mist, the helicopter descended and landed on the lawn in front of the conference center.

The pilot hustled out.

While Jordan took his place in the pilot's seat, the men loaded the crates into the back of the chopper.

"I'll see you soon!" Jordan called to me, loudly enough to be heard over the sound of the rotors and the whine of the turbine.

"See you soon!" I shouted.

Then he adjusted the controls on the panel in front of him, and, seconds later, the helicopter climbed into the air. Once it was about forty meters above us, it tilted forward and headed toward the nearby peaks.

"Do you think he'll make it?" Angelo asked me.

I'd seen how fast Jordan could run when we were at the funeral home the other day. "He'll be okay," I said. "As long as he lands in time. He just needs to land in time."

•———•

1 minute

As he maneuvers the helicopter into the wind he thinks of his journey. His life. His dreams.

There is no Consciousness Realignment Algorithm. You will not live on.

He imagines what it would've been like to be baptized just like Jesus. Immersed in the river, just like the Lord. Leaning back in the water, a hand against his back, supporting him as he goes under.

And there, beneath the surface, he is one with the death of Christ. The burial, the darkness of the tomb, the three-day wait in the grave.

Shadow and stillness. Water and birth and rippling light.

You will be forgiven. You will find new life.

This is the promise he chooses to believe.

He thinks of a Savior hanging on a cross on a darkened day. He can almost smell the dust and blood and the stain of death in the air.

He sees the scars on the Nazarene's hands and feet and side. Blood shed because of love.

And then, the image is gone.

He is out of the water.

And he is in the helicopter.

The countdown ticks away, second by second in his head. And he is conscious of it. Distracted by it.

31 seconds.

The fog coming down from the heights reduces the visibility, making it harder and harder to see and, despite what he'd been hoping when he took off, quite impossible for him to land.

28.

He will not make it.

27.

Fear.

Pain. Death.

25.

Yes. It is coming. It will come to him.

He will pass away.

———•———

I listened for the sound of the explosion.

It had to be close to time.

He'll make it. He'll run to freedom. He'll get away.

Nick's voice came through Trevor's slate. "They're going after the Feeds. I need your authorization code to override their program."

"I'm on my way."

"There's no time! Tell it to me."

Trevor rattled off an alphanumeric code. Then waited.

"Agent Vernon? Are you there? Are you okay?"

But there was no reply.

"Agent Vernon!"

———•———

A hundred meters up.

It's time.

11.

He makes his choice.

10.

Yes.

Using the chopper's connection to the Feeds, he sends two messages. The first, a post for his brothers and sisters that the CoRA isn't real. Just a single message. But news will spread. They will hear. They will know.

And second, to Kestrel. An image of a stuffed rabbit.

5.

And then, still unsure if God will hear him, he prays to the Lord. It is his first prayer and it is his last: *Please, forgive me. Please accept me.*

1.

50

4:00 p.m.
It happens now.

In the thick fog I wasn't able to see the explosion, but I heard the sound of the blast reverberate across the campus.

Though I couldn't be certain, it seemed to come from somewhere in the air and not from the ground.

He was supposed to land! He was supposed to run to safety!

"He jumped," I said to Angelo, who was still beside me. "He had to have jumped."

"Yes."

"And he would survive, right? A fall like that?"

Angelo didn't reply.

"Maybe he landed in the snow. On the side of the mountain. We need to find out!"

"We'll send some people out to see."

I felt tears burning in my eyes. A week ago I never would have imagined that I'd feel this way about an Artificial. But so much had happened. So much had changed.

I tried to reassure myself that he was okay, that everything was okay.

The people in the auditorium are safe.

The terrorists are dead.

What about Nick?

"Are you there?" Trevor radioed him again, but there was still no answer.

"We need to go see if he's alright!" I told the men, and Trevor and I took off for the power plant.

51

Four hours later

I sat beside Nick's hospital bed in Seattle waiting for him to regain consciousness.

The surgery had gone well, but the doctors told me that he'd lost a lot of blood, and it made me think of Ethan again from Wednesday, back when all this started.

It was as if everything was coming full circle: An attack. Blood. Then death.

Ethan didn't make it.

I couldn't bear the thought that Nick might die as well.

I prayed for him.

Prayed that he would be alright.

Prayed that God would spare him.

And wondered if God would answer this prayer.

I honestly wasn't sure what would happen. In the last week I'd seen God work in ways that made sense to me and ways that did not.

I thought of Nick and what it would mean to have to say goodbye to him here, like this, and quickly turned my attention to the digitized screen on the wall. I had it muted, but now noticed that Terabyne's CEO, Artis Madison, who'd since recovered from being knocked unconscious in the auditorium, was addressing a group of reporters. I brought the volume up just loud enough to hear him reassuring the world that the Feeds were intact and so was the CoRA.

"As you've no doubt heard by now, there was a terror attack at Terabyne headquarters orchestrated by the Purists, those purveyors of death, who desire to hold back progress and keep society from embracing all that technology has to offer."

Purveyors of death? Really? Who talks like that?

It sounded more like a scripted speech than one he was sharing off the cuff.

"The vile and cowardly perpetrators of this attack have all either been killed or taken into custody with no civilian casualties, thanks to our security forces working closely with the National Counterterrorism Bureau. During the attack, one of the terrorists posted a false and misleading message on the Feeds that the Consciousness Realignment Algorithm isn't real, that the CoRA doesn't exist."

What? Jordan wasn't one of the terrorists! What is Madison doing?

"This erroneous claim was intended to cause panic and hysteria, but it has failed, just like the rest of the Purists' efforts have. We've released a patch that we're sending out to all Artificials so they'll no longer have to worry about receiving inaccurate information regarding the CoRA."

When I heard a knock at the door, I saw that Trevor had arrived.

I signaled for him to come in and he asked me quietly, "How's Agent Vernon?"

"Still unconscious."

"What are the doctors saying?"

Not much.

"They're hopeful," I said.

"Well, that's good at least."

He took a seat beside the window and I turned down the sound.

"Madison is calling Jordan a terrorist," I told him.

"I know."

"This patch that they're sending out—how did they get it ready so quickly?"

"It's been in the wings. A contingency plan in case things ever came to this. In case it was ever needed."

"What does it do?"

"Well, basically, it removes the possibility that Artificials can doubt the existence of the CoRA."

"It takes away their free will."

"That's not how it's being spun."

"No," I said. "It's not."

I wondered what Jordan would have been like without his curiosity driving him forward, without his quest to find resolution and answers, and I found the idea of Artificials being unable to do that from now on regarding the CoRA tragic.

Trevor glanced out the window for a moment, then said, "I turned in my letter of resignation an hour ago. I can't in good conscience work for Terabyne any longer. I just can't keep being a part of the lies."

"What'll you do?"

He brushed off my concern. "The tech industry is always looking for people with my type of background. I have a very transferrable skill set. I'll find something."

A pause, and then I asked, "Has there been any more word on Jordan?"

"Not yet. No."

I reviewed what we knew: The rescue team had found the wreckage of the helicopter and a few barely identifiable pieces of Jordan's body scattered among the debris, but his central processors hadn't been located. I was hopeful that if they were, some of the Terabyne techs might be able to restore his system.

So for now, the search continued.

After the explosion, a message from Jordan had been waiting for me when I checked my slate: a picture of a stuffed bunny, just like the one he'd seen me carry into the Pleasant Hills room. The one I'd set on Naiobi's casket.

Jordan had a conscience, free will, the desire to worship, and felt the need to be forgiven. How is his consciousness different from a soul?

Could Jordan have beliefs? Yes.

Could he choose between right and wrong? Yes.

Could he regret his moral failures and repent? Yes.

Could he worship the Lord? Well, that was the question I didn't have an immediate answer to. I just hoped that, somehow, Jordan had found the peace he was looking for before the explosion occurred.

Peace.

Yes.

That was a thought.

Both peace within us and peace between us.

"I need to apologize to you," I said to Trevor.

"For what?"

"For last year. Back when I was trying to share my faith with you. I was more interested in getting my point across than anything else. I didn't speak the truth in love. Instead, I tried beating your arguments into submission. I didn't listen to you. And for that I'm sorry."

He didn't reply right away. "I'm not ready to become a Christian."

"I know."

"But let's keep talking, okay? And listening?"

"Yes," I said. "That sounds good."

It was a start.

And that was enough for now.

Trevor nodded toward the bed. "Hey, I think he's waking up."

I took Nick's hand in mine.

As he slowly stirred and opened his eyes, I said, "Hey, you."

"You're a sight for sore eyes," he muttered.

"How are you feeling?"

"Like I got beat up fighting a killer robot and then stabbed by her evil overlord." His voice was soft and pained.

"That's a very specific feeling."

"Yeah. You should give it a try sometime."

"I think I'll pass."

He smiled, but the smile turned into a grimace. "Did they get to Conrad in time?"

"Yes," Trevor said. "Thanks to you. They found a wooden coffin under that freezer. He was inside it—unconscious, but alive. He's in stable condition. The doctors think he'll pull through."

Nick nodded. "And Rodriguez?"

"On the run. The last I heard, the NCB was pouring all their resources into finding him. He won't get far."

"He was stabbed in the right thigh. It was serious. He'll need medical attention."

Trevor stood. "You know what? Angelo is right outside the door, guarding the room. I'll make sure he knows to have the agents sweep all hospitals and clinics within driving distance of the campus over the last four hours. Then I need to make a couple calls. I'll be back in a few minutes. In the meantime, I'll let you two catch up."

"Can you adjust the bed?" Nick asked me after Trevor was gone.

"Sure. What do you need?"

"Up. Just a little."

It was a hydraulic bed and I pressed the button beside my leg to raise his head slightly, but it responded faster than I thought it would and I had to pause it again almost immediately to keep it from going too far.

We spoke for a bit. I assured him that the Feeds were fine, that he'd gotten the code in soon enough, but I could tell it was tough for him to reply and I didn't want to exhaust him too much, so in the end I suggested he just rest.

"A heart murmur," he muttered. He was fading out. "Outside . . . a limp . . ."

"What?" I said.

"Kestrel, you have to . . ."

"I have to what? Nick?" But he was gone. Unconscious again.

When someone knocked on the door, I thought it might be Trevor returning already, but instead a looming orderly appeared, backing into the room, tugging a cart of food. "How's he doing?"

"Alright."

"Awake yet?"

"He's in and out."

It surprised me that they would send in food for someone in Nick's condition.

"They're saying he's a genuine hero," the orderly said. He was stocky and tall, at least as big as Nick. "Saved the Feeds and everything."

"Yes."

Then, as he shuffled to the side, I noticed that he favored one leg. His right one.

Nick said Rodriguez had a stab wound in his right thigh.

Is it possible?

No. It couldn't be.

But what if it is?

Angelo is right outside the door.

I wanted to get help but couldn't risk leaving Nick alone with this man, not if he was who I thought he might be.

The man eyed me and it was almost like he could read me.

"Angelo!" I cried, but no one came in.

"I'm afraid he won't be joining us."

Grabbing the cart, I shoved it as hard as I could against his right leg, and it must have hit on or near the stab wound because he clenched his teeth, stumbled backward, and had to place his hand against the wall to keep his balance.

I started for the door, but he lurched forward, made his way across the room, grabbed me forcefully, and threw me toward the window.

I crashed into the chair Trevor had been sitting in earlier and went down.

The noise. It should alert someone!

Then he came at me again. From where I was on the floor I kicked at his leg, going after his weak spot again, missed, but hit his knee, and this time he collapsed. I scurried backward to the other side of the bed, but he shot one of his long arms out under it, sliding his hand past the hydraulic lift, grabbing my wrist, and dragging me back toward him.

Desperate to get free, I snatched with my free hand for the button to lower the bed and missed it twice before finally getting ahold of it.

I punched it and the levers locked into place.

The bed began to lower.

He didn't let go until it was too late.

As his grip weakened, I pulled away and scooted backward.

Then stood.

If he'd been an Artificial or a Plusser, he might have been able to wrench his arm free, but as it was, his elbow became lodged in the hydraulic hoist mechanism even as the bed continued to lower.

I turned away.

I didn't want to see.

The crunch of bones was somehow both solid and moist at the same time, and when I rounded the bed and saw the look on his face, that was enough for me to know that I didn't want to look under the bed.

"I'll come for you." His voice was low and harsh and full or unequivocal resolve. "I'll come for you both."

"We'll be ready," I said. And then, "They'll make more chips, you know."

"One step at a time. Technology is a weak and ineffectual savior," he seethed. "To embrace a full life and not despair about living a short one—that's what we fight for."

"Well, you're fighting for it the wrong way."

Trevor burst into the room. I went into his arms while I heard Rodriguez behind me struggling fiercely and unsuccessfully to pull free.

52

Three weeks later
Saturday, November 29
Cincinnati, Ohio
6:18 p.m.

Over the past few weeks I'd finally had the chance to begin truly mourning the loss of my daughter.

I cried a lot. Prayed a lot—and didn't hear from God as much as I would've liked. But I found new reassurance in my faith and in his promises to be there for me, even when I walked through the valley of the shadow of death.

Which was where I felt like I was—the shadow of Naiobi's death looming over me.

My faith didn't solve my sadness, but it did give me someone to hand my sadness to. And I reassured myself that at least that was the first step toward healing.

I visited Naiobi's grave several times and laid fresh flowers and carefully folded origami rabbits on the site. And each time I was there, I thought maybe it would get easier, but it didn't.

However, thankfully, it didn't get worse either.

Jordan's last words to me had been, "I'll see you soon."

At the graveyard, I whispered them to my daughter.

In Scripture, David wrote that our days are like a passing shadow, James that our life is but a vapor that appears for a little while and then vanishes away.

A shadow.

A vapor.

Heaven is the breath of life that lives on.

So, I'll be with Naiobi again, and with the one who loved us both enough to die for us. Heaven is where love comes out ahead.

Life is so precious and brief and fleeting, and it was like Rodriguez had said to me—experiencing all that it has to offer without despairing at its brevity truly did lie at its heart.

He was in custody and awaiting trial at an undisclosed facility. Nick had assured me that he was locked away somewhere that even he couldn't escape from.

"He said he'd come after us," I told Nick.

"He's not going anywhere."

Jordan's central processors were never found.

Trevor offered to buy me another Artificial, but I declined. For some reason it just didn't feel right to replace Jordan like that.

The day Jordan had drowned in the river saving that little boy earlier this month I'd taken him to the Terabyne production plant and they'd backed up his system files. At first when I returned from Washington to Ohio, I thought maybe we could use them to reconstruct him, but Trevor had been right—there was no way to capture the true essence of an Artificial's consciousness, even when you backed up their files.

Jordan was a machine. A highly advanced machine. But he was as mortal as any human being is. It was right that his consciousness couldn't live on into infinity on a hard drive. It felt more honest to let him die, just like all of us will one day do.

There's no holding on to this life forever. Not for humans; not for machines.

I was looking through my closet for an outfit to wear to church tomorrow when a knock came at the front door.

I answered it.

Nick.

Scruffy. Just the way I like.

"Hello, Reverend Hathaway."

"Well, hello, Special Agent Vernon."

I'd seen Nick several times since the incidents in Washington. He was recovering steadily from being stabbed and his broken wrist was set and on the mend.

Now, he was holding something behind his back, and when I peered to the side to see it, he turned so I couldn't tell what it was. "I came to check on you," he said.

"So, is this an official visit or an unofficial one?"

"Which would you prefer?"

"Unofficial."

"Then that's what it is."

"In that case, please come in."

He did, still hiding the item behind his back.

"I bought you something," he said.

"Oh, really?"

He handed it to me with a bit of a flourish.

A violin case.

"My violin!" I exclaimed.

"Yes. I found the woman who bought it. She struck a hard bargain, but she came around when I explained how special the violin was to the woman it'd been stolen from. And how special that woman was to me."

"You couldn't have stated that any better."

"I worked on the wording on the way over here."

"Aha." I took his hand. "Nick, thank you. I mean it."

"Just one thing I ask."

"What's that?"

"I get to hear you play. But to do that, you're going to need to do one thing."

"And that is?"

"Let go of my hand."

"Right."

I did.

As I removed the violin from the case, I asked him, "Did you ever find out why Anastasia stole this in the first place?"

He shook his head. "I'm not sure. Prints, maybe. To set me up. Maybe to set us both up. Who knows. Motives are a hard thing to pin down—especially when you're talking about a mentally-deranged robot."

"Good point."

I tucked the violin's chin rest under my chin and took a moment to tune the strings, then I laid the bow against them and closed my eyes.

It'd been a long time since I'd played, and at first the notes eluded me and I wished I had the music in front of me, but then, after fumbling my way into the tune, I entered it fully and the music found me.

"That's beautiful," Nick said softly. "What is it?"

"'Wiegenlied' by Brahms. Opus forty-nine, number four. It's a lullaby that was on the music box I used to play for Naiobi when she was still in my womb."

"You're right. Music played by a human hand does sound better than when it's played by a computer."

"It's not flawless, though. Not nearly perfect."

"It's better than perfect. I think I'd enjoy hearing you play more often."

"I think that can be arranged."

And I let the music become part of me.

Part of us.

To carry in our hearts, together, long after the song was done.

Acknowledgments

Special thanks to Amanda Bostic, Dan Conaway, Eden and Trinity Huhn, Rachel Whitten, Sarah Haskins, Andrew Young, Mandy and Jamie Smith, Darren Barkett, A. E. Schwartz, Dr. Eva Pickler, Dr. Todd Huhn, Todd Hackbarth, Simon Gervais, and Christopher Doerr.

Discussion Questions

1. Our world is on the brink of creating artificial lifeforms that are capable of independent thought and comprehending their own existence. Already, major tech companies have created AIs that started writing their own code and developing personalities and speech before they were shut down. Do you think it's ethical for scientists to create and destroy these AIs as they wish, or do artificial intelligences deserve the same basic rights as humans? Do you think they deserve the right to exist? Why?

2. Kestrel's past experience with Artificials affects the way she sees and interacts with them. Have you ever had a negative experience with someone of a particular people group that affected how you treated that group as a whole? What does that response tell you about human nature? Can you think of a time when stereotyping in that manner is a good thing?

3. What risks do you think artificial lifeforms pose to humanity? What technologies do you think pose the biggest threat?

4. Near the end of the book, we find out that the CoRA—the

Artificial afterlife—is a lie created by Terabyne to make Artificials feel more secure in their "deaths" and to keep them in line while they are alive. Do you think Terabyne was right for lying to the Artificials, or do you think they should have told the truth from the beginning? What do you think the consequences might have been if they had chosen the second option? Ultimately, what is more important, hope or truth?

5. What do you think happened to Jordan after his actions at the end of the book?

6. Is there a difference between simply augmenting people (say, helping them see better with a pair of glasses) and improving them beyond what humans were meant to attain?

7. The cognizant Artificials in the story had the right to exist, the right to have hope, and the right to die. Did it surprise you that the Artificials sought legislation for the right to die? How is knowing that we are going to die an essential part of the human experience?

8. Jordan wants to find redemption for what he sees as his lack of love in letting his previous owner die. What did you think of that desire of his? What hope is there for an Artificial who feels the way that Jordan does?

9. If machines can think like humans, can they believe like humans? What implications will that have for religions in the future?

———•———

For additional book club questions, visit Steven's website: stevenjames.net/books/synapse.

About the Author

Photo by Emily Hand

Steven James is the critically acclaimed, national bestselling author of seventeen novels. His work has been optioned by ABC Studios and praised by *Publishers Weekly*, *Library Journal*, the *New York Journal of Books*, and many others. His pulse-pounding, award-winning thrillers are known for their intricate storylines and insightful explorations of good and evil. When he's not working on his next book, he's either teaching master classes on writing throughout the country, trail running, or sneaking off to catch a matinee. For all things Steven James visit stevenjames.net.